I0577246

Sir John Bowring

Autobiographical Recollections of Sir John Bowring

Sir John Bowring

Autobiographical Recollections of Sir John Bowring

ISBN/EAN: 9783337014575

Printed in Europe, USA, Canada, Australia, Japan

Cover: Foto ©Raphael Reischuk / pixelio.de

More available books at **www.hansebooks.com**

AUTOBIOGRAPHICAL RECOLLECTIONS

OF SIR JOHN BOWRING.

WITH A BRIEF MEMOIR

BY

LEWIN B. BOWRING.

HENRY S. KING & CO., LONDON.

1877.

The rights of translation and of reproduction are reserved.

PREFACE.

WHILE arranging the papers of the late Sir John Bowring, I discovered a great number of autobiographical notes and recollections in his handwriting, which he had apparently intended some day to put into a connected shape. The majority of these fragments were composed about the year 1861, after his return from the East, but many were written when he was in China, while others again, relating to incidents in his earlier life, and to persons with whom he was then brought into contact, were recorded at the time. Unfortunately, these reminiscences were never collated nor revised by the writer, neither did he leave any instructions regarding their publication.

Although therefore, the following pages comprise the more memorable experiences of a very varied life, and may be deemed worthy of preservation, they do not constitute a continuous or complete memoir ; and while the task of eliminating doubtful matter has been comparatively easy, I feel that no one but the writer himself could have supplied what is defective, or have elucidated more fully those portions of his recollections which may seem to need more elaborate explanation.

In the brief account of his life which I have prefixed, I have said but little regarding his political opinions, and still less about his views on religious subjects, because with many of them I do not sympathise, and because he has sufficiently indicated what they were in his notes.

L. B. B.

TORQUAY, *May* 1877.

CONTENTS.

A BRIEF MEMOIR OF SIR JOHN BOWRING.

SIR JOHN BOWRING was born on the 17th of October 1792, and died on the 23rd of November 1872, having just completed his 80th year. His father, Charles Bowring, was the descendant of a Devonshire family, which had for many generations been engaged in the woollen trade, and his mother, Sarah Jane Ann Lane, was a daughter of the Rev. Thomas Lane, Vicar of St Ives, who, on the maternal side, was descended from Sir Andrew Henley, and claimed kindred with William of Wykeham. Sir John Bowring's ancestors formerly held a small property called Bowringsleigh, near Kingsbridge, and a deed is extant showing that in 1379 it was in the possession of one John Bouryng, from whose descendants it passed eventually by purchase, in the reign of William III., into the hands of the Ilbert family, who still possess it.

A branch of the Bowring family settled in Chulmleigh, where Sir John Bowring's grandfather's great-grandfather, named John, possessed a small estate, which he sold in order to enter the woollen trade, at that time a profitable pursuit in the west of England, much followed by Dissenters. He struck tokens in 1670, in his own name, the coins having a device on them showing his craft. On his death, his widow had the intention of repurchasing his landed property, but on

A

Monmouth's landing, having concealed all her money and plate in silver vessels, which she hid among the wool, her hoard was discovered, and her house ransacked by the soldiery, who carried off also two of her apprentices.

Her son John was a schoolmaster, and wrote a great many indifferent verses, some of which show violent animosity to the Jacobites, and great exultation at the victory of the Duke of Cumberland over the rebels. His son Benjamin carried on the pursuits of his forefathers, as did his grandson John. The latter was a man of great independence of character, and deeply imbued with religious sentiments, which he endeavoured to impress on his grandson, the subject of this memoir, in early childhood. In some of his letters he condemns in strong terms the attitude assumed by the English Ministry towards America, and in others expresses his sympathy with the efforts made in Pennsylvania and in England to bring about the abolition of slavery. On the former subject, he thus expresses himself in a letter to his cousin, dated 1st August 1778. "After the most deliberate consideration of the nature of the quarrel between us, I freely own it appears to me that they are right and we wrong, nor is there anything I more ardently wish for relative to our national concerns than a thorough change both of men and manners in the British Cabinet. Yet, as an Englishman, I by no means wish to see my country vanquished by the arms of France. That some more able and upright Ministry than those my country is now curst with may, by providence, be raised up in the place of the present, is more than my most fervent wish. Should I live to see my country once more friendly united with America, and the pride of France effectually humbled, it would afford me such real pleasure as true patriots only could feel, though too great for the pen of eloquence fully to express." Again, in another letter, he observes, " it appears to me indisputable that we had *no right*, as it possibly may to you that we *had a right*, to tax America. Just in the same manner as this claim appears right in your eyes, I suppose it did formerly to King James, that he had an indisputable right to tax his subjects, nor can I see how the man (supposing him to act consistently) that blames the Americans but must in like manner disapprove of the glorious Revolution. I would by no means suppose you admit the conclusion drawn from the above argument, yet I own I cannot see how it can fairly be contradicted."

The precepts early instilled into John Bowring's mind by his grandfather tended much to form his character, and when at a later period he devoted his energies to carry out the principles inculcated by Jeremy Bentham, the Queen Square Place philosopher found a willing hearer in one who in childhood had been trained to an intense love of liberty and independence of opinion. The religious germs in his character, which formed a marked feature of it through life, were implanted by his grandfather at an impressionable age, and were developed under the teaching of Dr Lant Carpenter, who was an intimate friend of his family. In his earlier letters, written when he was twelve or thirteen years old, there prevails a strong religious feeling, tinged with a somewhat didactic and moralizing tone, which seems strangely at variance with the natural buoyancy of youth. Reflections on death, and juvenile verses on the shortness of life and its sorrows, are interspersed freely in these productions, while even in his later years such thoughts constantly sprang up, and acted as a counterpoise to his zest for new impressions. So strong indeed were these sentiments in his mind, that had not destiny opened out to him a far different field, it is probable that his natural inclination would have led him to become a Dissenting Minister.

On leaving school, he entered a merchant's office at

In 1816 he married Maria, daughter of Mr Samuel Lewin of Hackney, and during the vicissitudes of forty-two years, in which were blended, as in most human lives, much of happiness and much of sorrow, his wife, by her noble character and equanimity under heavy trials, proved herself a worthy partner, rejoicing in his successes and strengthening him in his reverses.

In 1819-20 he travelled extensively on the Continent on commercial business, visiting Spain, France, Belgium, Holland, Russia, and Sweden. During this long absence he formed the acquaintance in Spain of many well known liberals ; in France he gained the friendship of Abbé Gregoire (Bishop of Blois), Laroche, Thierry, Cuvier, Humboldt, and other prominent politicians and learned men ; while elsewhere he met many illustrious literary characters, with whom during several years he maintained an active correspondence. At Paris he was charmed with the perfect equality which prevailed among literati of all ranks, and observed in one of his letters, "It will be the height of my ambition to do something which many connect my name with the literature of the age." The tendency which he now began to exhibit to deviate from the career which he had originally chosen, and to enter upon the literary field, was no doubt detrimental to the successful prosecution of commercial pursuits, but the attraction was too powerful to be resisted, and immediately after his return from Russia in 1820, he published a small work called "Specimens of the Russian Poets." The translations in this volume are on the whole felicitous and truthful, and the book, having the merit of novelty, obtained sufficient success to encourage him in rendering into English the productions of writers in the cognate Slavonic tongues.

In 1821, having been entrusted by Milford and Co. with a power of attorney to prefer certain claims of theirs against

the Spanish Government, he again proceeded to the Peninsula, stopping at Paris, where he made the acquaintance of
the Duke of Orleans, afterwards Louis Philippe, who received him.with marked kindness. At this time intrigues
were on foot to bring the Duke to the front, but he was far
too astute to reveal his secret designs, knowing how closely
he was watched by the elder branch of the Bourbons. Mr
Bowring writes, "several of the leading liberals here
have requested me to urge the Duke to mingle more with
the liberal party, and to become the rallying point of the
friends of liberty. I had been made acquainted with a
scheme now at work for changing the government, which
everybody says will not last. The Duke said, ' I know my
strength. The crown has been offered to me again and
again, but I will only take it when I ascertain that it is the
general wish of the nation. I am sure the present state of
things cannot and will not last. I am the object of repeated
—of daily repeated insults, in the belief that I will bear
them, but they do not know that I may stretch out my
hand, and possess the superiority whenever I set my strength
in motion.' "

In his letters written from Spain at this time, Mr
Bowring gives graphic accounts of a terrible epidemic of
fever which prevailed throughout Catalonia and in the southern provinces, and which on several occasions led to his
undergoing the duress vile of quarantine in its most repulsive shape. In Barcelona 18,000 persons are said to have
perished, and many towns were nearly depopulated by the
disease.

In 1822, he was again in Paris, where he was the object
of attentions on the part of the Duke of Orleans, Lafayette,
and various prominent members of the anti-Bourbon section
of politicians, but his expedition terminated disastrously, for
on his arrival at Calais he was arrested, and thrown into

prison at Boulogne, where he was confined six weeks, and was only released on the urgent demand of Mr Canning that he should either be formally tried or set free. The ostensible charge against him was that he was concerned, together with Colonels Fabvier, Dentzel, and other noted French liberals, in endeavouring to effect the escape from prison of the four Serjeants of Rochelle, who were executed for conspiracy. An account of this episode will be found in his notice of France, but there can be little doubt that his imprisonment was owing to his known sympathy with the advanced reformers who were engaged in undermining the throne of the Bourbons, and who regarded with jealous eyes the intimacy which subsisted between the Orleans family and the English radical party. On his release, he was prohibited from ever re-entering France, and in fact he did not again visit that country till he came as the bearer of a congratulatory letter from the citizens of London to the Parisians on the events of the *three glorious days of July* 1830.

On his return to England he threw himself heart and soul into literary pursuits, his principal writings being translations from Spanish and Dutch, a second volume of Russian Anthology, "Matins and Vespers," which obtained an extensive circulation, and an English version of Chamisso's charming German tale, "Peter Schlemihl."

About the year 1821 he had been introduced to Jeremy Bentham, who conceived in 1824 the idea of starting the *Westminster Review* as an organ for making known the views of the so-called philosophical radicals, and advanced nearly £4000 towards its establishment. Many of the articles published in this magazine showed consummate ability, and as a means of ventilating the doctrines of the advanced liberals the *Review* was of great use, but, notwithstanding that it commanded the services of such men as the

two Mills, George Grote, and other well-known writers, it
never proved a good financial speculation. Mr Bowring
was joint-editor with Mr H. Southern, and wrote the political articles, contributing, however, also interesting papers
on the Runes of Finland, on the Frisian and Dutch tongues,
on Magyar poetry, and other literary subjects.

In 1827 he published a little volume called "Servian
Anthology," perhaps the best of all his translations, in
which the wild beauty of the Servian ballads is faithfully
rendered into English. He also brought out a selection from
the poems of Polish writers, but his devotion to literature
prevented his concentrating his mind on business, and he
consequently met with commercial disasters, which induced
him to seek for employment under Government. This was
not, however, entirely a new idea, for he had been recommended in 1821 to the Portuguese Minister of Justice by
Bentham, who, writing of him, said :—" Avez vous besoin,
vous autres Portugais, d'un homme qui est propre à tout,
pourvu que cela ait rapport au genre humain ? Il est actif,
infatigable au plus haut degré : meilleur cœur n'a jamais
existé, et n' existera jamais. Vous m' avez appellé citoyen
du monde, et je le suis, mais je ne le suis pas plus que lui.
On ne risque pas en donnant des éloges à cet homme là ;
il a autant d' amis qu' il a de connaissances." Bentham's
affection and regard for his favourite disciple were unchang-
ing, and it was probably owing to his good offices that
Bowring's name was laid before Government for employment.

In 1828, a Finance Committee of the House of Commons
recommended his appointment as a commissioner for reform-
ing the system of keeping the public accounts, and Mr J.
C. Herries, the Chancellor of the Exchequer, accordingly
nominated him, but the Duke of Wellington, who took
umbrage to his radical opinions, insisted on removing his

name from the commission. He was, however, deputed to Holland to examine the method pursued by the financial department in that country, and prepared a report, the first of a long series on the public accounts of various European states. These papers are models of perspicuity, showing considerable power in grasping facts, and in arranging them lucidly and intelligibly.

In 1829, he received from the University of Groningen, in Holland, the diploma of LL.D., a title by which he was subsequently generally known. The document runs as follows :—

" RECTOR ET SENATUS ACADEMIÆ GRONINGANÆ
VIRO ERUDITISSIMO JOANNI BOWRING.

Quam opinionem de eximiâ tuâ eruditione fama apud nos excitaverat, eam tuus in hanc urbem adventus non tantum confirmavit, verum etiam auxit. Cujus rei ut te certiorem redderemus, simulque palam ostenderemus. unius cujusque, etiam exteri, de re literariâ meritit suum apud nos constare honorem. Te, vir eruditissime ! Philosophiæ Theoreticæ Magistrum et Literarum Humaniarum Doctorem *Honoris causâ* creavimus. Ergo Diploma, quod hos honores manifestet, legitimo modo conscriptum et confirmatum, cum his literis ad te mittimus, sperantes fore, ut hoc nostræ de te opinionis documentum tibi non ingratum sit. Cœterum vale, vir eruditissime ! Tibique persuasum habe, te a nemine quam a nobis pluris æstimare posse.

" Scripsimus Groningæ pridie Kal : Feb : MDCCCXXIX.
" Senatus Acad : Groning : nomine
G. WOLTERS, *Rector Magnificus*.
J. ten Brink, Sen : Acad : h. t. ab actis.

In addition to this diploma he received during his life more than thirty other certificates of honorary association from various learned societies and institutions in different parts of Europe.

In the month of April 1830 he paid a visit to Abbotsford, of which he gives the following account :—

" I could not resist the fascination of Sir Walter's repeated invitations, and nothing could exceed the kindness with which he has welcomed me.

I found him writing for the "Waverley Novels," but he locked up his manuscript, and has devoted to me every moment of his time. He has led me over his grounds, talking of all possible things—his discourse rich, racy, and delightful, though he has been a little overwhelmed by the news of the sudden death of a ward of his (Lady Northampton) the mother of eight young children.

"His style of living here is far more expensive than I imagined. It is a sort of baronial abode, the servants being numerous, the house splendid, and the rooms decorated with rich works of art and remnants of antiquity, contributions from every part of the world. In one is his bust by Chantrey (of whom he told me some anecdotes—of his ecstasy when he caught a huge fish in the Tweed, &c.), and the famous silver cup filled with human bones, sent him by Byron. He showed me his grandfather's picture, with his long beard, which he had vowed never to shave till the Stuarts were restored; and, à propos of this, he mentioned some delicious conversations with the present king, who insisted on knowing what Sir Walter would have done had the Pretender appeared in his time. He said that the king always called Charles the *Pretender*, while he (W. S.) always called him the *Prince*. He gave me many curious particulars of his early history, and said he had forgotten nothing that had occurred to him since he was three years old. He told me many interesting things respecting his novels, and the personages in them, his interviews with the late queen, the Princess Charlotte, Burns, Byron, and others. More eloquent men I have known, I think, but I never knew any one so attractive. The variety of his conversation is stupendous, while it overflows with the most agreeable anecdotes, and almost every person who has figured in modern times has in some way or other been connected with him. His manner of talking is without the smallest pretence, and is gentle and humorous. His eye has a constant play upon it and around it. His dress is that of a substantial farmer—a short green coat with steel buttons, striped waistcoat and pantaloons, and he put on light gaiters when we sallied forth."

In this year Dr Bowring published a volume called "Poetry of the Magyars," a work not without merit as an attempt to popularize a language which is both difficult and unique, but the public were rather tired of translations from little known tongues, and the following amusing squib upon it appeared in *Fraser's Magazine*.

" *Te Pikke Megge.*	" *The Pious Maiden.*
Hogy, wogy, Pogy !	Holy little Polly !
Xupumai tïtzāāā bnikttm.	Love sought me but I tricked him.
Pogy, wogy, hogy !	Polly little holy !
Bsduro plgvbz cttnsttm	You thought of me, 'I've nicked him.'
Wogy, hogy, Pogy !	Little holy Polly !
Mlòsrz vbquògp fvikttm."	I'm not to be your victim."

The French Revolution in July of this year, which led to the dethronement of the Bourbon dynasty and the elevation to power of the astute Louis Philippe, took Dr Bowring to Paris, to offer to the French the congratulations of the people of London, and for some time he indulged the hope that the citizen King would lead the van of the Liberal party, but the newly-made sovereign was not long in showing his monarchical tendencies, and in adopting a line of policy nearly as arbitrary as that of his predecessors. He ceased to take Dr Bowring into his confidence, and speedily alienated the affections of all his old friends among the advanced reformers.

Dr Bowring warmly interested himself in the declaration of independence by Belgium, and was the medium of introducing M. Sylvain Van de Weyer to the political world in England, but his sentiments on this subject gave great offence to his Dutch friends, who accused him of ingratitude, and stigmatized his partizanship as betraying ignorance of the facts. In a letter to his old acquaintance, William de Clercq, he thus refers to the question:—"I have some claim on the candour, at all events on the just judgment, of Hollanders. When they have been wronged, what pen has ever been so prompt as mine in their defence? Has any living stranger laboured as I have laboured to obtain for their individual virtues and national literature the homage which is so justly their due? * * * I have never altered my tone nor changed my language in this matter. In a thousand conversations on every appropriate occasion, in articles in the newspapers and in reviews, in correspondence and in books, I have always preached from one text on this subject, and always developed one commentary, that the union of Batavia and Belgium was fraudulent and foolish—a blind sacrifice of the interests of both—that time, far from producing sympathy, was daily sowing stronger and stronger antipathy—that a rupture, either by consent or violence, was inevitable, and that such a rupture would bring with it many advantages to both. * * * The simple, the all-important fact is this, that a real union was impossible. Language, literature, religion, manners, historical recollections, political associations, everything proclaimed its impracticability. It was a most unhappy wedlock, and necessity (would it had been the calm controversy of friends, and not the bitter animosity of foes) necessity has forced a divorce. What becomes the duty of the friends of both? To teach a speedy forgetfulness of the days of bloodshed—to establish those relations of peace and good neighbourhood, of friendly, social, and commercial interest, which will add far more than political amalgamation can do, or has ever done. In a word, to bring about a benevolent rivalry, unchecked by those discords and discussions which were the natural consequence of the false position into which you were thrown."

In 1831 Dr Bowring was associated with Sir H. Parnell in the duty of examining and reporting on the public accounts of France, a task which was so satisfactorily performed that he was appointed secretary to the commission for inspecting the accounts of the United Kingdom. All the French authorities spoke in the highest terms of the report on the finances of France, and the Lords of the Treasury signified their approbation of the talent and labour which it exhibited. He was shortly afterwards appointed one of the Commissioners for discussing the commercial relations between England and France, his colleague being Mr George Villiers (afterwards Lord Clarendon), with whom he maintained for many years a close intimacy, in which the latter invariably evinced the greatest kindness and good-feeling towards him. The negotiations, however, as will appear elsewhere, proved nearly abortive, and it was not till the time of Napoleon III. that a satisfactory commercial treaty was effected by the exertions of Mr. Cobden.

While engaged in this undertaking he visited the celebrated Lafayette, of whom he gives the following description :—

"LAGRANGE, 4th November, 1832.

" I came here for a day or two, and send you a word from a spot so illustrious and attractive. I am contrasting my recollections of Abbotsford with those of Lagrange. There was a great man, surrounded by a thousand interesting things picked out of history and romance, and charming conversation, but the whole a little damaged by aristocratical vanities. Here is the representative of one of the oldest noble families of France, who will have no title but General—who, with a large fortune, has no powdered and liveried lackies, no parade of carriages and horses, no armorial bearings thrust forward at every step, but every conceivable comfort, abundant attendance, simple but excellent fare, and a family of four generations around him, all looking up to him, the patriarch of all, with an affection so generous and confiding, with an admiration so single and high-minded as to create a very atmosphere of love. And the good old man, benign and gentle as a beautiful sunset, who could believe him to be the hero of two worlds—the bosom-friend of Washington, Franklin, and Jefferson—the pole-star of three revolutions—the standard to which every nation has rushed when any dawning hope of liberty has kindled enthusiasm for him whom all men deem its seer ? The chateau is many centuries old, in the centre of a beautiful park, and is entered through a fine archway covered with ivy, which owes its existence to Charles James Fox, of whom the General speaks in language of admiring recollection. When all the guests have assembled, the gentlemen escort the ladies to the breakfast-room below, down a stone staircase, over which are suspended a number of flags, to each of which a story of fame is attached—flags telling the tale of the first and second revolutions of France—that of America— that of Poland, &c. Breakfast over, I went with the General to his farm, looked at his seven hundred and fifty merino sheep, his Cashmere goats, his Baltimore pigs (the only pigs I ever saw in France, where they give the name of pigs to snouted greyhounds), his aviaries, his grand turkeys, his cows and horses, and dairies, of which he is very proud. Lafayette is lame, as Walter Scott was, and, like him, hangs heavily upon the arm on which he leans, and this—the sense of his presence—is a very agreeable sensation."

On 6th June 1832 his revered friend Jeremy Bentham died in his arms, making him his executor, and leaving to his care for publication all his manuscripts, which Dr Bowring edited in a work comprising twenty-three volumes, to which was attached a biography of the renowned jurist. Whether from the recondite nature of many of the productions in this collection, or from the circumstance that Bentham's writings were far in advance of the age, the publication did not attain extensive popularity—in fact the philosopher's dogmas, as dressed up by Dumont, appear to have commanded more attention in France than did the originals in England. Bentham's singular disposal of his body by his will is well known, and he is still to be seen, dressed in his usual clothes, in University College, London.

When the Reform Bill was passed, Dr Bowring presented himself for election at Blackburn, but though enthusiastically received by the mass of the people, he was rejected by the electors, his opponents beating him by several votes.* On looking back at the electioneering contests of that time, one cannot help wondering at the vehement invective and unsparing abuse which were freely bandied about. Every kind of gibe, jest, satire, and insinuation was brought into play at Blackburn, nor was the hostility to Dr Bowring confined to words, for a large stone was thrown into his bedroom, which passed close to his head. His friends, however, on their side, manifested their regard by presenting his wife with a handsome service of plate.

* The Poll stood as follows :—Fielding, 376 ; Turner, 346 : Bowring, 334.

Defeated in the political arena, he resumed his commercial negotiations in France, where he received a cordial welcome from all the authorities wherever he went. His letters of this period contain much curious information on the state of affairs in that country. Letter-writing was to him one of the greatest charms of life, and he persevered in it to the very last.

From France he proceeded in 1833 to Belgium, where an incautious speech of his at the Hotel de Ville at Brussels elicited a reprimand from Lord Palmerston, who deemed it injudicious on the part of one entrusted with official negotiations. The particular phrase to which exception was taken, but which he disclaimed, was, "que le peuple Anglais n'était pour rien dans la conduite de la diplomatie," but, in submitting his explanation to Lord Palmerston, he observed that the British minister (Sir Robert Adair) persisted in regarding Belgium as a conquered country, which the Holy Alliance had a right to dispose of, treating the revolution of 1830 as rebellion, and deeming it the duty of England to do everything by coercion. He thus alludes to the attacks made on him by *The Times* on this occasion :—"I *know* their correspondent wrote of me and my speech in the most favourable terms, and I have now *their* letter to him, saying, 'We don't agree in your opinion of Dr B., and you must express *our* opinion and not *yours!*' But he says he will not do this. He will be silent about me, but will not write dishonestly." It would appear from the correspondence that Messrs Barnes & Murray, two of the proprietors of the *Times*, wrote in friendly terms ; but a third called Dr Bowring a visionary, and said that if he were to be *well* spoken of, the Belgian correspondent (Mr Turnbull) must not speak of him at all.

In 1834 he published a work called "Bentham's Deontology," that is, the knowledge of what is right or

proper, as especially applied to the subject of morals, or
that part of the field of action which is not the object of
public legislation.   This collection of maxims was in preparation for the press when the earthly labours of the
octogenarian philosopher were near their end.   It attracted
some attention in France, though one of the Paris newspapers, *Le Messager*, observed that it only added one
more to the many sophisms with which the moral and
political world was already inundated.   In the same year
Dr Bowring wrôte a pleasing little book called "Minor
Morals," in which an attempt was made to set forth the
above principles in a series of conversational tales adapted
to the capacities of youth.   This production was illustrated
by Cruikshank, and was well spoken of.

    In the month of June Dr Bowring returned to England
with the *ordonnances* issued by the French Government,
removing the prohibition on several articles of British
exports, such as cotton-twist, lace, iron cables, Russian hides,
rum, &c., but such difficulties had been thrown in the way
of the English Commissioners that Mr C. P. Thomson, who
had succeeded Mr Villiers, did not hesitate to stigmatise
M. Thiers as a charlatan for having violated promises made
under his own hand.

    Later in the year, Dr Bowring proceeded to the wine-
producing departments of France, visiting Champagne,
Burgundy, and Languedoc, and mentions in his letters that
wine was so abundant that year (1834) that in some places
it did not fetch a halfpenny a bottle, or ten shillings a
hogshead, and that any one would give a hogshead of wine
for an empty hogshead; that is to say, if people brought
two hogsheads, they might fill and carry away one, on condition that they left the other.

    In 1835, after standing unsuccessfully a second time for
Blackburn, he was elected member for Kilmarnock, but it

does not appear that his first speech in the House of Commons attracted attention, and before he had any opportunity of becoming better known, the Tory régime came to an end, by the resignation of Sir Robert Peel, on 8th April, the Whigs being again in the ascendant. This led to his being deputed to visit the manufacturing districts of Switzerland, and, in 1836, Italy. Regarding the former, he writes, "By a system of free-trade, Switzerland has overcome every natural difficulty, and created for herself a real superiority over the protected manufactures of *all* the surrounding nations." He was struck by the general prosperity and the financial and trading prospects of the people ; but, on the other hand, his visit to Italy, although he was most courteously received by the Grand Duke of Tuscany, appears to have been premature, and nearly barren of results.

The death of King William IV. in 1837 led to a fresh general election, when he was unseated for Kilmarnock, his opponent being Mr Colquhoun. He attributed his defeat to the combined influence of the Kirk, the Lairds, and the Tories ; but the true cause might perhaps have been found in the fickleness of his democratic supporters. Shortly afterwards he proceeded again to Italy, and thence to Egypt and Syria. Of his adventures and experiences in these oriental countries, some account will be found in this volume. He conceived, and certainly not without ample grounds, a great admiration for the ability and shrewdness of Mehemet Ali, the celebrated Viceroy of Egypt, and objected to the policy of England which enforced the dependence of that ruler on the Sublime Porte. The vicissitudes of sovereignty in oriental countries, where despotism universally prevails, are not to be regulated by principles which may be salutary in civilised states, and the several attempts made by the British Government to uphold

B

the tottering sovereignty of the Sultan, to the prejudice of
feudatories who might have proved useful allies to us, have
alienated the regard of those who looked to England for
help, and have failed to maintain the integrity of Turkish
dominion. The obstacles thrown in the way of Mehemet Ali's
founding a strong Arabian kingdom, including Syria, which
he had virtually conquered, have tended to perpetuate
anarchy and misrule from the Black Sea to the Persian
Gulf. Mehemet Ali sought the friendship of England, but
was repulsed, and the consequence was that France obtained
for many years the ascendancy in Egypt. Apprehensions
regarding Russian aggressions, well or ill founded, served to
throw a veil over and obscure the real interests of England,
which would have been best secured by supporting Mehemet
Ali, and allowing him to consolidate his authority over
the kingdom of Syria. Dr Bowring took great interest in
the Eastern Question, and wrote several articles on it in the
Morning Chronicle, in which he argued that Mehemet Ali
was in possession of Syria, that it was granted to him by
the convention of Kutayah, and that the attempt to dis-
possess him would lead to the disturbance of peace, while
there was no reason to believe that the Syrians had any
affection for Osmanli rule.

In 1839 Dr Bowring attended, at Manchester, a crowded
anti-Corn Law meeting, the proceedings at which laid the
foundation of the famous league which subsequently, under
the championship of Cobden, Bright, and other leaders, broke
down with irresistible force, the barriers which stood in the
way of free-trade. The evil effects of the prevailing restrictions were brought prominently to Dr Bowring's notice in
the same year, when, in pursuance of instructions from his
government, he proceeded to Prussia with a view to inducing
that country to modify her tariff on English manufactures.
He was at once met with the objection that so long as the

English Corn Laws imposed a prohibitive tariff on foreign grain, it was useless to ask Germany to relax her heavy duties on English goods.

The conviction that the abolition of the obnoxious corn laws was an imperative measure, rekindled in him the desire to re-enter Parliament, his exclusion from which had been a great disappointment to him. He accordingly stood for Kirkcaldy, where he was defeated, but was some months afterwards (in 1841) elected for Bolton, which he represented till 1849. His friends at Kirkcaldy, being desirous to recognise the value of his labours in the cause of free-trade, and for the amelioration of the condition of the working classes, presented to him a handsome silver salver. Similar tokens of esteem were offered to him by the people of Kilmarnock, and by the Maltese, whose claim to have a voice in the administration of their island he had advocated in Parliament. The Manxmen also testified their acknowledgment of his friendly offices in effecting their release from ancient feudal customs by a like mark of their gratitude.

While member for Bolton, he embarked all his fortune in ironworks in Glamorganshire, an enterprise which, though at the outset promising to be highly remunerative, proved eventually to be most disastrous. In 1847, the depression in the iron-trade caused him great anxiety, as the balance-sheet of his company showed a considerable loss on the business of the year. In 1848, however, he looked forward confidently to the restoration of prosperity, and with that buoyancy of disposition which characterised him, and enabled him to rise up again after temporary depression, he took great pleasure in witnessing the successful progress in life of his sons. Later in the year he began to be seriously alarmed at the state of affairs, and consequently applied for and obtained, through Lord Palmerston's friendship, the appointment of Consul at Canton.

A critical period in our relations with China had just arrived, for although the Chinese government had hitherto evaded the condition that the gates of Canton should be opened to foreigners, it had been understood on both sides that the privilege should be conceded in April 1849. Dr Bowring entered upon his duties in the hope that the local mandarins would at least receive him officially within the city, and that the way would thus be paved for the entrance eventually of all Europeans, but he miscalculated the obstinacy of the Chinese, who treated him with the same contumely as they had treated his predecessors. Seu, the Governor-General, wrote offensive letters, declining an interview inside the walls on the plea that the people were strongly averse to the desired concession, and that he could not control their excitement. Dr Bowring, in his numerous letters, bears testimony to the good feeling exhibited towards him by the Cantonese wherever he went, and proves that the opposition presented arose solely from the obduracy of the Mandarins and their repugnance to foreigners. Cooped up in the prison-house of the Canton factories, debarred from all access to the higher officials, far removed from the political and literary world, and restricted to the dull routine of purely consular duties, he realized in all its sadness the truth of the poet's saying, " Better fifty years of Europe than a cycle of Cathay," and found his position almost unendurable. He mixed much with the people, however, and gave in his letters curious and interesting details of their religious and social life, their occupations and amusements, their usages and their superstitions.

From his age and experience the new consul was not perhaps well fitted to serve in a subordinate capacity, nor was he entirely in accord with the Plenipotentiary, Sir George Bonham, as to the proper course of action to pursue. The consul wished to enforce treaty obligations which had been persistently ignored by the Chinese, and practically abandoned by ourselves up to the time of his assuming office, while the plenipotentiary was quite willing to let matters remain as before, and did not wish to have his serenity disturbed by any dispute with the Mandarins which might compel him to take active measures. Seu was, of course, on his part, ill disposed to allow the consul to introduce an innovation which the English plenipotentiary was content to leave in abeyance, and was shrewd enough to perceive that if he gave way to the demands of the former, all the opprobrium of abandoning the old system of exclusiveness, which maintained the power of the mandarins, would fall upon himself. In this disagreement lay the germs of the subsequent war.

In April 1852, Dr Bowring received temporary charge of the office of plenipotentiary from Sir George Bonham, and on the latter returning in February 1853, applied for leave of absence for a year, visiting on his way home the island of Java, of which some account will be found in his Recollections. In 1854 he was appointed to succeed Sir George, and was knighted by the Queen before his departure. Immediately after his return to Hong Kong, the war with Russia broke out, and he proceeded at once with the Admiral, Sir James Stirling, to the north of China, the admiral hoping to intercept the fleet under the command of the Russian Admiral Poutiateen. The latter had, however, received prior intelligence of the outbreak of hostilities, and had disappeared with his fleet long before the English men-of-war arrived off Chusan.

The state of affairs at this time at Shanghai, and in the Kiangsoo province, of which Nanking is the capital, was most alarming, the whole country being overrun by marauding parties of Taipings, who had successfully resisted the imperial authorities and seized Nanking itself. Shanghai also was

held by a gang of unkempt rabble, the leader of whom had
been, it was said, a horseboy at Canton, and trade was
consequently nearly at a standstill. The Taiping insurrection was so formidable, that Sir John Bowring determined
to send a mission to Chinkiangfoo and Nanking to inquire
into the resources and designs of the rebels, for whom considerable sympathy had been excited in England, under a
mistaken idea that they had adopted a pure form of Christianity. The report brought back by the officers delegated
by him demonstrated that the whole Taiping system was a
gigantic imposture, but this document was never published,
and it was not till many years afterwards that the fraud was
fully exposed, and the Taiping power annihilated by Colonel
Gordon.

Meanwhile trade languished, and owing to the inability
of the Taoutai of Shanghai to collect the imperial dues,
smuggling was largely carried on, and Sir John Bowring's
endeavours to put a stop to such proceedings gave him not
a little unpopularity. An arrangement was made by him,
with the concurrence of the United States Minister, that a
European Inspector should be appointed to collect tempo-
rarily the export duties payable to the Chinese government,
a plan which was readily accepted by the Taoutai or native
collectors of customs, but which was not very palatable at
first to some of the merchants who, taking advantage of the
prevailing disorder, had previously ignored the payments
due under treaty on the plea of non-protection.

On his return in August 1854 to Hong Kong, Sir John
Bowring was much mortified to find that the Home government, acting under the advice of the Crown lawyers, had
ordered the restoration to the parties by whom they were
given, of the bonds for payment of arrear duties, which
some of the merchants had executed and handed over to
the consul. Adverting to this much disputed question, Sir

John Bowring writes in one of his letters, " These unhappy Chinese, out of whose hands we took the collection of duties, and would not allow their officers to remain in charge, had never any doubts of getting their dues, and every encouragement and protection was given by them to goods shipped at Shanghai, which of course they would have stopped, and compelled to be sent to other ports, had they dreamed that repudiation was contemplated." It may perhaps be thought that he had too lofty an idea of his plenipotentiary powers, and that he ought not to have given any opinion on the merits of the dispute without first ascertaining the views of the Home government, but, in explanation of his proceedings, he stated that he had discussed the matter with Lord Clarendon before leaving England, and he added, " I only gave an opinion that the Consular Courts should be opened to the enquiry as to whether the duties were due, and upon this action of mine, the merchants (who, as I have reason to believe, had obtained an opinion from the legal authorities here that they had a bad case, and who, moreover, saw that all the American houses had shrunk from the enquiry of the Consular Court which had been opened, and had solicited the United States Minister to arbitrate amicably, and pledged themselves to accept his decision), the merchants applied to me also to arbitrate, and I most unwillingly undertook the task, and was engaged in the investigations when the mandate of the government came, to which I submitted, and did nothing but release the merchants from the arbitration bonds." Whatever may be thought of the time or manner in which he expressed his sentiments, there can be little doubt of the justice of Sir John Bowring's view of the transactions mentioned.

In 1855 he concluded a treaty with Siam, which was a most successful effort of diplomacy, and was remarkable alike for the promptitude and sagacity with which it was

carried out. Being to all intents and purposes purely a commercial treaty, it had a better chance of being durable than
most conventions with oriental powers, who are only too
ready to break through diplomatic engagements whenever
it may suit their convenience. The treaty opened a wide
field to commercial enterprise in a country which had previously been almost wholly inaccessible to western nations.
The happy termination of this undertaking, for which he
received but scanty thanks, was a great solace to him for
the unmerited obloquy he had suffered in connection with
the question of the arrear-duties at Shanghai, and for a
fruitless attempt made by him to gain access to the court
of Peking, a proceeding which was rather sharply criticised
by the Home Government.

In pursuance of instructions from England, he was con-
templating, in conjunction with the American and French
ministers, another visit to the Gulf of Pecheli, when the
outrage on the Lorcha " Arrow " by the Canton authorities,
in October 1856, involved him in hostilities with the Chinese
Government. Most unprejudiced persons will admit that
it was an error to allow the British flag to be abused by
unscrupulous Chinese traders, and it is evident that the
vessel in question had no right to carry it, the term of
registry having expired. The dispute was in fact regarded
as a means to an end, that end being the free admission
of foreigners to the city of Canton, and although Yeh's
conduct was defiant throughout, and his resolute determination not to hold intercourse with high European officials at
his Yamun exhibited a lamentable perversity, it is a subject of regret that a better cause of quarrel was not found
than the " Arrow " affair. Sir John Bowring's justification of his view that the expiry of the license did not
authorize the violence perpetrated by the Canton authorities
was—1. That they did not know of its expiry, and never

alluded to the circumstance. Had they done so the consul was the referee under the treaty, and a complaint of abuse of the English flag would have met with prompt enquiry. 2. Looking at their intentions by their acts, he considered that there was a distinct purpose to violate the privileges of the British flag. 3. The surrender of men, who believed that they were entitled to the protection of that flag, to so blood-thirsty a man as Yeh, would have been unpardonable. 4. The case of the "Arrow" was but one of a succession of outrages for which no redress had been given. 5. The expiry of the license and the failure to renew it placed the ship under colonial jurisdiction, the Chinese having no title whatever to interfere with her, except through the consulate. The ship's papers, whether in order or not, were deposited there, and if the Chinese had acted according to the conditions of the treaty, and put themselves in communication with the consul, there would have been no collision. The papers granted were of undoubted validity against any but British authority—the authority which alone granted, and which alone was entitled to withdraw protection. Lord Clarendon, in writing to Sir John Bowring on the debates in Parliament regarding the dispute, though pointing out the weakness of the case as to the expiry of the licence, observed:—" I think you have been most unjustly treated, and that, in defiance of reason and common sense, the whole blame of events, which could not have been foreseen, and which had got beyond your control, was cast upon you."

In January 1857, the colony of Hong Kong was startled by a diabolical attempt to poison the residents by putting arsenic in the bread consumed by them. Not one of the Governor's family escaped, and his wife's constitution was so fatally undermined that she was obliged in the ensuing year to leave for England, where she died soon after her arrival. When hostilities broke out, a price was placed by the Mandarins on Sir John Bowring's head, but he was of too fearless a temperament to be disturbed by the announcement.

Lord Elgin, on his return from Calcutta, whither he had at first proceeded on hearing of the Indian Mutiny, was constrained to adopt Sir John Bowring's views that the reduction of Canton was a necessary preliminary to an expedition to Pecheli, which latter the home Government had deemed of primary importance, and the place was carried with little loss or difficulty. The ambassador, however, tried the fatal experiment of a mixed Anglo-Chinese government, contrary to Sir John Bowring's recommendation, the result of such a dual administration being naturally to produce mutual distrust and clashing of authority, the Mandarins still exercising an amount of jurisdiction which led the Court of Peking to infer that the barbarians had not really conquered the city, and encouraged it in resisting Lord Elgin's treaty demands. Sir John Bowring rightly opined that Canton should have been held by the European military authorities pending the result of the negotiations in the north of China, and that a strong, wise, and just government of this kind would have produced the best impression on the minds of the people, and have restored confidence and trade.

The year 1858, besides diplomatic and domestic anxieties, was fruitful in local squabbles which disturbed the peace of Hong Kong, and towards its close Sir John Bowring proceeded to Manila on a visit to the Philippine Islands, of which he published an account the next year. He returned to China in January 1859, and in the month of May resigned his office, after more than nine years' service in the East, being nearly worn out by incessant care and anxiety. On his way home he was shipwrecked in the Red Sea, but reached England in safety.

The remainder of his life was not characterised by any incidents of a striking nature, but he was never unoccupied. Besides concluding several commercial treaties between the Siamese and Hawaiian courts and various European states, he was an active member of the British Association, the Social Science Association, the Devonshire Association, and other institutions, often contributing papers to their proceedings, and taking a prominent part in their discussions. He wrote many articles in periodical magazines, as well as fugitive pieces of poetry, and constantly gave lectures on oriental topics, and the social questions of the day. The subjects which specially interested him were prison labour, the metric system, religious progress, universal suffrage, national accountancy, and various statistical matters, his publications of this nature evincing wide information, and, generally speaking, correct and sound views.

In 1860 he married Deborah, daughter of the late Thomas Castle of Clifton, his second union contributing much to the comfort and serenity which attended his latter days.

In the last year of his life (1872) he was still physically strong, while his mental faculties seemed to be quite unimpaired. In the summer, at the meeting of the British Association at Brighton, he delivered an eloquent and effective speech, welcoming the Japanese ambassadors, in response to a sudden call from the President of the Geographical Section. Two months before his death, at the Plymouth meeting of the Social Science Congress, he spoke two or three times a day at some length; while at a temperance meeting, held on the same occasion, he addressed an assemblage of 3000 persons with all the energy of a young man, making the platform shake with his earnest action. He celebrated his eightieth birthday surrounded by his family, when he expressed great pleasure at having

received from Hungary some German stanzas congratulating
him on having attained so great an age. But the silver cord
was soon broken. In the middle of November he purposed
to proceed to London, but feeling indisposed, postponed his
departure, then became worse, and finally took to his bed,
from which he never again rose. It is a singular fact that,
after a long life crowded with so many incidents and strange
adventures, he enjoyed the privilege of dying where he was
born, his eventful career closing at Exeter, almost within a
stone's throw of the house where he first saw light.

In his private life he was the most affectionate of
husbands and fathers, and the firmest of friends. He
never varied in his regard for his early associates, and in
his own family his name was always mentioned with love
and sympathy. In society, which he greatly relished, he
was a most agreeable companion, having a fund of information and anecdote, while his genial and buoyant nature
made him a general favourite. As an old man, his serene
demeanour testified that, notwithstanding the assaults of
time and the vicissitudes of a chequered life, in which there
had been many and rapid alternations of joy and sorrow,
his existence had been on the whole a happy one.

L. B. B.

AUTOBIOGRAPHICAL RECOLLECTIONS

OF

SIR JOHN BOWRING.

EARLY RECOLLECTIONS.

MY GRANDFATHER.

My grandfather's house was adjacent to my father's, and when I was a very little fellow I was accustomed to crawl up the steps which led from our house to the court in front of his domicile. Kneeling at his feet, I said my morning prayers, and many a sweet and kind counsel fell from his lips. Well do I remember the emphasis with which he repeated to me hymns and passages of poetry, which left an indelible impression upon a somewhat susceptible mind. One passage comes back to my thoughts as vividly as when I heard it more than three-score years ago :—" To be good is to be happy. Angels are happier than men, because they are better. Guilt is the source of sorrow. It is a fiend— the avenging fiend which follows us behind with whips and stings. The good know none of this, but rest content in peace of mind, and find the height of all their heaven in goodness." I thought this eminently sublime, and it took me as far into the cloud-land of imagination as my young intellect was capable of proceeding.

My grandfather was a man of strong political feeling, being deemed no better in those days than a Jacobin by politicians and a heretic by churchmen. The truth is that the old Puritan blood, inherited from a long line of ancestors, flowed strongly in his veins, and a traditional reverence for the Commonwealth was evidenced by a fine mezzotint print of Oliver Cromwell, which hung in his parlour. He took a strong part with the Americans in their war of independence, was hustled by the illiberal Tories of the day, and was, I have heard, burnt in effigy in the cathedral yard at the time of the Birmingham riots, when Dr Priestley was compelled to flee his native land. Many prisoners from America were, at the time of our hostilities, confined at Exeter, and my grandfather was much persecuted for the attentions he showed them, and for his attempts to alleviate their sufferings. When John Adams was in England, he, with his wife (who, by the way, was a connection of our family),* visited my grandfather at Exeter as a mark of his respect and regard.

My grandfather's business was that of a fuller, who prepared woollen goods for foreign markets, and especially for that of China, the monopoly of which was in the hands of the East India Company. He had a considerable library. The regular arrival of the *Gentleman's Magazine* was in those days a great event, and a long series of volumes, from its very commencement, occupied no small space on the library shelves, being to him and to me a field of constantly instructive and amusing reference. I breakfasted with him daily, sitting on a trivette (tripod) kept in a state of beautiful brightness, with a game-cock in the centre, a great object of childish admiration.

MY GRANDMOTHER.

My grandmother had a great passion for flowers, and I have very distinct recollections of the fierce war she made upon snails, slugs, and other invaders of her beautiful flower-beds. Every Sunday morning, when I was a child, she led me up the steps of her garden, and never failed to adorn me with a nosegay of the gayest produce of her

* Abigail Adams was the daughter of the Rev. William Smith and Elizabeth Quincy. She married Mr Adams in 1764. Her elder sister, Mary, married in 1762 Richard Cranch, who became a judge of the Court of Common Pleas in Massachusetts. He was a cousin of Sir John Bowring's grandfather.

floral cares, to be exhibited in my button-hole to the whole congregation at church. Of her anemones and ranunculuses she was particularly proud, and not the semblance of a weed or a blade of grass was visible in the plots of ground where these roots had been planted. The tulips, too, were among the grandees of the place, and she used to point out to me with no small complacency the varieties of their stripes and the richness of their colours. My father, her only son, was her pride and glory, and to me, *his* eldest born, she transferred her warm affections. I was in the habit of admiring the very sweet expression of her small mouth—handsome in her old age—and she would then tell me tales of the admiration she had inspired in her youth, and what a pretty girl she was when my grandfather fell in love with her. The vanity, the coquetry of the maiden, is not quite extinguished in the heart of the matron, and very winning indeed was the smile and the toss of the chin which accompanied the words " Ah, John ! had you seen me when I was young ! " Her father's name was Hutchings, her mother's Gifford. The latter was of the same family as Sir Robert Gifford, Attorney-General in George the Third's time, and raised to the peerage. His father was a hop merchant in Exeter, and I think it was in his place of business that I saw Lord Nelson, either returning to, or, coming from Plymouth. He looked to me the shattered fragment of a diminutive man. He wore several decorations and a large cocked hat. There was the empty sleeve of his right arm, and a patch upon his eye, but withal a sort of mysterious greatness about him. *Nelsonem tantum vide.*

MY FATHER.

Of all the men I ever knew, I think my father possessed the sweetest temper, and on only two occasions have I ever seen it ruffled. Once, when I was a child, and gathered a

handsome peony, which flowered at the entrance of the
garden, and of which he was very proud. I gave it to my
sister Margaret, of whom he was singularly fond, but I
incurred his transient displeasure. The other outbreak was
more serious. When a little boy, I was beaten and misused
by a big fellow, named Ben Hutton, the son of a drunken
old fellow, who was in my father's employ, and my father
was passing in the street when he saw me maltreated. He
pounced upon the injurer with the fierceness of a tiger, and
gave him a very severe dressing. My father, though a
sound and thoughtful liberal, took little share in party
politics, and when the Municipal Reform Bill passed, refused
an offer of the citizens of Exeter to be the first Liberal
mayor. His great enjoyment was reading his favourite
author, Shakspeare, and it would have been difficult to quote
a passage, either in the plays or poems, of which he could
not immediately cite the place where it was to be found.
Philip Quarles' "Emblems" was also much appreciated by
him, and he kept an early edition in his bureau, ornamented
with *cuts*, which now and then the children were allowed to
see. I remember my father's extreme delight when Sir
Walter Scott invited me to Abbotsford, an honour which he
deemed of the highest order, and the anxious inquiries which
he made as to every particular of that, to me, so interesting
a meeting.

MY MOTHER.

My mother was one of the most excellent of women.
She was, with many brothers and sisters, left an orphan,
her father and mother having been carried off by a pestilential disease at St. Ives, in Cornwall, where he was the
rector. My father met her by accident at the Exeter
theatre, and their married life was one of great felicity,
though her later years were troubled with that mortal disease

to which she fell a victim. I write this in the Bay of Pecheli, on the anniversary of her death, which took place on the 24th October 1828. I was at Leeuwarden, in Friesland when I heard that her end was approaching, and I hastened home, merely to see her pale emaciated countenance in the black coffin where her body was deposited. Everything looked awfully desolate. ˌI went into the room, removed the cover of the coffin, where lay the cold clay of her I had loved so tenderly, and whose exhibition of affection for me had been the daily delight and cheerful duty of her life. Two of my children had been the consolation of her declining days. They stood by me and wept, for they had learned to love her. Winter was coming on, and few flowers were to be found, but I rushed into the garden, gathered such as I could collect, with holly branches and evergreens, and with those I surrounded the corpse and then closed the coffin over it. She had extraordinary aptitude for mental arithmetic, and kept the house accounts in admirable order. Up to the time of her death, my father's affairs went on prosperously, and she bore her part with great propriety, but her health was always feeble, and her looks were those of a confirmed invalid. Nothing, however, paralysed her industry, or interfered with her excellent and economical management of household affairs.˙ Education and affection made her devout, and the Bible was a source of habitual enjoyment to her, but her religion was unostentatious and silent, though on all becoming occasions lessons of virtue and wisdom were conveyed to her children. She used no other discipline than that of kind reproof, and in her presence I knew not the emotion of fear or awe. All her influences were gentle and patient.*

* Her father left three sons and three daughters. One of the former entered the naval service, and was a favourite of Lord Collingwood, who addressed to him a charming letter on the duties of a midshipman, which is preserved in the Admiral's memoirs.

ST. LEONARD'S PARISH.

In the parish where I was born, and at the time when I
was born in it, there was neither doctor nor lawyer, clergyman nor publican, tax-gatherer nor soldier. There was
little disease to be cured by the physician, no squabbling to
provide for the attorney, little vice to be reproved by the
clergyman, no pothouse or tavern to encourage drunkenness,
no riots to be suppressed, and there being no paupers, there
were no poor-rates to be collected. I have seen great
changes in that happy spot. The population of St. Leonard's on the southern outskirts of the ancient and loyal city
of Exeter—"*Semper fidelis*" is its motto—has become
multitudinous. With the bills of mortality and the cata-
logues of diseases, there is no want of medical practitioners.
Barristers and solicitors have erected their talking and
scribbling mills, to which the accustomed grist has been
brought by the litigious portion of the community. Divines,
both orthodox and heterodox, have found materials for their
pulpits and their prayers, and parish squabbles have not
been wanting to give their gay variety to the local history.
Many a licence has been granted to beer-shops and public-
houses, whence many a drunkard now reels homeward after
the setting of the sun. The quarterly visitant, demanding
house taxes and parish taxes, and water rates, and lighting
and paving rates, is now the unwelcome but never-failing
disturber of the domestic serenity. I saw a large barrack,
even while George the Third was king, and the noise of the
drum became a daily, and the thunder of artillery not an
unusual, invader of the sweet silence of the scenery. There
was, indeed, a church remarkable for its beauty, its tower
hidden under masses of green ivy, through which the outlines of some Gothic arched windows could be imperfectly
traced, but the clergyman who served in it was no inhabi-

tant of the parish. There was one great squire, the head of the Baring family, the member for the city, whose ancestors sleep in the churchyard under the shadows of some magnificent elms. There were a few seats occupied by country gentlemen, and a few *tuckers* engaged in the preparation of woollens—mostly for the markets of China. Of these (a portion of the representatives of the protected staple trade of the capital of Devonshire, the once renowned Exonia) not a fragment is now left. The coal-mines and the steam machinery of central and northern England have crushed the ancient industry of the West. The chapel of St. Leonard's was destroyed by the violent spirit of innovation. Well do I remember how often rambling artists committed to paper the transitory beauty of the edifice, with which many traditions were associated in my memory, particularly one of a lady who lived in a cave which had been formed out of a bank close to the chapel, where it was said she consoled herself for a long life of sorrow by the devout performance of religious rites in the ivy-covered chapel, whose very altar was darkened by the leaves which excluded the light from the windows, and gave to the whole edifice a damp and gloomy character. Within a stone's throw of the chapel was a little stream, which ran into a shallow receptacle called Parker's Well, the water of which was thought to possess medicinal and even miraculous virtues, especially for eye diseases, and I have often in my childhood seen the afflicted seeking relief from its supposed excellences.

GEORGE'S MEETING HOUSE.

Our place of worship was called "George's Meeting House." The congregation had migrated from a chapel built in the reign of King James, and thence bearing his name, to the new church to which their loyalty gave the name of the reigning sovereign, George. Exeter had been

for generations the seat of fierce religious controversy, and
the place of gathering of many a dissenting synod. It has
the honour too of being associated with noble efforts for
establishing the right and proclaiming the duty of private
judgment. It was there that Mr James Pierce attacked the
doctrine of the Trinity in the beginning of the eighteenth
century. Among the objects of interest connected with
George's Meeting House was a marble tablet in the vestry,
commemorating the fact that after his death the bigoted
Church of England clergyman of the parish in which he
lived, died, and was buried, had denied a "just memorial
on his tomb." This was the parish of St. Leonard's,
and I had often looked with some sentiments of pride on
the massive stone monument bearing the words, " Mr James
Pierce's tomb." It was surrounded by iron rails, and used
to be covered with flowers of the wild convolvulus, growing
over and half hiding the briars below. Two simple things
in the meeting-house always attracted my attention. In
the very centre was a large brass chandelier, looking always
bright, suspended by a twisted rod of iron from the centre,
in the midst of which were two letters, S. S., wrought in
gilded work, most mysteriously intertwined, so as to be read
either backwards or forwards, commemorating the initials of
the name of the donor, Sarah Stokes, who, to my youthful
thought, was thus elevated into regions of immortal fame,
and seemed ever looking down from the entangled glory
upon the congregation below. Then there was a clock—a
broad-faced clock—the movements of whose minute-hand
it was my comfort and amusement to watch when the sermon was particularly dull, or when my thoughts had nothing
else to do. Upon that white field, with its figures that
never moved, and its pointers that were always moving, one
most visibly and the other invisibly, how often did my
thoughts repose. The two hands were the images of know-

ledge and faith. The progress of one I could trace from "tick to tick"—of the other I only felt that it moved, but could convince myself that it *had* moved if, for a few minutes only, I turned my eye away. Over the clock was a golden sun half emerging, but I never knew whether it was intended to exhibit the rising or the setting of the luminary. Opposite this was the scythe of Death, gilded too. I well recollect my affliction when, one Sunday, I discovered that the blade of the scythe had fallen, and nothing was left but the handle. That blade was never restored. I think I made some effort to obtain its restoration, but its fall was an appropriate lesson, and had its becoming moral.

In that meeting-house I well remember my grandfather's venerable form, his tall person, and white hairs. He stood (for from the beginning to the end of the service he never sat down) behind one of the square fluted pillars, upon a peg of which his hat was hung, a model of devout attention and an image of serene piety.

UNITARIAN MINISTERS.

There were no less than three ministers who served that congregation. There was Mr James Manning, an Arian, who was the most popular with the poor, whom he often visited, and always addressed in sweet words and gentle manner. There was Mr Timothy Kenrick, a courageous Unitarian, who was the chosen one of the more intellectual and inquiring; and there was Mr Joseph Butland, from whom I do not remember ever to have heard a doctrinal sermon, but who was a great mathematician, a laborious student, a lover and observer of nature, and an amiable and excellent man. His mode of life and manner of dress were alike simple. It was said, and I believe it is true, that his supper consisted of a far-

thing's worth of periwinkles (wrinkles is the Devonshire
name), on which he fed himself with a pin. Certainly I
have often seen the wrinkle-girl at his door in the evening,
and I know from my own experience that she was in the
habit of selling a small tea-cupful of her ware for a farthing.
I was fond of Mr Butland, who taught me how to avoid
the sharp winds in my walks by walking as much as possible with the wind. His style of preaching, though sometimes quaint, was often practical and eloquent, and there is
a passage in a sermon he published on the death of Mrs
Elizabeth Rowe, which runs for nearly a page into excellent
blank verse. I could repeat it from memory. It runs—
"Not long ago thou wast what I am now—one of the
actors in this passing scene. To all thy woes I lent a
pitying ear,"—and so it ran on in natural flowing harmony.
Yet the latter end of the good man's life was disturbed by
the introduction of an organ into the meeting-house. It
led to a rupture with the congregation, and even as a hearer,
I believe, he never attended when the pipes were called into
play. I have seen him glide in to unite with the rest in
partaking of the Lord's Supper, and I think, when it was
known he was to attend, the pealing organ was locked into
silence. His household affairs were managed by his wife,
a quiet, taciturn, good woman, who had been his servant,
and who, reverencing him as her "lord and master," provided for all, and more than all, his daily wants, never
intruding upon those tranquil studies to which his hours
were devoted. Mr Kenrick was of a more ambitious
nature. He was a Welshman, and on a visit to a Welsh
friend died of apoplexy in the prime of life. I remember
that the bigotry of the time attributed his death to a divine
judgment upon his heresies ; but not long afterwards, when
a very orthodox minister of a very intolerant congregation
committed suicide, nobody ventured to discover in that

providence the outstretching of the hand of heaven. Mr Kenrick's style was rational, dry, and cold. He reasoned well, and encouraged freedom of thought by precept and example. His eldest son, John, has won for himself a high reputation as a classical scholar, and well deserves the reputation he has won. Mr Kenrick's first wife died soon after giving birth to his youngest son George, who afterwards married my eldest sister Margaret, who died in 1824. Mr Timothy Kenrick's second wife was the sister, and the very image of the Rev. Thomas Belsham, the successor of Theophilus Lindsay in Essex Street Chapel, London. Mr Kenrick's conversation was most acceptable to my grandfather, at whose house he invariably spent his Friday evenings, talking of the politics and the religious controversies of the times, topics on which, in those days, it was not always safe to talk, for Exeter was one of the chosen seats of bigotry and intolerance, and to burn Socinians in effigy, and to insult Jacobins in the public streets, was no uncommon amusement of the inhabitants of that episcopal city. Mr Manning was intellectually superior to his colleagues. He was the immediate successor of Micaiah Towgood, and published, if I mistake not, a biography of that excellent man. He also translated Zollikoffer's sermons. There was always a sort of rivalry between him and Mr Kenrick, and if he had been as zealous for the propagation of Arianism as Mr Kenrick was for the diffusion of Unitarianism, I hardly know how the congregation could have held together. Arianism, however, was much on the decline, and Mr Manning quietly submitted to its gradual extinction. I do not believe he cared much about the matter, or would risk the unpopularity to which polemic zeal might have exposed him.

DR LANT CARPENTER.

On the death of Mr Kenrick, Lant Carpenter, afterwards made an LL.D. by the University of Glasgow,
was chosen to succeed him. He was exceedingly and
deservedly beloved by the congregation, and to the
young catechumens (a very grand name, which conveyed
to all of us some notions of dignity) was an object
of the highest reverence, almost of worship. I owe
to Dr Carpenter a boundless debt. He.developed much
that lay hidden in my nature, and was one of the most
virtuous and religious of men, being and doing all that he
taught others to be and do. There was at times a precision
and attention to the minutest things that seemed narrow-
minded, as if great things and small things were of the
same importance, and deserving the same amount of care,
caution, and concern. Nor could he always understand or
pass by little aberrations of thoughts and feelings which, in
his extreme susceptibility, he fancied might lead astray. On
one occasion he called on me to narrate, in my own words, the
Scripture account of our Saviour's interview with the woman
of Samaria. At the point where, availing herself of the presence
of so high an authority for the solution of a question fiercely
disputed between Jews and Samaritans, I inserted the
phrase "impelled by a natural curiosity," I was reproved
for the introduction of a something not to be found in the
gospel narrative. So, on another occasion, when I was
certain that I had a more thorough knowledge of the subject
under examination than my competitors, the prize was given
to me for a verbal accuracy quite compatible with inferior
acquaintance with the whole, and I felt greatly aggrieved,
and treasured up the memory of the wrong. These were
small defects in a character which I shall always contemplate
with grateful affection. How he laboured—how lovingly,

how untiredly he laboured for the improvement of his pupils—how lucidly he taught, how practically ! As regarded the young people of his congregation, it was all gratuitous service. He lectured, he catechized, he exhibited experiments in chemistry, electricity, and galvanism—he taught us geography, astronomy, and the use of the globes, and wrote a book of Scripture geography, principally for our instruction. For many a year I deemed him the wisest and greatest of men, as he assuredly was one of the best. Others had the title of Doctor—there were Doctors of Divinity, Law, and Medicine, but he was *the* Doctor, far above all, and to dispute his authority or to doubt his judgment, would have appeared to me almost sacrilegious.

WORKMEN.

I remember well the groups of workmen in my grandfather's employ. There was a surly foreman of the name of Simmonds, who was thought wise because he was taciturn. There was an old fellow of extremely diminutive stature, whom the others called "The Pixie," and who was the object of the daily jeers and jests of his fellows. He was rather given to tippling, and I remember on one occasion, when he refused to make up a quarrel over the ale-pots, an inscription was written on the walls of one of the workshops, far above the pixie's reach,—on such a date "Pixie Soper refused beer," which remained a record of his infirmity for many a year. There was an apprentice called Jack Kelly, who was always lost in arithmetical and mathematical abstractions. A sprightly sexagenarian was the genial spirit of the place, and was habitually called "Young Omer," his real name being Oram. He had a stupid sort of a son, who bore the designation of "Daddy Omer," by contrast. The great event of the year was the jollity of Christmas eve, when the great logs were burnt, and the ale and bread and

cheese went round with jokes, tales, and songs.   There was
one in particular, of which the burden was—

"St George he was for England, St Denis was for France,
   Sing 'Honi soit qui mal y pense.'"

which was sung with immense emphasis in chorus, thus—

" O-nai so-ait Kwai mal why pence."

These are recollections of a state of things which has
passed away.   In my youth a great proportion of the
working people at Exeter were engaged in the woollen
trade.   They wore green serge aprons with scarlet strings.
There was an influential guild, whose magnates met in an
ancient building in the main street of the city, called the
Tuckers' Hall.   Time was when the merchants, fullers,
tuckers, weavers, dyers, pressmen, and packers of Exeter
held the representation of the city in their hands.

SCHOOL LIFE.

I was sent to school at Moreton-Hampstead, then one of
the rudest spots in Devonshire, the joke being that it was
made out of the rubbish that was left when the rest of
the world was created.   There were then no roads pass-
able by wheel-carriages of any sort, and everything was
conveyed to and from Exeter on *crooks*—bent branches
of trees which were fastened to pack-saddles — seated
on one of which I departed from home.   The schoolmaster's name was Bransby—James H. Bransby.   He was
the son of an instrument-maker at Ipswich, I think, and,
being dissatisfied with the orthodox faith of his fathers,
deserted to the Unitarians, and was educated by Mr T.
Kenrick in an academy of divinity established in Exeter.
He was not a very wise, nor a very honest man, but had in
him some dry humour, some knowledge of old books, some
amusing stories, and was of what was called an affectionate

nature. I recollect the first sermon he preached to his
country congregation at Moreton-Hampstead. The text
was "Fulfil ye my joy." He represented himself as bound
to his hearers till death—bound by inseparable links.
Afterwards a larger salary was offered to him at Dudley,
which, naturally enough, he accepted, but how bitterly was
he reproached by the Moretonians. The "fulfil ye my
joy" sermon, with all its protestations, all remembered, all
recorded (for they had been most flattering to the pride of
the rural flock) was flung at his head, and cast into his
teeth. Poor man! he did not inspire his pupils with much
respect, for they found out that he could tell little fibs and
do little dishonesties. He was accustomed to accompany
his scholars in their country walks. On one occasion he
tumbled over a stone, and told us he had hurt his shin and
must go home, but that we were to continue our walk, and
return by the same road. With the common perverseness
and disobedient spirit of boys, we determined to go home
by a different road; and lo! at about a mile or two from
the town, on the opposite side from that by which we had
gone out, we suddenly stumbled upon our master, seated on
a stile, with the young lady he was courting, and reading
love-poetry to his "mistress' eye-brow." The words we
heard were—

> "Humid seal of soft affection,
> Love's first snow-drop—virgin kiss!"

He had not the courage to reprove or punish us, and we
had among us some wicked wits, who would certainly have
given him a Roland for his Oliver. On another occasion,
however, he did punish us, and that also was connected
with the history of his lady-love. Her name was Isaac, and
she was the daughter of a Welsh Baptist minister who kept
bees, wrote a book about them, drank nothing but mead or
metheglin made from his own hives, and rejoiced greatly in

a pun of his own making—that he ruled over one of the most ancient nations of the world, the *Hivites*, proudly referring to the Bible for his authority. Mr Bransby was passionately in love with his fair one, and sometimes sadly neglected the duties of the school, in order that he might enjoy her company, for she lived in an adjacent street. Our evening lessons were frequently left without superintendence. Our schoolroom was over a cellar, in which was a pump, and one evening, when our tutor had run away to pay his devoirs to his chosen one, it was determined that all the school should retreat to the cellar, that the two lowest stairs should be sawn away, and the cellar then be filled with water from the pump, while the heroes were to keep themselves dry on a heap of coals that lay in a corner. In due time the master came home, found the schoolroom empty, wandered over the house, where he discovered nobody, and at last, hearing some noise (intentionally made) in the cellar, came down in a great rage, himself and the lighted candle (soon extinguished) falling into the water. While he was splashing about in the dark, the lads managed as best they could to make their way up the stairs. The joke was too good a joke to be repudiated, as everybody in the school was concerned in it, and openly avowed it, and I believe there was not one who would not have suffered the penalty over and over again for the enjoyment of the fun, so we all submitted cheerfully to our castigation.

My schoolmaster afterwards committed a forgery, hid himself in Wales, where he became the editor of a country newspaper, and died in obscurity. But I owed him something. He had some knowledge, more taste, and was full of pleasant anecdote. He gave me encouragement, and set my cheeks glowing when he told me I had written a very good line when he gave me "death" as the theme. It was—

"Monarchs must die as well as meaner men."

But, to say the truth, it was stolen property, for there was a picture in an old book—I believe it was Drelincourt on "Death," at the foot of which was this inscription "the philosopher tells the king that in the grave, monarchs and meaner men were all alike." However, mine was truer, and makes a tolerable line of poetry. I sometimes attempted a little poetry then. There was a boy who excited much envy and jealousy. His name was Moore. He entered the army, turned out a sad profligate, and was killed or died in very early life. A subject was given out, it was "orchard robbing," and he read a poem he said he had written, beginning—

> "A boy ascends the tree,
> To steal another's pears,
> And thinks no one will see,
> And if they do—who cares ?"

The boy's heroism, and the poet's verses were equally applauded, and Moore was the hero of the hour ; but, alas ! the following day the poem was discovered *printed,* and Moore's reputation was suddenly lowered, notwithstanding his solemn averment that he had written a poem on apple-stealing, and had, by mistake, confounded his composition with the printed and lauded poem.

I have some distressing recollections of school-life. One of my masters was a man named Tucker, and I remember his fascinating my father by exhibiting a picture of the "Haven Banks" at Exeter. He was a drunken good-for-nothing fellow, but was himself the son of a schoolmaster, and wrote a fine hand. He was an accomplished flourisher of swans, and eagles, and angel's heads and wings, with which he adorned the first pages of our writing and cyphering books ; and of his exploits in this part of the field he was very proud, as I learned to my shame and sorrow. Well do I recollect the schoolroom, on whose walls he had inscribed in big black letters, "Let emulation prevail." There was only one boy about whom I cared a rush, and his name was Edward Pearce. He was fond of drawing, as was I, but he was incomparably my superior, and I looked at his work as something unapproachable. He loved his books too, was gentle in manner, and kind to me, his junior, asking me to his uncle's house to see his pictures. I had a new arithmetic book, on the title-page of which Tucker had exhibited one of his finest specimens of ornamental penmanship. He was delighted with his work, and so was I, its possessor. I was hanging over it with a pen full of ink in my hand, when a large drop fell from the pen, blotting and obscuring the glories of the artist. He was in a desperate rage, and determined to visit me with condign punishment. I believe I had never been punished before— certainly never whipped, but I was conducted into the cellar, my trousers pulled down, and Edmund Pearce (my friend) was sent for, the birch was put into his hand, and he was ordered to lay it on severely, which he did. It was one of the bitterest moments of my life. To be so punished for what was at worst but a little carelessness, to be punished by the hands of him whom, out of the circle of my family, I loved best in the world! I thought at the moment "Edmund will not flog me, or if he flog me, I shall come off with a slight visitation. I could not flog him. No! I would die first." From that hour I hated the master, from that hour my feelings towards Edmund Pearce became frozen (I believe he was afterwards frozen to death on Dartmoor), and the early lesson of human faithlessness was engraved on my heart. As to Tucker, had the opportunity been in the way, the will was not wanting to inflict upon him summary vengeance. It was perhaps well for him and for me that we never met in a solitary place after I grew strong enough to revenge a wrong of which I retained so bitter a memory. New scenes brought other thoughts, and I mention the matter as an additional evidence of the ill-digested plans of education, and an example of the ill-judging and improper instruments to which, in the last century, the formation of character was confided.

We were only eight boarders at Moreton, but were as mischievous as any eighty or eight hundred could be ; and the little respect in which we held Mr Bransby left our wicked propensities full play. A cane lay on his desk for flogging the boys, which we cut up into small pieces, and it was fine fun to see what an impotent instrument of punishment he held when he took it up, intending to lay it on the shoulders of one of us sinners. On one occasion, the boys made an excursion to a place called Sentry Field, where, to the great annoyance of the inhabitants of the town, they filled up a well with stones, so that no water could be drawn. At another time, one of the boys fired small cannons into the bedroom of an opposite neighbour, filling the family with alarm ; and it was no unusual thing to put gunpowder into the snuffers, which exploded when they were used. Once, when our master neglected his school for his lady-love, whom the boys pleasantly called *Miss Saucer-eyes*, they blackened all the desks with ink, and told the tutor they had gone into mourning for his absence. They disturbed him at night by their racket, and always pretended to be asleep when he entered the bedroom, attributing the noise to cats and rats.

MORETON CHARACTERS.

Moreton, like most small towns, had its celebrities. There was a man who mended our shoes, who bore the illustrious name of Ptolemy. The tonsor who cut our hair was always called " Dip my head, sir ! " that being the form of ejaculation with which he interlarded his discourse. There was an old woman who lived in a hut filthier than herself, with no end of cats around her, in whose skins, and those of hares and rabbits, she traded, and whose hovel, holding our noses, we sometimes visited. One day she asked us what was o'clock, and offended us (as we were all Presbyterians) by answering, " Aye, yours is a Presbyterian clock ! " meaning, of course, that it was not to be trusted, but I doubt if the beldame ever went to church. Had she done so, the congregation would assuredly have soon taken flight.' Cats prowled about her garden, occupied her cottage, and were carried about in her arms. They shared all she had in her of tenderness and kindness. Could a creature so hideous ever have loved ? I never heard that she had an acquaintance, still less a friend, and her domicile was at some distance from the road, and far away from other dwellings. Among the characters was the Welsh Baptist minister, father of Miss Saucer-eyes, whom we used to call Parson Jacob Isaac, or Farmer Isaac Jacob, the King of the Hivites. He used to say that he ruled over a very irritable and ungrateful community, who often stung him in recompense for his care and kindness, and whom I have often seen him approach, shrouded under the protection of a heavy black veil, and wearing thick leather gloves. His scheme consisted in stealing the honey without destroying the bees, and I understood that the whole secret of his management was traceable to his intimate alliance with the sovereign queens. By his influence behind the throne, he contrived to direct the policy (whether or not he won the affections) of the whole Hivite nation. I remember well the indignation of our teacher when one of his congregation asked him if Miss Saucer-eyes (she had large bright eyes) were well. He blushed like a peony and exclaimed ' " For shame ! " but the Moreton-Hampstead rustics were not distinguished for refinement, and a joke was not the less appreciated because it was coarse.

DARTMOOR.

Those were most happy days. Our rambles were delightful. We were accustomed to trace the hill streams to their very source, to scramble over the rocks, and to visit the waterfalls, of which one—Becky Fall—has much local celebrity. We went to the hamlets and villages that skirt the dreary Dartmoor, upon whose verge Moreton (whence the name Moor-town) stands. The last house in the town was a small inn bearing a sign, on one side of which was written—

> "Before the moor you strive to pass,
> Take here a good refreshing glass."

And on the other—

> "Now the moor you're safely over,
> Drink, your spirits to recover."

The moor was, indeed, in winter a most dreary and desolate place, on which people were not unfrequently frozen to death when they lost their way in the midst of its pathless snows. There were, besides, numerous cromlechs and other Druidical remains, rude fortifications, both British and Roman, among which I recollect Cranbrook Castle, a circle of stones, forming a vast encampment on a very elevated spot, down whose steep banks the most beautiful wood scenery descends to the Teign below. The rivers which take their rise in the forest of Dartmoor glide or hurry through the most lovely varieties of mountain and valley, their clear streams, bright and musical, bordered with flowers and filled with fish. But to trace them in their windings in the light-hearted days of healthful, joyous boyhood, that was indeed a bliss, and I felt—how often!—all that I afterwards read in the finest passages of the "Excursion" or "Childe Harold." At the top of one of the Dartmoor tors, was a church whose curate told me his congregation was sometimes the clerk alone, and sometimes the clerk and a wandering butterfly. It was at the time when the admission of the Catholics to civil rights was fiercely debated, and somehow or other the topic was introduced into our conversation. As the simple-hearted parson poured out the most extraordinary vitupera-tions upon the Papists, talking of them with as much horror and repugnance as if they were all incarnate fiends, I quietly asked him, " Have you ever known a Roman Catho-lic ? " On which the good man vehemently answered, " O Lord, sir ! No ! God forbid ! " Yet he was not tormented like the unfortunate madman who, having been in his time one of the most passionate opponents of the Catholics, fancied that his right leg—his favourite leg—had become a Papist, and was tormented from morning to night by the thought of its disagreeable adjacency, availing himself of all possible contrivances to keep it, as he said, at a distance, and invari-ably putting it out of bed before he composed himself to sleep.

YOUTHFUL ASPIRATIONS.

It was a longing desire of my boyhood to be trained to what is called the ministry, but I never gave open ex-pression to my wish, and never even hinted it to my father or to any of my friends. It seemed too lofty an ambition, and I felt as if it would be impertinent and presumptuous to indulge in such aspirations. I cannot now unravel the thoughts which intruded between my desire and disappoint-ment. I sometimes fancied that it would be suggested to me, or planned for me, and with what delight should I have welcomed the proposal ! The utterance of a single word would have changed the whole course of my existence. Instead of a life of vicissitude, I should probably have spent the years of mortal existence in silent monotony—instead of wandering over the wide earth and the still wider seas, I should have been located in a narrow sphere, and associated

with the scenery of the fields and the streams of some
country town—instead of intercourse with multitudinous
man, with those who have moved in and moved the great
events of our time, my acquaintances would not have
stretched beyond the narrow circle of family and household
friends—instead of occupying myself with the concerns of
the world, I should have had charge of a country congregation—and instead of launching (ever too rashly) into the
literature of remote nations, it would have been my pride
and my duty to solve theological problems, and to find
acceptance in the columns of a provincial newspaper (for
the itch of writing was upon me from my very boyhood)
would have been a great gratification. I had perhaps
hardly defined to myself what a dissenting minister was, or
ought to be, but in the circle where I moved, he was an
object of boundless reverence, his visits were anticipated
with awe, and sometimes with apprehension, and always
recollected among the memorabilia worthiest of note. Then,
he was the principal actor in the most impressive family
scenes—he gave their names to the children when life
began, he spoke the eulogiums of the dead when life was
ended, he counselled, encouraged, reproved all from the
pulpit, and was entitled to speak as no one else spoke in the
household. He knew most of hidden things, most of
heaven, hell, and God, and had little to do with the working,
every-day world. It was indeed a great thing to be a
minister of the Gospel, too great a thing for me, and so I
glided into other studies and pursuits, still looking back
upon that to which I felt I was not worthy to be called.

POLEMICAL CONTROVERSY.

I was engaged for years in a fierce polemic struggle with
a cousin, whose talents I was taught to hold in high
respect. He was afterwards a successful Chancery barris-

ter, but died young. As to the results of the religious controversy, they were exactly what they ordinarily are. Neither made any advances towards the conversion of the other. We became angry, each despising his adversary for being blind and deaf to the counter-arguments which each deemed irresistible. How stupid that you do not understand *this* reasoning! How intolerable that you will not acknowledge *that* fact! But every boy is a miniature man, little quarrels are but the type of great ones, and too many a controversy has been, I fear, rather instrumental in developing impatience, ignorance, intolerance, and evil passions, than in furthering the progress of truth and charity.

FIRST LAUNCH IN LIFE.

On leaving school, I was placed in a house whose principal partner, Mr Robert Kennaway, was engaged at the same time in the wine and spirit and the Manchester trade. He was very kind to me, lent me books, and assisted me in acquiring the Spanish, Portuguese, and Italian languages. French I learnt from an emigrant named Coupé. I was greatly aided in the study of Italian by the emigrants who then visited England in great numbers, selling barometers and other instruments. A merchant of the name of Churchill helped me to acquire German and Dutch. In those days the Exeter merchants were mostly travelled men, with a practical knowledge of other tongues, and the Quay at Exeter was crowded with the ships of all nations, carrying away the staple produce of the county, which consisted of a great variety of woollen goods, baize, serges, druggets and many others. The tenters' grounds, called rack-fields by the fullers, displayed all the colours of the rainbow, but not a vestige is now left of things that were. My father was one of the last representatives of the ancient woollen trade of Exeter, and saw its final decay and departure to the north.

COMMERCIAL EXPERIENCES.

In June 1811, I was settled in London as a clerk in a merchant's counting-house. I had not many friends, but such as I had received me with singular kindness. I cannot forget the hospitable attentions I found under the roof of Mr and Mrs Parkes, who were then, from a situation of great worldly depression, gradually rising in wealth and prosperity. I looked upon Mr Parkes with great respect, for he was an author, and a popular one. All literary objects I was disposed to venerate, and though Mr Parkes over-estimated his own powers, and was too fond of appearing to be acquainted with matters of which he was ignorant, yet his calm sound sense, and the industrious habits of his mind, made him a valuable friend and a judicious counsellor. I owe him much, but will give an instance *ad docendum* of his weakness. He was engaged in a controversy as to the greater or less safety of employing oil in sugar-refining, and wrote a pamphlet—clever enough but ill-tempered—which was full of Latin quotations, furnished him by some too busy friend. They had nothing to do with the matter in dispute, and were personal, but they had a classical air. Now Mr Parkes could not understand, far less apply them, and when accused of calling in auxiliaries to his help, he never had the courage to desist from taking all the credit of the quotations to himself, and though he would not tell a falsehood about the matter, he always insisted that he had all the books quoted in his library, that he could point out every passage, and that he had learned Latin at school.

He had a great passion for literary distinctions. It was his ruling passion, in truth, and his industry and intrepidity in hunting them out, his delight in obtaining, and his un- subdued ardour when he failed to obtain them, altered in my mind very greatly the estimate I had formed of their value. I have received many such honours, and if they have an interest, it is because they were not obtained by canvas or by self-esteem.

My commercial history may be shortly told. I went to Spain in my twenty-first year, where I had sometimes ten or a dozen vessels consigned to me, in several ports, at the same time. I lived for some months at Bordeaux. I after- wards went to Lisbon, in order to obtain a settlement of the claim I had upon the British Commissariat for supplies furnished through me to the English army. Never was a war conducted with more improvidence and disregard to economy than that of the Peninsula. Everything was bought at extravagant prices, and the want of ready money had thrown British pecuniary reputation into such distrust that large fortunes were made by the purchase, at an enormous discount, of the promissory notes of our Commis- sariat officers ; 60 to 80 per cent. less was not a uncommon depreciation. The exchange upon London was immensely disadvantageous to the British government, and instead of providing money by drafts on the Treasury, supplies of hard cash had been sent out. Probably more than half the expenses of the war might have been saved to the public. Our army was at the mercy of contractors, jobbers, speculators in exchange, and a thousand classes of adventurers, native and foreign. Almost everything being bought at most extravagant rates, this added to the enormous increase of prices which increased demand always produces. There was the additional augmentation, justified by supposed risk as to ultimate payment, and certainty of delay in the examination and settlement of accounts. It was some of these accounts in arrear whose payment I was sent to claim, and the payment was enforced by me. I was not satisfied with the estimate formed of the value of my services to my principals, and the consequence was a separation. I had acquired a small property, amounting, I think, to about £1500, and was about to engage in some trading adventures with a Bordeaux house, which would have taken me to the Mauritius, but the project was finally abandoned, and I became a merchant on my own account. My capital was too little, and I was too adventurous. I stumbled, rose again, and found a partner. Stronger than I, he was too weak to support me, so we tottered together. Released, and after some years' experience and much travel, I found capital and strength—too much strength, for it crushed me. I have passed through all the vicissitudes of the uncertain career of commerce. At one time I had realized about £40,000, a sum that ought to have satisfied my ambition. Not once, but twice in my life, I have been possessor of this more than competency, and twice I have lost more than I possessed. I abandoned commerce, for which, in some respects at all events, I was not unfitted. I had a thorough knowledge of accounts, and have, I hope, turned that knowledge to the public benefit by my successful efforts to reform our national system of book-keeping. I had a knowledge of languages, superior to that of most of the merchants in the Royal Exchange. The causes of my failure I can now calmly estimate and thoroughly understand. I had too much confidence in unworthy men, and was altogether of too adventurous and speculative a nature. Had I been associated with persons of a less sanguine character, and possessing qualities in which I was deficient, I should probably have ended my commercial career in much prosperity and opulence. Perhaps, through much suffering, it was good for me to be placed in another part of the field of activity. I had buoyant spirits, which supported me like life-buoys on the ocean of adversity. Shipwrecked, I was not wholly lost, and the very waves that rolled over me seemed to freshen and strengthen me for new exertions. Besides, I had made many friends, and faithful friends they have proved themselves.

SUCCESSFUL CRŒSUSES.

Many of the men who have been most fortunate, as it is deemed—I mean those who have amassed the largest sums of money—have generally succeeded by the persevering application of some very simple principle, which they have established as the general rule of their proceedings. Ricardo said that he had made his money by observing that people in general exaggerated the importance of events. If, therefore, dealing as he dealt in the stocks, there was reason for a small advance, he bought, because he was certain the unreasonable advance would enable him to realise ; so, when stocks were falling, he sold, in the conviction that alarm and panic would produce a decline not warranted by circumstances. Morrison told me that he owed all his prosperity to the discovery that the great art of mercantile traffic was to find out sellers rather than buyers ; that if you bought cheap, and satisfied yourself with only a fair profit, buyers— the best sort of buyers, those who have money to buy—would come of themselves. He said he found houses engaged with a most expensive machinery, sending travellers about in all directions to seek orders, and to effect sales, while he employed travellers to buy instead of to sell, and, if they bought well, there was no fear of his effecting advantageous sales. So, uniting this theory with another, that small profits and quick returns are more profitable in the long run than long credits with great gains, he established one of the largest and most lucrative concerns that has ever existed in London, and was entitled to a name which I have often heard applied to him, "The Napoleon of shopkeepers." Hudson had his theory too, and a very simple and sensible one. He saw how unnecessarily expensive was the machinery of railway management—that the same staff and plant, generally very costly, while directing only one railway concern, might, with a small additional charge, be applied to many. Hence, fusions and absorptions, and junctions and unions—the *personnel* improved in quality by the selection of the most efficient, and the *material* economised by a great extension of its employment.

LITERARY REMINISCENCES.

My first literary production printed was a short skit I wrote when Wordsworth first obtained a government appointment, on the recommendation of Lord Lonsdale :—

> "When favour's golden hook is baited,
> How swiftly patriot zeal relaxes ;
> In silent state see Wordsworth seated,
> Commissioner of stamps and taxes.
> Wordsworth, most artless among bards,
> Who talked of Milton and of freedom,
> Scorned service purchased by awards,
> And pitied those who chanced to need 'em.
> Some poets are but men, 'tis said ;
> The question may be well disputed,
> If they can eat corruption's bread,
> And still continue unpolluted."

I should have added—

> "And can the lesson taught the child
> From God's authority—the Bible ;
> Who touches pitch must be defiled,
> Become an actionable libel ?"

This was printed in the *Examiner*, then edited by Leigh Hunt, whose personal acquaintance I made in Horsemonger Lane Jail, to which he and his brother John were committed for two years, for having said, in answer to some foolish verses, written by "Laura Matilda," in which all the graces were attributed to the Prince Regent, that this paragon of graces was "a fat gentleman of forty," the libel being that such an averment tended to the degradation of the sovereign authority in the opinion of his liege subjects. Upon such basis stood the monarchy in those persecuting, or, in milder terms, prosecuting days. It was then that William Hone, arraigned before Lord Ellenborough for his libellous and profane publications—very popular they were—drove the judge into a towering passion, by referring to the tolerant spirit of his father Bishop Law. "It is as false as hell," was the passionate and undignified retort of the man in ermine.

I have published between forty and fifty volumes—in every case with some pecuniary profit—and several pamphlets less known of course — one on the absurdities of the Quarantine Laws, another on my arrest by the Bourbons in 1822, two in Spanish, of which one was on the slave trade, in reply to O'Gavan, an Havana deputy to the Cortes, while the other was a translation from Clarkson's tract on the opinions of the early Christians in reference to war. I was liberally paid as editor of the *Westminster Review*, for which Jeremy Bentham originally provided the funds, and in which I wrote a great many articles. I also contributed largely to the *London Magazine*, in which Elia (Charles Lamb), William Hazlitt, Leigh Hunt, Charles Elton, and many other well-known names were writers.

WILLIAM HAZLITT.

What anecdotes cross my mind, illustrative of the character of each ! Hazlitt was a dirty fellow, and seldom washed his hands. When playing at whist with Lamb, the latter said to him in his stammering way, "Haz-Haz-Haz-l-l-it ! if dirt were trumps, what hands you'd hold!" Hazlitt occupied the house in Bentham's garden, where Milton lived while secretary to Cromwell, and a great plague he was while he inhabited it. He never paid any rent, and wherever there was any white paint to write upon, he covered it with his superscriptions. The philosopher was much perplexed by his pertinacity in not quitting the abode upon notice being given, but (probably persuaded by Leigh Hunt, who owed many favours to Bentham) he was at last induced to surrender a domicile which he had so comfortably and cheaply held. I have some recollection that the garden in which Milton's house is is somewhere referred to by the blind bard, but my memory fails me as to the locality of the description. I remember the old sage, when he passed before it, pointing out to his guests the inscription, "Sacred to Milton, Prince of Poets," which Hazlitt had caused to be engraved on a stone, and, lifting up the stick with which he always walked, and which he called Dobbin, raising it over the shoulders of his companion, saying, "down on your marrow-bones."

GEORGE DYER.

George Dyer, the author of the "History of Cambridge," and of "Poetics," in which are one or two of the best hymns in our language, was a frequent subject of Lamb's jests, though he loved the old man dearly. Dyer was the most absent person I have ever known. He was once seen in Fleet Street without his stockings, and he took off his inexpressibles to give them to a poor man who was wretchedly clad. At a party he took up a coal-scuttle instead of his hat, and its contents fell into his neck and down his back. He once walked during his reveries into the New River, and, as Lamb said, was "fished out" by his sister with her parasol. I was requested once to ask George Dyer to write a sonnet for a lady, and to take care that it consisted of *fourteen* lines. He told me he *had* been very careful about it, but, on counting it, there were only *thirteen*. I have seen him at his own table put his fingers into the mustard-pot, mistaking it for the sugar-basin. When I went to Russia, he urged me to present to the Emperor Alexander a copy of his letters on the English Constitution. It was splendidly bound for the occasion, and I told him he must write a proper inscription. He made a flaming dedication to the Emperor *Joseph !* I happened to look at the title-page, and discovered his mistake. When the book was sent to him, he pasted over the erroneous page, and rewrote the inscription, but the word Joseph was most visible through the paper, and the amendment was sadly botched and bungled. The emperor sent him no ring, as he did to me.

THOMAS HOOD.

I was acquainted with the editors of several of the annuals, in most of which I was in the habit of writing. With Thomas Hood, the conductor of *The Gem*, I was more specially allied. He had attained great celebrity from his "Eugene Aram," and his "Bridge of Sighs," every verse of which is a touching picture, and greater still, from his "Song of the Shirt." The anti-Corn Law League was desirous of making him their poet-laureate by engaging him in their service, and I invited Cobden, Bright, and some others of the leaders of that formidable body to meet Hood at my table, but his death put an end to any such arrangement. Poor fellow ! From his death-bed he sent me an engraving of his bust, with his autograph at the foot. He once addressed me in the following lines :—

> "To Bowring ! man of many tongues,
> (All over tongues, like rumour),
> This tributory verse belongs,
> To paint his learned humour.
> All kinds of gab he knows, I wis,
> From Latin down to Scottish—
> As fluent as a parrot is,
> But far more Polly-glottish.

No grammar too abstruse he meets,
    However dark and verby ;
He gossips Greek about the streets,
    And often Russ—in urbe.
Strange tongues—whate'er you do them call,
    In short, the man is able
To tell you what's o'clock in all
    The *dialects* of Babel.
Take him on Change—in Portuguese,
    The Moorish, and the Spanish,
Polish, Hungarian, Tyrolese,
    The Swedish, or the Danish :
Try him with these, and fifty such,
    His skill will ne'er diminish ;
Although you should begin in Dutch,
    And end (like me) in Finnish."

Hood never took a prominent part in conversation, but
what he said was always pointed, and his puns were most
pungent and biting, and always appropriate.

THE "WESTMINSTER REVIEW."

THE *Westminster Review* was the first attempt, and a thoroughly successful one, on the part of a body of men known as "the philosophical radicals" to find a voice. That voice spoke loudly, and its echoes formed an era in the history of political progress. "*Blackwood's Magazine*" at once recognised the advent of a new power. Of the writers in it almost all have obtained honourable distinction. It was universally acknowledged that Radicalism had its historians, philosophers, and poets, and that they brought their full contributions into the treasury of letters. The *Westminster Review* has frequently shifted hands, but it still retains an honourable place in the literary world. Many of its teachings have become laws, and it took the lead in the questions of free-trade, popular education, codification, reforms in the administration of justice, the poor laws, the representation of the people, usury, colonial government, and many other evidences of progress. If universal suffrage, shortened parliaments, and the ballot are among matters in abeyance, they are only suspended for a time, and the same processes of reasoning, the same tide of tendency which has driven forward the successful issue of some of these questions will bring round the consummation of all. The leaven is in the meal, and the whole lump will be leavened.

JEREMY BENTHAM.

In the very centre of the group of persons who originated the *Westminster Review* stands the grand figure of Jeremy

E

Bentham. Though closely resembling Franklin, his face expresses a profounder wisdom and a more marked benevolence than the bust of the American printer. Mingled with a serene contemplative cast, there is something of playful humour in the countenance. The high forehead is wrinkled, but is without sternness, and is contemplative but complacent. The neatly-combed long white hair hangs over the neck, but moves at every breath. *Simplex munditiis* best describes his garments. When he walks there is a restless activity in his gait, as if his thoughts were, " Let me walk fast, for there is work to do, and the walking is but to fit me better for the work."

The first steps taken were in communication with Longmans & Co. When the negociations had reached what seemed a conclusion, the proprietors of the *Edinburgh Review* objected to the arrangement, as the starting of the *Westminster* was likely to be prejudicial to the interests of the *Edinburgh*, whose interests the Longmans represented in London. This led to a correspondence with Baldwins, to whom the publication of the *Westminster* was finally committed, and it launched with the printing of two thousand copies, which were rapidly sold, and another edition of one thousand copies followed. The funds were furnished by Bentham, the editors being Henry Southern, who had charge of the literary department, while the political was committed to my care, the money being confided to me.

H. SOUTHERN.

Southern was a very clever man. He was a son of a barber at York, but his precocious talent recommended him to some opulent patrons, by whom he was sent to Trinity College, Cambridge, where though he did not specially distinguish himself, he made many friends, among whom was Charles Barker, brother-in-law of Perronet Thompson, and who was

afterwards associated with him in his literary undertakings
—the *Retrospective Review* especially and the *Westminster*.
I afterwards recommended Southern to Lord Clarendon,
who, being in search of a private secretary, found in him all
the devotion and ability he desired, and recommended him
particularly to Lord Palmerston, from whom he received
sundry diplomatic · appointments, among them that of
Minister Plenipotentiary to the Argentine Republic, and
that to the Brazils. Southern's sense of honour was so
blind that I had the greatest difficulty in extorting from
him the repayment of a hundred pounds, due to his tailor,
the non-payment of which would have prevented his leaving
England for Madrid, where Lord Clarendon had nominated
him for the secretaryship. He laughed at the idea of its
being a debt of honour, and asked me whether he was the
first gentleman who did not pay his debts.

WRITERS IN THE " WESTMINSTER."

The *Westminster Review* created a great sensation, both
in the political and the literary world. The field had been
almost monopolised by the blue and yellow of the whigs,
and by the graver grey of the Tories, but the Radicals had
no quarterly representative. Blackwood hailed their
appearance in the field as evidence of discord in the Liberal
camp, and certainly the Whigs were not spared in the exceedingly pungent articles which emanated from the pens
of James Mill, William Johnson Fox, George Grote, Roebuck, and many others who came forward in the van. But
it certainly was a discovery that in the Radical field men of
the highest order of intellect were earnest labourers—that
historians of the first class, eminent poets, several of the
wisest and the wittiest of our literary men, political econo-
mists of the highest authority, statisticians, men well known
in the arena of public life, came forward to represent that

great and growing class which belonged to neither section
of the British aristocracy, and whose standard took the
emphatic device, "The greatest good of the greatest
number."

JAMES MILL.

The biography of James Mill has not, I believe, been
written. He was the son of a farmer who was a tenant of
Sir John Stuart, who made the earliest experiments in removing great trees, and whose exploits were recorded in the
Quarterly Review by Sir Walter Scott, who followed his
example at Abbotsford, which he found bare of wood, and
surrounded with woodland scenery. The now distinguished John Stuart Mill had his name from his grandfather's connection with the Stuart property. His father
came to London, made the acquaintance of David Ricardo, and through him was introduced to Bentham, who
was wont to say, "I begot Ricardo, and Ricardo begot
Mill." Mill and his family lived with the philosopher at
Ford Abbey, in Devonshire, a place which the latter had
rented for several years. He was occupied with his "History of British India," and wrote several articles in the
"Encyclopædia Britannica" on politics and political
economy, which gave him great reputation as an acute rea-
soner and an original thinker. It was, however, from Bentham's mind that his own was impregnated, but he must be
considered as Bentham's best interpreter. Dumont, indeed,
has popularized Bentham on the Continent, though his style
was less incisive and condensed, and thence, perhaps, more
acceptable. Mill's book on India, in which he endeavoured
to demonstrate, and by many has been thought to demonstrate successfully, that the remoteness of an observer from
the scenes he describes is likely to produce a less prejudiced
and partial, and a more general and accurate estimate, led

to his appointment to one of the most influential positions in the administration of British India, that of Examiner, in which he was associated with Peacock, the author of " Headlong Hall," and M'Culloch, and afterwards with his own son, John Stuart Mill. As to the Examiners all important despatches were referred, and as all the answers to those despatches were prepared by them for the approval of the Court of Directors, the Examiners were really the rulers of India, and among them James Mill undoubtedly exercised the supreme authority. He was the great gun of the *Westminster Review.* His object was to crush aristocratical influence, whether Whig or Tory, and he saw little distinction between the tactics of either party. Both were equally moved by a passion for place and power, both seemed to claim an hereditary right to govern, and both concurred in the policy of absolutely excluding the middle classes and the people from any influence in the Legislature, excepting so far as that influence could be made to serve their own purposes. Mill marked out the strong demarcation by which the subject many were separated from the ruling few —and asserted that the two factions were disposed only to grant such reforms as they could turn to their own account, but that the great interests of the people were opposed to the views of the aristocratical sections. In every part of the field of Government he showed how the greater interests were sacrificed to the lesser—Parliamentary representation, with its rotten boroughs and narrow boundaries—corn-laws and monopolies, which enabled Lords of the Upper House and Lords of the land and their colleagues in both Houses, to pillage the people—the army and the navy, the church and the state, all made the pasturage for the privileged orders— offices without responsibility—appointments without deservings, covering the whole area of administration. When the pressure from without forced concessions from the Govern-

ment, there was heard the cry, so often repeated, of
" Finality," or " Rest and be thankful," and that cry is still
uttered from high places.

GENERAL T. P. THOMPSON.

Thomas Perronet Thompson was one of my most honoured
and beloved friends. No one is more alive than myself to
the peculiarities of his character, but his slight defects,
which were the cause of his exclusion from Parliament,
were as nothing compared with his moral and intellectual
excellences, and ought not to have been weighed in the
balance against the good services he rendered to the cause
of reform, and especially in the field of Free Trade. His
father was Thomas Thompson, a banker at Hull, who was,
I believe, the first Wesleyan Methodist who ever obtained
a seat in Parliament. Perronet received his education at
Cambridge, and was a favourite of Dr Isaac Milner, one of
the celebrities of his day, and the object of great admiration
on the part of young Thompson. When a youth he went
to sea as a midshipman, afterwards entered the army, and
was made a prisoner at Buenos Ayres, while under the
command of that general whose name may be looked for in
the enigma—

> " My first is an emblem of purity ;
> My second of security ;
> My whole is a name 'twere a sin and a shame
> To hand down to futurity."

In consequence of the intimacy of the Thompsons with Mr
Wilberforce, and of their known abhorrence of negro slavery,
Perronet, then a lieutenant, was appointed to the Governor-
ship of Sierra Leone. I have heard it said that his sympathies with the black population were so strong that, in
any question between an African and a European, he was
sure to decide in favour of the coloured man, and no doubt

such decision would generally be in the right. In the House of Commons, on one occasion, much impatience was exhibited during a speech of the "honourable and gallant member for Hull," when he said he hoped some indulgence would be accorded to so rare a personage as a *living* Governor of Sierra Leone. The appeal was quite successful, and he was allowed to say his say, after a cordial laugh from both sides of the House. Thompson served for some time in India. An admirable Arabic scholar, he was sent up the Persian Gulf in command of a troop, to act against the Wahabees, a fanatical sect of Moosulmans who had captured the Holy Cities (of which Ibrahim Pasha afterwards dispossessed them), whose leaders were, at the time of the expedition from Bombay, holding the fortress of Rás el Kamar. Thompson was very desirous to avoid bloodshed, in fact he had a strong sympathy with these reformers, who lived lives of singular abstinence, and neither drank coffee nor smoked tobacco, the two great and allowed indulgences of Islamism. He summoned the citadel to surrender, but in vain. The answer of the Wahabees was, "we will not surrender, we wait the will of Allah!" No man was better read in military matters than Thompson, and Jomini's writings were one of his text-books. It is said that, in ordering the attack, he exclaimed, "Jomini, chapter the seventeenth, I have them!" but the Wahabees knew nothing of Jomini, nor of European warfare, and our soldiers on that occasion met with a severe defeat.

Thompson, with his wife, returned from India by the Red Sea, then a most tiresome and difficult enterprise, which they were among the first to attempt. They could only slowly make their way by Arab boats, and instead of reaching Suez and Cairo as now, they passed by Kench, far to the south. His father wished to surprise him by purchasing for him, according to the usages of the day, a seat in Parliament, and I was charged with the negotiation. A rich Indian, named Farquhar, had purchased Fonthill Abbey, to which the rotten borough of Hindon was attached, with its two members. The price asked for a Session was £5000. The arrangement, however, was not made, and Thompson was brought into the House for his native place, by the radical party, at no small cost, augmented by a petition presented against his return. He owed much of his reputation to the " Corn Law Catechism," one of the most masterly and pungent exposures of fallacies which ever passed the press. Its circulation was great. Thompson became one of the most efficient auxiliaries of the Anti-Corn-Law League, which, I think, somewhat under-estimated the value of his services and sacrifices. He had a theory that the mathematical laws of order might be applied to musical compositions, and that what is called " temperature" is a practical heresy. He had a piano constructed so as to fulfil all the conditions of his theory, as were the guitars he used. While in Parliament, he adopted the practice of periodically addressing his constituents on the topics of the day. These addresses form several volumes, and every page is marked with the characteristics of a strong and original mind.

He became the editor and proprietor of the *Westminster Review* about the period of Bentham's death. The strong Anti-Catholic feeling which he inherited lingered in his mind, a mind singularly stern and resolute. He lived to the age of eighty-six, but his later years were spent in comparative seclusion.

CHARLES BARKER.

Charles Barker was the brother-in-law of Thompson. He had been educated at Cambridge, and was H. Southern's best ally. He was the critic of a large portion of the light literature noticed in the *Westminster*. His style was free and flowing, his habits most industrious, and his pen was always ready. He met his death by a sad accident. Having swallowed an ear of barley-corn, gathered in the field, the beard stuck in his throat, inflammation ensued and proved fatal. He was a man of very gentle manners, highly accomplished, but little known beyond a narrow circle. He had aided Southern while editing the *Retrospective Review*, whose purpose was to call attention to the literature of the past, and not to the literature of the present, except as illustrating ancient books. Barker belonged to a literary and artistic family, his brother being a contributor to *Punch*.

W. J. FOX.

William Johnston Fox wrote the first article in the first number of the *Westminster*. He made his way from a very low position to the distinction of M.P. for Oldham. His sole resources were the profits of his pen, derived from his sermons, and from his contributions to sundry periodicals. His first anonymous or pseudonymic designation was "A Norwich Weaver-boy." In his early days Norwich presented a very literary atmosphere. Mrs Opie, the Taylors, the Austins, and many distinguished persons, gave eminence to the capital of Norfolk. Taylor (but he was a bachelor, and of a family distinct from the Taylors and Austins) was an intimate friend of Robert Southey, a good scholar, the translator of Lessing, and one of the first to call attention to German literature. Edgar Taylor, the translator of Griesbach's New Testament, was one of our allies, as was Henry Roscoe, the son of William Roscoe of Liverpool, and the father of the still more distinguished professor of our day. Fox was a man of singular eloquence. He spoke seldom in the House of Commons, but when he spoke was listened to with a very marked attention. His works have been edited by Dr Hodgson in a Memorial edition of

twelve octavo volumes. Fox was one of the best speakers
at the great gatherings of the Anti-Corn Law League, and
his Bill, introduced in 1830, for promoting the secular
education of the people in England and Wales, was one of
the most important steps taken in an unsectarian direction.
Of the *Monthly Repository*, the then representative of Unitarian opinions, he was for several years the editor. Before
his death, he was disassociated from the Unitarian body,
and he informed me that his later creed was grounded on
the views of Dr Strauss.

SOUTHWOOD SMITH.

Southwood Smith, who had been a Unitarian preacher
and abandoned pulpit teaching for the medical profession,
was a frequent contributor to the *Review*. His article on
the " Use of the Dead to the Living," prepared the way for
that reform in our legislation which provided subjects for
dissection from other sources than body-snatching and murdering. He attacked successfully the theory as to the
contagion of plague, and exhibited the worthlessness and
the silliness of the quarantine laws. He also wrote much on
Hygiene, and was afterwards associated with the Board of
Health. When Bentham died, his body was delivered to
Dr Southwood Smith for dissection, and he delivered over
it (amidst a storm of thunder and lightning) a beautiful
lecture on the character of the great legist. The skeleton
of Bentham, clad in his own garments, and seated in his
own chair, the face being reproduced in wax, was for some
time in Dr Smith's keeping, and was presented by Lord
Brougham (to whom it never belonged, and who had not
the least authority for his intrusion) as a gift to the London
University College. I presented to the College a portrait
of Bentham, to the London University his bust by David,
and to the National Gallery of Portraits a full-length picture,

painted when, at the age of fourteen, he obtained the applause of Dr Samuel Johnson for a Latin poem on the death of George II. and the advent of George III.

ALBANY FONBLANQUE.

In Albany Fonblanque wit and wisdom were admirably blended—the wisdom suggesting the wit, and the wit decorating the wisdom. An article of his on Robert Montgomery's "Satan," is singularly clever and characteristic. Montgomery's real patronymic was Gomery—the son of the clown of that name—but he sought to aristocratise his designation, and wished to be called "*The* Poet Montgomery," an ambition which gave no little offence to James Montgomery, the veritable poet, whose hymns live in many of our collections, and are among the best of sacred songs. He stands in the first line of devotional minstrels. Fonblanque was one of Bentham's favourites, and while the editor, and, I believe, the proprietor, of the *Examiner*, lent most useful aid to the utilitarian creed. His mind was very differently moulded from that of either of the Hunts, whom he succeeded in the direction of the newspaper, and whose pecuniary difficulties were the source of much vexation to their many friends. His "History of England under Seven Administrations," afforded him a fine field for the display of that acumen which distinguished his pen. It is to be regretted that few of his witty sayings are preserved. They are as incisive and humorous as any of Douglas Jerrold, and far more philosophical than the best outpourings of Theodore Hook.

J. A. ROEBUCK.

John Arthur Roebuck was an able but unmanageable man, sharp, severe, but unsympathising. Bentham once said to him that his temper would do him more mischief than his intellect would ever do him good. Had his caustic oratory been associated with more moderation in his expressions, more communion with others, or, rather, more respect for the opinions of others, his might have been a brilliant instead of a chequered career. The articles he wrote in the *Westminster Review* are all remarkable for their soundness of view and clearness of expression. He brought as much common sense into his writings as ever did Cobbett, and far more of instruction—the result of study and reflection. In the House of Commons his courage was admirable, and he enforced respect where he could not induce sympathy or co-operation.

WILLIAM ELLIS.

William Ellis has obtained distinction and realised a fortune as manager of the Mutual Marine Assurance Office. His articles on subjects of political economy have all the clearness of a singularly lucid mind. His publications of the true principles of education, and, what is far more important, his application of those principles to a large field of practical instruction by the establishment of excellent schools, have made him, though perhaps not extensively known—for he is as modest as he is benevolent—one of the most efficient of the philanthropists of his day. When I think of the variety of talent which was brought into the service of the *Westminster Review*, and of the influence which its contributions have had in the vast arena of reform, both within and without the parliamentary circle, I feel pride in having been a fellow-labourer with them, and in having found friends and associates with whom pleasing intercourse has been preserved to my old age.

J. HOGG.

Hogg, a barrister, made many contributions to the classical articles in the *Review*. He was a strangely capricious, unmanageable creature, who prided himself, and with some reason, on his erudition, but his articles had not the superlative merit he ascribed to them.

JOHN AND CHARLES AUSTIN.

John Austin wrote only one article in the *Review*— namely, on Law Reform. It is a very remarkable production. His extreme fastidiousness made him dissatisfied with everything he did, and unwilling to do what he might easily and satisfactorily have done ; *easily*, I should not say, for he elaborated everything. His was a perpetual " Limæ labor," and the more he filed away, the more he desired to file, not but that the matter was substantially good, yet he always found something to be improved in the form or expression.

Charles Austin contributed more frequently. , He was the readier, but not the abler hand, yet his success at the bar was prodigious, while his brother was little known. Charles, at one time, was reported to make £30,000 a-year by parliamentary practice. He stood foremost among orators, if oratory can be said to belong to those who plead before committees on private bills. John Austin is better known as the husband of Mrs Austin, who was one of the distinguished family of the Taylors of Norwich—the German scholar and translator, and the mother of Lady Duff Gordon, who well maintained her mother's literary reputation.

WALTER WATSON.

Walter Watson, then editing the *Traveller*, which was afterwards linked to the *Globe*, a ready writer and an able lawyer, was among our contributors.

ELECTION EXPERIENCES.*

FEW men have had more experience than I of the various incidents connected with contested elections. Personally I have been engaged in seven, and have come to the conclusion that though the ballot would not effect all the objects which some of its advocates anticipate, and may not be of much value where the constituencies are so large and independent as not to be seduced by bribes or menaced by threats, secret suffrage would nowhere be an evil, and in very many cases a positive good. The arguments against it appear to be most frivolous and unphilosophical, and such as only become those who desire to wield an irresponsible and dangerous power. That the sober intelligence of mankind has generally adopted it, that it is inwrought with almost every form of representation in foreign countries— to say nothing of its adoption in our own clubs and other associations where a free opinion is really desired, especially where the most privileged classes are concerned, would seem to add much weight to the teachings of observation. No one knows how much suffering is inflicted on many by their being compelled to violate their consciences, nor how much pleasure is denied to others who, in order to avoid "trouble," refuse to vote at all. Bribery has its attractions and its recommendations for the bribers and the bribed—it is pleasant to be able to make money by the exercise of a privilege and the discharge of a trust; but in the case of a coerced will, there is nothing but disgrace to him who employs the dishonest influence, and nothing but dissatisfac-

* Written in 1861.

tion for the poor victim of oppression. The ballot struggle can finally have only one settlement, namely, the adoption of the principle. It is the quietest of reforms, it will act as quickly as showers and sunshine upon the summer flowers and autumnal fruits, genial and grateful, and the time will come when men will wonder that a remedy so gentle should have been repudiated with so much pertinacity.

My experience would show that if corruption be more general among the unopulent, far grosser cases occur when people of some social position traffic with their electoral privilege. The tales one sometimes hears from the poor of their distresses and embarrassments, of their being a little behind-hand with the world, of rents due, debts unpaid, and threatened proceedings, are quite intelligible, but I remember a case where a person of wealth called me aside, and said, "I shall be frank with you. I have so many voters who wait my bidding, but my price is an East India cadetship." Cadetships I had none to give, and believe the money value of such an appointment was several hundred pounds.

On two or three occasions, my supposed heterodoxy was thrown into the scale against me, and was sometimes urged in a somewhat amusing form. I was inquiring into my chances of return for Penzance. My maternal grandfather was a minister of the Church of England in that part of Cornwall, and I learned that his name was very popular among the people. Both he and his wife died victims of their attention to the poor during a desolating epidemic. An old man came to me on behalf of the Wesleyan Methodists, and told me it was reported I did not believe in the Trinity, and therefore I must pay double for their votes. They fancied, no doubt, that they ran some additional risk to their souls' salvation, and were therefore entitled to get some premium for the perils they incurred. In one of the Clyde Burghs, a letter was shown to me in

which were these words, "we will have a religious man to
represent us, even if we go to hell to find him." Everything seems allowed in the heated passions of an electoral
struggle. I have seen myself placarded in Scotland as an
atheist, an unbeliever, an unfaithful husband, and a disre-
putable head of a family. No small difficulties these for an
Englishman seeking a seat for Caledonian burghs; but I
triumphed over them, and was returned by a large majority
over one of the leading local lairds. The seeds of slander,
however, produced after-fruit, and I lost my seat, I believe,
principally on account of my opposition to Sir Andrew
Agnew in his attempts to establish "the bitter observance
of the Sabbath," as the *Examiner* called it. A certain
Scotch member who, in committee, strenuously opposed Sir
Andrew's legislation in the case of a railway bill, to my
utter astonishment and disgust voted with him in the House.
He represented a constituency adjacent to mine, and on my
reproaching him for his desertion and double-dealing, he
very coolly said, "Do you suppose I would be such a fool
as to put my seat in danger." It is to be hoped that such
exhibitions are rarer now than then.

The excitement connected with popular elections has lost
much of its intemperance, and on the whole the expenses
have been considerably reduced. The scenes which took
place at Westminster, when the poll was kept so long open,
are of historical notoriety; acts of outrage and violence,
particularly directed against the candidates and their
partizans, were quite the practice of the day. In Preston,
I remember that a body of bludgeon-men were brought into
the field to support the claims of one of the candidates.
When I was first defeated at Blackburn, the mob menaced
with destruction the houses of those who had taken a part
against me, and it was with some risk to myself that I
managed to obtain the dispersion of the infuriated crowd.

But in Cornwall, the deadening influence of the rotten borough system was such that it was impossible to secure a moment's attention from any auditory, the non-electors deeming it no concern of theirs, and the electors making the best bargain they could for themselves, or following, sheep-like, the lead given them by the proprietor of the borough. In Scotland, since the Reform Bill, the constituencies are infinitely less corrupt than in England, expectations of reward for electoral services being by no means universal. I was once invited to contest an Irish borough, but on inquiry found that the defilements through which one would be compelled to pass were of so degrading a character that I withdrew from the controversy.

PARLIAMENTARY RECOLLECTIONS.

WE have all of us our special missions. I believe my
efforts were instrumental in putting a stop to the annoy-
ances caused by the passport system to aliens who came to
England, to the tyranny of the press-gang system, which
there was an attempt to legalize, and to flogging in the
army. I was censured by the Duke of Wellington for the
part I took in this last matter, but I had the satisfaction
afterwards of hearing from his own lips the frank and
honest avowal that I was right, and that the practice ought
to be abolished.

Of the questions which constitute what are called party
politics I say nothing. In these I had only to take my part
with the Liberal section of M.P.s, but I had the satisfaction
of laying the foundation of the decimal system in our coinage, and of obtaining the issue of the florin, the tenth part
of a pound sterling. I sought to introduce an explanatory
mode of designating value, namely the pound, the decime or
dime, the cent, and the mil, and to divide the pound into
one thousand mil instead of 960 farthings, but I failed.
It was proposed to call the cent a " Queen," but the Prince
Consort objected that he would not like to have the
Queen's name given to any coin that was not of gold, and it
would be impossible to alter the name of the sterling pound
or sovereign, a household word on the lips of the whole
people, and a designation derived from the highest antiquity,
though the value was much greater in Saxon times than now.
There is no name so familiar throughout the globe as the

pound sterling. Much has been said in favour of "the poor man's penny" as the integer of value, but the knowledge of this coin is confined in other countries to a narrow circle —at all events beyond European lands. The same may be said in objecting to the adoption of the French franc, which has been urged as a means of introducing a general system of coinage, which, it was said, would not derange our currency, the value of our 10d., a decimal element, being the same as that of the franc—which it is not, and could never be, inasmuch as the legal tender in France is silver, and in England gold, so that fluctuations in the agio would be constantly disturbing the relative value of the precious metals. As the report of the Committee of the House of Commons, presented by Mr Cardwell (but written by my son Edgar), recommended the adoption of the pound sterling as the integer, and the opinion in its favour is supported by the highest mathematical authorities, such as Sir John Herschell, Professor de Morgan and many others, there can be little doubt that when, as Mr Gladstone requires, the matter has been sufficiently ventilated, the thousand mil project will be adopted. But we move slowly, almost always in the same track, and enquiring not "*quo eundem est, sed quo itur.*" The "*stare super antiquas vias*" seems almost as much a law as was the foolish old declaration of the Barons of Runnymede, "*nolumus leges Angliæ mutari,*" as if the business of Parliament was not mainly to be changing laws, removing absurd and pernicious acts of former legislation, and introducing the improvements demanded by progressive civilization.

My attempts to obtain modifications of the Quarantine Laws were not without success. I obtained on three occasions Resolutions of the House recommending a less stringent administration, and had thoroughly convinced myself during my residence in the Levant of the non-contagiousness of

plague out of the miasmatic locality. I had travelled with
the Greek doctor, Hepites, who had sought to communicate
the plague to himself by inoculation and had failed. Clot
Bey told me that, though he and his assistants had carried
on the autopsis of hundreds of corpses dead of the plague,
there had been no instance of its conveying infection.
The Emperor of Russia sent many criminals to Egypt, who
were compelled to sleep in the beds of plague-patients, but
not one of them caught the disorder. From Malta I obtained a return of persons who had waited upon plague-
patients or manipulated the articles called susceptible
during nearly two centuries. The return was *nil*, for
there had not been a single instance of the communication
of the virus. A large quantity of cotton, impregnated
with pus from Fellahs who had died upon it, had
been sent to England and distributed among manufacturing districts — nay, so little is plague disposed to
spread, that I have been informed there is seldom a year
that plague, with its characteristics of carbuncles and
buboes, is absent from the London hospitals. The plague
has never been known to penetrate into the Fayoum, close
to Cairo, or to visit Upper Egypt, and though it frequently
accompanies the caravans bound to the Holy Cities of
Mecca and Medina, there is no example of its travelling
further east. Lord Auckland nominated a commission of
medical men to report whether it was desirable that he
should establish a sanitary cordon on the frontiers of our
East India possessions, but they unanimously reported in
the negative, and no mischief or danger has resulted in
consequence.

Another of my Parliamentary objects was to secure the
payment into the Exchequer of the gross amount of public
revenues from the department of receipt, and to check the
departments of expenditure from raising money by the

transfer of stores or other means unauthorised by the House of Commons. Seven millions sterling annually escaped the notice of the supposed " guardians of the public purse." I carried by a small majority a vote in the House condemnatory of the existing system. I was opposed by the Whigs, but the battle was really won. To Mr Disraeli, while Chancellor of the Exchequer, belongs the honour of abolishing the old and introducing the new arrangements. Lord Congleton had unsuccessfully pleaded the case in his book on Financial Reform.

In my struggles for the representation I was thrice successful, and four times defeated. I twice lost Blackburn by only five votes. The last time it occurred on a Friday, and on the following Tuesday I was returned by an immense majority over the Tory, Downie of Appin and of Glencoe, and the Whig, Dunlop of that ilk, the head of a very influential family in Ayrshire. I was afterwards unseated by Mr Colquhoun of Killermount, in consequence of my pro-Catholic and anti-Sabbatical votes in the House of Commons. Such was the purity of election in those days in the newly enfranchised Scotch burghs that my election did not cost me a farthing. I failed at Kirkcaldy, "the lang toun," though I had the promise of a majority of the voters, in consequence of the great but deserved local influence of Colonel Fergusson and his family. I might mention that when so honourably returned for Kilmarnock, I had not a single acquaintance in any one of the returning burghs; indeed, I had never set my foot in any one of them, except in Rutherglen, a suburb of Glasgow, and then not as a public man. I twice carried Bolton, once without any expense; on the second occasion it cost me £500.

Parliamentary life, independently of the social distinction, and the field of public usefulness open to those who are

willing to serve the community, is very agreeable. The
House of Commons has been called, as it deserves to be
called, the best of clubs. A gentlemanly spirit prevails
among the members, and the authority of the Speaker, to
which every member pays the utmost deference and
promptest obedience, preserves an admirable spirit of order,
which forms a remarkable contrast to what I have seen in
other representative assemblies. Three usages of our House
of Commons seem to me most influential in preserving harmony—the necessity of addressing, not the assembly, but
the Speaker, so that one is in a state of habitual submission,
as it were ; then the prohibition of all written discourse, by
which arrangement public business is despatched, and debates left in the keeping of those best able to elucidate them,
whereas written discourses frequently repeat what has been
said before, and fail to answer what has been elicited in the
arguments brought forward in the progress of the discussion ;
and finally, the veto which is put upon the use of any
member's name, so that the sharpest observations lose much
of their acerbity. It is always "the Honourable" or
" Right Honourable Member for," "the worthy alderman,"
" the gallant officer," " the learned doctor," &c. I do not
know whether there is as much wisdom in our Wittenagemote
as ought to be found there, but I am sure there is an abundance of wit, ready and à propos. When Sir Francis Bur-
dett, after ratting from the Liberal cause, closed his apolo-
getic speech by saying, " There is nothing I so detest as the
cant of patriotism ; " " Mr Speaker," retorted Lord John
Russell, who rose immediately, " there is one thing worse—
it is the recant of patriotism." When Paul Methuen endeavoured to stop the interruptions of a tipsy brewer called
Kearsley, the latter, amidst the roars of the House, shouted
" Paul ! Paul ! why persecutest thou me ? " When John
Walter of the Times had flitted with five others from the

Liberal to the Tory side of the House, Dan O'Connell exclaimed—

> "And down thy steep, romantic Ashbourne! glides
> The Derby dilly, numbering six insides."

And while he was hesitating before he followed his leaders, Dan applied to him the title of "the last rose of Summer," which became his cognomen.

FREE TRADE RECOLLECTIONS.*

THE founder of the Zollverein, Dr Frederick List, is dead. He died by his own hand, and a mystery hangs over his fate. He laboured—laboured with indomitable perseverance and energy to accomplish a great object, and he accomplished it. It was a triumph of mingled good and evil—good and evil on a large scale. He broke down the barriers within the German circle, enabled twenty-five millions of men to traffic and travel without let or hindrance, overthrew all the custom-houses within the limits of the commercial union, created a compact national interest, and revived an almost extinguished German patriotism. But, at the same time, he prohibited the trade of those twenty-five millions with the rest of the world, did all he could to limit their exchanges to their own productions, raised a wall of brass against the invasion of the cheaper and better commodities of other nations, limited the field of political sympathy to narrow bounds, and levelled to one monotonous system of protection and prohibition every commercial code within the union which was marked with liberality, or distinguished by low fiscal duties.

The question has often been asked whether List was sincere. I doubt his sincerity. I believe he was not unacquainted with the true theory of political economy, and that, if strong and sinister interests had not. acted upon him, he would have been a free trader, and an advocate of free trade. But he launched a speculative

* This appears to be a fragment only.

theory, which suited the interests of German manufacturers, and of Prussian politicians. He was lauded, encouraged, and driven forward. What was an interest at first, became a prejudice. His name, his reputation, his influence were associated with his system. So he wrote and wrote, and was never weary of writing—first in one newspaper, then in another, till he got a newspaper of his own. He was rewarded by all the manufacturing interests for whom he found reasons why there should be a monopoly of sale in the German markets. He was flattered by all those who had mourned over the scattered fragments of German nationality, and were delighted to see Prussian and Saxon, Bavarian and Würtemberger, &c., all blended in one German name. But I doubt if he had any real faith in his own doctrines. It is a fine thing, no doubt, to talk about *nationality*, as if nationality implied or necessitated the repudiation of other nationalities. It may sound well to write in honour of independence—self-standing (to use his own phrase)—but who, after all, *is* independent, who *does* stand alone? Be he who he may, he is a most pitiable object, a mere cumberer of the ground.

It was not long before List's death that I discussed some of his opinions with him. He was what the world calls a jolly, jovial fellow, and had certainly the virtue of not taking offence at pretty severe criticism. I asked him pointedly, "Now, do you, can you believe what you have written in favour of the protective system?" He had not the courage to avow that he did—nay, he acknowledged that he could not defend it on the economical or commercial ground. "My object," said he, "was political." He came to England to see the downfall of the very system that he was seeking to build up in Germany. His defence appeared to me very hesitating and feeble—the ordinary fallacy that what may be true to-day will not be true to-morrow, that

what is true here may not be true elsewhere, and that
nothing is true without many exceptions.   It is a sad sight
to witness the endeavour to escape from a felt and acknowledged dilemma—acknowledged, if not in words, in evasions
and in retreatings.

LANGUAGES.

In the study of languages for practical purposes, I have found that courage in speaking is the very best means of advancing. Far more is learnt by the exercise of the tongue, which is necessarily active, than by that of the ear, which is nearly passive. It is a common vanity for people to say that they understand better than they can talk. Such cases are, I believe, rare. Generally speaking, it is more easy to convey one's thoughts by signs and language to others than to receive their thoughts. The art of language-learning is one that requires no superior capacity. There is not much difference in the ages at which different children are able to express their emotions, and if languages were learnt as children learn them, they would be found easy of acquirement. It is scarcely more difficult to acquire five languages than one, and I have known many instances of five or more languages spoken with equal purity and perfection. The proof of the thorough possession of a language is that you are able to think in it, and that no work of translation goes on in the mind. For myself, I often dream in other languages than English, and find that associations with particular countries and particular studies do not take the form of English phraseology; but this of course depends upon the extent to which foreign languages have been employed in the daily business of life. I learnt Italian from intercourse with itinerant instrument-sellers, a race of men that have disappeared; while French I picked up from a refugee priest, and from seeking the company of French prisoners, of whom there were many in Devonshire on parole.

In my travels, I have never been very ambitious of the society of my countrymen, but have always sought that of the natives, and there are few men, I believe, who can bear a stronger or a wider testimony to the general kindness and hospitality of the human family when the means of intercourse exist. My experiences of foreign lands are everywhere connected with the most pleasing and the most grateful remembrances.

ADVENTURES.

On several occasions my life has been exposed to great danger. In my boyhood, I fell from a high wall in the Topsham Road at Exeter, and was found senseless in the dust by my grandfather, who was then taking his wonted walk, though little able to move from an attack of palsy. It was long before I was brought round.

I was once frozen in for some hours in the Gulf of Bothnia, crossing from Åbo to Upsala, the cold being so intense that we used a hatchet to cut our bread, while the brandy was frozen. I lay down under some furs, expecting to die, but at length the ice around us broke, and we were enabled to make a perilous way between the ice-islands that were floating about.*

Not long after, when returning from a dinner-party at Gottenberg, the driver of the vehicle which conveyed me, having imprudently indulged in the after-dinner enjoyment of the bottle—a vice to which the Swedes are somewhat addicted—the horse ran away with the carriage, which was dashed against the postern of a bridge, and I was thrown with considerable violence some yards from the vehicle on the stones. Both my wrists were severely strained, but no serious injury was inflicted.

Travelling from Scanderoon to Antioch on an extremely beautiful and spirited Arab stallion, which had been lent me by the Governor (a mark of singular attention, as the steed was of great value), the large blue velvet saddle, being badly

---

* A detailed account of this adventure will be found further on, under the head of " Sweden."

girthed, annoyed the horse, and as we were ascending a
mountain, he sprang away from the road, among the rocks.
The saddle turned round, and I fell, the heels of the horse, as
he dashed off, just escaping my head. He left me scrambling
amidst brake and briar, *quitte pour la peur*, but it was some
time before the animal could be secured.

In 1847, while being driven by my brother in a gig from
Bridgetown, in Glamorganshire, to his residence at Bowrington, in the mountains by Llynfi, we were met by two
Irish footpads, who presented loaded pistols to our breasts,
and, as we were wholly unarmed, robbed us of a leathern
bag in which was a sum of £1000 intended for the payment
of the workmen at the Bowrington Ironworks. They shot the
horse we were driving through the brain, the poor animal
falling instantaneously dead. They confessed afterwards
that they had made up their minds to murder, had there
been the slightest resistance, and we learned that they had
been practising at a target for several days before, while
one of them had been seen sharpening a large knife, which he
acknowledged was to have been used if the shot had failed.
There was some delay in getting out the bag from the other
things in the body of the gig, and I heard the leader utter
the word *fire!* the moment before I put the straps of the
leathern bag in his hand. When brought to trial, they
pleaded " guilty," and were sentenced to transportation for
life. They were both captured before night, a large part of
the money being found on them. The robbery took place
at midday, on a public road, and close to a house, from
which a boy saw all that occurred.

I was run away with by a racer belonging to Mr Jardine,
in January 1851, and was thrown to a considerable distance,
my coat being torn in shreds from my back. The horse sprang
over a wide ditch and dismounted me. I was weak from a
fever, which had prostrated me for some months before, and

was wholly unable to restrain the horse, which was excited by the presence of other horses then exercising on the race-course at Hong Kong.

On my way from Colombo to Galle, a native horse sprang into a deep ditch dug for the protection of the cinnamon grounds against cattle, and my five companions and myself, with the carriage, were all tumbled into the ditch, but without any grave injury, though the horse was killed, and we had to pursue a journey of many miles in the sun.

In January 1857, an attempt was made to poison the European residents of Hong Kong by putting arsenic in the bread consumed by them. Not one death ensued at the time, for uneasiness and vomiting so soon followed the use of the bread, that the cry of " poisoned loaves" ran like an electric shock from house to house, and immediate measures were taken to get rid of the perilous stuff. Not one of my family escaped, and my wife suffered much.

In June 1859, I left Aden in the " Alma," with my daughter, and on the 12th we heard *crash*, CRASH, CRASH. The ship was wrecked. The water rushed in like a flood through the ports, and there were horrible shrieks, " we are lost! we are lost!" prayers, and invocations. The vessel was almost on her beam-ends, and it was difficult to hold on, but I endeavoured to escape through the port. There was neither rope, however, nor chain, nor hand to help, nor ear to hear, so I returned and tried to get to the door of the saloon, but it was under water, and out of my depth. Then the sea broke in and extinguished the lights, and all was darkness, the water still rising and rising, till we thought there was little hope, and committed ourselves to Him who wisely ruleth all. Those around us thought that nothing remained but calmly to die, but at this moment a rope descended, friendly hands were stretched out, and we were dragged, one after another, through the skylight. We had

nothing on but our night garments. We were helped to
crawl up the deck, and get over the bulwarks to the outside
of the ship, and were then lowered into a boat which was
full of water. We were rowed to a coral reef, where we
landed, barefooted, the coral tearing our feet like jagged
knives, but we were delighted to see, from the deposits of
the birds, that the sea did not ordinarily wash the higher
parts of the island. Arrangements were made to save what
could be saved, to organize, to arm, to bring sails for shade
against the burning sun, and spars, and stores, and liquids.
There was no water for the men, for this, brackish though
as it was, was kept for the women and children and the
sick. The men took their posts gallantly, keeping watch
by night, for we did not know whether the Arabs might
not attack us, and we could not trust the crew, who were
clamorous for water which we could not give, and who
began to break open and plunder the baggage. We constantly bathed our heads with sea-water, and though there
were many sad cases of sunstroke, there was only one death,
that of the purser, who was killed by over-exertion and
anxiety the first day. An officer left for Mocha to send us
water, and to communicate with Her Majesty's ships of war
at Aden. On the fourth day the "Cyclops" appeared, and
well did the brave captain and crew exert themselves, conveying all the passengers to that place, where we were
hospitably received by Colonel Coghlan. We had some first-
rate men among the Indian officers, who exhibited presence
of mind, a calm foresight, and a disposition to make the
best of and to do the best in everything.

I remember on one occasion, after I had returned from a
Continental tour, that I received a hint from the Earl of
Durham, then a member of the Cabinet, that I should be
very cautious as to what I wrote, for my letters were among

those stopped in the Post-Office, and that he had seen one of them on the table of the King (William IV.). We certainly live in days when the tone of public morals has been greatly improved. Jeremy Bentham told me that he learned from Lord Shelburne that the practice of opening private letters was carried on with great activity during the reign of George III., as a means of government, but I expect for one example of genuine light a hundred jacks-in-the-lantern would lead the spy astray. The government dared not avail itself fully of disclosures disgracefully reached, and always imperfectly understood. The most dangerous persons are generally the most guarded, and those who talk most loudly, and speculate most loosely on political or public matters, are generally persons little disposed to energetic action, and little suited for perilous and daring combinations. But they are precisely the people to awaken the alarms and anxieties of timid and distrustful governments.

G

COUNTRIES VISITED.

I EMBARKED for Spain in 1813 on board the "Telegraph" at Plymouth. The captain (Scriven) was at the same time one of the most brave and modest of men. He had, not long before, attacked a large fleet convoyed by vessels of much greater force than his own, and brought away no less than six of the enemy's ships. I had occasion to witness the coolness with which he encountered danger, for in the Bay of Biscay we fell in with a man-of-war of four times the force of his own. He told me there would probably be a severe action, and that I must choose whether I would serve with the rest on deck, or be sent below to take care of the wounded. I then noticed that, though a braver crew than that of the "Telegraph," who had so often been victorious over the enemy, never existed, the men showed that after all a fight at sea was no trifling affair, and almost every one went to perform what the French call *le petit besoin*. The decks were cleared, and we bore down upon the supposed foe, when suddenly she hoisted the Union Jack, the captain informing us that he had concealed his nationality in order to see whether Scriven would have the impudence to attack him, as he must have been annihilated or captured had he done so. There was no swagger, but only an honest smile on the countenance of our hero when he said it was his undoubted purpose to do his best, as he had done before when he mastered a French war-ship of much greater power than his own.

On reaching the Biscayan shore I was placed on board a

Spanish Quechemarin (coaster), which conveyed me to
Deva, a pretty little village, where 1 was hospitably received
and entertained by the Spanish captain's family. I there
saw for the first time some of the beauties of southern
scenery, and was particularly struck by the trellised vines,
whose bunches of grapes hung over the arched trellise
which formed the entrance to the cottage. A young maiden
took possession of my portmanteau, and 1, on horseback,
followed her to the neighbouring town of Bilbao, where I
took up my abode at the Posada de San Nicolas. I had
scarcely ever till my landing in Spain spoken Castilian with
a native, and I rejoiced to find myself so much at home, as
I really was, in mastery of the language, in which, by the
way, I afterwards wrote, *currente calamo*, a book (published
at Madrid) against negro-slavery, and I enjoyed the title of
el Español Ingles.

Having been sent to Spain as the commercial agent of a
London merchant, a large amount of transactions was placed
under my guidance. I bought myself a tractable mule, and
vibrated frequently between the ports of Bilbao, St. Sebastian, and Passages, and the River Adour (Bayonne being
still in the possession of the French). Numerous cargoes
were consigned to me in all these places, consisting principally of wheat and stores for the British army, the headquarters of which were then at Leraca, a Pyrenean village,
which I afterwards visited, crossing the Bidassoa near
Fuenterabia. I heard there of the extraordinary severity
of Lord Wellington, who punished with death the slightest
offence of roving or robbery committed on the Spanish
peasantry, such as robbing their roosts or other pecca-
dillos. The Duc d' Angoulême accompanied him. He
wore pea-green trousers, and was reported, whenever a battle
was expected, always to find some excuse for retreating a
good way to the rear.

I had soon occasion to see war with all its attendant horrors. Visiting Vittoria, I found that its fine amphitheatre was covered with cannon taken from the French. I went to St. Sebastian, which I entered by the breach by which our soldiers had penetrated, the fire upon them being so fierce that the British regiment at first halted and hesitated. It was indeed a dreadful spectacle. The course of the stream which runs by the side of the city was diverted by the multitude of corpses over which we had to pass, many of which stuck between the stones of the brook. Everywhere were shattered limbs and brains, tattered garments, and other marks of desolation, while, on entering the streets, I saw the hands of dead soldiers protruding from fallen houses, and grasping the soil beneath.

On visiting Madrid I made many acquaintances among the distinguished men of the time—Moratin and Gorostiza, the dramatists—Garrido, the satirist—Navaretto, the historian—Mariana, the author of the "Teoria de las Cortes" —Orchell, the Hebrew scholar—Mora, the political writer, and a long list of less eminent authors. Most of the patriots of the day I knew intimately. There was Arguelles, whom they called the silver-tongued—Isturia, afterwards ambassador at the Court of St. James—Alcalle de Galiano, who did not prove a very honest politician—Count Toreno, Don Francisco Martinez de la Rosà, the chronicler of Granada, and Villanueva, the Valencian scholar. Popular enthusiasm was at its height, and the clubs in the Puerto del Sol echoed with the speeches of impassioned orators. Riego's " Hymn," and the " Traga lo perro—Constitucion !" were everywhere heard in the streets. Riego was afterwards hanged, a victim to the brutal and ungrateful Ferdinand VII., and his brother, the Canon, fled to England with the widow, finding an asylum, and being well received by a large circle of acquaintance. At this time I formed an intimate friendship with General Espoz y Mina, which continued to the end of his life, and has been prolonged in that of his amiable and heroic widow.

Every town and important village had then its *piedra de la Constitucion*, which it was hoped would prove more enduring than *l' arbre de la liberté* in France. There was much to gratify the friends of progress. Schools for popular instruction were everywhere started, multitudes of newspapers were published, and a free press gave the desirable influence to all the master-minds of Spain. The democratic constitution of 1812, which established universal male suffrage, appeared a great success. Lord Holland at that time wrote to me, requesting I would furnish the *Edinburgh Review* with an article on the Spanish position and prospects. I did so, but it was found too Radical for the Whig organ and was never inserted, so I had my labour for my pains. It appeared to me that the great error committed by the patriots was the attempt at centralization. The preservation of the local liberties would have been most welcome, but those liberties were all sacrificed. The Aragonese would have been delighted to have heard again the ancient oath which accompanied their recognition of the King, " Nos que valemos cuanto vos, y podemos mas que vos, os hacemos nuestro Rey y Señor con tal que guardeis nuestros fueros y privilegios—y si no, no." The Biscayans would have rejoiced in being again called to fling flowers into the stream, exclaiming "So long as thy course is towards the sea, so long shall Biscay be free ; " and the Guipuzcoans would have been proud again to sit under the oak of Guernica, there to repeat the traditions of their forefathers, there to sing again the songs of freedom, proclaiming that all the inhabitants of the Bascuence provinces were noble by birth, that they could not be taxed by the sovereigns of Castille, and that their ports and communications were to be for ever free.

There is more of provinciality than of nationality in Spain, and the Castilian has not superseded the local languages. Catalan is universally spoken in Catalonia, Valencian in Valencia, Galician in Galicia, and Euscarra or Biscayan in Biscay. It is not as in France before the Revolution, when only one-seventh of the population understood French, whereas it is said that now there is only one-seventh of the population which does *not* understand it, for the French Biscayan, formerly used between Bayonne and the Pyrenees, is dying, while the Gascon and other dialects are dead. In Spain, beyond all other countries—for there is no abstract Spain, as every Spaniard is prouder of his province than of his country—the provincialities were the true elements of freedom, and should have been carefully and cautiously watched. We ourselves owe much to the pertinacity with which we hold to ancestral traditions and ancestral usages.

It is difficult to say which part of Spain has most attractions. It is everywhere the land of romance. When I was there, nationality was preserved in every shape, and French costumes, French books, and French phraseology were objects of detestation. No word was more offensive than *Gabacho*, the name given to Frenchmen, and to the partizans of French politics; *Pepinos*, or cucumbers, was another degrading appellation.

But, as it was, the government of Joseph was more tolerable than that of the beloved Ferdinand, who was perhaps one of the most infamous of modern princes—low, sensual, mendacious, superstitious, treacherous, and malignant. How often have I heard the chant, "Viva Fernando, y vamos robando."

Cordoba is a city of which I was very fond. Moorish manners have left their unmistakeable vestiges, even in the food and costumes of the people, and Spain owes a debt to the Moosulmans which she will not willingly acknowledge. The cathedral of Cordoba has served alike for the heathen services of the Romans and the rites of the Islamites, and now the Catholic worship has of course superseded the others. At the entrance in ancient times were two majestic date-palm trees—one of which was still standing—the beauties of which have been celebrated in Arabic verse. Granada and its Alhambra are better known than Cordoba and its temples.

Spain is also greatly indebted to the learned Jews, the catalogue of whose writings forms two large folio volumes. Of the great Hidalgos of Spain—the sons of something, as the word implies—the dignitaries of the *sangre azul*, there is scarcely one whose ancestry is not mingled with the Hebrew races. Those races have been equally the objects of persecution with the Moors, but they have not been extirpated. I have often met with Jews in Spain, whose religion was concealed from their Catholic neighbours, but who did not hesitate to avow their faith to those they deemed worthy of their confidence. They absented themselves on some plea or other during the time when the *viejos cristianos* are required to attend the confessional. Of the two races of Jews, the Spanish and the German, I believe the former are by far the more enlightened, and deemed a superior race to those of northern Europe. In the case of the Jews, persecution drove them from the ordinary pursuits of life to money-making and usury (I attach no disgraceful meaning to the word), just as our Dissenters, tormented by the Test and Corporation Acts, betook themselves to merchandise and manufactures, and, in both cases, the results have been eminently successful. The Rothschilds and Barings may attribute their present opulence to the sufferings of their forefathers.

The nationality, to which I have above referred, penetrated into every department of the social and personal life of the Spaniard. Among the women, not one would have dared to show herself in any other garments than those made of the black, or very dark plum-coloured Alepin, with the velo, mantilla, and basquiña (a portion of the dress attached to the waist, whence black silk cords were suspended, which swung backwards and forwards with every movement of the body). The abanico (fan), which has been called the lady's weapon of war, was then, and is now, never wanting as a female accompaniment. But these nationalities have passed away, the ladies of Spain all seek to imitate Parisian fashions, and in the colonies, as in the capital, French milliners and mantua-makers make the dresses of all who can afford to employ them. Men, too, have adopted the *froc* of civilization, and the *Capa y Espada*, so well known to the Spanish drama, are never seen. The gastronome has everywhere nearly the same opinion as to what a good dinner is, or ought to be ; but I hope that certain first-rate Spanish dishes will not be abandoned. Fowls à la Valenciana, and Bacalas à la Biscaya are much to be commended, and the province of Granada could afford welcome contributions from Moorish sources.

It has been truly said that he who has thoroughly mastered the pages of Don Quixote and Gil Blas will find nothing new in Spain. This *was* true, but is now only partially so. No doubt the gentlemanly spirit of the knight-errant would be found among the high-bred Hidalgos, and there is not a peasant who would fail to string like onions the multitudinous proverbs with which discourse is constantly interlarded. All the natural objects remain unchanged. Windmills, shepherds and shepherdesses will still be found, and goatherds watching their flocks. Hundreds of ancient castles and edifices were destroyed by the French during their invasion — an invasion, by the way, which cost the lives of more than a million of French, and was the real cause of Napoleon's downfall. In connection with this, I remember a circumstance worth recording. The Emperor had invited the Portuguese minister to meet him at Bayonne, with the hope of talking him over, and inducing him to concur in the policy which Buonaparte wished to carry out. The Lusitanian exclaimed, "Não!" "I never heard anything so sublime as that Não!" said the Emperor after the conversation, and certainly it had a sublimity not akin to the ridiculous, which, however, has been averred to be the constant companion of the sublime.

Though Spain moves slowly forward, there is movement. In my youth there were no stage-coaches, no means of conveyance, even in the *caminos reales*, but a *silla de posta*, and in the by-ways mules alone were employed. I once travelled with the mails from Madrid to Cadiz in a vehicle without springs, lying upon straw, and arriving at the end of the journey absolutely black and blue with bruises. But the horses on the high roads were excellent, all *caballos enteros*, and I once rode two hundred miles in twenty-four hours. The courier of Lord Wellington told me he had ridden eighteen hundred miles in nine successive days. He was like a centaur, seeming part of his horse, and he slept as soundly in his saddle as if in his bed. In my long ride, on dismounting, I fell asleep on the ground from pure fatigue, but, being roused, was soon awakened by the fresh air, with which the rapid motion of the steed fanned the cheeks. The horses were of Arab breed, so sure-footed that I have never known them stumble, and they needed neither the guidance of the bridle, nor the impulse of the spur, knowing well when to hasten or slacken their speed, and still better, when and where to rest.

At Alcalá de Honores, I was enabled to ascertain that

the manuscripts which Cardinal Ximenez used for the composition of his polyglot Bible still exist unmolested in the library. It had long been believed that they had been sold to and used by a rocket-maker.

There is no province of Spain which has not something specially remarkable. The orientalism of the streets of Cordoba, resembling those of Damascus and Cairo, struck me much, as did the manner of life of the Cordobese. The streets admit with difficulty a beast of burthen, while the lanes are absolutely impassable, and are so constructed, no doubt, as a protection against the heat of the sun. The plain of Valencia is beautiful from its varied fertility, that of Orihuela not less so, as the Spanish proverb says, "Llueva o no llueva, hay pan en Orihuela," "Let it rain, or let it not, Orihuela bread has got." Castilian pride is notorious. Columbus was not a Castilian, nor a Leonese, but the adage is not the less frequent on Spanish lips, "A Castilla y à Leon, nuevo mundo dió Colon." The enthusiasm of the Galicians for their patron saint, Santiago de Compostella, equals that of the Neapolitans for their St Januarius.

The language of Spain is one of the most sonorous spoken by man. Castilian poetry has a peculiar rhythm called the *asonante*, usually employed by the improvistas, who are common even among the peasantry. The rhythm, as is well known, is found in the closing vowels and not in the syllable. Padre, for example, would be a correct asonante with sastre, quiero with negro. I have known a muleteer pour out his spontaneous verses in the cadence of song for half-an-hour together, somewhat in this strain :—

> "O, my mule ! thou must be weary,
>   So am I, and how I *wish*
>   That our journey's toil were ended,
>   And that we had reached our *inn*.

There, that smiling maid, Maria,
 Has a smile for me, which *I*
Will, with many a kiss repay her.
 Is she not a charming *prize ?*
He who woos her, and who wins her,
 Will, indeed, enjoy a *bliss,*
Far beyond a monarch's sceptre ;
 Would such heavenly bliss were *mine.*

The Catalan idiom is one of the favourite tongues of the Tro-
badores (Trouveurs—*Gallice*), and has in it some extremely
pretty poetry, particularly that of Ansias March. It fills
up the space between the dog-latin of the monks and the
classics of the sixteenth and seventeenth centuries, and has
none of the guttural sounds which the Moors introduced
into the Castilian, nor of the nasals which are thought to
disfigure the Portuguese. There is in it a close resemblance
to, but not identity with, the Valencian, but I am not aware
of any Valencian poet who has obtained the same reputation
as March. Some modern writers, however, and among
them the Padre Villanueva, one of the Valencian Deputies
to the Cortes, have written works of some merit in their
native idiom. The Castilian language is seldom understood by the peasantry of Valencia. The Biscayan is giving
way. It is one of the oldest of living languages, but is
supposed to be so difficult of acquirement that the title of
a certain Euscarra grammar is "El imposible vencido."
Evidence of its antiquity is found in the fact that modern
names are given to all the products of civilization, as
latigua (whip), candela (candle). The name of God is *Jan-
goicoa* (the J being a guttural), the Lord above ; *egusquia*
(the sun), the giver of day ; illarguia (the moon), the light of
the dead ; *subea* (bridge), two trees across the water ; *aber-
atza* (rich), abundant in cattle, which last two words prove
the antiquity of the language, as modern bridges would not
be described by such a phrase, and we know that in olden

time riches consisted in the possession of herds of oxen ; *e.g.*, *pecunia*, from *pecus*. The plural is formed in *ac*. The best account of the language with which I am acquainted is that given by Adelung in his " Mithridates." Thirty or forty volumes have been printed in the Bascuence. I endeavoured to ascertain whether there was any popular or traditionary poetry, but found only one piece, which had not an historical character.   A man called Erro published a book to prove that a certain vase bore an inscription to the effect that it had been used by the priestesses for worship in the temple of the sun, but it was really a modern German pipkin which had dropped into a well, the words on it being, " Gott ! erbarme dein armes würmchen ! " Nothing in the extravagances of Sir Walter Scott's " Antiquary" approaches this.

The Biscayan never fails to tell you that he is, and that all his countrymen are, noble, that he never allowed the King of Spain to call him subject, nor gave *him* a higher title than Señor, but national character is more strongly marked in Spain than in any country with which I am acquainted, though it is blended with and subordinate to what is local and provincial, and a Spaniard is only national when in intercourse with other nations.   He is proud alike of the past glories of his country, and convinced of its infinite superiority to all other lands.   I remember a muleteer, with whom I was travelling on the skirts of the Pyrenees, asking me to tell him something about England and France, and having listened for some time, shouted " España ! diciendo España, el orbe tiembla."   " When the word *Spain* is pronounced, the world (no ! the *orb*, for the phrase is very grandiloquent) the orb trembles."   Among the different races of Spain there is much jealousy, hatred, and hostility. The Biscayan will talk of the Galician, or Castilian, or Manchego with infinite contempt, while the Aragonese will elevate his Zaragoza above a hundred Madrids. The Andalusian despises all capitals but his own Seville, the Galician glories in his Santiago de Compostella, nor is the Catalan less proud of Barcelona, nor the Valencian of his principal city. Their pride and prejudice have passed into local proverbs, and there is scarcely a town which has not some addendum (generally laudatory) to its name. Sometimes the epithet is sarcastic as " el ayre de Madrid mata à un hombre, no apaga un candil." "The air of Madrid kills a man, but does not put out a lamp."

Spain was, when I visited it, covered with bandits, with whom the government could not cope, many of them being popular with the peasantry, and having done good service in guerilla warfare against the French. Strange marks of barbarism were visible, both in the highways and byways through which the traveller passed. To say nothing of the many crosses that marked the spots where murders had been committed, iron cages were often seen holding human heads and limbs which had belonged to robbers who had fallen into the hands of the authorities. Once, travelling from Andalucia towards Alemtejo in Portugal, in company with a band of smugglers, to be with whom was a great protection, we tarried to take our noonday meal under a large tree, and looking up, saw a number of human skulls among the branches. The contrabandistas were public benefactors, who saved the people from some of the privations and many of the heavy charges which, what was called a " protective system," imposed upon the community, and no song was more popular on the stage than one, often introduced in the presence of royalty itself, beginning " Yo que soy contrabandista." It was very amusing to journey in the company of these men, who were generally on excellent terms with the custom-house officers, who preferred pocketing bribes to encountering danger, for the smugglers were always well armed, and had the best mules in the country, and assuredly would not have come off second best had they met with resistance. Gibraltar was the principal depot in the south, the free ports of Biscayan Guipuzcoa in the north, and Lisbon and Oporto in the west, whence they drew the articles clandestinely introduced, among which tobacco and English cotton goods held the first place. Men were not the only instruments employed in the contraband trade, multitudes of dogs being used on the land frontier to convey prohibited articles. Even in our own country, the science of smuggling was, in those days, carried on to an extent, and with a success, which would now seem incredible. The mischief was not confined to mere frauds upon the revenue, for the encouragement of a large body of men, whose practice and profession it was to violate the laws, could not but be a gigantic evil.

Once, while travelling with some friends from Cadiz to Gibraltar, we met in a forest a party who had a short time before been pillaged by a band of robbers. We continued our course, being well armed and in considerable numbers, and shortly fell in with the marauders, dismounted from their horses and mules, and enjoying their repast, seated on the ground. They saluted us as "*caballeros,*" and asked us to partake of their meal, after which we proceeded on our way, being persuaded that they would not risk an encounter in which they would probably be worsted. They waited for other victims, and we afterwards heard that the party which followed us had been thoroughly sacked by our hosts.

On another occasion, when bound from Bilbao to Vittoria, we were informed that a horde of robbers had been committing many devastations on a mountain over which passed the direct road. A good many travellers were then on their way to Vittoria, and the more timid determined, for the sake of safety, not to go by this road, but to pass along the foot of the mountain by a much longer and less frequented route, which added another day to the journey. I joined the cavalcade which resolved to proceed direct, and on arriving at the spot where the two ways met, we found our companions tied to trees by the bandits, having been despoiled of everything they possessed. It is impossible to describe the disorganization of the Peninsula at this period, when the guerilla warfare was at its height, and men were one day patriots destroying the French, and another robbers, attacking all travellers without distinction. A notion of their brutality may be formed from the fact that one band, after murdering an officer engaged in their pursuit, flayed him, and after sewing up and inflating his skin, suspended it to a branch of one of the trees of the forest.

PORTUGAL.

In 1815 I visited Portugal. I was familiar with the language, whose beauties have not been sufficiently appreciated, nor has its literature received the attention it well deserves, although the Lusitanian chronicles especially are of singular value. The language is so like Latin that pages may be written in which not only would every word be intelligible to an ancient Roman as to a modern Portuguese, but every word would be grammatically correct. Whole passages in Camoë's Lusiad may be quoted, as flowing and as harmonious as anything in Tasso or Ariosto. For example—

> " Estavas, linda Inez, posta em socego,
> De teus annos colhendo o doce fruto,
> Na quelle engano d' alma tão ledo e cego
> Que a fortuna não deixa durar muto :
> Nos saudozos campos do Mondego,
> De teus formosos olhos nunca enxuto
> Aos montes repetindo e ás ovinhas
> O nome que no peito escrito tinhas."

Portugal was at the time mentioned recovering from the effects of the French invasion, and the spirit and the love of liberty were moulding its institutions into constitutional forms. There, as in all Catholic countries, the influence of the clergy was the great barrier to improvement, but many of the nobility were friendly to reform, and civilization was making progress, though but slowly. In the Cortes there were eloquent speakers. The influence of English residents and the intercourse between Portugal and Great Britain, were favourable to the developement of the Portuguese mind. England and Ireland were the great consumers of the Portuguese wines, and large amounts of British capital were brought into the Oporto market. Under British commanders, the Portuguese troops had been trained to discipline, and were more to be relied upon than the Spanish, who were often led by inefficient officers. Spanish pride constantly repudiated foreign assistance, and yet I frequently found among the peasantry a latent feeling of respect for England, a proverb often repeated being " Paz con Inglaterra, y con todo el mundo guerra."

Lisbon is a much larger town than I expected to see, but its size and population are greatly exaggerated by the Portuguese historians. Oliviera says " it is without doubt the largest city in Christendom, and if we leave vain speculations and consult facts, we shall find it the largest city in the world." The Portuguese have a proverb " Quem não ha visto Lisboa, não ha visto cousa boa." With the exception of five or six noble streets (some unfinished, for the Portuguese forget the advice of one of their best writers, " Be flexible in resolving, and inflexible in performing," and begin a hundred things which they leave incomplete), Lisbon was but an immense mass of irregularity and illcontrivance. The streets were made the depositories of all the filth of the filthy city. Multitudes of dogs (the Lisbon scavengers) patrolled their different quarters in the evening, and removed some of the nuisances, but it was impossible to walk in any but a few streets, without observing innumerable dead animals, and being almost overwhelmed with the abominable stench. If the air of Lisbon were not extremely salubrious, it would have been quite the headquarters of pestilence. It was amusing to mark the names of some of the streets, as, for instance, " The Street of St. Anne of the Great Cross of the Happy Death," " St. Antonio of the Place of the Convent of the Heart of Jesus," the street of " Jesus, Joseph, and Mary." Then there were the Streets of "The Holy Old Men," the " Shoe's Toe," the " Soldier's Dogs," and lastly that of " St. John of the Happily Married," which some say ought to be without inhabitants.

Portugal, though one of the smallest independent states of Europe, and at that time a century and a half behind many of the northern nations in the arts of life and the cultivation of the mind, once extended its influence through every quarter of the globe, and though the people were completely subdued by the Moors, and kept in a state of the worst slavery, they succeeded in chasing their conquerors from their borders, took many important places from them in Morocco and Arabia, and spread their victories " even from the Isle of Ormus to the coast of China." In the sixteenth century Portugal became subject to Spain, but they freed themselves from this yoke in 1640, João de Braganza was proclaimed King, and his family have retained the sceptre ever since, but the country was dreadfully impoverished by its severe masters, who, in about one hundred years levied from it as tribute no less than two hundred millions of gold crowns. Since then Portugal has been often invaded, her strength and influence declined, and without the assistance of England, she would, I think, have become a province of Spain. The administration of justice

H

was tardy and arbitrary. It was the custom for the "Society of Mercy" to supply the instruments of punishment, by bribing whom, the most atrocious criminals escaped from death. They were always present at executions, and, when sufficiently paid, provided rotten ropes, which broke with the guilty person, and when he fell, they covered him with the flag of mercy, and he was out of the reach of the civil power. I often saw in the streets robbers and murderers chained together, who sold cigars as they went along, and seemed quite insensible to their crimes.

I visited the extreme western point of Europe—the rock of Lisbon. We hired donkies, which were universally employed on all expeditions among the rugged and pathless hills. An immense pillion was fastened on them, which had no stirrups, and they were usually ridden as ladies ride in England, but always with the left hand towards the head of the beast. Passing through Colares, a village famous for its vines, we reached the cliffs, against whose feet the waves of the sea are dashed, and whose hollows echo back the roaring of the surges. A number of men who accompanied us descended the frightful precipice, and I scarcely know how I could have looked on with so much calmness, as it is a bare smooth rock, and the stones which we hurled from the top fell with a horrible noise to the bottom of the cliff. I also went to the Pena Convent, which towers over the highest of the precipices. The rude path which leads to it winds round the rugged steep, and if ever there was a spot fitted for those who would withdraw from the world, it is this. Here might misanthropy revel in perfect abstraction, for scarcely could any earthly idea enter into that secluded and weather-beaten temple. The clouds gather round the building, the wild wind whistles shrilly through its alleys, it totters in the earthquake, it is scorched by the suns of summer, and frozen by the wintry hail-storm. Part of it was shaken and overwhelmed by the earth's convulsions. In the highest tower I read the name of Byron, and I ventured (for almost the first time in my life) to scratch my own. It may recall to some future wanderer the name of one he knew when the hand that wrote it has decayed in dust; I remarked that the birds which flitted round the dreary retreat seemed scarcely to consider it inhabited by man. The lightning and thunder which flash and growl there are sometimes horrible, but I observed that even here worldly cares and worldly passions had found an entrance.

I visited also Pombal, which was built by the great minister whose name it bears. It was the triumph of his glory, and the witness of his disgrace. I know of no one to be compared with him but Wolsey, whom he resembled in his pride, in his vices, and in his fall. His rule was despotic and inflexible, and he scrupled not to employ the basest means to accomplish his ends. Whatever he determined on, he carried into effect, and was in vain resisted by the whole influence of the nobility and ecclesiastics. Once, he ordered one-third of all the vines in the kingdom to be rooted up, and corn to be planted. At another time he commanded half the inhabitants of a province to change their dwellings; but he purified and gave respectability to the University of Coimbra (before an Augean stable of corruption), he overthrew the gigantic power of the Jesuits, he overawed the Inquisition, he diminished the influence of the Fidalgos (nobles), he filled the impoverished treasury with riches, and obtained for all the inhabitants of the Portuguese colonies the privileges of citizens—in a word, had he been less vindictive and tyrannical, he would have been a model for ministers, but his enemies at last made head against him with success, his decline was more humiliating than his rise had been surprising, and in the retreat of Pombal he ended his days. The nation had

become sensible of its loss in the removal of such a man,
they remembered him with gratitude, and spoke of him with
reverence. He was once very hard pressed by the French
and Spanish ambassadors to declare war against England.
They had been making long speeches, and concluded by telling him that, if he did not immediately decide to comply with
their demands, an army of ten thousand men would be sent
against his country. He replied quite calmly, " O Portugal,
he muito pequeño—não cabé tanta gente." "Portugal is very
small—it would not hold so many people." We applied
for permission to see the coffin which contained his remains,
his body having never been buried, but in vain. So much
respect had the French for his memory, that during their
invasion, when everything was devastated by the soldiery,
the French commanding officer ordered to be inscribed over
the spot where he was laid, " Respeitao este tumulo ;" but,
on their retreat, nothing could restrain their wild licentious-
ness, they destroyed the coffin, and his ashes were mingled
with those of meaner men. An attempt was made to
collect them in 1811, and they were deposited in another
case, but with them is mixed the baser clay of the humble
villager. It was a promiscuous heap, which would be
eloquent to the child of pride.

Coimbra was to Portugal what Santiago is to Spain, the
grand vortex of ecclesiastical power. There were immense
numbers of religious establishments and orders, and it was
to the monks what Gibraltar was to the Jews—an earthly
paradise. I went over the " Mosteiro da Santa Cruz," or of
" St Vincent." Within it was every luxury which wealth
can purchase, or worldliness desire. Extensive orange
groves and vineyards, plantations of olive trees, gardens
glowing with beautiful flowers, magnificent arbours, long
shady walks impenetrable to the hottest sun, aviaries and
fish-ponds, baths and grottoes, bowling-greens and billiard-

tables, chess and backgammon boards, cellars stored with rich wines, and magazines full of fruits and luxuries. Some of the monastic institutions, however, were as rigid as others were comfortable. In that of St Teresa, the nuns led a life of constant suffering. Once immured, they never saw a friend, wore no dress other than the coarsest woollen, no shoes or stockings, but a rough unpolished sandal. Besides the daily services of religion, they chanted matins at midnight.

O Porto, the second city of Portugal, is said to have given a name to the whole kingdom. Camoēs says or sings, "That noble city which, as told by fame, gave Portugal its great eternal name." The rapidity of its rise was wonderful, for in 1732 it only contained about 20,000 inhabitants, while in less than fifty years this number was trebled, and in 1815 the population probably amounted to 80,000 or 90,000. Its trade was so great that England alone took yearly 30,000 pipes of wine. The Douro, though not a very large river, discharges a great abundance of water into the ocean. They have a proverb, "O Tejo tem a fama e o Douro as aguas." Its stream was so rapid that there was no bridge across it (in Portugal at least), but there was a bridge of boats, which was obliged to be removed whenever there was a flood. As the course of the river is between mountains, so that it cannot overflow its banks, the perpendicular rise has been known to be as much as 40 feet.

RUSSIA.

In the winter of 1819 I went to St Petersburg, posting from Hamburg, and passing along the Kurische Haf. It was bitterly cold, and among the most delicious moments of my existence was that of our arrival at a warm and comfortable inn called the Krasnoi Kabák, or beautiful inn, the last stage before reaching the Russian capital. I took lodgings on the Vasiliostrov (the Island of St Basil), which forms a portion of the city, reached by a bridge of boats, which are removed for a short time when the ice breaks up, and the navigation of the Neva begins to be freed.

I neither found St Petersburg to be that magnificent and wonderful city which it is represented by some, nor so shabby and contemptible as described by others. The contrasts exceeded all belief and all description. There are in it palaces and mansions of great splendour and solidity, buildings of enormous size and imposing appearance, but the shabbiness of many of the abodes, and the foul filthiness of others, showed the utter want of sanitary regulations, and the absence of efficient local police. It was sometimes difficult to make one's way through the ordure found on large staircases and unswept courts. The houses were kept warm by stoves and double windows, and had many more winter comforts than summer accommodations, so that a visit to Russia in the cold season is to be preferred to one in the hot. Ingenuity, in truth, can make much more satisfactory arrangements against a low than against a high range of the thermometer. What can a man do to protect himself against tropical heat? He may agitate the air with punkahs, but it is but the air of an oven—he may wear the lightest dress, but he cannot lower the temperature around him many degrees—he may exclude the sun, but there is intolerable warmth in the shade—he may slightly mitigate, but he cannot escape the mighty, the irresistible influence of the god of day. But, in the Arctic regions, the temperature can be raised to any height by artificial means. The peasants of Russia, in the bitterest winter, keep their log-houses at a temperature of from 80° to 90° by stoves and fires. Any amount of garments may be worn, and the same furs which protect the quadrupeds—the foxes, the wolves, and the bears—or the more delicate creatures, as the ermine, whether in the Arctic or Antarctic zone, contribute to the wants of man, and most successfully so.

I had occasion to see much and hear much of the character of the government and institutions of Russia, which were corrupt and barbarous. The proprietor of the house in which I lived had, many years before, committed forgeries in one of the public offices, but he was perfectly free. The judge to whom his case was referred was a military officer (a general), who had a pile of documents, the records of various offences, the latest of which was placed at the bottom of the file, and as they were cleared away, one after another, the lowest document gradually mounted. My host, a few days before his case reached the summit (which was about once in three years), received from the general's secretary a notice that an adjudication was at hand, upon which a bribe was sent in according to arrangement, and the case was removed to the bottom of the pile. I have often seen public functionaries, whose pay did not exceed £60 to £80 a-year, driving their carriages and four horses through the streets of St Petersburg. Now and then, extortion received a check, when by some means or other a case of cruel injustice reached the Emperor's ears, but the Emperor was nearly as inaccessible as the God of heaven, or implored only by prayers and groans which he never heard. The constant aspiration of the injured was, "Could the Emperor but know! but Bóg (God) and Tsar are equally distant." It was of course alike the art and the interest of every functionary, both high and low, to keep the Emperor within an impassable circle, so that the relief which unlimited power might bring to redress oppressive acts was seldom available.

There is great fascination about the Russian Court. The variety and costliness of the costumes, the splendour of the

equipages, the extent and beauty of the imperial apartments, and the grandiose character of the whole display,
are found in scarcely any other European capital. I was
once present at a court ball—I think it was on the New
Year's Day—to which, it was said, 30,000 persons were
invited from all parts of the empire, and an extraordinary
sight it was. There were Manchoos, Mongolians, and Chinese, representatives of all the tribes and tongues from
Kamtshatka to the Gulf of Finland, from the White
Sea to the Crimean peninsula, all the Caucasian races,
Georgians, Circassians, and Armenians, Turks and Greeks,
to say nothing of all the envoys of European sovereigns.
Through the crowded multitude the imperial family swept,
a passage being made for them by the courtiers in attendance, who announced their approach. I was talking French
to a Swiss lady, when a general, covered with orders, came
up to me and said " vous êtes des étrangers. Permettez
que je vous fasse voir l'Hermitage." He beckoned us to
follow him. The crowd gave way before him, and he led
us through a long suite of apartments to the Hermitage,
which was brilliantly illuminated. I said to him, " veuillez
donc me dire à qui nous devons cette attention si distinguée.
He replied, " à personne. Je suis très flatté de vous avoir
été de quelque utilité." I ascertained afterwards the name
of this officer, who was, I think, General Miloradovich, the
head of the police, a great favourite of Alexander, and one
of the most distinguished noblemen in Russia.

In St Petersburg I made many agreeable literary acquaintances, and among them the younger Adelung (Friedrich),
who was deeply engaged in philological researches, and had
just published his list of languages, amounting to about
3500. It was he who asked me to translate Chamisso's
" Peter Schlemihil," which my friend George Cruikshank
illustrated by his humorous etchings. Philology is a popular

study in Russia, and the Empress Catherine gave a great impulse to it. We are but at the threshold yet of lingual philosophy, and, compared with the vastness of the field, the harvest is small and unsatisfactory. As regards our own tongue, we are tracing it to its sources, and inquiry will probably exhaust all that is practicable or useful to know, but what languages have been spoken and have perished for ever, what languages are perishing even now, we know but little. It will probably turn out that, so far from the number of languages having increased by ramification from a common root, that number has been in constant process of diminution by the progress of time and the extension of intercourse. Every tribe had once its own language, which has been lost by being moulded into the language of districts—the language of districts lost by being absorbed in the language of nations. We have seen with our own eyes the process in our own country. The British language is dead —the Manx, the Erse, the Welsh, the Gaelic are dying. In France, before the Revolution, less than five millions of people spoke the language of Paris, which is now spoken by more than thirty millions of Frenchmen. In Australia, the primitive state of things exists in all the remoter and less accessible regions, the number of persons speaking the same tongue is small, and there is little resemblance between the various idioms where there is little intercourse. In Africa, fifty-six different languages have been found in a not very extensive tract of country. Everything shows that the various nations who inhabited ancient Italy had each its separate dialect, though of scarcely one does a fragment remain. No doubt, without any affinity, or with a small affinity of words, there may be much resemblance in character and construction.

I was much pleased with the conversation of Horch, the political economist, who complained of the impossibility of pursuing investigations into scientific questions under a despotic government. " You walk where you will," he said, " but we are cramped in an infant's cradle," and this is perhaps one of the worst consequences of arbitrary power, for discussion would soon undermine its foundations, while the proclamation of sound principles would shake its fiscal, judicial, and administrative organization. There is no safety for it unless the press is shackled, free thought discouraged, and the exercise of the noblest faculties of man restrained and paralyzed.

Kruilov, the fabulist, amused me much. He resembles La Fontaine in the facility of his versification, and the same droll, dry spirit of jest and fun runs through all his compositions. He was public librarian at St Petersburg. He seemed to eschew clean linen, and looked as if he thought the washing process an intolerable intervention.

Karamzin, the Russian historian, was then at the height of his reputation. I found him an agreeable and intelligent man, but I remember nothing in his conversation that betokened a high order of intellect. It was his object to flatter the Emperor, and to draw brilliant pictures of the progress, position, and futurity of his native country. His writings are among the best specimens of Russian prose. The Russian tongue has, in the course of three or four generations, been raised to be a fit instrument for representing an advanced civilization. It does not repudiate foreign aid, but, on the contrary, foreign words meet a ready acceptance in consequence of the extensive employment of other languages by the higher classes in Russia. In the field of poetry, Lomonosov laid a noble foundation in a style essentially popular and national, for he was a serf without education, and unacquainted with any idiom but his own. Derjàvin brought a higher elevation of style and a more dignified and sonorous versification, but Karamzin was the first to obtain for any serious prose work a general acceptance and applause. Multitudinous writers on almost all topics (excepting those connected with political speculations) have brought their contributions to the various departments of literature, but the influence of French authors, especially in the region of the *belles lettres*, is still paramount.

I found at St. Petersburg some interesting documents among the manuscripts, namely—the original letters of Mary Stuart, written while in prison, and an immense mass of papers purchased by the Russian ambassador at Paris during the Revolution. I saw the missal of the unfortunate queen, in which she wrote up to the time of her death. She made it an album, and appears to have requested the celebrated personages who visited her to write their names in it. Bacon's name is among the rest. Some of her own verses bewailing her fate are beautiful. From the letters of Mary to the French court and others she seems to have been treated by Elizabeth with monstrous brutality. In one of them she complained that her guards insisted on her sleeping with their wives and daughters. Elizabeth's answers to several potentates who interceded for Mary bespeak a cold-hearted cruelty and pride which do her little honour. At the time of the Revolution these letters were scattered among the mob, to be trampled on as the works of " kings and queens," and were most of them purchased for a trifle. Some hundreds of letters of Henri IV. cost forty francs.

At St. Petersburg I acquired a knowledge of the Russian language sufficient to enable me to give the first specimens ever presented in English to the public. The first volume was successful. The second I wrote in 1822 while in Boulogne Prison, and forwarded a copy to the Emperor Alexander, who sent me a large amethyst ring surrounded with diamonds.

Alexander, though idolized by his people, was a weak, vain, and impressionable man. His policy changed as frequently as the wind, for one day he would passionately urge the progress of public instruction, and the next, alarmed at that progress, he would suddenly check its course. He was most accessible to flattery, which was administered to him in large doses, but he seemed scarcely able or willing to distinguish between the value of praise awarded for great services rendered to his people, and the compliments paid to him on the cut of his uniform, or the graceful manner in which he bestrode the floor. He was much under the influence of a fanatical impostor, one Madame Krüdener. At this epoch foreigners were in great favour at the imperial court, and many departments of government were under their direction. The commanders of the Russian fleet were a Scotchman and a Hollander ; the head of the engineer department of the army (Betancour) was a Spaniard ; Capo d' Istria, a Greek, and Pozzo di Borgo, a Corsican, were two of the most distinguished Russian diplomatists ; many of the ministers were not Muscovites by birth ; the most eminent professors of the universities were strangers, settled in the country ; while most of the literature of the country was moulded to a foreign, and principally to a French, type. Since then a great change has taken place ; almost all the high offices of government are now filled by native Russians, and the books of Russia have acquired an independent and even a robust nationality. Though many foreigners are settled in Russia, especially those connected with industrial establishments, the capital is mostly provided from native funds.

What most characterized the social state of Russia was the utter absence of a middle class, or *tiers état*, to fill up the vast chasm between the noble and the serf. The condition of the millions of the servile races was exceedingly various, some of the more liberal of their lords allowing them to amass wealth, and I heard of instances where £60,000 to £80,000 had been saved by their industry. Count Tsheremetiev was wont to boast of having 100,000 peasants, and was satisfied with a yearly contribution from each amounting to twenty shillings sterling, but the whole property of the serf was at the absolute disposal of his lord, who might at any time dispose of whatever belonged to him, so that the serf's condition of course depended upon the character of his master. A necessitous noble, given up to habits of profligacy, or to gambling, which is too common in Russia, would frequently not hesitate to pounce upon the hard-earned savings of his dependants. It was often represented to me, though the witnesses were no doubt interested parties, that the peasants were generally well satisfied with their condition, that they desired no change, and that those living upon the estates had the first claim to its produce for the supply of their own and their families' necessities, while of those who were removed the situation was generally bettered. Multitudes of peasants are settled in the larger towns as shopkeepers and merchants, and the boy who attended me was one of a very numerous body engaged as domestic servants, whose earnings belong to their owners.

FINLAND.

I returned from Russia to England through Finland and Sweden. Finland, which was so cruelly wrested from Sweden by the despotic autocrat of all the Russias, still cherishes its ancient nationality, and looks back with deep affection upon the period when the representative principle existed, in however rude a form. I travelled through its silent and solemn forests, looking at the tracks of the wolves on the snow beneath, and listening to the crashes among

the trees of the dense woods whose branches, bound together
by icicles, were shaken by the stormy winds.   The language,
the poetry, and the traditions of the people were full of
charms, having for their special interpreter Tengström, the
Archbishop of Åbo.   The Finnish tongue has been represented by some as bearing much resemblance to the Magyar,
and by others to the Laplandish, the fact being, however,
that very few words of either are to be found in it.   Most
of the poetry of the Finns is written in that peculiar metre
to which Longfellow has given a certain popularity in his
" Hiawatha," but I believe I may take credit to myself for
having been the first to introduce it into our language in
an article which appeared in the *Westminster Review* of
April 1827.   In the long and severe winters which confine
the Finlanders to their wooden cottages, their ancient
mythical poetry serves to shorten and soothe many an
evening hour.   It may be remarked that, notwithstanding the rigour of the climate, the proportion of persons
who reach extreme old age is very great.   The gods
and demigods of their old mythology have merged into
a Christian deity and Christian saints, and the name of
Wäinämöinen now represents the Jehovah of the Hebrew,
and the paternal God of the Christian dispensation.

I found among the Finns a civilization far superior to
what I anticipated.   The gastgiväre, or public hotels, in the
main roads are excellent, and I was once conveyed in my
sledge eighty miles by four ponies abreast, almost without
stopping, more rapidly than the ordinary stage coach would
have carried me in England.   Almost all the educated
people in Finland speak Swedish, that liquid language
which has been called the Italian of the North.   The
Russian is almost confined to the Muscovite functionaries,
in whose offices alone did I see either Russian books or
newspapers.   There is a good deal of resemblance between

the Finlanders and the Esthonians and Livonians on the opposite shores of the Baltic. There was a parish clergyman who, some fifty years ago, collected the Livonian popular songs, and, in the absence of any accessible printing-office, himself set up the types, and worked off an interesting volume, a copy of which reached Sir Walter Scott, who requested me to write some account of its contents. This I did in an article which was published at the time, but where I have now forgotten.

In my intercourse with the leading men, I found that they had, like the Poles, an earnest longing for the return of their independence, but they were fully convinced that it was hopeless to dream of any such felicity. The immense power of Russia, acting upon the weakness and the divisions of the several countries she has absorbed into her huge empire, has imposed a yoke which, heavy though it be, must be borne. These regions are no doubt among the "oppressed nationalities," and the best that can be anticipated is that such concessions may be made by the wisdom and fore-thought of the Russian government as will remove any fair grounds for popular discontent. It is not for us, who have imposed our dominion upon many a once independent people, to be hasty in condemning the usurpations of other powerful states. The progress of time may bring to many a nation the blessings of self-government, and may instil into the hearts of their conquerors the conviction that they may safely and wisely leave many of their dependencies to take care of themselves. That time is undoubtedly rapidly advancing as regards several of the British colonies, in some of which the influence of the mother country is practically almost annihilated.

In the University of Åbo, the most accredited Swedish authors are used as text-books, and some of the sciences which have been cultivated with special success among the

Swedes, such as botany and chemistry, under the great names of Linné (Linnæus) and Berzelius, appeared to me to be the objects of particular attention among the Finlanders. A short time before my visit, a dreadful fire had destroyed the university library, and I had the pleasure, with the aid of friends, to send a pretty large collection of English literature, helping in a small way to fill the melancholy vacuum left by the ravages of the flames.

Finland furnishes to Russia some of her best mariners, the naval service being one for which she has some difficulty in finding a supply of experienced men. Down to the time of the first Alexander, foreign maritime nations generally furnished officers of the highest rank, but of late she has found among her own people men sufficiently instructed and experienced to take charge of her fleets, and this is to her all the more important as her ships of war will undoubtedly find an outlet in the Tatar seas, which is denied to them from the Baltic or the Bosphorus. Whenever any great naval power opposes their exit through the Sound or the Belt, that exit is impassable during the winter season, and Turkey, feeble though she is, can always prevent their passage from the Euxine to the Mediterranean.

The habits of life of the Finlanders are necessarily very simple, and, from the rudeness of the climate, the inhabitants have been sometimes compelled to mix the bark of trees with their bread, in order to provide sufficient aliment for their wants. Torneå, at the head of the Gulf of Bothnia, is sometimes visited by travellers as a place where, in summer, the sun never sets, and in winter never rises. Most of the country is covered with pines, which form a considerable export trade. Wiborg and Helsingfors are, with Åbo, the principal ports, and furnish the best supply of sailors for the Russian navy.

SWEDEN.

In order to avoid the long and weary land journey round the Gulf of Bothnia, by Torneå, I engaged, at Åbo, a small boat with four men, and sledges to go on as far as possible, hoping in this way to cross to Sweden. We went on very well for six or seven miles, when the great chasms between the masses of ice (one of the horses having fallen through, and several of the men) induced us to send back the sledges, and to try to drag our little boat to the furthest possible point. The labour of hauling it thus for several miles, surrounded as we were on every side by hills of ice, and by large holes where the ice had been broken by the storm, was extreme, but we reached at last open sea, and launched our boat, hoping that our difficulties were over. We encountered, however, large islands of ice, and found the water freezing around us, so that we had soon to cut our way through ice an inch thick. The cold and frost increased, and at sunset we found ourselves completely frozen in, no land to be seen, cold and darkness over and around us, in an open boat, and in a latitude of 60 degrees. I had always found fortitude under bodily suffering, and my spirits did not flag. I wrapped myself in my wolf-skin and slept, thinking of my friends, the North Pole Expedition, and the second part of Don Juan. We had a couple of days' provisions, no compass, and our food was frozen to ice. I had once or twice expected, in the course of our land journey, that we should have been lost in the snow, but now I thought of a worse fate. I was calm, however, and rejoiced to think that nobody knew where I was who cared a pin about me.

We lay thus for nine hours, and at break of day were so fortunate as to discover an open sea before us, and, with the assistance of the wind, we cut through the ice, which

I

had been much agitated through the night and was breaking around us, and reached again a space where we could use our oars. The Finn sailors seemed less pleased than I, for the ice islands, broken by the storm, were approaching us, and they feared that we might be carried away by them. However, amidst their crashing and noise, we made great progress, and drew near the coast of Sweden. The seals were playing about, which portended a storm, but we made for the shore, and as the port of our destination was surrounded by ice, we reached land at some distance from it. I suffered more fatigue in getting to Griselhamn along the cliffs, which were rugged and pathless, covered with snow and smooth with ice, with a part of my baggage on my back, than I had ever experienced before. I often sank into the snow, and several times fell among the icy rocks. Two or three of the men slipped over the cliffs into the sea, which was fortunately not more than two or three feet deep, so they escaped with a wetting. The wind was bitter and bleak, but I was so hot with exertion that I devoured large pieces of ice. 1 was also sadly encumbered with furs. However, arrive I did at Griselhamn, and drank nearly two bottles of the best beer I ever tasted. The first words I heard were, " Komm lät oss gå," which have exactly the English sound.

From Griselhamn I proceeded to Upsala where, in company with Professor Aurivilius, I visited the tomb of Linné, bringing away with me some of the earth which covered his honoured remains. Among my acquaintances in Sweden was Berzelius, whom I saw, where such a man is most advantageously seen—in his laboratory — and engaged in his scientific pursuits. He was then occupied with experiments on the human skin, and he told me that there was no substance in nature which could bear such vicissitudes of heat and cold. He was dressed in garments most appropriate to the work which occupied him, and mentioned with much hilarity how long he had been detained when calling on our chemist, Sir Humphrey Davy, in London, who thought it necessary to dandify himself, and to appear in spruce apparel, in order to welcome the Swedish philosopher.

I spent a few agreeable days with Franzen, Bishop of Örebro, next to Tegner the most popular of the modern poets of Sweden. My vanity was not a little flattered by a circumstance which he mentioned to me. A vessel from Calcutta had been wrecked in the Baltic Sea, and a native Hindoo who escaped saved a little book of mine called " Matins and Vespers," which, he told the good Bishop, had been a source of great comfort to him. He presented the volume to my kind host as a token of gratitude for the attentions he had received, and the Bishop had kept it in his pulpit, little expecting to have the author as his guest. He wrote some pretty verses in my album, in which he compared friendship to the rainbow, whose arch stretches over and smiles on many lands at the same time.

I found the Swedes a courteous and hospitable people, never given to luxury, more observant of forms and fashions, and generally less contemplative than their neighbours the Danes, but fond of dance and song, with which they make their cold winters bright and gay. They have been called the French of the north, and no doubt their choice of a Frenchman to be their king had made Parisian tastes and fashions and the French language popular. Bernadotte seems to have understood them well, and founded the present reigning dynasty, to the hopeless exclusion of the ancient royal race.

The Swedish language is remarkable for its sweetness, and for the great number of vowel terminations by which, like Italian, it is characterized.

FRANCE.

In the year 1822 I visited Paris on commercial affairs. My known opinions, no doubt, made me an object of attention to the police, and I had reason to believe that my bureaux were opened by false keys at my lodgings, and my papers examined, while my steps were constantly watched by spies. I was then intimate with the Duke of Orleans, who was in disgrace at Court. He had been denied the privilege of sitting in the Chamber of Peers, no higher title than Serene Highness was conceded to him, and it was believed that he was the centre of a hundred conspiracies to overturn the government. It was supposed, as I had travelled much, and had had much intercourse with the liberals of Europe, that I was a secret agent, as I undoubtedly was a personal friend of Louis Philippe, to whom I had been originally introduced by General Dumouriez, than whom a more acceptable usher could hardly have been found. I believe the accusations against the Duke of being a conspirator against the senior branch of the Bourbons were wholly groundless, for, though talkative and somewhat swaggering, he was really a very timid man. I know of more than one flattering offer made to him by malcontents, which he invariably repudiated and discouraged, but he had a notion certainly that the absurd policy of the elder Bourbons, and especially of " Frère Philippe" (Charles X.) would, in the natural course of events, waft the crown of France towards him, and that it would fall on his head. In fact, his work was better done by his foolish relations than he could have done it for himself, and he preferred a safe to an adventurous policy. He was wholly without enlarged ideas, but saw clearly enough in a narrow circle. He was surrounded by spies, and I remember his whispering to me, when on one occasion he proposed that we should leave the dinner-table for a walk in the gardens at Neuilly, that he had not a servant in attendance whom he could trust, and that he believed they were all in the pay of the police. That day was to me a memorable one. It was then that the " quatre Sergens de la Rochelle" were guillotined, and I heard, in the presence of Louis Philippe, the artillery which he said announced their decapitation. They were young men of good family who had been convicted and condemned to death for singing republican songs. It was at a moment when political passion was at its height, and the Bourbons were revelling in the blood they shed. The fate of these youths excited great interest in Paris, and an attempt was made by Generals Fabvier, Dentzel, and others to save their lives. The jailor was tampered with, and he promised to facilitate their escape if the sum of 10,000 francs were given to him. The money was raised and paid to him, but the scoundrel denounced the plot to the police, and an order was given for the immediate execution of the young men. To crown all, the Bourbons gave a great fête and *bal* the same evening, which led to the circulation of the following couplet—

" Pour le peuple Français O ! quel heureux jour !
On égorge à la Grève et l'on danse à la Cour."

When Fabvier was arrested, a bill of exchange was found with my name endorsed on it. It formed a portion of the money raised in order to save the unfortunate victims. This fact was afterwards made the excuse for my arbitrary arrest, when Mr Canning insisted on knowing the cause of my detention and imprisonment. But the government dreaded discussion and exposure, and did not venture to bring me to a trial, which would have infallibly led to both. They had suffered much in public opinion by the exposure in Lavalette's affair, and the business of the young serjeants was still more sanguinary and indefensible.

I was accustomed to attend the house of a literary lady,
Madame de B——. After the Revolution of 1830, I had an
opportunity of ascertaining that she was in the habit of receiving the sum of (I think) 6000 francs a-year, to cover the expense of her entertainments, to which multitudes of people
were invited, whose conversation was regularly reported to
the police. The ramifications of the French police were at this
time so extensive, that I found I was honoured in my house
at London Field, Hackney, where I had a sort of conver-
sazione on Thursday evenings, with frequent visits from
police agents, who managed to get themselves invited in
consequence of letters they brought, or on their introduction
by personal friends. I saw at Paris the record of conversations which had taken place in my drawing-room, which
were given with no small accuracy. Great numbers of
refugees, who had sought an asylum in England from political persecution, and many of whom I had known in their
native countries moving in the highest circles, were in the
habit of visiting me, and in the melée no doubt were some
who became the willing instruments of French, Austrian, and
Spanish surveillance. But the grand organization of the
system of espionage was united in Paris, and the Pavillon
Marsan at the Tuileries, the portion of the palace occupied
by the Comte d' Artois (afterwards Charles X.), was one of
the places where the gathering and distribution of political
secrets were in a state of the greatest activity.

One evening, at the house of Madame de B——, a gentleman who called himself the Marquis de——, I have forgotten
the name—was exceedingly assiduous in his attentions to me.
I saw him for the first time. He expressed great interest
in England and English institutions, and said he had determined to send his son there for his education. " Would I
take charge of him ?" I hesitated, said it would be an
embarrassment to me, as in fact I had not settled when or

how I should travel, and finally declined the proposal. On the following day a livery servant called with a message from the Marquis, who hoped I would change my purpose, and was exceedingly anxious to know when I meant to depart. My suspicions were aroused, and I sent a person to follow the footsteps of the liveried gentleman, who went directly to the Pavillon Marsan. I was arrested at Calais, on my way to England, by a telegraphic order, and was conducted by the gendarmerie to the Maison de Ville. Among my compagnons de voyage was Mr Mark Phillips, afterwards M.P. for Manchester. He was with me when, at the moment of leaving the shore, a gendarme put his hand on my shoulder, stopped the embarkation of my baggage, and bade me accompany him. Had I been alone, probably nothing would have been heard of my arrest, and I might have been detained a prisoner as long as it suited the purposes of the French government. While in the Mayor's chamber, he was called out, and I took up the papers on his table. They were communications from the Minister of Police, in which my conversations with the *Marquis* were fully reported, and they were to furnish materials for the interrogatories to which I was to be subjected. But I believe the more immediate object of my arrest was to obtain possession of despatches of which I was the bearer from the Portuguese Minister to his government in Portugal. I was at first thrown into a vile and offensive dungeon at Calais, having for my companions forgers, from whose own lips I heard a confession of their guilt.

Canning was then Prime Minister of England, and as soon as he was informed of my arrest, he insisted on my release, or an *acte d' accusation* which would justify my detention. At last, charges were made against me, first of being the bearer of letters, and secondly of being concerned in the attempt to effect the escape of the Sergens de la Rochelle.

Both of these accusations had, in truth, some evidence to support them, for I was the bearer of despatches from the Portuguese minister, his own couriers being tampered with, and I was a party, with the generals I have mentioned, in the endeavour to procure the *evasion* from their prison of the condemned youths. The despatches were of great importance, as they announced to the Portuguese ministry the intended invasion of the Peninsula by the Duc d' Angoulême. It may be observed that, in reply to an enquiry made by Mr Canning on this subject, such intention was distinctly disclaimed, and he was assured that the troops collected along the Pyrenees were intended only as a *cordon sanitaire* for the protection of France.

I was several times escorted by French soldiers to the *griffe*, where examinations, which lasted several hours, were conducted by the Procureur du Roi, in order to extort from me materials out of which to frame an indictment. As to the two charges on which the French Government chose afterwards to rest their justification for my detention, I did not hesitate to avow my guilt, and told the Procureur that I would have given my right hand to save the youths from the fate to which they had been so cruelly condemned. I said, moreover that, when brought to trial, I should justify all I had done, and call attention to facts exceedingly discreditable as to the manner in which judicial proceedings were conducted in France. I had applied for the presence of the Consul or an interpreter during the interrogatories, but was told that as I knew French perfectly well, their intervention was needless. I protested, inasmuch as my case might be made a precedent where individuals knew much less than myself of the French tongue, and moreover that, as regarded the phraseology and technicalities of the proceedings, I was not so much at home as in the colloquial language, but I protested in vain. I was, however, never brought to trial, and was surprised one morning, six weeks after my arrest, by the entrance of the jailor of the Boulogne Prison (to which I had been removed five days after my first detention), who informed me that I was a free man, and that a King's messenger was waiting to convey me to England.

My arrest was the subject of a motion in the House of Commons, as it was thought I had claims to indemnity for the injuries done me, but it was stated by Mr Canning that he had consulted the highest French authorities, and as I had suffered no grievance other than that with which a Frenchman might have been visited, I, a foreigner, could claim no redress which would be denied to a native subject. I was informed that I should not again be allowed to enter France, but, after the Revolution of 1830, I conveyed the congratulatory address of the citizens of London, which I had written, and which was voted in Common Hall. A public dinner was given to me at the Hôtel de Ville by Odilon Barrot, the Prefect of the Seine, and I was the first person received by Louis Philippe after the British Ambassador had announced to him that he was recognized by the English Government as King of the French.

Louis Philippe was the most insincere of men, and Thiers once called him "le plus grand fourbe de l' Europe." Though physically brave, he was a great political coward, and it must be owned that a good deal of poltroonery was inherited by some of his sons, who abandoned their wives in the moment of danger. The Prince de Joinville was certainly absent at this juncture, but for him there cannot be much genuine sympathy in England. He was the author of the pamphlet which his father corrected for the press, whose object was the humiliation and subjugation of the British navy. I remember Charles Napier, the admiral, saying to me, "If I ever catch that fellow, I will fling him into the sea." There

are indeed few, if any, of the Bourbon race distinguished
for bravery.   I think it was Boileau who lauded Louis XIV.
for keeping out of danger, and waiting *sur la rive* while his
army crossed the river.   Louis Philippe could not stand up
against any stout resistance.   Dupont de l' Eure told me he
applied to him, when Minister of Justice, to nominate to a
judgeship a magistrate unfitted for the post.   Dupont
steadily refused, but the King returned again and again to
the charge, which made Dupont only the more obstinate,
and he at last said, " If Your Majesty persist, I shall fling
up my appointment."   The King surrendered, but he took
the earliest opportunity of getting rid of the party to
which he owed the sceptre, and of taking into his confidence the Doctrinaires, who proved his willing tools, helped
him in the disgraceful affair of the Spanish marriages, and
were willing (though some of them, and notably Guizot and
Duchatel, were not corrupted) to do all his behests.   Corruption was indeed the great instrument of the Orleans
dynasty, and a majority of the House of Deputies under its
régime were place-holders.

Guizot was the most influential representative of the
Doctrinaires—a cold, hard man, who had the reputation of
Liberalism, but was essentially harsh, despotic, and untrustworthy.   Personally he was not corrupt, but was extremely
vain and ambitious.   His hatreds were bitter, but there
was no relying on his love.   He had the credit, and deserved
it, of having diligently studied English history, but he failed
to learn the emphatic lessons which it teaches, possibly
thinking a régime of despotism best suited to France.
When disorders broke out at Lyons, and so many of the
workpeople were slain by the soldiers, he announced his
policy to the Chambers by saying, " Rassurez vous,
messieurs, les ordres sont impitoyables," and pitiless they
were.   Had he been born in Spain in the sixteenth century,

he would have been the most merciless of inquisitors. He consented to hold office long after he knew that the King carried on a personal correspondence with his foreign ministers, pursuing a policy of his own without the knowledge or consent of the ministry. The intrigues connected with the Spanish marriages were, I believe, unknown to the Paris Cabinet, though Guizot afterwards undertook to defend the double-dealings of the King. The French Minister at Madrid (Bresson) committed suicide to escape, it was said, the opprobrium of the proceedings which took place.

My acquaintance with Louis Napoleon commenced at Arenenberg, where he was living with his mother Hortense, the ex-Queen of Holland. Her manners were so fascinating that I can well understand the influence she exercised over her imperial step-father, of whom she spoke in terms almost of idolatry. She took me to her boudoir, and showed me a number of interesting relics—the sash which Buonaparte wore at the Ponte d'Arcolo—the various presents he had received from different monarchs—the wedding rings and jewels of the members of the Napoleon family—the pictures of the Empress and the King of Rome, on which Napoleon looked when he was dying—the ornaments found on the breast of Charlemagne, when his coffin was disinterred and his corpse exposed to public view, and a number of other things equally historical. She gave me a copy of her account of her journey incognita to Paris, notwithstanding the banishment of the whole race by the French Chambers.

Louis Napoleon was at this time much engaged in military studies, and gave evidence of the talent which he subsequently displayed in the Italian campaign. His book on the artillery service obtained for him a high reputation among the greatest authorities, and in these days one may safely affirm that no man can have written the best book on any subject, without being gifted with more than

common sagacity. It has often been said that the merit of
the work was not his own, but was due to his instructor
General Dufour. I had occasion to meet the General at
Berne, and took the liberty to enquire how far he had been a
party to the composition, but he disclaimed all participation
in the work, saying that the Prince was a superior military
genius. I have since closely watched the progress of Louis
Napoleon's career, never concurring in that depreciatory
estimate of his intellect which the Orleanist party assidu-
ously sought to circulate. He was, at the time of the
Strasburg and Boulogne expeditions, the object of much
contemptuous ridicule, but those expeditions were very
near success, and one of them would almost assuredly not
have failed, if the officers in command had not been superseded by the government in consequence of some revelations
that were made. The primary object of these attempts was
to keep his name constantly before the French nation, and
to associate that name with acts of daring, which he was
well assured would popularize it, and the result responded
to his expectations.

It is impossible to deny that he succeeded in winning
the suffrages of the great majority of the French people,
and that he elevated his country to take the highest rank
among the continental nations of Europe. The tendencies
which latterly characterized his reign, the greater latitude
given to public opinion, the abolition of the passport-system,
and the distribution of many of the powers of the Central
Government among the Departments, are evidences of
liberal and enlightened views. Once, calling on Casimir
Perrier, while he was Minister of the Interior, and when all
the functions of domestic government were concentrated in
that ministry, I saw a heap of despatches, reaching from
the floor to the table, waiting for his signature. I asked
how it was possible he could master, or even make himself

tolerably acquainted with, the contents of the multifarious documents. He said that would be impossible, that they were prepared by the different heads of departments, and that he was compelled to rely upon their sagacity and honesty for the decisions which he had to affirm. It seemed a strange mode of government, but so France was then governed. Centralization had so completely usurped all authority, and so much time was necessarily lost in the various claims upon attention, that the decrees were almost invariably behind hand, and inadequate to the removal of the grievances they were intended to redress. Whatever advantages may attend the consolidation of power in the hands of the Home Minister in Paris, as regards foreign nations, its effects upon the well-being of the French subject are undoubtedly pernicious.

Among my most intimate acquaintances in Paris was Appert, known for his works on prison discipline, who was the almoner of the Queen of the French. In that capacity, she transferred to him masses of letters, in which persons of all classes applied to her for assistance, and at the foot of every communication were instructions, written with her own hand, for the guidance of the dispenser of her bounties. The tales of human misery which were sometimes revealed exceeded anything which fiction has ever painted, showing from what heights and into what depths the victims of vicissitude may be flung, especially in a country where political changes have been so frequent and appalling. Nothing could be more admirable than the attention which this excellent woman paid to petitioners, or the trouble she took to ascertain the truth of their representations.

With Appert I visited many of the prisons of Paris. In that of Bicêtre there were four thousand five hundred persons. I saw one hundred and sixty chained together, iron collars being rivetted round their necks. There was among them a boy of only sixteen, who was a chief of bandits, and they could scarcely find a collar small enough to secure him. Some of the prisoners were going to the galleys, and of all the scenes I ever witnessed it was perhaps the most extraordinary. Some had dressed themselves in a grotesque and fantastic manner, with ribbons, swords of straw, and other absurd decorations, while others were almost naked, and there was scarcely one who felt the shame and ignominy of his situation. They jested, they laughed, they sang, they danced, one man having blackened himself to look like a negro. These were of course the most hardened, and they formed a strange contrast to the young, who were weeping, and the old, who were despairing. Before they were marched off, they gathered round one of the convicts, who sang a song, in the chorus of which they all joined (and it was very affecting), to the effect "that though they were chained now, they should one day find freedom."

I afterwards visited the three great depôts of felons at Brest, La Rochelle, and Toulon, being provided with official letters which enabled me to witness all their horrors. At Rochefort, there were about six hundred or seven hundred men condemned for life, and about five hundred for a longer period than ten years. They were all heavily chained, and were the most horrible collection of human beings that one could imagine, about half of them being murderers. I had some conversation with the famous Collet, and bought from him some of his work as a memento. He had appeared in France some years before as an archbishop, had levied contributions from the clergy, and had ordained so many priests that the Pope was obliged to confirm his acts. He next appeared as General Inspector, called out and reviewed the troops, distributed decorations of the Legion of Honor, and drew money from the military chests. He began his career as a monk, got to be the *boursier*, and ran away with all the money of the convent. I suppose so illustrious a swindler never appeared, and I found that he exercised the greatest influence over the wretches around him, who all spoke of him as Monseigneur. He was a monarch in hell. The felons were all chained together in pairs, and were occupied with one solitary thought—how to escape? The overseer was obliged to employ men among them as spies, but he told me that when the others discovered a spy they invariably murdered him.

At Brest there were over three thousand three hundred galley-slaves, the most renowned of assassins and robbers, and I bought some beautiful carvings from one of them named Contrefalto. Among them was a man who single-handed robbed a diligence with fifteen passengers, five or six of whom were military officers. He arranged along the road a number of straw figures, which he armed with sticks pointed at the diligence. It was nearly dark, and the passengers thought they were a troop of bandits. ' He made all the passengers fall on their faces, telling the men of straw to fire if there was the slightest opposition, and he robbed the whole party alone. They remained on their faces nearly half an hour, and when they rose, found that the bandits were nothing but straw, covered with old clothes! Among these wretched beings reigned a sort of fidelity. They always settled the day for every individual to escape, and on that day he received every assistance from all the rest. When they discovered a spy among them, they invariably destroyed him by means concocted, but seemingly accidental, such as allowing a beam of timber to fall upon him, precipitating him from a height, or some other device which might free the perpetrator from the charge of homicide. I heard of one case in which a man was conveyed away in the ordure of the criminals, and other cases scarcely less extraordinary had occurred. Revolts sometimes took place, which were pitilessly dealt with by the musketry of the soldiers. The felons had for their beds rough planks, to which they were chained at night, and marvellous it seemed that any slumber should "weigh the eyelids down" of so much wretchedness.

Appert once invited me to a dinner such as could only be given in Paris, the guests being Sanson, the hereditary executioner, Vidocq, the thief-catcher, some authors, artists, and myself. Sanson and Vidocq made on that occasion their first personal acquaintance, though they seem to have had much connection with each other in their separate and singular spheres of action. Sanson talked very willingly of the management of the guillotine, which he called "la mécanique," of his ancestors, the former *bourreaux* of France—and of his son and successor, whom he afterwards introduced to me. He said that the families of the different executioners in France almost always intermarried, and that there was a strong clanship among the members of this life-destroying community. He asked me to his house in order that he might exhibit the operation of "la mécanique," and I went thither, accompanied by Lord Durham, Mr Edward Ellice, and Mr Dawson Damer, whom, by the way, I had known in Egypt, where his wife was introduced to old Mehemet Ali, whom she much amused.

Sanson's house was a little way in the country, was prettily furnished, and had quite the air of respectability and comfort. He showed us the volumes of the *procès verbaux*, which were detailed records of what occurred at every public execution that had taken place in Paris. The books were very neatly kept, and bore the signatures of the parties who had assisted at the dread exhibitions. Some one asked Sanson whether, after decapitation, he had ever seen any movement in the head after its separation from the body, as a theory had been put forward that sensation was not immediately extinguished by the operation, but he said that he had never observed the slightest movement. He conducted us to a large outhouse in which the fatal machine was kept. It was painted scarlet. *Un homme de paille* was prepared, and the usual assistants were summoned, in order that we might witness the whole mode of proceeding. We were struck by the heaviness and sharpness of the knife, which, falling from a great height, could not but do its bloody work most effectually.

While seated at dinner with M. Appert, Vidocq questioned Sanson as to the manner in which many acquaintances had met their death. He mentioned, among other things, that, when connected with the police, he had associated himself with a band of robbers and murderers, whom he promised to deliver over to the authorities while they were engaged in a large scheme of plunder at the Batignolles. An arrangement was made by which, on his firing a pistol from a window, the house was to be surrounded and the felons captured, as they were. Vidocq said they never discovered his treachery until they saw him in the street on their way to execution. The account he gave of his courtship and marriage with a woman who was his fellow-prisoner was most romantic, but as the details of his life have been published in memoirs written by himself, they may be referred to as furnishing the sort of material of which his conversation was composed. Probably no man knew more of the organization of the thieves and burglars in Paris than did Vidocq, whose own offences were condoned when he was admitted into the service of the criminal police, of whom he became a most efficient instrument. He had also a little private profession of his own, and was frequently employed by individuals to assist in the detection and conviction of robbers. In his person there was nothing remarkable, but he was singularly self-possessed and dis-

K

posed to be loquacious. Sanson, on the contrary, was a tall heavy man, of taciturn habits, from whom information was only obtainable by its being specially sought. The son had rather a cadaverous appearance, but took little share, when his father was present, in the colloquies that passed.

The whole system of criminal proceedings in France is singularly contrasted with that which prevails in our country. We expect a prisoner always to plead "not guilty," he is recommended to say nothing by which he may inculpate himself, and the judge before whom he is tried is called his counsel, and is expected to point out to the jury those points of evidence which are favourable to his defence. In France, on the contrary, everything is done by the magistrate to extort confession, to involve him in contradiction, and, even before his defence is heard, to give a strong opinion as to his guilt. The number of condemnations to capital punishment is very great, but, as the general character of the French is really humane, the verdict of "guilty" given by juries has often attached to it "*avec des circonstances attenuantes,*" equivalent to our "recommended to mercy," even in cases where, to the calm eye of reason and justice, the offence has in it everything that could aggravate its criminality. My experience has led me to the conclusion that the interests of society will be best served by the absolute abolition of capital punishment, and that O'Connell was perfectly right when he said, "The worst thing you can do with a man is to hang him."

My mind is often filled with gloom when I remember that, neither in my reading nor in my own personal experience, has France, in the midst of all her political vicissitudes, ever really enjoyed the blessings of good government. Under the ancient Monarchical despotism— amidst the liberty, or rather the licence, of the Revolution of 1792—under the Consular or the Imperial dynasties—with the modified form of the Constitutional Charter under the elder Bourbons—in the concessions made by the semi-legitimacy of Louis Philippe—or in the advent of Louis Napoleon to the throne of France, I find nowhere any of the guarantees for personal or public liberty which have become a part of the social organisation of Great Britain and her dependencies. Thiers once cleverly and happily said that France was governed more by a "*phrase*" than by a principle, and after what have been called "the glorious days of July," I found everybody in Paris occupied, not with the establishment of national freedom on broad and solid foundations, but with the consideration whether Louis Philippe should be called "King of France" or "King of the French," whether "parceque" or "quoique Bourbon," whether La Fayette's interpretation "une monarchie entourée d' institutions républicaines" was to be accepted as a final solution of the political problem, or some other such really comparatively unimportant topic. The simple fact is that the general distribution of property—there being, I believe, more than five million owners of land, and twenty million separate estates in France—has made universal suffrage almost a necessity of government, which, if it obtain the good opinion of these multitudinous proprietors, is little likely to be overthrown. We commit a great error in supposing that French institutions can be modelled on our own, but if the small number of our land-holding gentry, and the growing concentration of estates in the hands of the opulent, to the exclusion of the ancient yeomanry, be contrasted with the precisely opposite state of things among our Gallic neighbours, a key will perhaps be found to the understanding of much that takes place in the course of events at home and abroad.

The bitter reproach which was formerly addressed to the

French that they were either tigers or monkies, can certainly be no longer with any truth or propriety applied to
them. Wordsworth, in one of his sonnets, contrasting the
intellectual position of France with that of England in the
time of the Commonwealth of the illustrious names which
shone upon our annals, says that the history of our neighbours
exhibited " equally a want of names and men." But books in
every portion of the field of thought, and men honouring
the highest seats of action, have, for the last century at least,
been associated with French history and the French language. Much of the old levity has passed away, and
the nation can boast of philosophers more severe and profound than those who have made up the reputation of the
great people on the other side of the channel. Not that the
sprightly gaiety of conversation, and the sparkling of ready
wit have disappeared, for the soirées of Paris have a charm
in them which I have nowhere else discovered. The light-
heartedness of the masses, the cheerfulness with which
they submit to what is inevitable, are still their characteristics, and they can joke on subjects from which other races
would turn away in disgust. I remember when the allies
entered Paris that the letter *A*, meaning Alexander, was
(probably by the Russians) made to supersede the *N*, for
Napoleon, and the calembour of the day was, " Autrefois il
y avait des *N* mis (ennemis) partout. Maintenant il n' y
a que des *A* mis." I had once a fencing-master, who narrowly escaped death for having, in his zeal for legitimacy,
thrown an orange on the stage, exclaiming, " Otez l' écorce
(le Corse, *i.e.*, Buonaparte) et gardez lui (Louis)."

HOLLAND.

Perhaps there never was a monarch so keenly engaged in
money-making as was Vader Willem, as he was familiarly
called by his Dutch subjects. When he was exalted to the

Hague, after the French were driven out of his country, and before any tariff of duties was established, he shipped a large cargo of tea, without the payment of any impost, which he sold at an enormous profit. In almost every successful industrial undertaking he was a sleeping partner, and in the bank at Brussels, the receptacle of the State revenues, he held the largest number of shares. When the Civil List was settled at a certain pecuniary amount, he managed to get the money value changed into real property on terms which enormously increased his yearly income.

In the year 1828, I was sent by the British Government to examine into the state of the national accountancy of Holland. I soon discovered that the establishment called the *Sindicaat* was made the instrument of great abuses, and my investigations into its doings were suddenly arrested by special orders from the King.

Whatever may have been the intentions of the Congress of Vienna, or the hopes of the Dutch from the union of Belgium to Holland, the policy was a very mistaken one, and there never was a real fusion of the heterogeneous elements. Belgium was the more populous country of the two, and was just as unwilling to submit to Dutch authority as the Hollanders were anxious to enforce it. In many respects Holland was the more enlightened of the two countries, for the spirit of toleration, or rather of religious freedom, was there generally diffused, and all sects were equally patronised, if they desired to receive pay from the State. No one sect looks with distrust or disdain upon another, and it is quite common to hear different doctrines preached from the same pulpit, the Dutch pastors willingly lending their churches to those of different opinions from themselves. A very liberal system of theology has taken deep root in Holland. Instruction is widely diffused among the people, without the heartburnings and jealousies so com-

mon in Belgium, and few countries have so many well-ad-
ministered charitable institutions.   The national credit
stands high, and there is a great distribution of wealth
among the more privileged classes.   Holland is one of the
most heavily taxed countries of Europe, but the burdens
are not felt to be oppressive, and are the subject of little
complaint.   Where she is most at fault is in her protective
system.   Under the pretence of favouring the interests of
navigation and commerce, the Bataavsche Maatschappij is
a monstrous monopoly to which the general interests are
sacrificed.

When I visited Holland in 1828, my name was not
unknown in the country, for, in association with Harry S.
Van Dyk, I had published a volume of translations from
the Dutch poets, and had been honoured with a gold medal
from the king in recognition of my services.   I made the
acquaintance of most of the literati of the day—Tollens,
Bilderdijk (perhaps the most distinguished of their modern
poets), Cappadoce and Da Costa (converted Jews), Siegen-
beek, who remodelled the Dutch orthography, and many
others.   William de Clercq was then in his glory, and his
improvisation in a language seemingly so little fitted for the
purpose was much applauded.   I found social life in
Holland very much resembling that of ancient times in
England, the ladies taking a much more active part in
domestic and culinary arrangements than is the practice
now in our country.   The distinction between the dresses
of the female servants and those of their mistresses was still
preserved.   I met everywhere with great hospitality, and
ready entrance to the social circle, and discovered that there
was no ground for the reputation of inaccessibility, at least
for those who are acquainted with the language of Holland,
without which little can really be learned of the inner life
of the nation.   The wealth of the Dutch merchants, and the

extent of the Dutch colonies, give them a European position higher than their small population would seem to warrant, and their position excites no jealousy.

Of all the Netherlandic provinces, Friesland had for me the greatest interest. The Frisian language more nearly resembles the Anglo-Saxon than any other tongue, and the proverb—

> "Butter, bread, and green cheese,
> Is good English and good Fries."

is often heard from Frisian lips. It is a curious fact in modern history that the Frisians had no proper family names until the conquest of their country by Buonaparte, when, for the purposes of conscription, the baptismal designation was insufficient to identify the individual. So every man selected the name that pleased him, and very many were taken from Roman history—John the Smith becoming Julius Cæsar, and Peter the Longshanked being converted into Virgil. Posthumus was the name of a village pastor living at Waaxen, whose translations from Shakspeare much more resemble the original, and as perfectly convey the sense as the best translations (and they are most excellent) of the scholars of Germany. The Frisians have a poet, Sapiex, of whom they are proud, and who was a school-master at Bolsward. The well-known Francis Junius spent some years in the country, in order to study its language and literature, and presented to the Bodleian Library the results of his researches. Rask, the eminent linguist of Copenhagen, wrote a Frisian grammar. A literary society exists at Leeuwarden, which publishes a periodical, and has done good service by collecting the various works, printed and manuscript, which illustrate the history of the province. An article which I wrote in No. XXIII. of the *Westminster Review*, on Frisian literature, gives an account of my inquiries in the country itself.

I was accompanied from Lecuwarden to Leer (in Germany)
by an itinerant French conjuror and his family, who fancied
that he had been commissioned to enlighten the world by
his "talents dans les belles sciences," to use his own words.
He had been a farmer, a soldier, a dancing-master, a
merchant, and a corn-factor. The revolution took away his
farm ; he deserted from the army ; he was persecuted by a
priest for having taught a "danse immorale," which he
averred was admired in the very first circles ; the English
captured his ship, which, he said, was known in every port
from Bordeaux to the Isle de Ré ; and he lost his factor's
ticket for something he had done "pour faire enchèrir les
grains." The interesting family had been making the tour
of Holland, and the fellow assured me that he had been
"abimé, pillé, ravagé, écorché, brulé, volé, violé, crevé,
massacré," and a hundred things besides, in all the towns
and villages of the Netherlands.   His conversation was
made up of the most vehement interjections, "O ! les
assassins ! les gueux ! les scélérats ! les voleurs ! les tigres !
les monstres ! les bêtes ! sans foi, sans loi, sans honneur !
qui devraient être foulés à pied mais qui sont trop indignes
même pour cela." He had the impudence to send the boatmen to me that I might pay his fare, saying that it would
be very unjust to demand it from "un professeur comme
moi, qui travaille pour gagner la vie," and that they might
ask it from me "puisque Monsieur était Anglais, et que
tous les Anglais sont braves, riches, et généreux."   On my
refusal, he came himself and strutted up and down as if he
were the king of the conjurors, but as I continued obdurate,
he left me with a majestic air, saying, "Monsieur, je vous
croyais Anglais. Si vous l'êtes, ce que je doute, vous êtes
peut-être un de ces chétifs commis qui viennent vendre les
marchandises de leur maîtres, sans avoir rien à eux." I had
hardly reached my inn and seated myself at the table d'hôte,

at the head of which, as usual in Germany, the good woman
of the house was presiding, ere I was tapped on the shoulder
by an officer of gendarmerie, who, after many expressions
of regret at being obliged to perform so disagreeable a duty,
gave me to understand that the police had been struck by
my resemblance to a " Lord Murray," whom they had orders
to arrest, the "lange nase" being the first article in the
description. After some explanations I convinced him that,
though I might have a long nose, I was no Lord, and,
moreover, that the description did not suit me in other
particulars. I found afterwards that the conjuror had had
something to do with it. He had been summoned by the
boatmen for not having paid his fare, and revenged himself
on me by such a description of me as led to my being
waited on as I have described.

DENMARK.

At Copenhagen, the interesting capital of Denmark, I
enjoyed, in 1829, the friendship of many eminent men,
among whom was Henry Wheaton, the United States
minister, a well known writer on International Law, and
a man held in high esteem by his brother diplomatists.
Though no partisan, he was sacrificed to party, and died
poor and neglected, his fine intellect having sunk under
the burden of dejection and disappointment. I met also
Oehlenschläger, who wrote poetry and dramas with equal
purity and success in German and Danish ; Finn Magnusen,
the Icelander, the illustrator of Runes and Runic history ;
Rask, whose knowledge of languages was as extensive, and
far more profound than that of Mezzofanti ; Thiele, the biographer of Thorwaldsen ; and the Bishop, a most learned
man, whose absence of mind often led to most amusing
scenes.

A rather curious circumstance occurred when I was introduced to the King. I was kept some time waiting at the palace, in consequence of the meeting of a council of ministers, and meanwhile one of the courtiers apologised for telling me that His Majesty had a singular aversion to spectacles, and suggested that I should remove them when admitted to the royal presence. When the ministers came out, I, whose vision is not very perfect even with these aids to deficient eyesight, moved forward, expecting, as is usual in such cases, to pass through a succession of apartments, instead of which the King was near the door of the first. I walked blindly on, and nearly knocked down His Majesty, who was an exceedingly small man. He staggered and looked at me, my embarrassment of course being extreme; but he behaved with great good nature, and we were soon engaged in an interesting conversation, in which he naturally took the initiative, asking me what had struck me most in visiting his dominions. I answered—and the circumstance was a very interesting fact—that I had not in my travels found a single Danish subject unable to read and write. He said it was a good thing to teach people, as it then made it difficult to deceive them, and certainly nothing could be more creditable to the despotic character of his rule than that despotism should have been exercised for purposes so beneficial.

Prince Christian, the heir-apparent, was in all respects superior to the King, and his wife was one of the most beautiful princesses in Europe. She spoke with enthusiasm of the novels of Sir Walter Scott, which were then exciting so great a sensation through the European world. On one occasion they so completely absorbed her attention that, while reading them in bed at night, the curtains caught fire, and she was in consequence exposed to great personal danger. Nothing could have been more courteous than the Prince's reception of me. He was very anxious to hear all

about the London University, enquired after Mr Fry, and
desired me to assist the literary researches of one of his
friends who was proceeding to London.

Of the three great branches of the Scandinavian stem,
the Swedish, Danish, and Norwegian, the Danish is characterized by the most marked nationality. Copenhagen is
the centre from which most of our knowledge of the earlier
history of Iceland is derived, while the Danish mind is
more thoughtful and philosophical than that of the Swedes,
and less engrossed by the attention to trade and shipping
so universal in Norway. I am disposed to regard the
civilization of Denmark as being of a somewhat higher
character than that of its neighbours, and to think that the
despotism of the old government was often used for excellent objects. Danish nationality is kept constantly on the
alert in consequence of its union with the provinces of
Schleswig and Holstein, where the German element is
generally diffused, upon which the German Powers are
constantly acting to the great disgust of the Danish Court.
The late introduction of a more liberal policy into the
councils of Copenhagen does not seem to have diminished
the deep hostility fanned and fostered by the most influential
portion of the German press. The patriotism of the Danes
at home, and the interest which they have inspired abroad,
may indeed prevent any serious rupture, as there is certainly no disposition among European Powers to lower the
influence of an enlightened and pacific people, who count,
as they ought to count, for much in the balance of European
policy. What is to be desired is the consolidation of all the
Scandinavian interests into one, and time may see a fusion
of Danish, Norwegian, and Swedish authority, and the
consequent concentration of elements so great and important
as to place these nations among the most influential of
northern states.

On my homeward way I visited the Duke of Schleswig-Holstein at his palace. He was deeply engaged in the study of the Phallic rites, and the history of Isis and Osiris, some curious pictures found in the tombs of Thebes having specially interested him. Had he but lived to hear of the extent to which the worship of the Phallus exists in Japan down to our own days, he would have rejoiced at the information. A very curious collection of the appurtenances of this singular religion was made by Dr Witt, and, accompanied by Charles Dickens, Bishop Colenso, and several other gentlemen, I visited the doctor, who displayed and explained his museum, in which all the Priapean illustrations were gathered together. The collection was presented by him to the British Museum, where it can be seen on special application.

An accident, scarcely less unfortunate than that which occurred in my interview with the King of Denmark, befell me with the Duke. He was exceedingly excited during our conversation. He was suffering from a severe attack of gout, his feet being wrapped in flannel. I know not whether it was his fault or mine, but my boots came in contact with the gouty part, and the consequence was a loud cry, the memory of which still vibrates in my ears. I was glad to find, however, that he was able soon to resume his favourite topic, and to establish what he deemed a sufficient foundation for his theories in the paintings of Egyptian temples, in the tombs of the Pharaohs, and in the fragments of history which have conveyed down to us some knowledge of the rites and superstitions by which the priests ruled the ancient inhabitants of Egypt.

BELGIUM.

The Dutch were not fortunate in their rule over other races, and seldom succeeded in winning the affections and friendly feelings of their foreign subjects. Nothing could have been worse than their management of Belgian affairs, nothing less calculated to conciliate and win over the Flemings, Brabanters, and Walloons, those various tribes—clans in truth—which the ill-devised and hastily concocted Treaty of Vienna transferred to them—a treaty which shows how little modern statesmen have advanced beyond the civilization of the middle ages, when the arms of a conqueror, and nothing else, disposed of territory and peoples, for, in the case of Belgium, nothing but the will of conquerors was considered. It was a redeclaration, a new teaching to souls enslaved and realms undone, of the " enormous faith of many made for one—that proud exception to all nature's laws," which, being built upon rottenness, is perpetually tottering to its foundations, and must finally give way piece-meal. It required only the movement of the French Revolution in 1830 to tear Belgium from the Dutch sceptre, a consummation which, however wounding to the pride of Holland, has in no respect been pernicious to her true interests or to the prosperity of her people.

It was the fate of the House of Nassau to do everything unseasonably, and, in consequence, amiss. The first murmurs of the Belgians asked for the redress of a very simple grievance—the dismissal of a single obnoxious minister, but, though demanded by tens of thousands, it was obstinately refused. The Belgians then said, " We will now ask for a better administration, both legislative and judicial." The King got alarmed, and offered to dismiss Van Maanen, but would not hear of the second proposal. Then the Belgians answered, " Nor will *we* now. We demand complete separation from Holland." His Majesty was advised to say, " I agree to your second proposal," but it was too late. They who have won the battle may use very different language, and propose very different terms from

those which would have satisfied them before the combat.
The King determined upon the unfortunate royal "ultima
ratio," attacked Brussels, where his troops met with a signal
defeat, and Brabant to a man rose against him.   There was
still a door of salvation open, for the Prince of Orange had
kept aloof from personal compromise, and would certainly
have been elected king, had he not chosen to appear as a dic-
tator at the head of a Dutch army.   He had numerous
partisans in Brabant, which his brother had managed to
alienate, but it was his ill fortune to win the execration of
the Flemings, Antwerp having been ruined by the Dutch
troops and frigates under his command.   A few days before, the Prince was, what the "Courrier des Pays Bas"
called him, "the inevitable man," but afterwards none was
to be found to suggest his name.   The destruction of the
Entrepôt at Antwerp brought ruin upon thousands, and it
was said that the value of goods destroyed was nearly two
millions sterling.   The Belgians threatened to cut the dikes,
by which the whole country would have been overwhelmed,
and which would have been a retaliation such as might have
been expected from those who had suffered as the Brabanters and Flemings had done.   Brussels, the liveliest
place in the gay world, became one of the gloomiest, the
houses in the higher parts of the town being riddled with
balls, while many were burned, and more deserted.   The
population were all armed, and I saw groups of sorrowful
and suffering, but revenge-threatening men.   The deadly
hate against the Dutch grew stronger and stronger, and this
was the result of the Metternich policy.   It is quite true
that the Constitution, which was drawn up by twelve
Dutchmen and twelve Belgians, provided for a general
equality between the races, but the idea of "Orange
boven!" (Up, Orange!) was still predominant in the minds
of the Hollanders, and practically they gave little effect to

the promised conditions, and excluded the Belgians from participation in many privileges which they contended were their own exclusive and inherent right, while onerous taxes were imposed to which the Belgians were wholly unused. The Dutch, naturally enough, in the case of public employments, gave the preference to their own people, whose loyalty was more assured, and who certainly had abundant aptitude for any official post. The Belgians, moreover, shared few of the advantages which the Dutch enjoyed in their large colonies in the East and West Indies, and in their fisheries on the coast of Europe.

After the Revolution, there were three parties in the field. First, the Republicans, who desired the establishment of a Commonwealth, with De Potter as a president, but their views did not meet with much acceptance in the minds of the people, and would assuredly have created much dissatisfaction among European Powers. Another party was exceedingly desirous to call one of the sons of Louis Philippe to the throne, but this faction was even less popular than the Republican, and met with no encouragement from the governments. Then there was the National party, who succeeded in placing the sceptre in the hands of Prince Leopold, undoubtedly the wisest policy which could have been adopted. The Dutch were recovering from their first panic, and there were not wanting in the Flemish provinces many auxiliaries disposed to make great efforts and sacrifices on behalf of the House of Orange, supported, as it undoubtedly was, by the instincts of all the despotic and monarchical influences of central and northern Europe. Belgium had on its side the cordial sympathies of the French nation—the King's cordiality being, however, wholly subservient, as was all his policy, to the narrowest calculations of personal and family interest. England remained aloof, and the fate of Belgium certainly depended upon her fiat—

not the ultimate and final condition of Belgium, for in some way or other the force of events must have produced a separation from Holland, and either an independent government or an annexation to France; but the solution of the then existing complications depended wholly upon the Cabinet of Great Britain. I had much intercourse with the members of the Provisional Government, and pointed out to them that in London, and not in Brussels, the Belgian question must be discussed and decided. I recommended that M. Van de Weyer should be immediately despatched to England. My views were adopted, I accompanied him to London, and introduced him to that political circle of which he has since been so distinguished a member.

I had two official missions to Belgium, both connected with commercial objects. There was much hostility to free trade among the manufacturers, but it was a good deal modified by the desire of keeping on good terms with the French, into whose markets there was a large importation of Belgian produce, which was favoured by the differential duties of the French tariffs.

There are two parties in Belgium engaged in constant conflict—the Liberals, who comprise the most intelligent persons in the country, and the extreme Catholics, headed by the ecclesiastics, who no doubt represent the masses of the people. The battle-field is generally that in which the modes of public instruction are debated, and the Government often has great difficulty in steering its course amidst these hostile influences, but, on the whole, has managed so well as to give little offence to either party. I found at Rome that the Belgian volunteers were among the most earnest to do battle in favour of the Pope.

King Leopold once told me that I had by my writings and discourses made all his people free traders. There was a movement at one time for the abolition of all custom-houses in Belgium, and a grand work will be done when this is accomplished anywhere.

TUSCANY.

I have most pleasant reminiscences of the Tuscan court. In 1836, I visited Florence on a mission from the British government, and had the good fortune to enjoy the confidence of, and to experience much kindness from, Leopold, the Grand Duke. After my first formal official introduction, he said he should like to see me divested of my court costume, that he would direct me to be admitted to him by a private staircase, and that at 10 a.m. I should always find him in his library, a privilege of which I availed myself almost daily. He was then less an Austrian than a Tuscan prince, and was much disposed to listen to any suggestions of a practical and improving character. He said to me, " J'ai mes défauts, mais j'ai une grande responsabilité, et je cherche à m'instruire." Railways were then beginning to supersede less convenient and rapid modes of communication, but the Grand Duke expressed his apprehension that their introduction might interfere with the interests of his " póveri vetturini." I assured him that there was no cause for alarm, and that railways would not lessen but augment the demand for conveyances, and the value of the horses employed, of which in England we had abundant experience. He liked to talk of the Medici, and presented to me a copy in four volumes of the history of that illustrious family.

He asked me to accompany him in a visit he was intending to make to his southern provinces, an invitation too flattering to be rejected, and a most pleasant time we passed among the peasantry, with so little *gêne* that we did not even dress for dinner. I even remember an embarrassment for the want of a corkscrew, which I was fortunately able to supply. We visited Piombino, which, a few years before, was almost

L

uninhabitable, and which Dante compared to hell. Almost all the children born there perished in infancy, and the population, yellow, wretched, and diseased, wandered like spectres over the surface. A gradual change was going on, and all sorts of works in the way of draining, clearing, &c., had been introduced, so that the Maremma was becoming productive, and the country every year more healthful. My visit was not in the pestilential season, and the climate was divine ; but in Fellonica, where there were then fifteen hundred inhabitants, not a single one was left during the summer, except three soldiers and one custom-house officer, who invariably sickened and sometimes died, although relieved two or three times in the hot weather. In 1836, an experiment was made to keep the labourers through the pestilential months, but not one escaped, and it was sad to see the yellow, cadaverous, and gloomy expression of their sickly countenances, but they are a kind and gentle people, and it touched me to hear them adding, "illustrissimo" to every word they uttered, and showing a zeal to serve which was most striking.

I went into the mountains, to visit the copper-mines, and was most hospitably entertained at Massa, which was an independent Republic in the middle ages. A large body of men, with lights, lanterns, and torches, escorted me to the great alum-caves. We went in a long procession in the dark up the mountain side, and were conducted in solemn silence to the wonderful vaults, which were dug in the time of Napoleon's sister Eliza, who was the proprietress of the mines. They were illuminated, and in the different galleries the miners were seen, each holding a light, which, reflected on their sallow Italian faces, produced an effect which Gerard Douw would have been in raptures to see. We descended through passages hewn out of the solid rock (in several of which were scattered men and boys bearing lamps), from cavern to cavern, each more beautiful than the last, and when we reached the lowest of all, an explosion was prepared, and a huge fragment of the rock fell in honour of the visitor. The miners then all came forward to escort us home. In spite of the beauty of the scene, their spectre-like looks, pale but dark, gave the whole affair the character of a dead-march. It was, I confess, a relief when, returned to our house, a living " viva! viva!" fell upon my ears.

At the Duke's request, I went to see one of the pestiferous lakes (Lago Rimigliano), and found nothing but a thermal stream, pure and bright, while the miles over which it had flowed for ages were ripe for cultivation. I told the Grand Duke (which was true) that he was gradually rescuing the Maremmas from the Inferno, transferring them to the Purgatorio, and that they would soon form a part of Paradise.

When I arrived at Grosetto, the Court were attending a *joust*, in which the peasants were exhibiting feats of horse-manship, by endeavouring to carry off on their lances a ring held by a painted figure dressed like a Saracen, which they passed at full gallop. The Grand Duke directed the principal engineer of the great hydraulic works to accompany me through the district, and I had a very instructive though toilsome tour through the neighbourhood. I went in one day nearly fifty miles on horseback, and fifteen in a boat, through the pestiferous marshes, which they were filling up. One of these, the Padule di Castiglione, is nearly forty miles in circumference, and for many months in the year condemned the whole population to disease. In making my way through the woods, and reaching the mines, which the Grand Duke made a point of my seeing, my clothes were nearly torn from my back. Sometimes it was necessary to dismount, while the horses leaped from rock to rock, and for miles together the path was through

rough masses of schist and granite, over rapid streams, and
through bogs of deep mud. I was generally eight or nine
hours a day on horseback, and had the Director of the Mines
as my companion, together with some Tuscan guards. After
visiting the boiling borax-lagoons, the fancied entrance of
hell, I went to Monte Cattini, where the sovereign took me
with him into the copper-mines, into which we descended,
and after breakfast he departed, and I proceeded to Volterra.
This tour was to me a memorable one, for I caught the
marsh fever, which nearly cost me my life.

The Grand Duke afterwards became a servile tool in the
hands of the Vienna Court, and his son even joined the
Austrian armies in their campaign against the Italians,
which made all reconciliation impossible, the Italian feeling
being so strong on the subject that a friend of mine, Count
Serristori, who, out of personal respect and affection for the
prince, endeavoured to bring about kindlier sentiments,
quite lost the confidence of the patriotic party, and his later
days were embittered by the thought of his failure. It
was well for the welfare of United Italy that Leopold was
ill-counselled on this occasion, for his existence as an independent sovereign, and that of Tuscany as a separate State,
would have been a serious complication and embarrassment
to Victor Emmanuel as King of Italy. Wonderfully have
events assisted the progress of Italian emancipation, and
the establishment of good constitutional government. Whatever has been done in hostility to freedom has but served
freedom's cause, and all things have worked together for
good. Austria has paid the price of her obstinacy, and
Italy has reaped the benefit of her patriotism and foresight.

ROME.

In December 1836, I was presented to Pope Gregory
XVI., in company with Mr. J. C. Herries, and a Colonel

———. We went through seven ante-rooms before we reached His Holiness, the Swiss guards and soldiers presenting arms to us as we passed. In the last room but one —where were friars with long beards—we were received by the Maggiordómo, who was, I believe, the Archbishop of Philippi, and a direct descendant of one of the ancient Roman Consuls. At last the door of the room opened in which was the throne, and at the end of it stood the Holy Father, dressed simply in white, with a white cap, and a large ring on the middle finger of his right hand. He had a benignant, but not an intellectual look. He beckoned to us, and the Hanoverian Minister (English there was none, and Canning was wont to joke about the perils of a prœmunire hanging over the head of any minister who might approach the Pope) presented us. The Pope asked which was the "famoso letterato" of whom he had heard, and then said some flattering things of me. The Hanoverian minister said I was an Irish member, which I was obliged to correct. The Pope said to Herries that he was obliged for all the kind things the English Government had done "per i miei figli." (I fancy he knew little of the part Herries took in the Catholic question). He said that it had never occurred to him before to have *three* Englishmen presented, with all of whom he could talk Italian. We then got a little on Italian literature, and he said that one of Dante's verses was addressed to a room in a convent in which he had been a monk. He asked me how I had learned Italian so well, when the minister said that I was a distinguished linguist. "Then," said the Pope, "I suppose you have seen Mezzofanti?" I answered no, but that I meant to do so. "He is our great philologue," he added. I told him the object of my mission, when he remarked that England must not raise her commercial prosperity on the ruin of other nations, and that she should not absorb

the trade of the whole world. I answered that she could
only trade as much with others as others would trade with
her, and that trade was but the interchange of common
interests, all nations having the same interest when rightly
understood. He said that trade was a circle, in which there
was a great centre.

He was, I heard, a good theological scholar, but knew
little of positive science or political economy. His manners
were mild and gracious, and he held the minister's hand all
the time he was speaking to us, which may have been
twenty minutes. We were told it was not usual for Pro-
testants to kiss his hand, so we did not. I think, however,
that he meant that it *should* be kissed, but, as I followed
Mr Herries, I could not of course do more than was done
by a Right Honourable and ex-minister.

The parade of introduction was very curious—the mixture
of Church and State—the ancient costumes—the long road
to the Vatican about and above St Peter's—the simple dress
of the Holy Father, surrounded (but not in his hall of
audience, for there he was quite alone) by scarlet-stockinged
cardinals and purple-stockinged archbishops and bishops—
the various dresses of monks and friars—the military and
official state—the pomp and circumstance—all was curious
—and the being himself, the abstraction, was more curious
still. I had, I confess, an odd feeling in the Pope's presence.
It was the unveiling of the prophet.

He maintained to the last the system of despotic misrule,
which was then in the ascendant in most of the Catholic
courts of Europe, and which was superseded by the elevation
of Pius IX. to the Papal throne, of him who declared that
it was his purpose to establish a free and constitutional
government, and to give liberal institutions to the Roman
people. Rossi, who was afterwards assassinated (a foul deed,
the mystery of which has never been unravelled), is said to

have given the Holy Father wise and judicious counsels on this occasion. It was supposed that a new era of hope and happiness was dawning on the Catholic world, and the name and policy of Pio Nono began to be almost adored among the friends of freedom and progress; but other influences obtained the ascendancy, and the Pope became, not the representative of a liberal policy, but one of its most decided opponents. Beyond the field of ecclesiastical authority, his influence upon the minds of intelligent Italians has passed away. Even among the peasantry, the hold of the clergy is much loosened, and they have learned to despise the thunders of excommunication, which have threatened the persons of Victor Emmanuel and his partisans. It was reported that the priests had cursed the vineyards and the lands of those who favoured the new order of things, but as the character of the vintages improved after the malediction, the people began to call the best wines by the name of "Scomunicati," and they were applied for and known by that designation in the *alberghi* and wine-shops of Tuscany, and perhaps in other parts of Italy.

In 1861 I had a private audience with Pope Pius IX., which lasted exactly half-an-hour. He was habited in a simple garment of white flannel, and seated me opposite to him at his table, on which lay a few official papers for signature. His reception was very cordial, and on my leaving, he shook me most warmly by the hand. He expatiated on many matters—Chinese, of course, especially,—asked for a variety of information, and himself introduced the subject of Italy. I did not conceal my opinions as to the policy which ought to be pursued, and I must say that he listened with the greatest amenity and good humour while I gave reasons for not concurring in his conclusions. I thought it would be a blessing for him to be disembarrassed of his temporal sovereignty, with all its financial cares and complications, and I felt assured that the removal of the French troops would immediately lead to the loss of his temporal dominion. He acknowledged that there was something great in the idea of a united Italy of twenty millions, with Rome for the capital, but said the thing was impracticable. I did not think so, and saw no other safe or satisfactory solution.

ITALY.

The spy system was carried to perfection in Italy, and I had often occasion to see it exhibited, as my name figured in that *black list* of dangerous men, which the despotic governments on the continent pass from one to another for their mutual information and security, the presence of any such person being a subject of perpetual alarm. When I went from Turin to Genoa, on a commercial mission from my government, I was particularly recommended by the Sardinian Court to the Marquis Paulucci, the governor of the latter city, and no doubt the recommendation to his courtesies which I brought was preceded by an official one recommending me to attentions of another sort. I soon found that, wherever I went, I was dogged and pursued by spies, and on one occasion, when one had followed me up a thoroughfare to the house of a friend I was visiting, I stopped the fellow, and threatened to break his head with a trusty stick which I carried with me. He cried out " Perdona, Signore !" and, on inquiring about his profession, he told me what he was paid, who employed him, and that he was especially charged by the police to look after me. Upon which I went to Paulucci, and told him that, as I was a public functionary of the British government, I requested to be spared the civilities with which he honoured me, both personal and political ; that I would most willingly give him more correct information of all that I said or did in Genoa than he could obtain from the gentleman whom he employed to follow my footsteps ; that I would furnish him with a list of all the persons I visited in Genoa, and moreover enlighten him as to the topics of our conversation, and that if my government had, as he supposed, any secret objects, I was the last person to whom the trust would be confided, for my opinions as to Italian princes and Italian politics were notorious to everybody. I added that, though a sense of public duty restrained me from meddling in any way with Italian affairs, my notions as to the state of Italy would be somewhat strengthened by displays of the mode of governing, such as those he had exhibited towards myself. He said he acted according to his instructions, but would in future refrain from what I thought an improper persecution, and certainly, if the spies continued to track me, their persons were changed.

That I *was* in the black list of dangerous persons I had special evidence at Leghorn. I was on my way to Naples as a British commercial commissioner, and on applying to the Neapolitan Consul to endorse my passport, he refused to do so, saying I could not proceed to Naples. On my request being strongly enforced, and an urgent representation made of the responsibility he was incurring by denying his signature to a British subject charged with a public mission to his own Government, he produced a paper containing a list of names of those who were prohibited from entering the Neapolitan territories, among which mine undoubtedly appeared. I transferred, of course, my indignation from the Consul to his superiors, and soon received an apology from Naples, and a declaration that it was all a mistake on the part of the Consul—that it was never intended to stop me in my progress to Naples, &c. I afterwards found that, knowing my appointment, the foreign Neapolitan minister had sent to Paris, and to the other places through which I was likely to pass, desiring that no impediment might be put in my way. Leghorn was out of the ordinary line of travel, and had been forgotten. The prohibitory list contained many well-known names, with which I could only deem it an honour to be associated.

My experience of the spy system as an instrument of government is that it leads to the communication of ten times more falsehoods than facts to those who employ it, that it serves to mislead and embarrass infinitely more than to instruct and to guide, that the very persons whom it employs have a greater interest in deceiving than in instructing their masters, that the information they communicate adds to the darkness and difficulty in which distrustful and despotic governments habitually live, and that the knowledge they obtain as to secret machinations, plots, and confederacies is seldom furnished by the emissaries they employ, but by treacherous persons of another class, who are the occasional tests of authority. As regards the costly machinery of political *espionage*, as it is organized in most of the Continental monarchies, I believe it is utterly inoperative for any good purpose, and renders a beggarly return for all its infamies and outlay.

An opportunity of better acquaintance with Garibaldi's inner self has unveiled points of character little suspected by the world. Everybody recognizes his patriotism, honours his disinterestedness, marvels at his wonderful success, but understands the influence he has acquired over his countrymen. If Cavour occupied a higher position in the estimation of statesmen, Garibaldi has had a stronger hold upon the affections of the Italian people, and it is as much to the enthusiastic ardour of the one as to the cool statesmanship of the other that Italy owes her redemption, and the occupancy of a position of which her best loved sons had never dared to dream. It may be remarked that even in the faint hopes breathed by her poets, there prevails a tone of dejection and despondency as touching as it is eloquent. The citizens were "schiavi, si, ma schiavi ognor freménti," yet her destiny was proclaimed to be "per servir sempre, o vincatrice o vinta." Out of this degradation she has been raised, and undoubtedly the honour is mainly due to the sagacious minister and the brave soldier of whom I have spoken. But in Garibaldi's heart of heart there is a deep religious feeling, a constant recognition of a Providential guidance, an earnest aspiration after ecclesiastical as well as political reform, a strong conviction that the triumph of the one will herald the advent of the other, and a longing for the time when the arts of peace shall be more devotedly cultivated than is now the science of war, and nations shall repose in the security of peaceful commerce and progressive civilization.

There is much of poetry in Garibaldi's mind, and the following lines are nearly a verbal translation of an address to the scenery around him at Caprera when retired there from the toils and turmoils of his excited political existence.

> " Upon thy granite summits I inhale
> The breath of liberty—far, far removed
> From the corruptions of a palace court,
> Caprera wild and lonely!   For my park
> Thy bushwood, while, in thy imposing shades, ·
> I find safe domicile—if unadorned,
> Yet freed from servile vassalage.   Thy few
> Rustic inhabitants are rude indeed,
> As are the craggy rocks that form thy crown,
> But, like them, proud, like them, disdaining too
> To bend the prostrate knee.   The only sounds
> Are of the storm-winds in the asylum deep,
> Which neither slave nor tyrant sheltereth.
> Rugged may be thy pathways, but no train
> Of insolent courtiers there will cross my track,
> Or turn me from my course, or with vile mud
> Defile my uncontaminated brow.

> The Infinite I contemplate, removed
> From fraud and falsehood, the stupendous works,
> Spread 'neath the broad horizon, I admire,
> Grand, infinite, unlimited, immense,
> Unveiled by the Eternal to the great
> High priests of truth—to such as Kepler was,
> Newton, and Galileo."
>
> G. GARIBALDI, 25*th May* 1861.

He has shown that, while ready and willing to act when the fit occasion arrives, he can check his impatience, and wisely bide his time in the interests of his fatherland. Shakspeare has pertinently said "ripeness is all," and the maxim is applicable to all the concerns of life, whether public or private. It is, in truth, but an earlier form of Bacon's great aphorism, " respice finem," a teaching which, if it became the world's guide, would prevent the mischiefs which Madame de Stael pourtrayed when she said, "le mieux est le grand ennemi du bien."

It is not difficult to trace the causes of the decline of Catholic influences through the whole of the Christian world. Formerly, it was the noble ambition of ecclesiastics to lead the van of civilization and progress. Not only were the convents the distributors of bounty among the necessitous, providing for wants in which the laity seemed to take no interest, but the higher orders of the clergy were frequently the protectors of the poor against oppression, standing between the feudal lord and his serf with courage and success. The monks especially often took the initiative in agricultural improvements ; they repaired roads, threw bridges over rivers, and in one of the titles of the Pope himself—that of Pontifex, or the bridge-maker—His Holiness was presented to the people as a public benefactor. Most of the Books were written by the clergy, and most of the manuscripts copied in the monasteries. At a later period, Rome formed a glorious alliance with the arts, and made architecture, sculpture, and painting subservient to her influences. But when an impulse was given by the Reformation to the new elements that were called into the field of public improvement, the Papacy altogether failed in turning them to any account. Navigation went forward with its great discoveries ; commerce and colonization changed the character of the eastern and western world ; but the Church of Rome had little to do with these victories. She sent forth her missionaries, it is true, but they had small power to direct or control the proceedings of either the Spanish or the Portuguese conquerors. They could not check the fierce and exterminating policy of the former in the new world, and in the East they were principally occupied in the work of conversion, in which, no doubt, they were aided by military influence. In periods still more recent, when improvements in every species of communication have made such astounding advances, no helping hand has been stretched out, no sympathy exhibited by the Papacy, which has looked with a cold eye upon the progress of manufactures, and, as regards philosophical discovery, would willingly have punished all whose superior knowledge led to the abandonment of the Ptolemaic system. Steam engines have revolutionized the application of labour ; railways have facilitated communication throughout the civilized world ; electric telegraphs have annihilated distance ; and social improvements, too many and too various to estimate, have added countless enjoyments to man's existence, but with all these neither Pope, Bishops, nor clergy have had ought to do. Who, then, can wonder that Rome has ceased to be what Rome once was, the polestar and the guide of Christendom ?

EGYPT.

The vicissitudes of mortal existence are nowhere exhibited in a more contrasted form than in the Ottoman Empire. There, one man occupying a most exalted and confidential post to-day may be degraded and decapitated to-morrow, while another, upon whom the sunshine of imperial favour falls, may be elevated with equal rapidity. The most remarkable example of almost unchecked success is that exhibited in the history of Mehemet Ali, the Viceroy of Egypt. I think that a great political error was committed by the British government when they lent themselves to the views of the Ottoman Porte, and determined to coerce Mehemet Ali into subjection, instead of encouraging his desire for independence. His plan was to gather all the Arabic-speaking nations under Egyptian rule, and to establish the foundations of a great Arab empire ; and had we been a party to this arrangement, there is no doubt that we might have exercised at Cairo an influence far more potent than we could ever expect to do at Constantinople, which is the very focus of intrigue, where all the great powers are constantly struggling for ascendancy, and where our policy is often thwarted by the action of Russia, France, or Austria. The geographical position of Egypt—standing midway between England and her Indian possessions—the great highway of a constantly increasing communication—must have a political importance of the highest order. When the French first invaded Algiers, they made to the Pasha the most seductive offers to recognise his independence of the Porte, if he would co-operate with them in their intended African expedition. He communicated this information to the Duke of Wellington, who recommended him to repudiate the offer, stating that, if he did so, the service rendered to English interests would not be forgotten.

Referring to this subject with some bitterness, he once told me that he would at any time have despatched ten thousand of his regular troops to assist in maintaining our authority in British India, and though their services might not have been of much value, the offer was evidence of the friendly animus which inspired the Viceroy.

Mehemet Ali was born at Cavalla, in Roumelia, in the memorable year 1769, the year in which Wellington, Napoleon, Humboldt, and many other celebrated persons first saw the light, and was the son of a dealer in tobacco. He may be said to have changed the face of Egypt by his sagacious views, but he did not learn to read and write till he was forty-six, and it was utterly impossible to create in him any of those more refined and exalted tastes which distinguish civilized nations. For example, when remonstrated with on the destruction of some of the finest specimens of Pharaonic antiquity, he asked what they were but old stones, which might be usefully employed in building edifices or making enclosures. Though he kept up his reputation among fanatical Moosulmans by erecting mosques and protecting religious endowments, he was eminently tolerant, and laughed at an over-zealous Quaker, who put a New Testament into his hand, and recommended him to become a Christian. On another occasion, when a missionary had been preaching against the false prophet of Mecca, and exposed himself to the indignation of the people, Mehemet Ali interfered by representing the imprudent zealot to be a lunatic, knowing that madmen are always treated by Mahommedans with a certain degree of reverence. .

The Pasha received me in his palace at Shoubra, in the month of November 1837. We were preceded by a Janissary with his silver staff, on horseback, and were accompanied by a number of men, who turned aside the camels, overturned the donkeys, beat the children, collared the men, and shoved away the women, it being as difficult to thread the streets of Cairo at sunset as it is to force a passage through the Royal Exchange at mid-day. The Pasha's secretary awaited us, and conducted us into the place of audience, in the centre of which were three huge silver candlesticks with lighted wax candles. In the corner stood Mehemet Ali, with his white beard, soft and fair hands, and fiery eye. He beckoned us to approach, and squatted himself in the corner of the *diván*, on a carpet of green and gold. Next to Colonel Campbell, the Consul General, I had the seat of honour, the interpreter standing before the Pasha. Coffee was ordered in, and conversation began. He told us of the bad education he had received, said that he had never seen civilised nations, that he had been thrown among barbarians, of whom, when he came to Egypt, scarcely one could read, but that he was endeavouring to instruct his people, and had ten thousand in different schools. He added that though he had often been at war, it was against his wish, and necessary for his protection, and that he wished to live ten years more in peace, in order to show what Egypt was capable of becoming. He told us that, when the insurrection broke out in Syria, the Russian and French consuls told him that he should study *history* in order to learn how to govern. "My son wrote to me," he said, "for orders. I thought the best thing was to go myself, so I went, and settled everything in a week. That was practical government—better than I would have learned from history." The fact is that he went to Jaffa, seized and hanged the leaders of the revolt, and returned to Egypt in a month from the day he had left it. Colonel Campbell, who went with him, told me that he never saw such an example of energy.

Nobody could fail to be struck with his suavity of

manners, his natural ease, his good humour, his smile, and his penetrating eye. Who, in that fine old man, stroking his long beard, white as snow, and wiping his lips with a fair and fine pocket-handkerchief, could imagine that he saw the slaughterer of the thousand Mamelukes, his guests and dependents, the conqueror of the Wahabees of the holy cities, the man who had bearded the Sultan, and subjugated the half of Arabia, the hero of Syria and Candia ? There he sat in the corner of the *divân*, his words bearing life and death. It was altogether a most interesting scene.

I had heard in Alexandria that the Pasha's troops had been carrying on the slave trade to a frightful extent, but I did not like to introduce the matter until I had got together better evidence. When I had obtained sufficient facts from eye witnesses, I determined to try to induce Colonel Campbell to go with me at once to the Pasha, and at all risks to break the matter to him. I had met a gentleman who, in Senaar, saw a soldier fondling a young slave on his knees, who had been caught in a slave hunt (as they called their chase of human beings, in which hundreds of slaves were taken by the soldiery), and when the General enquired why he was busied with the child, he found it was his brother. " What is the value of the boy ?" inquired the General. " Five dollars," they answered. " Let him take him for this, and deduct it from his pay." Districts had been depopulated, the poor inhabitants being smoked and burnt out of caves to which they had retreated ; and I saw myself in the slave-markets the emaciated children who had been marched over the burning sands for hundreds of miles, a large proportion of them perishing on the journey. But to talk of such a subject to Mehemet Ali in Egypt, the country of slavery even from the Bible days, to a Mahom- medan tyrant whose religion authorised the crime ! Colonel Campbell, without waiting for instructions from home, fell

M

into my views, acted nobly, and before the first sun-set
after we had got the facts, we mounted our horses, and went
to the Pasha. The fate of thousands, of tens of thousands,
hung upon our success. Might not, too, my own mission
be thwarted, and was it not a foolish risk to run? Would
he tolerate a lecture from us, shocking all his prejudices,
and bearding his power? Might we not fail from mis-
management, from over-excitement, or from respect for a
sovereign—for this Mehemet Ali, the murderer of the
Mamelukes, the terrible of the terrible? How I watched
his countenance as we entered! He was smoking a pipe
resplendent with hundreds of diamonds, a snuff-box even
more splendid being at his side. The room was cleared, the
interpreter stood before him, and we seated ourselves close
to him on the *divân*. Colonel Campbell opened the matter.
The Pasha's eye of fire glanced lightning, and he stroked his
long white beard with his beautiful small hand, while the
words, "slave-hunt"—"your Generals," fell on his ear. I
cannot describe what passed, but we carried our point
triumphantly, and the old man acted superbly. The first
shock over, we talked to him of the opprobrium from which
we sought to relieve him, and of the honour and reputation
he would win, if he would terminate the horrors that were
being committed. He asked for delay, said he would like
to enquire, and offered to pay the expenses of any Englishman going up to Senaar, accompanied by an agent of his
own to verify the real state of things; but we urged the
danger of delay, and succeeded in obtaining from him an
order to the Governor of Senaar to put an immediate stop
to the slave-hunts, and to the payment of his troops in
slaves. We obtained also his promise that he would, as
soon as he could, and by degrees, put an end to the slave-
trade altogether in his dominions. The order to the
Governor of Senaar concluded thus, "Know thou that I

will make no profits from a trade which does me no honour, and even though its abolition should require some sacrifices, I am willing to make them."

Mehemet Ali had six sons, of whom five were by his favourite wife. They always approached him with the wonted obeisance paid to princely rank, but I was present on one occasion when a little boy, the child of his old age, who bore his name, instead of kneeling reverently before him, scampered away, which only elicited a shrug of the shoulder and a smile from the old Pasha, to whom I said, " he is your pet, I observe," a remark which he received with considerable complacency.

When the tribute to be paid by Egypt to the Porte was under consideration at Constantinople, and the line of succession was to be settled, there was some doubt whether European law, by which the eldest son succeeds the father, or, on failure of direct descent, the next of kin, was to regulate the futurity of Egypt, or whether the Mahommedan law, by which the eldest living member of the family continues the line, should be adopted. The latter course was eventually followed, and on the death of Ibrahim Pasha, Mehemet Ali's eldest son, Abbas Pasha, the next son, was called to the throne to the exclusion of Ibrahim Pasha's children. Doubts have been expressed whether Ibrahim Pasha was the legitimate or only an adopted son of his father, but on my once asking Mehemet Ali what was the truth, he answered that he was undoubtedly the first-born of his wife, who was also the mother of several of his brothers. Abbas Pasha, who was for a short time Viceroy, was a great bigot, resembling his father in no respect, while in Ibrahim Pasha was to be seen the coarse but very obvious likeness to his more illustrious sire. Saïd, the third Viceroy, was somewhat rigidly brought up, and, being inclined to corpulency, was subjected to severe exercises by command of his father, who directed that from time to time he should be weighed, and reports be made of the discipline. It failed, however, and Said Pasha became a very unwieldy personage. He had a Frenchman for one of his teachers, and spoke the French language well. His only son frequently visited England, where he often saw the Queen, and it was said that on one occasion, when she offered to kiss him, he gracelessly said that he preferred giving a kiss to the Princess Royal. He had an English nurse from his childhood, and afterwards an English tutor was appointed to direct his studies.

Mehemet Ali, in his rude way, did wonders for Egypt, caused vast tracts of land to be redeemed from the desert, introduced the fine sea-island cotton, which has become so important an export from Alexandria, made canals, though at a fearful sacrifice of human life, introduced into the army the military organization of Europe, so that he overthrew again and again the forces of the Sultan in Syria and Asia Minor, put his ships of war into good condition, and appointed French officers to the supreme commands, both in the army and the navy. He had applied to our government to obtain the services of British officers, but met with a refusal. The French government, however, willingly granted his request, and in consequence French interests in Egypt have not unfrequently circumvented British policy. He saw the importance of facilitating communication across the desert, which he cleared from predatory Bedouin Arabs, so that, even before the laying down of the railway, it was as safe to travel from Cairo to Suez as from London to Bristol. No man was ever more fitted to deal with the inhabitants of the wilderness than he. He subjugated the Wahabees when they had obtained possession of the holy cities, and when caravans were robbed, he extorted from the Bedouins many times the value of the plunder they had appropriated. Under his rule the Egyptian revenues increased enormously, the commerce of the country was greatly augmented, and the flags of all nations were seen to crowd to the port of Alexandria. He had his territory explored in different quarters in the hope of finding coal, and on one occasion, for the purposes of visiting his dominions, went up the White Nile, far beyond its confluence with the Blue Nile at Khartoum.

His conversation was lively and original. He was fond of talking of his plans for the improvement of Egypt, and said to me, " I have hitherto only scratched the earth with a pin, or tilled it with a hoe, but I mean to go over it with a plough." He took great interest in steam navigation, and when I asked him how Moosulman pilgrims going to the holy cities could venture to employ the steam vessels of the infidels, he answered, "there is not a word said against steamers in the Koran. You Englishmen have done many great things, but nothing so great as the application of steam to shipping." I observed that the first successful experimenter was Fulton, who was an American, not an Englishman, on which the Pasha retorted,—" He never would have done what he did if he had not had Englishmen for his ancestors." When Mrs Dawson Damer was introduced to him, she asked him for a lock of his hair as a memento. He refused the favour, probably thinking it would be an improper and un-Islamite concession to a Christian woman, but said, " No; I can't give you a hair now; but when I am dead my whole head shall be at your service."

During my residence at Cairo, corn got up to a famine price, and there was much misery among the people. Mehemet Ali, with a short-sighted but not unnatural policy, published decrees ordering that wheat should not be sold in the markets above a certain sum, a politico-economical mistake, for which he might have found a justification in the example of the first Napoleon, and in the legislation of more than one European country. He, at the same time, prohibited the export of corn from Egypt, the result being what greater sagacity might have foreseen, namely, that wheat was sold clandestinely at a much higher rate than it would have obtained under the ordinary action of supply and demand, inasmuch as the seller made an extra profit to protect himself from the penalties of having violated the law. Very small quantities were brought to the market, and the quality of that openly sold was of the worst kind. Thus the evils were greatly augmented, the country was menaced with absolute famine, and public discontent began to show itself, for it is well known that there is no rebellion like that of the belly. Knowing that I had constant access to and frequent interviews with the Viceroy, a deputation came to me, imploring me to represent the condition of the people to his Highness, which I willingly consented to do. Fortified by incontestible facts, and what I deemed irresistible arguments, I entered upon the discussion with the wily old man, who at first would not hear of any opposition to his ordinances, or admit that the value of a commodity was beyond his control to regulate. I launched all the reasoning at my disposal against his views, which he valiantly defended, and, though he made no concessions, I thought my arguments could not but produce some effect on his sagacious mind. The next day, the colloquy was resumed. He had expected that the high price of wheat would entice adventurers to bring it to the Egyptian market, but I showed him that, while the prohibition to export continued, prudent merchants would not incur the risk which the lowering of prices might entail. I recommended the abrogation of all restrictions, and the proclamation of free trade, both for the export and import of corn. He adopted this counsel, the mischief gradually diminished, prices fell to their natural level, and the disquietude and murmuring of the people as naturally ceased. This was some years before our legislators had the wisdom to pursue a similar course.

While I was at Damascus, the Greek Bishop brought to me some of the families of merchants to whom Mehemet Ali had lent large sums of money, which they had lost by imprudent speculations. As they were unable to discharge their obligations, the Pasha ordered them to be seized, and condemned to the punishment of the galleys. They implored me to lay before him a statement of the misery inflicted on their innocent families, and to entreat him to revoke the decree which had subjected the merchants to so severe a penalty. I doubted whether I could venture upon so delicate a topic, and only promised to do so should I find a convenient opportunity, but I determined if possible to find such opportunity, and asked for an interview with the Viceroy. I am not aware how he had learned that I had undertaken the mission of imploring his clemency, but soon after I entered the hall, where he was seated in a corner of the *diván*, he rose, and placing his scimitar, as he was wont to do, against his back, and supporting it with his two hands, he said, " I know what you are come about. It is to speak to me on behalf of those rascally merchants, but you will speak in vain, and they must pay the price of their knavery." He did not, however, enforce silence upon me, and I ventured to say that he would be touched could he but witness the misery into which the wives, children, relations, and friends of the peccant traders were plunged. I said it was a noble privilege to possess power, but that the exercise of the attributes of mercy and forgiveness was the noblest of all. " But the women," said he, " about whom you have been talking to me, have been recipients of the spoils, and have received from their husbands presents of diamonds and other jewellery, paid for from the funds out of which I have been cheated." Ignorant as I was of the circumstances of the case, I could say nothing in answer to this statement, and I left the Pasha under the impression that he would be inexorable. The next day, however, I received a message from him that he would not enforce the penalties against the merchants, and that their sole punishment would be exile from Egypt.

The name of Boghos Bey, his Armenian Prime Minister, is closely associated with the history of Mehemet Ali, his position having frequently been compared with that of Joseph at at the Court of Pharaoh. The viceroy gave way occasionally to violent outbreaks of passion, and once, being exasperated against his minister, ordered him to be thrown into the Nile. An intimate friend, a Hungarian of the name of Walmas, who had received many favours from the Bey, determined to screen him from the effects of the viceroy's resentment, believing that the tempest of wrath was only temporary, and that the time would come in which Mehemet Ali would regret the sacrifice of so faithful a servant as Boghos had always been. He therefore concealed him, and it was not long before the viceroy gave evidence of the value he attached to his services, expressing annoyance that there were always people to be found at court to give effect to the hasty mandates of the sovereign. When matters went wrong, he would remark that had Boghos been alive, this would not have happened. " Oh, that I had the benefit of his judicious counsels ! " At last Walmas informed the Pasha that his orders had not been carried out, and that Boghos was still alive. The Pasha sent for him immediately, an interview and reconciliation followed, the minister was restored to his former high position, which he continued to fill till the day of his death, and was the individual through whom the representatives of foreign Powers carried on the whole of their negotiations.

Mehemet Ali had heard that I had been engaged in enquiries as to the system of public accountancy. He told me
that he was much dissatisfied with the manner in which this
department of the government was conducted, and that he
could never comprehend what was meant by the word
balance, which he found in all the accounts laid before him.
I told him that in that word all perplexities were concentrated, and that the most judicious course he could adopt
would be to allow no balances to remain in the hands of the
receivers of his revenue, but to require their immediate
payment into the public treasury, employing a separate set
of officials for all purposes of expenditure. He asked me
whether I would look into the accounts, which I expressed
my willingness to do, and he directed Abbas Pasha, who
afterwards succeeded him as viceroy, to hold a *diván*, to
which the finance minister and the principal receivers of the
public monies were to be summoned. It was a curious
scene. The state account-books were brought on camels'
backs, and I was amused at seeing Abbas throw a golden
snuff-box at the Coptic Finance Minister. The idea of
examining the huge volumes which were brought in was
absolutely ridiculous; the conference ended in nothing, and
I could only repeat that I saw no solution of the difficulty
but in the adoption of the plan I had suggested, namely,
that all public money should be paid without deduction or
delay into the exchequer. It may be remarked in passing
that this system has only of late years been adopted in
Great Britain, and that formerly only the net revenues were
handed into our treasury, nearly seven millions sterling
being detained by the departments of receipt and expenditure, and disposed of without the authority of Parliament.

I paid an interesting visit to the Shereef of Mekka, one
of the most sacred persons among the Moosulmans, and a
direct descendant of the Prophet. Mehemet Ali, being

afraid that he would insurrectionize Arabia against him,
invited him on board a vessel of his in the Red Sea to a
grand festival, and, as soon as he had him on board, ordered
him to be brought to Egypt, where he was kept in a sort of
honourable durance, being much distinguished, and of course
closely watched.   He was something like Pius VII. in
Buonaparte's custody.   He had heard of Buonaparte, wanted
to know how he was overthrown, asked particulars of our
Sovereign, and was astonished to hear we had a Queen who
dined in public unveiled, as well as her mother and other
ladies.   He enquired what was the cause of the rise and
fall of the sea, and why it was that the moisture of the eye
was salt, of the mouth sweet, and of the ears bitter ?   I remarked, " You are a Mahommedan, and those who surround
you (there were 30 or 40 Moosulmans seated on the *Diván*,
and listening in a large circle about us), and we are Christians, but we can agree in this, that though we cannot
understand many things, we all understand that God is wise
and good, and that all He does is wise and good."   His
eyes brightened with fire, and he exclaimed with enthusiasm,
" It is so—it is so," and an audible murmur, an universal
response, went round the room " tayib—tayib," meaning, "it
is good—it is right."

The state of society in Egypt is such that there is no law
but the law of violence, and every master beats his servants.
The Minister of Public Instruction gave two thousand three
hundred blows on the feet to one of his dependents, who
died the next day, but he paid £45 to the family, and the
affair was hushed up.   I saw a young man take off his sash
in the street, throw it round the neck of an old man, and
nearly strangle him in the presence of the lookers-on.   The
Dufturdar, in order to punish a smith who had shoed his
horse badly, ordered the shoe to be taken off and nailed to
the feet of the smith, which was done.

We explored the Nile beyond the first cataract into Nubia,—the Nile venerated by the modern Egyptians as it was by their more civilized predecessors. The Copts say, "what champagne is among wines, the Nile is among waters. No one ever drank of it without longing to taste it again." In my travels, having to visit a spot where I could not lead my horse, I left it in charge of an Arab woman, and on my giving her a few small coins for her trouble, she said, "May Allah bless thee, as he blessed the sources of the Nile." On my leaving Cairo for the South, the Pasha gave me one of his beautifully adorned boats, with a great number of rowers; a Bey, who had been educated in France, for a companion; a French cook, with a large supply of provisions and wine; and a Teskerch, commanding all his vassals to supply whatever I might require. I of course paid, though it was not expected, for all I demanded, but Prince Pückler Muskau, who had just preceded me, was not so considerate, and I heard that he had even exacted wax candles, and would not give a *bakhshish* in return. In visiting the pyramids, I witnessed a curious example of oriental notions of justice. In one of the dark chambers I was robbed of the purse which I carried concealed in my sash. We had been followed by a crowd of Arab boys, and on my telling Selim Bey of the robbery, he offered to hang them all on the spot, so as to make certain of having punished the thief.

At Assouan I had for my guide an intelligent native, who escorted me about that wild and wondrous scenery which forms such a contrast to the pure marble temple of Philæ, sacred to Isis and Osiris. From him I learned marvellous stories of Jins and other fabulous creatures, some of which I turned to account in "Minor Morals," which George Cruikshank illustrated by characteristic etchings. We stopped at the different spots of interest, which we visited by day, always returning to our boats at night,—" our boats,"

I say, for we had one belonging to Mr R. H. Galloway of Alexandria, and another to Mr Baillie Cochrane, so that our voyage was eminently social. We found that in many cases interesting monuments had been recklessly destroyed, a very needless devastation, for chance and change are but too busy, and need not the co-operation of thoughtless man. A beautiful sphynx was dug up while I was in Egypt, and bore the name of that Pharaoh who knew not Joseph. I presented it to the British Museum, but through careless-ness it was disintegrated and destroyed in the fire which took place in the Plymouth dockyard, and the monument which had been spared for thousands of years was lost in consequence of the neglect of its keepers, who had forgotten to report its arrival, and to forward it to the Museum authorities.

I witnessed at Cairo a scene which could not but remind me of that which preceded the crucifixion of Jesus Christ. A man was brought before the tribunal, being accused of burglary. There was an immense clamour in the court, and loud cries of " let him be hanged—let him be hanged," and the judge instantly condemned him, and ordered him to be conveyed to the gates of the city, to be suspended there. The judge enquired of me how such a criminal would be dealt with in England, to which I answered that he would probably be transported to a distant colony. " And at what cost?" asked he. I mentioned some amount that ap-peared monstrous to his imagination. " And what, in your country, is the cost of a rope ? " " A few paras (pence)," I answered. " Then, I think," said he, " you must be great fools."

SYRIA.

The Pasha gave us one of his vessels, the " Timsah" (Crocodile), to convey us to Scanderoon (Alexandretta), and on our voyage we had strange evidence of the credulity of the Mahommedans. They enquired whether our European doctor had any marrow taken from dead men's bones, which, it was reported, he used for ointment, as if so, being of evil augury, it must be thrown into the sea. They pointed out a place on the hills which, they said, Adam had visited, leaving footmarks traceable by white spots. So careless were they, that we found one of them seated on a barrel of gunpowder smoking his pipe, though, from inattention in packing, grains of the explosive material might have been lying about. We, however, reached Scanderoon in safety on 8th April 1838, but had such reports of the extreme unhealthiness of the place, that we hurried on to Dana, which geographical descriptions represent as an important town, but we saw only miserable ruins. We ascended with some danger and difficulty up rotten stairs to the room where we were appointed to sleep, which was peopled by rats and smaller vermin. The Orontes is a beautiful river, Mount Taurus being visible in the distance, and we made our way to Antioch, one of the least changed, least visited, but at the same time one of the most interesting cities of Northern Syria. There it was that the disciples were first called Christians, and the places where they worshipped among the rocks are still pointed out to visitors. Wherever we went, crowds of people came, having heard that we were accompanied by a great foreign physician—they "came to be healed," and seemed to think that our friend possessed miraculous powers.

Aleppo interested us much, though the streets were in ruins, having been overthrown by an earthquake. It had a considerable trade, and some British merchants were established there, who received us with cordial hospitality. There were a good many Jews, whose outward appearance gave no indication of the wealth they possessed, nor of the luxuries we found in their dwellings. They had large quantities of precious stones for easy transport in case of danger, but with which their wives and daughters adorned themselves when they received visits from strangers. There was not the same difficulty of access to the Hebrew families as to those of the Mahommedans. Attended by domestics, the young ladies brought coffee to the guests, and furnished them with smoking materials, giving them the choice of the chibook or the narghileh, the latter being preferred by the women. The Jews live in constant fear of persecution from the Moosulmans, and, sad to say, the native Christians give them little protection or sympathy. I had a servant, named Joseph, who one day said to me, " Was not your prophet a Jew ? " I answered, " Undoubtedly he was." " Then," said he, "What must his brethren think of *him*, if he taught you to persecute us, and what must we think of *you*, if he did not so teach you ? "

On our way to the South we visited Homs and Hamah —the Hameth of the Scriptures. Many of the cities have retained their ancient names. We had been furnished with excellent horses by the Governor of Antioch, but we found it very difficult to provide for them a sufficiency of food, and were obliged to return them to the kind donor in a very emaciated state. Food for ourselves we could purchase, and shared now and then our bread with our four-footed companions, but that was insufficient for their support, and as the resting-places where stabling or shelter was to be found were frequently distant from one another, we had often to lament the sad state of our cavalcade. Things became worse as we approached the Hauran, where Ibrahim Pasha had gone to suppress an insurrection, but the Ansari tribe had been ravaging the country, and we found it unsafe to travel without a military escort, whose wild freaks and oriental apparel added not a little to the picturesqueness of our train. We had a Syrian dragoman, an Armenian servant, a Greek cook, a wild Bedouin Arab, a Constantinopolitan Turk, an Aleppine muleteer, and our scarlet-cloaked escort. I had the Sultan's firman, as well as Mehemet Ali's, and that of the Governor of Aleppo, besides being furnished with letters to all the principal people, so we obtained every attention, and were considered very great personages.

Our stopping-place, after leaving Aleppo, was Khán Shékhuné. We met on our way caravans of camels, an immense body of Armenians returning from Jerusalem, hundreds of pilgrims—many of them old, feeble, lame, and wretched—men, women, and children, who had been travelling fifteen hundred or two thousand miles on foot to perform their supposed religious obligation, and numbers of Christian Persians, of whose existence I was not aware.

The Sheikh received us hospitably, and while with him, a dervish introduced himself into the *diván*, professing to be able to deprive any one of speech, and he certainly practised successfully on one of our attendants, a *mascara*, or story-teller, who had been given to us as a companion by the Aleppo Governor. When he was forced into the presence of the magician, who was a man clad in black flowing garments, and wearing a green turban as a descendant of the prophet, with a stern black eye, he trembled violently. The dervish said loudly, "I strike you dumb." The man stuttered in absolute agony, but was unable to utter a word, and his suffering was so great that I implored the necromancer to release him. Giving him a cup of coffee, he said "Speak!" upon which the poor mascara fled, concealing himself in a neighbouring mountain, and did not join our party till we were far from Khán Shékhuné on the following day.

We had heard much of the extreme beauty of the Sheikh's

young wife, and I had a natural curiosity to get a glance
at the inaccessible lady. Fortune seemed to favour my
wishes, for the Sheikh informed me, with expressions of
great grief, that his infant child—the child of his old age
and of his lovely spouse—was dangerously ill, and as I had
the credit of being, and indeed bore the name of "El
Hakeem el Kebeer" (the great Doctor, for they were not
learned enough to distinguish between a Doctor of Laws and
a Doctor of Medicine), I was supposed to be able to effect
marvellous cures. He entreated me to cure his little boy,
which I expressed my willingness to attempt, but said I
must see the mother, and talk with her of the child's ail-
ments. He said that was impossible, as an unbeliever
could not be introduced into the harem of one of the faithful, but the child would be brought to me. I said that I could
not prescribe for the child without seeing the mother, but
he repeated, "That cannot be." I retorted "Your child
will die." He left the room the picture of despair, but in
the evening came again, saying that I was very unkind,
but that he would do anything to save the boy's life, and
that he would show me the way to the harem. He led me
to a room where I saw a poor, emaciated child on a rug,
his body covered with various charms, such as sentences
from the Koran, and bending over him was a veiled woman.
My curiosity was, of course, on the stretch, and I addressed
the mother with some enquiries as to the symptoms. She
answered, but I said I could but imperfectly understand
her, as she spoke Arabic, and I asked her to remove her
veil. She resisted, when I observed that European phy-
sicians studied the diseases of children in the countenances
of the mothers. I became peremptory, and at last she
slowly raised the veil, when, instead of the angelic beauty,
I was confronted with the face of a hideous hag, who said
to me, "I am the old wife." The Sheikh laughed, as in-

deed he had a right to do, and I could not but join in the laugh, for the trick had admirably succeeded.

The Orontes runs through the town of Hamah, where there is a water-wheel of gigantic size. We were amused by the tale-telling and song-singing of our professed buffoon, and on his dismissal I gave him a piece of gold, which he flung indignantly away. The Moofti at Hamah, a jolly fellow, asked whether we had brought any " moya inglis " (brandy) with us, and whether I could get him a young and pretty handmaid for a sum representing about £300. I replied that our fair maidens were beyond all price, though what he offered was about the market value of a handsome Circassian. There was a good deal of business in the bazaar, and troops of all sorts were moving about, as Ibrahim Pasha was then making war in the Hauran. His father, Mehemet Ali, who was very proud of his eldest son, especially after his success in conquering Mekka and Medina, having heard of his being ill, sent Clot Bey, his principal physician, to minister to him, but the Bey was met by a messenger sent to say that he did not want any physic, but if he had brought a supply of champagne he would be welcome.

Of the cities of the Holy Land, Damascus ranks next to Jerusalem in order of sanctity. The Orientals call it " the Pearl girded with Emeralds," and it well deserves the name, for its whitened walls are surrounded by beautiful gardens freshened with Abana and Pharphar, which shine with ever-living green. The architecture of the city is probably not changed since the days of Abraham. The houses present bare white walls towards the streets, but their interior is charming, with marble floors, in the centre of which are fountains perpetually flowing, while all around are beautiful flowers.

The Pasha gave me a splendid dinner, consisting of one

N

hundred and fifty dishes. He had hired a Turkish, an Arab, and a French cook, the last having served under Napoleon, and each was ordered to provide fifty *plats.* We were a company of thirteen—the fatal number, as superstition says—and in this case the event was inauspicious, for the Pasha was beheaded for treason to his sovereign shortly after. He amused us with his stories after dinner, *moya inglis* being the topic. He said he had learned that a Mahommedan shopkeeper in Damascus had been clandestinely selling the liquid prohibited in the Koran. He sent for the sinner, who tremblingly confessed that he had six cases with six dozen in each, on which the Pasha said, " I am doubting whether I shall hang you or not, but send the cases to the palace, and I will look into the matter myself." The cases were sent, and the Pasha was tempted to taste. " I liked it," he said. " I was going to take a ride, but I got up the wrong way on the horse, and found that I caught hold of the tail instead of the bridle, but I thought the *moya* very good, and I am sorry to say none is left to offer you."

Damascus had not then undergone the changes which have since altered its character. A man could scarcely pass through the streets in a European dress without being insulted—a stranger especially—and a Jew was only allowed to ride on a donkey. The Jews were more numerous and richer than those of Aleppo, and were most hospitably disposed towards European officials.

At Hasseyah we found the government of the place entrusted to a lad only twelve years old. We had *Teskerehs,* enabling us to levy contributions for our wants, which we only asked when money availed not. Having purchased some eggs of a Syrian woman, we offered her a glass of wine, which she refused, shaking her head, but soon after, to our surprise, she returned and claimed the proffered gift, which she did not drink, but poured it over her head.

At Sahalieh, we went to dine with Ali Aga, a jovial Mahommedan who, no doubt made bold by wine, proposed to show us his harem, and we were glad to take advantage of the opportunity. He conducted us to a room where female garments were strewn about, and a number of ladies, who were seated on the *diván*, screamed out, " Oh, infidels! What business have you here?" There was one very sweet voice, and I said, "I am sure that sweet voice must belong to a very pretty woman, whose face I should like to see." She put aside her veil, which concealed a very handsome person, and screamed out louder than before, "Ya Giaour!" covering her face suddenly again. It was an unaffected—I may perhaps say an affected—display of feminine vanity. I remember that in Turkey, where the ladies are concealed by screens from the male guests, they manage to make holes through which their bright eyes are to be discovered, and that they put out their pretty feet under the carpet that they may be admired, but the old and ugly seldom unveil.

Galilee and Samaria were to me the most interesting parts of the Holy Land. At every step, as we proceeded to the south, we were met by the most absurd and baseless traditions, but Nazareth and Nablous—the Sechem of the Old Testament, the Sychar of the New—stand forth in all their ancient simplicity and truth, reproducing the Bible of yesterday in the pictures of to-day. We crossed the Jordan at the bridge of "Jacob's Daughter," and met numberless pilgrims going to or returning from Jerusalem, though many perish on their way before they reach the sacred city. The river's banks were crowded with people, Christians, Jews, and Mahommedans, all bathing in the crystal stream. It was with singular pleasure that I dipped my feet in its waters, and, strange to say, of three fresh-water shells which I took out, one was very rare, and the others, till then,

unknown.   I filled a bottle with water, which I presented
to the Queen, and from which the Crown Princess Imperial
of Prussia was baptized, as were the children of Lord
Clarendon.   Our pleasure was somewhat diminished by the
enormous quantity of vermin which we found in a shed
where, for a short time, we tarried, in which a caravan of
camels had been housed.   We sent one of our servants to
explore, and he was absolutely blackened by the quantity of
fleas that covered every part of his person which was
exposed, so we determined to sleep on our rugs under the
clear canopy of heaven, but even then we were persecuted
by such multitudinous visitors that, as Curran said, if they
could only have agreed to pull one way, I might have been
dragged into the Jordan.   Travellers must expect to find
the plagues of Egypt in Syria, added to other vermin not
mentioned in holy writ.

"How beautiful," I exclaimed, "is the Sea of Galilee!
How beautiful the wild flowers on its borders! beautiful
the barren mountains on the east, more beautiful still the
green valleys on the west!"

There was complete solitude on the lake—not a boat, not
a human being.   We sat on its shore looking above to
Magdala, where are the ancient graves hewn out of the rock.
As we turned to the lake, we witnessed one of the phenomena
which frequently occur in inland lakes.   There was a violent
hurricane coming from the opposite hills, which shook the
lake violently, and then, suddenly there was a great calm.
We sat down to take our meal by the side of a rivulet
running into the lake, the banks being covered with
flowering rhododendrons, while I gathered some of the
watercresses which grew there abundantly.   Everything
looked bright and happy, the fields were filled with oxen,
there were multitudinous wild-flowers, and numbers of
green lizards were running about the rocks.   Most of the

towns, once so thickly peopled, and of whose large trade on the Galilean Sea Josephus speaks, were but solitudes. We entered Nazareth close by the declivity down which Jesus passed through the crowd. Many women, the younger of them very pretty (and being Christians they were not veiled), were filling with water from the wells the vessels which they bore gracefully on their heads. In the streets there were loud songs and music, and a procession was escorting a bridegroom home. He wore a white turban, and was arrayed in handsome scarlet garments. Multitudes of children followed the trains of the bridegroom and the bride. We had just passed Cana of Galilee, and there was evidence enough that the wines were of an intoxicating character, the most celebrated being the "golden wine" of Lebanon. Cana is in ruins, as is Ramla, the Arimathæa of the New Testament, but the monks of the convent, of whom there were fifteen, escorted us to the "Holy Places." Many of the monks had forgotten their native language, but they were very civil, showed us the house where Joseph and Mary lived, and of course told us the story of the pillar miraculously conveyed to Loretto, the broken fragment of which was there to tell its own tale.

Passing to Nablous, we saw the well at the entrance of the city, where the grand words were uttered to the woman, "God is a Spirit, and they that worship Him must worship Him in spirit and in truth." A woman was there who offered us water to drink. It was indeed a realization of past history.

The governor, at whose palace we descended, lived in luxurious style, and we had beds of silk, stretched on the floor, with gold decorations. From the harem the ladies sent us sweetmeats, flowers, and embroidered handkerchiefs. The servants were numerous, and I was glad to learn that the secretary of the governor was the son of Aias Cohen, the high priest of the Samaritans. He accompanied us to Mount Gerizim, where we saw the famous Pentateuch written on sheep-skins in the ancient Samaritan language, and containing the celebrated verse not found in the Hebrew Septuagint—" In Mount Gerizim ye shall worship." The type of the Samaritans is not Jewish, and they bear the same antipathy to the Jews which their forefathers bore. Their numbers did not exceed one hundred and twenty. They told us how wonderfully their sacred book had been preserved, it having been several times buried, and once for eighty years in the bowels of the mountain. Its preservation uninjured they, naturally enough, deemed miraculous. I published a short account of my visit entitled " Samaria and the Samaritans." What most struck me was a conversation with a sheikh, who said he could not understand why European Christians were so much interested in a small tribe of men like them. I told him that there was a story which we were taught in our childhood of " the good Samaritan," a lesson taught us by our Master, and I narrated it to him. " Why! every word of that is true," he said. " We had a great and good physician among us, of whose kind deeds we have many traditions. He was accustomed to go into the highways, and to relieve and succour the indigent, and to heal the sick. You have been told a true story."

The governor was very curious about European customs, and had his children taught Turkish and Persian, as well as Arabic. The master used not the rod, but he spared not the kourbash, which is made of buffalo-hide. The boys were frequently introduced, only the youngest being allowed to sit in his father's presence, as is generally the case among the higher ranks of Mahommedans. A Christian youth was bought as a slave while we were there, the price paid being about £70, but domestic slavery is not oppressive, the slaves forming part of the family, as in patriarchal times, though they have no legal protection, and are disposed of at the master's will.

We found much civility, but little civilization in the Franciscan convent at Nazareth. A Spanish brother said he had never heard of such a person as " Don Quixote," but he was enlightened by another of the fraternity, who was surprised at his ignorance, and told him, and the company in general, that the king of France had sent a copy of " Telemachus" to Spain, and that the Spanish king returned the compliment by sending a copy of " Don Quixote." His most Christian majesty said that the author must be a very clever fellow, so he invited him to his court, where he was covered with honour and glory.

Sleeping at the convent, we were awakened by the tones of the bells, and our special friend, the Spanish friar Antonio, came with a cup of tea to speed the departing guests. Our goal was St Jean D'Acre—the Akka of the modern Arabs, the Ptolemaïs of the ancient Greeks. Recollections of home crowded on me when the clotted cream, which, it is said, the Phœnicians introduced into Devonshire and Cornwall, was given to me, and I saw the same kind of cob-walls—the clay mixed with straw, so memorable in the Egyptian history of the Jews—around me. Strange that the influence of those adventurous men, whose nation, whose language, whose memory has passed away, the great merchant princes of Tyre and Sidon, should still be visible in our western regions. At Acre we saw curious evidence of personal affection for one of the most brutal of tyrants. Jezzár Pasha, known by the name of " the butcher," had died. He was a most horrible example of a modern despot, and would put out the eyes of one of his vassals, saying, " you did not see a plot laid against me." He would cut off the ears of another, exclaiming, " you did not hear the

tales of the market-place, and report them to me." He cut
out the tongues of others, and said, "you knew what was
going on. What were your tongues given you for but to
tell me what you heard." And yet to this monster's
memory a shrine was raised, it was covered with flowers,
and streams of fresh water flowed from it. In spite of
the proverb, "Flatterers *have* friends, and tyrants *have*
worshippers."

We passed through Soor and Sayda, the ancient Tyre
and Sidon, cities whose merchant princes filled the world
with their fame, but the ports, once crowded by the largest
ships, will scarcely admit a fisherman's boat. Columns of
the old piers lay in the sand, the waters had invaded the
coast, and silence reigned where the noisy traffickers filled
the marts, and where the treasures of Ophir were bought in
exchange for the luxuries which the industry of Syria could
produce. Here we encountered a flight of locusts, which
darkened the air with their multitudes, and devoured everything green on the face of the land. A few hours brought
us to Beyrout, now the principal port in Syria, whence the
markets of Damascus are principally supplied.

While at Beyrout, I sent a message to Lady Hester Stanhope, who had established herself at Joun, a hill looking
down upon ancient Sidon, asking if she would do me the
honour of receiving me, as I was acquainted with some of
her family in England. She replied that she would receive
no envoy from Cupid (Lord Palmerston), but she had been
visited by Lamartine, Prince Pückler Muskau, and others.
She had written a letter to the British Consul General in
Egypt, in which she said, in answer to a claim which he had
been directed to prefer against her, that " She would recommend him to put on a wig, and give his orders from the
woolsack, servant as he was of the wise Lord Palmerston,
and he the servant of our magnificent Queen," and ended

by saying that she would not pay her debts, unless Her Majesty ordered her to do so. She lived, with more than a hundred and twenty armed people around her, like a sovereign, but Mehemet Ali told Colonel Campbell that she should have as many people, and no more, as were necessary for a lady, upon which Colonel C. said she might have sixteen, whereupon she called the old Pasha " a bloody tyrant," at which I daresay he laughed heartily. She coveted the title of Queen of Syria, and a mad fellow at Alexandria, who called himself King of Jerusalem, wanted to marry her. Mr C. visited her, and gave strange accounts of her manners and conversation. She said to him, "You are not such a d——d puppy as Byron was. You are lame as he was, but you don't come shuffling into a room as if you were ashamed of what is no fault of yours, standing before this picture and that, and making your way to a seat sidling, just to hide, what anyone can see, that one of your legs is shorter than the other." She told him, if he would stay, that she would send for a magician to take him to a place where was a serpent born before the world was created, and hidden under a rock, and that the serpent would show him a spot where treasures were concealed.

She had a great hatred for consuls, and one of our consuls, thinking she would be pleased at the compliment, asked her opinion as to the name he should give to his newly born son. She wrote him the following letter :—" Sir, call him Humbug or Fiddlesticks." I saw a copy of a letter which she wrote to that wandering fellow, Mr ——, which is really too good to be lost, and which she gave to Mr C. :—" Sir,—I am astonished that an apostate should dare to thrust himself into my family. Had you, whose real name I know not, been a learned Jew, never would you have abandoned a religion, rich in itself, though defective, for the shadow of one. Light travels faster than sound. Therefore

the Supreme Being could never have allowed His creatures
to remain in utter darkness for two thousand years, until
paid speculating wanderers think it proper to raise their
venal voice in order to enlighten them."

When pressed for payment of what she owed, she said,
" I have divided my creditors into three categories. Those
who have asked for their money, which I consider an insult,
shall never be paid, and the second and third who have
never asked, I shall divide into two classes, some of whom
I shall pay, and some not." Her dress was rather that of a
man than a woman. She talked of religious matters, saying,
that she had been looking into the respective merits of the
Bible and the Koran, and had come to the conclusion that,
on the whole, the latter was the better book of the two.
Her creditors endeavoured to lay hands on the pension
which her uncle, William Pitt, had obtained for her (she
had kept house for him), but she managed to receive
the money so cleverly through the French and not the
English authorities, that not a penny could be reached.

In the earlier part of her residence in Syria she was very
popular. She had a horse with a natural saddle (back), and
a handsome ass, which was to assimilate her entrance with
that of Jesus Christ, when she came to claim sovereignty
as the Queen of Jerusalem. She spent liberally, but borrowed on all sides, which soon dissolved the charm of her
presence, and in her later days her pride had a bitter struggle
with her poverty, and nothing in her life was so sorrowful
as its termination. Dr Merian published her memoirs,
which are interesting, though they throw but an imperfect
light on so singular a character.

Count Berthoud, whom we met at Beyrout, told us that
he had discovered that the level of the Mediterranean was a
hundred and twenty feet above that of the Red Sea. He
had, in his explorations, found out the site of Zoar, and

ascertained that a town, now in ruins, still bears the name of Wadi Moussa, the stream of Moses.

When at Akka, I heard of a case of plague, and was convinced, as I endeavoured to show in a paper on Oriental Plague and Quarantine, which I read at a meeting of the British Association, that plague cannot be communicated beyond the infected regions, and only in certain atmospheric conditions. I showed that, when the plague broke out among the Egyptian troops, and they were sent to the desert, its ravages were immediately stopped, that Clot Bey had dissected more than a hundred plague patients, and that Dr Hepites had inoculated himself with the pus, neither having caught the disease; that the quarantines, which confined sufferers to a particular locality, had immensely increased the mortality, while the dispersion of the infected had always diminished it; that in the Lazaret of Malta, where for centuries plague-infected persons and goods had been imprisoned, there had never been an example of its communication to a doctor, nurse, or attendant; in fine, that Quarantines, created and maintained solely for the benefit of the interested, and by the folly of the ignorant, were in themselves the veritable plague and pest of commerce and of communication, and ought to be abolished. I brought the subject more than once to the notice of the House of Commons, and there have been many modifications of the regulations which once existed. It has been declared, both by the Académie de Médicine in Paris, and by the College of Surgeons in London, that the disease is never latent more than *ten* days, and generally breaks out in seven. Hence the absurdity of establishing a quarantine of *forty*. But the time must come when the belief in the contagion of plague will be buried in the same limbo which holds other credulities of past times, such as the belief in ghosts, witches, and other marvels. The process is slow, for the belief is strongly impressed on the minds of the vulgar, and will long serve to decorate the fictions of the novelist and the artist.

We started from Beyrout for the land of the Druses, on a visit to the Emir Beshir. Both the country and the inhabitants appeared very superior to those of the district we left, the land being well cultivated, and the people having a noble bearing. The women were handsome, and wore the characteristic ornament of the silver horn, always "exalted," except when they bow at the entrance of their lowly doors. Almost every man was absent from home, the fields having been invaded by clouds of locusts, which the people were destroying with branches of trees, and burying in deep holes. The scenery was wonderfully grand. Many of the roads are like staircases, winding round and round the skirts of the hills. We reached a height, down whose sides streams of clear water were flowing, and there stood Bait-ood-deen, the palace of the Prince of the Druses. An immense number of attendants were in the court, which was filled with travellers and their horses, for whom every accommodation was provided. The Prince had been humiliated and disarmed by Ibrahim Pasha, but was able to maintain a certain amount of authority. Not long after our visit, however, he was banished to Constantinople, where it was reported that his eyes were put out, and that he was condemned to death. He came to welcome us with a most courteous reception. He was handsomely clad, and his watch-chain was decorated with brilliants. The walls of the apartments were gorgeously painted, fountains of water played around, and there were hundreds of servants. We observed that lightning conductors had been placed, and the Emir told us that, having seen them on the masts of English ships of war, and having ascertained their use and value, he had protected with them his palace from the lightning, which formerly did much damage to it. We were told that he had seven thousand men capable of bearing arms, but their arms were taken away by Ibrahim Pasha, and the Emir was compelled to witness their being broken in pieces in the court of his palace. A handsome dinner was provided for us in European style, and our sleeping room was that which had been occupied by Suleiman Pasha, the commander-in-chief of the Egyptian army. We had never seen such baths, nor smoked such tobacco (Latakia), as awaited our acceptance.

We visited the church, which was ornamented with several pictures sent from Rome, the service being conducted in Syriac. In the library was a collection of books in that language, and in the school attached to the church were about twenty Syrian ladies who were learning Arabic, but they were not taught Syriac, which is a sacred tongue, mainly useful to the priests.

The Emir was said to be a Christian, but most of the Druses of the mountain are faithful to their ancient religion, and observe the superstitious rites of their forefathers. The people told us that they had a temple for worship, but they would not say where it was to be found. I asked one of the attendants of the chapel whether they were Roman Catholics, and he anwered, "siamo figli della chiesa," but there are among the Druses a large sect of Maronites, who profess, however, devotion to Rome, and use the Roman services.

Syria is one of the most interesting regions of the world, and I had on my visit some special advantages, not only because I had a mission from my government, but because I had recommendatory *teskerehs* from the Sultan and from Mehemet Ali.

Nothing of particular moment occurred till I reached Constantinople, where every one was talking of the follies of the Sultan, who, while his country was invaded by Ibrahim Pasha, and his troops had been utterly defeated at

Konich and Kutayah, was amusing himself with frivolities. He ordered bows and arrows, and then flung them away. He entertained himself with childish toys. One day, when going up the Bosphorus, he saw a Greek priest, to whose cap he took a fancy, and ordered an attendant to follow him, but the priest escaped. A mandate was issued, and the priest was traced to his convent, where the cap was demanded from him. He handed over an old one, which was taken to the Sultan, who said that it was not the one wanted, and that a new one must be brought, which was done, and the priest was glad no doubt to escape on such easy terms. In his rage, the Sultan, one day, ordered all his Christian subjects to be murdered, but the Seraskier, happily for him, represented the perilous character of his proposed ordinance, and it was withdrawn. When at last the progress of the Egyptian army towards the gates of Constantinople was announced to him—which the English ambassador insisted should be done—he was found in his garden cutting down the rose-trees with his sabre, and exclaiming, " Thus I dispose of my enemies !" After the destruction of the Janissaries was determined on, and his orders given, his courage failed him, and he withdrew the mandate, but it was too late. He had confided the task to officers who delayed not to execute it. He was addicted to the inordinate use of spirituous liquors, and not unfrequently gave orders for the execution of officers, which he recalled when the bloody deed had been done.   .

PRUSSIA.

In 1839 I was sent by the British government to the meeting of the Zoll Verein at Berlin. The object was to ascertain how far our commercial relations with Germany could be extended, but the German delegates appeared to me for the most part very narrow-minded in their views,

opposed to free-trade, and afraid of competition, most of
them indeed being manufacturers, or the representatives of
manufacturing interests. They failed to see that if the breaking down of the barriers which had opposed the free circulation of commodities within the circle of the German Verein,
had been a great blessing to trade by leading to its augmentation, the application of the same principle to England
and the wide world, would, in proportion to the increased
area, have extended the common benefits. But Great
Britain was ill fitted to be a teacher when a restrictive and
prohibitory system formed the foundation of her commercial
code. Adam Smith, and a succession of distinguished
politico-economists had preached sound doctrines in vain,
and though I could easily and triumphantly answer the
reasonings of our opponents, I could not gainsay the fact
that our own tariffs, and especially those which most interested Northern Germany, by which the import of corn was
placed under severe and repelling restrictions, were altogether hostile to free-trade principles. But so little hopeful
were our prospects then, that when I returned to London,
and gave an account of my mission to Lord Melbourne, then
Prime Minister, telling him he must abolish the Corn Laws,
he looked at me with surprise, and exclaimed with an oath
(not an unusual ornament of his conversation) that I was fit
for Bedlam.

But the Corn Laws *were* abolished, and I had the honour
of laying the foundation of the Anti-Corn-Law League,
which grew out of a small meeting held at Manchester, and
acquired such a gigantic power, by creating an irresistible
public opinion, that Sir Robert Peel was convinced, and had
the honesty to own that Cobden had become his master.
So, in spite of the resistance and the vituperation of a section of the Tory party, headed by Lord George Bentinck,
D'Israeli, and others, we conquered the ill-judged resistance

of the landed interest, who proclaimed that they—the
farmers and the husbandmen, would be hopelessly and help-
lessly ruined, that the sun of England's glory would set for
ever, and—but the result has not warranted the awful predictions.   Rents are advanced, and wages too as a necessary
consequence, and well may we now say, " Fac recte, nihil
time."   Right *was* done, and there was no ground for
fear.

One morning at Berlin, while I was sitting at breakfast,
a stately person, booted and spurred, and wearing a gay
uniform, entered, and bowing low said, " You are invited
to dine with the King at Potsdam to-day at 4 o'clock."   I
accepted of course, royal invitations being commands, but I
went off at once to Lord William Russell, our ambassador,
expecting that he would accompany me, and aid me in sur-
mounting the difficulties which; in Courts so formal as those
of Germany, always attend the stranger.   To my surprise,
he said that neither he nor any of the foreign ministers had
ever been invited to dine with the King, it being a traditional counsel of Frederick the Great, still observed at
Court, not to allow foreigners to meddle with the affairs of
the royal family.   Lord William added that he saw him only
once a year, and then but for five minutes, while even his
ministers rarely got at him.   People waited three months
for an audience, and the King spent half his time with
dancers and ballet girls.

I went to Potsdam, and happily found Humboldt at
Court.   I was the sole Englishman introduced.   The King
asked me how I liked Berlin, and said he had heard of my
reputation from Humboldt.   Soon came in the Queen of
Bavaria, the Princess Liegnitz, the Princess Royal, and other
princesses, and some pretty children, among whom was
the son of the heir to the crown, a lad of ten or twelve.   At
about six we were summoned to the theatre in the palace,

which was superbly fitted up, and filled with guests invited by the king—some sixty or seventy persons. All the great actors of Berlin were there, but the ballet, which was the King's hobby, was specially good, and one part of it truly amusing. There were forty or fifty little children, four or five years old, playing the parts of men and women, and some did it admirably. One child, who was a grandmother, was perfect, and there was a good love scene, and an after-matrimony scene between a boy and a girl not above six years old. The soldiers with moustachios, the sappers with long beards, the postillions in their boots and with their tails, the lawyers in their gowns, &c., were *à mourir de rire*.

The King's dinner was unlike any I had ever seen. In the centre of the room was a table where the royal family took their seats, while around it were many other tables, arranged as at a French restaurant, the most distinguished guests being near enough to hold conversation with the royal family. The waiters were Chinamen wearing their national costume, whom the King told me he had imported to take charge of his gardens, but the project not having succeeded, he had turned them to other account.

Wandering through the gardens and admiring the collection of dahlias, Humboldt mentioned that all the dahlias in Europe were the descendants of a few seeds, which he had gathered on the table-land of Mexico and sent in a letter to Lady Holland, from whose gardens they have been so widely distributed that there is scarcely a garden unadorned with them, and they are to be seen near many a peasant's cottage.

The necessity of standing in the presence of royalty is a very painful duty, and must be dreadfully wearisome to the habitués of the Prussian court. I recollect that at a party given by the Crown Prince, to which I had been invited to come dressed *en bourgeois* because, in addition to the court

o

people, there were only to be some *gelehrten*, a message came to say that as the Dowager Queen of Bavaria, mother of the Crown Princess, was to be present, I must come in my court dress. The Queen invited me to converse about the Holy Land, saying she wanted to compare my impressions with the accounts she had received from her son, Prince Max, who had lately visited the sacred soil. While she stood, nobody could sit, and as it was in the evening, there was a large company of guests. The Crown Prince was impatient and very angry. " Ich bin so genirt," he said irreverently, speaking so loudly as to be heard by his mother-in-law, who, however, did not heed his rebuke. At Charlottenburg, where the Prince had built himself a house in the classical Roman style, with baths and all the appurtenances which an opulent patrician could desire, he rejoiced at being able to enjoy himself and entertain his friends without the fettering of court etiquette.

The Crown Prince escorted me through the Potsdam library, where are many reminiscences of Frederick the Great, and of his visitor, Voltaire. There was scarcely a German book on the shelves—indeed it is known that Frederick despised his native language and literature, which had little to recommend it, for the days of Goethe, Schiller, and the illustrious writers of Germany, had scarcely dawned. The furniture was of light blue satin, fringed with silver. The mill was still to be seen which the bold miller refused to surrender to his master. The statue of Queen Louise in the gardens appeared to me very beautiful. I shall always retain sweet impressions of Berlin. Mendelssohn was then in the full blaze of his fame, society was cordial, amusing, and instructive, the city was rapidly growing in wealth, and the suburbs were being covered with comfortable habitations. Who then could have dreamed of the wonderful events which have made the descendants of the Prussian King emperors of Germany, have reduced France almost to a state of vassalage, and given to the empire an ascendancy which entitles it to be ranked as the first of Continental Powers ?

I passed some time with Humboldt, who showed me the presents he had received from the Emperor of Russia, among which was a platina medal as large as a cheese-plate, of which only one other exists, and a collection of gold medals weighing, I should think, fifty sovereigns each. He said that he had had some misunderstanding with the Emperor, and when the quarrel was made up, Nicholas gave him this superb cadeau. He took me over his house to show me how he carried on his studies, how he arranged his books and maps, how he conducted his philosophical observations, &c. It was wonderful how he crowded so much into life, for he was constantly at court, attended all great parties, and yet produced the most profoundly elaborate and learned works that have ever been written.

At Berlin I met a well-known character, J—— F——, who by sheer, persistent, imperturbable boldness, had made his way to half the kings and courts of Europe, getting the various sovereigns to write their names in his album. " Now! look at that signature," said he, pointing to the handwriting of the King of Bavaria. " See what a passion that's written in ! Why, do you know, when I took out my album and asked the King to write in it, His Majesty said he wouldn't—positively wouldn't—never did such a thing—so I attacked him again, and he took up a pen, and see what a towering passion he was in when he wrote his name." F. said that the police were troubling him, and asked me to help him. He told me that a sovereign once said to him, " Get out of my way," on which he answered, " No, Sire ! I am an Englishman, and you may get out of mine." He said he had ordered Lord S. away from Stutt-

gardt, for the police, on an application of his, had dismissed
him. Some one asked him if he might refer to me about
him, but, as I had refused to lend him money, he replied,
"O ! that Dr Bowring is so caustic, and is an outrageous
radical, while I am a Tory—a true Tory to the backbone."

ISLE OF MAN.

The position of the Isle of Man formed a singular
anomaly in the dominions of the British rulers. It had formerly a language of its own, whose principal elements are
Keltic, with a few Scandinavian words introduced by
visitors from the north, and some English of still more
modern date, but the idiom has nearly died out, and at the
present moment the national tongue is used in all the
Church services. Many of the ancient usages and ceremonies, however, remain, and fragments of the Manx are
still used in some of the legislative proceedings, e.g., the
Tynwald, and the title of Deemster (Judge), while the
names of almost all the old towns, villages, and country
seats are Keltic, and such as still are found in Scotland,
Ireland, and Wales, namely, Douglas, Ralta, Curn, Avon,
and others. The surnames, too, resemble those of the
Gaelic races, with the prefixes of " O " and " Mac."

The rights of the lords, and the subjection of the vassals,
resembled those of feudal times. The rich paid no taxes,
but levied contributions from the poor ; the yachts of the
opulent entered the ports scatheless, while the boats of poor
fishermen paid taxes to the state ; the well-to-do had
licences for the introduction of foreign commodities, and
sold to shopkeepers and consumers the excess not required
for themselves, their families, and friends. I brought these
oppressions to the notice of Sir Robert Peel, and the abuses
were remedied to a great extent. The members of the House
of Keys, who, in earlier times, were nominated by the kings

of Man, and afterwards self-elected, are now chosen by popular suffrage. One of the earliest experiments in favour of Free Trade was made with complete success in this small island, which is the scene of one of Sir Walter Scott's most popular novels, "Peveril of the Peak," in which many illustrations of the old habits and history of Manxmen may be advantageously studied.

When I visited the island in 1843, I learned much of the history of the people, whose manners were quite primitive. I was told that in 1825 they drove away the Bishop and his family, owing to his extreme exaction of tithes, and that, when he sent his carts to collect the potatoes, they precipitated them into the sea. The Bishop then applied to the government for troops, whom the women surrounded, bound, disarmed, and sent away empty-handed. A deputation then went to his Lordship, and, on being admitted to his presence, told him that unless he signed three documents, giving them indemnity for the past, pardon for the present, and release for the future, they would burn his palace, farm, and ricks. The Bishop signed, but after continuing the struggle for some time, fled with all his family. My host, who was one of the prime movers in this rebellion, recounted all this with bright eyes, and added that the Bishop afterwards told him that if he had followed his (my informant's) advice he would have been Bishop still, and would have lived in peace and quietness.

SINGAPORE—PENANG.

What struck me most in visiting these places in 1849 was the immense number of Chinamen in the streets, in the shops, and in the water, all busily employed, or eager for employment. The excessive population of the "Central Kingdom" is constantly swarming forth in every direction, and the immigration of the black-haired races is changing the whole character of society, the Indian Archipelago being the field where the battle of the nationalities is constantly fought, and where the expulsion of the less civilised by the more civilized may be studied. The aborigines were ruled over by the more adventurous Malays ; then came from the shores of India the Klings who, under British rule, had acquired some elements of progress ; then the Chinese, far more industrious and economical, and with more temperate habits than their predecessors ; and, lastly, the English, of whom a very few have learnt to subject the very many of the now subordinate tribes. In proportion to the civiliza- tion is the growth of wealth and influence, the silent law of development is always actively, and somewhat mysteriously at work, and the tide of tendency moves on, ever flowing, seldom ebbing, or, if ebbing, only to obtain a greater and more active impulse. Singapore owes its great success to Free Trade, whose foundation was laid by John Crawfurd, the Malayan scholar, known in the clubs by the name of "the inventor of forty Adams," a title he obtained for repudiating the doctrine that the various races of mankind are descended from one single ancestor. He used to say that Max Müller's Aryan heresy respecting the Oriental and Occidental tribes of men was a grosser heresy in the philosophical field than was the Arian heterodoxy in the theological. Certainly, Singapore may be advantageously studied in comparison with, and resemblance to, Hong Kong, and in contrast with the French colonies in Cochin China and elsewhere, where the old taint of monopoly and national privileges remains associated with loss of wealth, of reputation, and of soldiers' lives. Many of the productions of the Straits Settlements have rendered incalculable benefits to science and to civil- izing comforts. The value of india-rubber—caoutchouc —was for some time confined to the artist's studio, but Macintosh introduced it for garments, and for a hundred other purposes. Gutta-percha has played a still more important part, for, while more soluble than caoutchouc, it is of far greater natural hardness. What cookery owes to the various spices, the pen of a more practised gourmand than myself must describe.

Penang had been described to me as a most beautiful island, and certainly its appearance, presenting one mass of gorgeous vegetation, with trees covering the sides, and crowning the tops of the highest hills, is singularly striking. The town looks like a fragment of China, torn away, and fixed in the straits. There was Chinese music in the streets, and Chinese water-sellers, fish-sellers, fruit-sellers, &c., everybody crying about his wares. We went into one of the opium-smoking houses, where lay multitudes, almost naked, in a state that seemed one of felicitous dreaming, while the fumes were inhaled. The dull eye brightened, the haggard look departed, and a smile succeeded the scowl, till sleep took possession, and then, alas for the wakening! A large proportion of the Chinese are addicted to this vice, which has none of the horrors however of our European drunkenness. It enervates and destroys body and mind, but so slowly and stealthily as to leave much controversy as to the extent of the evil.

We went to a Chinese theatre in the open air, where there must have been two thousand spectators; the actors, on a high stage, being gaily dressed, and the whole exhibition somewhat better than that of a country fair. There was a humourous buffoon, a troop of soldiers, and an audience at court, where the *Kotow* was performed. The music was very strange, and some of the speeches reminded me of the ravings of an ambitious village stage-player. Thence we went to the Joss-houses, where the priests were telling fortunes, the attendants making oblations and burning papers to the memory of their ancestors. There were some hideous idols, bedizened with scarlet and gold, but, strange to say, in the inner temple was a figure of the Virgin Mary, which the Chinese had found at sea and made a goddess of.

The beauty of Singapore is indescribable. Through groves of spice-trees, nutmeg, and clove, through a garden of fruits and flowers, amidst the songs of rare and beautiful birds, and enormous splendid butterflies, we reached the governor's bungalow, which is on the top of a hill overlooking all the town and neighbourhood—the centre of a magnificent circumference of sea and land. The governor had a large aviary, and while I was lying down, quietly reading a description of Singapore, a gigantic peacock of the Borneo race perched near me, and, after looking at me for some time, attacked me fiercely. I ran at him, supposing he would retreat, but no ! he came on again with redoubled violence, so I seized my umbrella, opened it, and by main strength forced the hero out of the window.

CHINA.

When I was a little boy, I had a singular dream. It was that I was sent by the King of England as Ambassador to. China. No doubt my head was filled with the gorgeous representations of Chinese life which are found in the narratives of the Macartney and Amherst missions to Peking, but of all improbable things nothing could appear less probable than the fulfilment of my dream, for I was living in the country, no ambition had been awakened in me, and, according to all appearance, I was destined to walk in the humbler path which my forefathers had trodden for many generations. But to China I went as the representative of the Queen, and was accredited, not to Peking alone, but to Japan, Siam, Cochin China, and Corea,—I believe to a greater number of human beings—indeed not less than a third of the race of man—than any individual had been accredited to before.

Lord Palmerston offered me the Consulship of Canton, where diplomatic questions with the 'Central Kingdom' were discussed. The engagement made with Sir John Davis that the gates of the city should be opened, and personal intercourse established between the Mandarins and the British authorities in two years after the treaty was signed, had been repudiated, and it was my business to enforce the engagement. I knew the importance of the question, for it was certain that if one could get into the presence of a Chinese official, with a sufficient force behind, he was not likely to be unreasonable. Year after year, I implored Yeh (the Chinese word means *leaf*) to admit me to his presence in his *yamun* (official residence) at Canton, or to visit me either at the factories or in Hong Kong, but he was deaf to every entreaty. I went to the Peiho, and was visited by Mandarins, but only to learn that Yeh's conduct was approved, and that we must not attempt to visit the capital.

My career in China belongs so much to history, that I do not feel it needful to record its vicissitudes. I have been severely blamed for the policy I pursued, yet that policy has been most beneficial to my country and to mankind at large. It is not fair or just to suppose that a course of action, which may be practicable or prudent at home, will always succeed abroad. You can no more apply exactly the same discipline, or the same character of reward and punishment to masses of men than you can apply them to individuals. The powers of reason fail when coming in contact with the unreasoning and unconvincible. No man was ever a more ardent lover of peace than I—in fact, I had been the Secretary of the Peace Society, and had always taken an active part in promoting the peace-movement— but with barbarous—ay, and sometimes with civilized nations, the words of peace are uttered in vain—as with children too often the voice of reproof. Better times may come, and the delightful anticipations of the poet may be realized, future ages bringing

> " Peace and good will, good will and peace,
> Peace and good will to all mankind."

I look back with complacency on my government of Hong Kong, which I held for five years, and on surrendering the post received the thanks of the Conservative Minister of the Colonies. I had during my tenure of office the pleasure of seeing the population nearly trebled, and the shipping trade increased nearly cent. per cent. I not only made the revenue, in which there had been a great deficit, equal the expenditure, but I left a large balance in the treasury chest. I carried out the principles of Free Trade to their fullest possible extent, and did not impose even a harbour-due to pay the expenses of the service. Vessels came from every quarter and from every nation. They entered, they departed, and no official interfered, except to record whence they came or whither they went. The tonnage increased from 300,000 to 700,000 tons of square-rigged vessels, to say nothing of the large native junk trade. The harbour (one of the finest in the world, having an extent of safe anchorage exceeding five miles) is always crowded with shipping, more than a hundred vessels being ordinarily in port, in addition to the steamers—frequently as many as twenty—and the ships of war of all the great maritime powers. An enterprising individual made docks equal, if not superior, to any east of the Cape, and there is no element of prosperity and progress which has not been wonderfully developed.

The revenues are furnished by the ground rent of houses, the opium monopoly, the judicial fees, &c., but there is no direct taxation. The value of land has increased rapidly, and indeed land is the main source of income. On my recommendation, the Legislative Council had an infusion of many non-official names, but I am not sure that the colony was ripe for this sort of representation, and I think that more might have been done by the executive without the popular element.

Some time ago there was a great deal of clamour in praise of Chusan and depreciation of Hong Kong, and Sir Henry Pottinger was blamed for having chosen the latter in preference to the former. Though the mortality among our troops in Tinghai was exceedingly great, the climate was represented to be more salubrious, the geographical position more favourable, and it was said that the greater adjacency to Peking would enable us to exercise far more influence than in the remoter island of the south, while it was averred that Chusan would give much greater facilities to trade than Hong Kong could ever offer. Experience has belied all these predictions. Hong Kong is as healthy as any of our tropical colonies, its trade is enormous and constantly increasing, owing to its being in the neighbourhood of Canton, and to its having always a large fleet in the bay, and it is an object of greater apprehension to the Chinese authorities than our possession of Chusan could ever have been; but the truth is that the influence of either at the Court of Peking has always been almost *nil*.

I do not know that I could better illustrate the character of the great *Kwans* or Mandarins of China, than by personal sketches of two or three of them, with whom I was more intimately associated while British Plenipotentiary in China, and I will select Yeh, the viceroy of the Two Kwangs; Wang, the viceroy of Fookien; and Keih, the governor of Kiangsoo.

All the superior authorities have received Imperial instructions, which may be summed up in two sentences—" Keep the barbarians at a distance," and " take care not to involve the Emperor in annoying disputes." It will be easily seen that the practical application of these two principles would depend very much upon the personal character of the individual authority. Yeh gave all his care to the first of these lessons, being very reckless as regards the second; for, while his measures were most repulsive to strangers, he forgot that they might involve his master in many disasters, as in fact they did, so that he brought upon China the last war, with all its mischiefs and miseries. Canton has generally been ruled by a man of more obstinacy than prudence. Kesheu had greatly offended the Emperor by telling him that he was unable to resist the power of the western barbarians, and the " Son of heaven " directed that he should be sawn in two for his inaptitude of judging of the foreigner; but having powerful friends at Court, the execution of the sentence was delayed, and it was afterwards commuted into banishment, from which he was recalled into the public service, and became the Chinese Ambassador at Lhassa, in Tibet, where Father Huc saw him. Huc had so completely mastered the Chinese and Manchoo languages that he was not discovered to be other than a Chinese subject, until Kesheu, who had had much experience of foreign nations while at Canton, found out that he was nothing better than a Christian Missionary.

Yeh succeeded two viceroys, each of whom had obtained considerable celebrity. The career of Lin, the most renowned of the viceroys in China, whose literary reputation was of the very highest order, was most disastrous, for he was the cause of the opium war, and suddenly fell in consequence from the height of popularity into the depth of degradation. He too was exiled into the cold country, for in China no man is forgiven whose policy has proved unsuccessful, but Lin also was summoned to court when the affairs of the empire were entangled in difficulty. He was despatched to the south, and on his way thither died at Foochow, the capital of the province in which he was born. Seu, who was then made viceroy, was less unfortunate in carrying out the policy of contempt for western nations, but he was made very uncomfortable in the latter part of his vice-royalty, when he was associated with Yeh, then governor of Kwangtung. Yeh was the very incarnation of wrong-headedness, and when I begged some of the mandarins of his council to induce him to make some small concessions,—all such as were promised by treaty engagements,—they answered that they might as well talk to the rocks as to the viceroy. Again and again I requested him to grant me an interview, which he perseveringly refused. He would not come to the consulate or to Hong Kong, nor receive me in his own *yamun*, under the pretence that he could not protect me from the violence of the people. This was a false plea, and I answered that I would bring with me a force sufficient to secure me from danger if he would consent to give me an interview. He was a most industrious administrator, wrote his own despatches, which, like those of Lin, were much admired for their correctness of style, and he obtained great credit at court and among his countrymen for knowing well how to manage the English barbarians. In the official papers which fell into our hands (on the capture of Canton), we found much evidence of the exalted opinion formed of his sagacity, his course of action being recommended to the imitation of the other viceroys. When Sir John Davis seized all the Bogue forts, and menaced Canton, Keying entered into an engagement that in two years from that period, namely, in April 1849, entrance into the city should be allowed to the British. The time being arrived, Seu refused to give effect to the agreement, but said he would refer the matter again to the Emperor, whose answer was, " Keep the barbarians out if you can." It is greatly to be regretted that this infraction of treaty rights was not there and then resented, but the British government, desiring to avoid controversy, and perhaps not attaching sufficient importance to the question, consented to leave it in abeyance, giving the viceroy to understand, however, that the treaty-right was by no means relinquished. The Peking Court was delighted with the success of Seu's policy, and a cornucopia of presents and honours was showered down upon him, and upon those whom he reported as having co-operated with him. The Emperor declared in an Imperial rescript that he had shed tears of joy on learning the success which had attended the wise but prudent course pursued by the viceroy, and six triumphal arches of granite were ordered to be erected in the name of the Emperor at the principal entrances to the city of Canton. A copy of the Imperial letter was engraved on each of the columns, with the names of the meritorious patriots who had laboured with the viceroy to maintain the dignity of China, and to bring about the humiliation of the foreigners. About the same time, a gathering of the dignitaries of the province took place at the famous Poloo temple, where a foreign idol is worshipped, the image showing that it must have been an Indian whose body was interred, and whose person was deified by the Chinese. It was represented that his influence over the British had led to their submission. Yeh, profoundly learned in the literature, and a master of the language of China, was, beyond all belief, ignorant of all that characterizes western civilization. He was given to the study of necromancy, and many astrological horoscopes were found among his papers. Being a thorough predestinarian, and believing that "the city of rams"* was under the protection of the five genii whose

---

* It is a tradition among the Chinese that when, in very remote times, the city was visited by famine, five rams entered it, each bearing a sheaf of corn, and that an abundant supply of food followed their advent. These rams were afterwards converted into the five tutelar genii, and five rude stones in the temple are still shown as their representatives.

temple in Canton was the object of the most superstitious reverence, he scarcely made any preparations for its defence, and though walled and fortified, and containing à million of inhabitants, it was captured by a small body of British and French troops and marines with a very trifling sacrifice of life.

Yeh was dreadfully sanguinary in his policy. The executions at Canton frequently amounted to many hundreds a day, and on my asking him, when he was a prisoner on board a British ship at Hong Kong, whether it was true, as I had heard, that he had caused the decapitation of seventy-two thousand persons, he answered, with a sort of triumphant energy, " more than a hundred thousand, of whom three thousand were chiefs." The Chinese code professes to be very tender of the life of man, and under ordinary circumstances no man is put to death except by a warrant from the Emperor, but there are cases in which this finality is suspended, and the powers of life and death are confided to a viceroy. How Yeh used this power is visible in the bloody records of his government, and it may be doubted whether any example is to be found of such holocausts of human sacrifice as took place under his rule.

After Yeh, on his capture, had ascertained that he was not to be put to death, a fate which he undoubtedly expected, he exhibited a stolid indifference to all that was passing. He wholly neglected his person, wore filthy garments, scarcely ever submitted himself to an ablution, and only on one or two occasions, such as on visits from myself or the Admiral, did he put on his mandarin costume. He complained, however, that he was given in charge of a captain with two gold stripes instead of three, which, he thought, was an offence to his dignity. When he reached Hong Kong, he professed utter indifference as to the aspect of the colony, saying he knew all about it, and had nothing to learn. On my enquiring whether I could render him any services, he said no, but after a few days he requested me to provide for him some medicine, which, he said, was necessary to his health, and some of the peculiar tobacco which he was accustomed to smoke. One lady was introduced to him by the general, but he turned away as if in disgust, and would not favour her with a single glance. On board the ship was the correspondent of the *Times*, to whom he took a great antipathy. On reaching Calcutta, he exhibited the same *insouciance*, saying he cared nothing about the place, but he was more than once detected looking out of the port-holes as the vessel passed up the Hoogly. After he landed, offers were frequently made to him to show him the city, but he always declined. I sent him the Imperial decree which announced his degradation, but he only said he expected it. An honourable M.P. who visited him said he had taken his part in the House of Commons, as he thought Yeh was right and Bowring wrong in the Cantonese quarrel, but when he was gone, Yeh exclaimed " Umph ! and do such men make the laws of England ? " A credit for money was sent to him, of which he never availed himself. He died in Calcutta, but his corpse was conveyed back to China, where it met little honour at the hands of his countrymen. The Indian government intended to bury him in the Chinese cemetery at Calcutta, but the people of that nation, who are almost exclusively of inferior rank, remonstrated, saying, " that the other ghosts would not like it."

Wang was a more timid and cautious politician than Yeh, and though he equally desired to keep foreigners at a distance, he avoided any steps which might complicate the relations of the empire with the Treaty Powers. When I visited Foochow, I sent him a message that I wished to pay him my respects in person, but he endeavoured on various pretexts to elude the interview, sending several mandarins of rank instead, whom I refused to receive, and insisted on the rights established to hold personal intercourse with the great authorities of the State. After much correspondence, in which, by the way, he employed some characters representing superiority, and opposed to that equality between the British and Chinese sovereigns fixed by treaty, he gave way, and appointed a time for receiving me officially at his *yamun* within the gates of the city ; but having been given to understand that it was his purpose that I should be met, not at the great portal, through which all the high dignitaries of the empire pass, but at the entrance used by mandarins of lower rank, I informed him that I must be received in the same way as the highest Chinese functionary. Accompanied by a large escort, our sedans reached the *yamun*, but we heard, as we passed through the streets, that our expectations would be disappointed as to the honours to which I was entitled. The bearers of the sedan deposited me at the great entrance, the doors of which were opened at the appearance of the Governor, who came forward, took me by the hand, and escorted me in the presence of a prodigious number of mandarins through a succession of apartments to the interior, where he placed me in the seat of honour. He apologized for the delays and difficulties which had taken place, exculpating himself without much regard to truth. I then pointed out to him the discourtesy in the phraseology of the letter he had addressed to me, when he declared that the fault was attributable to the ignorance of the scribe, whom he offered to summon and punish in my presence, but I assured him I should be perfectly satisfied if the becoming alteration were made, which was immediately done with all the forms of urbanity, and the expression of a wish to cultivate the most friendly relations with the subjects of Great Britain. He directed the immediate redress of some grievances which

P

I represented to him as complained of by our merchants, particularly in reference to obtaining legal titles to lands which they had purchased at Nantai, on the banks of the Min, where most of the foreign warehouses are built. Nothing could have been more satisfactory than the results of the conference, and I have generally observed in China that where matters in dispute can be discussed with the high authorities, amicable arrangements are the result. Had the viceroys of Canton been willing to hold friendly communications with our plenipotentiaries, both the Chinese wars might have been avoided.

Of all the mandarins of China, Keih had formed the most correct notion of the power of Western nations, and the desirableness of maintaining with them relations of concilia- tion and amity. He was killed, and his army utterly de- feated in a battle with the rebels at Chin-Kiang-foo. He had lived at Shanghai, where he had seen much of the wealth and prowess of foreigners, the trade of that place exceeding twenty millions sterling, and the receipts of the custom-house, collected with the assistance of foreign agents, amounting to from two to three million ounces of silver. On several occasions he was made the channel of intercourse with the court of Peking, where he represented himself to be very influential, assuring us that he should be able to prepare the way for the establishment of a more friendly policy towards the Treaty Powers, but in this he wholly failed, and the ministers were obliged to proceed to the Tientsin River, where they had no success whatever in ob- taining those reasonable modifications of the treaty which might have prevented collision. It was under Keih's government that the rebels held the city of Shanghai; many attempts being made at his request to get rid of their pre- sence by assuring safety to their persons, but they were obstinate and unmanageable. They were ultimately dislodged, and principally by the intervention of the French, after having committed incredible horrors in sacking the city and torturing the rich inhabitants.

My intercourse with Keih was not unfrequent, and on one occasion, when the admiral and I went to complain that by. the firing of his troops the lives of some Englishmen had been endangered, he sent for the six men represented as guilty, who were ordered to kneel down, and he offered to decapitate them there and then in our presence, which of course we declined. It was Keih's ambition to be appointed Imperial Commissioner at Canton, where assuredly his policy would have formed a favourable contrast to that adopted by the Viceroys in general. Keih was a Manchoo, and, as far as my experience goes, the Tatar mandarins have been better affected towards the representatives of foreign nations than have the native Chinese. This may be accounted for by the fact that the Tatars have had, from their adjacency to the Russian tribes of the same races, more opportunities of acquiring information as to western affairs than have been enjoyed by their Chinese brethren.

BRITISH INDIA.

When I visited Bengal in 1851, I came to an early, and, I believe, just conclusion that the popularity of the government and the happiness of the people depended far more on the conduct of our local functionaries than on any instructions received from Leadenhall Street or the Board of Control. I shall not now enquire as to the extent to which the prosperity of India may be promoted by its absolute transfer to the rule of the British sovereign, nor enter into the many intricate matters which that question involves. I certainly found among the most intelligent of the Hindoos that British rule was far preferable to that to which they had been subjected under Mahommedan sway, and there was a general confidence in the manner in which justice is administered, and a belief that our officials are not to be diverted from their integrity. I watched with great interest the proceedings of the supreme tribunals, and frequently attended the *kutcherries*, or subordinate courts, where there are so many opportunities of studying native character. One could not but be shocked by the mass of contradictory evidence and consequent mendacity. At that time, all was conducted by written depositions, often of the most elaborate and confused character, prepared by the native lawyers, crowds of whom were assembled, either in the chambers adjacent to the Kutcherry, or seated in the compound that surrounded it. There was generally a large auditory, appearing to take a deep interest in all that was passing. In the department of criminal justice especially every species of misrepresentation was employed, above all in defence of the accused, an alibi being the most frequent plea, and it required the utmost sagacity on the part of the judge to see his way through the entangled mass upon which he was about to pronounce judgment. Questions of property, and especially those connected with the soil, were in a most misty state, the removal of landmarks, the imperfect survey, and contradictory traditions involving these matters in obscurity, through which no penetration could discover a way. In England it is not unusual to talk about the settlement of these intricate subjects, as if the labyrinth could be explored by a stroke of the pen or an act of the legislature, but the practical difficulties can only be estimated by those who have local knowledge. It might no doubt be practicable in general terms to separate the rights of the Zemindar from those of the Ryots, but it is scarcely necessary to observe that these have varied in different parts of India from time immemorial, and that great divergence of opinion exists as to what would be, on the whole, the most satisfactory tenure of land.

I believe it has of late become more the practice to subject witnesses to personal examination, a course of proceeding in every respect desirable, and especially to interrogate individually plaintiffs and defendants, who know more of what is relevant to the question than other parties are likely to do. This great reform, so urgently insisted on by Jeremy Bentham, has at last become the law and the usage of England, and by it the ends of justice have been greatly facilitated. But the all-present evil in India is the curse of caste, an evil which one meets on every side, and which tends utterly to destroy that equality in the eye of the law which it is the object of sound legislation to introduce and maintain. It is impossible to calculate the mischief and misery, social and political, which the broad distinctions among the different classes necessarily create ; yet, so inveterate are the prejudices, and so deeply rooted are the habits of the Indian people, that it is difficult to suggest a remedy for so gigantic an evil, and it must be owned that we have in some respects augmented it by the deep abyss which we have established between the whites, who are the ruling few, and the coloured races, who are the subject many. I believe no large amount of military force, either European or native, would be necessary to maintain our domination, if more attention were paid to the usages and opinions of the people. These are often treated with great unconcern, yet I believe the late mutinies found their main strength in the erroneous estimate we had formed of what we called their superstitions. Our people are frequently in the habit of treating the Indians with contumely, and using expressions in their presence deeply wounding to their pride and self-respect. Even in acts, gross insults are sometimes inflicted, as in a case once brought judicially before me, where the captain of a British ship, who had been dissatisfied with the conduct of his Mahommedan cook, ordered a ham to be brought, with which he beat the offender cruelly about the head and even the mouth. It was an outrage of the grossest character, and as the tale would be widely told, one cannot but see how detrimental it would be to our reputation, and how aggravating to the susceptibilities of Moosulmans, who look upon the pig as one of the most unclean of animals.

Most beneficial, without doubt, are many of the schemes proposed for the developement of the resources of India— improved roads, river steam-navigation, and extensive railway lines producing important results ; but it is to irrigation we must mainly look, and anyone who will study the increased value of lands, which attention to the watercourses has given to Lombardy, or compare the great results in Egypt (a country resembling in many respects parts of our Indian dominions), from the overflowing of the Nile, the numerous canals, and the measures taken to carry out a general system of irrigation, will be struck by the enormous amount of produce which Egypt furnishes, contrasted with the miserably small returns from most of our Indian districts.

CEYLON.

The perfumed island, as Ceylon has been called, fragrant with cinnamon and flowers, presents a singular but welcome contrast to parched-up Aden, that volcanic record of prehistoric ages, at which the Oriental steamers touch, to be supplied on their transit with coals.

It is in Ceylon that Booddhism may be studied in its most orthodox forms, the Cingalese priests being deemed the highest authorities. Much of their time is passed in silent meditation, the principal topic of their contemplations being the mysterious manifestation of Booddha, and the manner

in which notions of his eternal existence can be conveyed to
his disciples. The unit of these calculations is a *Kalpa*,
which represents ten thousand of our numerals. Here is an
example of these teachings. There is a huge rock of granite,
and once in a kalpa of years an angel descends, and just
floats by the rock, touching it with the edge of a light
muslin robe. Now there can be no attrition without action.
When you can conceive that the whole of the granite stone
shall have been swept away by the angel's visits, you will .
have an idea of the time which represents the existence of
Booddha; or, suppose an enormous building to be filled with
sand, and that, once in a kalpa, one grain of sand is removed,
when not one is left, the life of Booddha will have but begun.
With such illustrations, the Bonzes profess to explain the
inexplicable, to grasp the infinite, but they certainly succeed
in producing towards themselves a great amount of reverence, greater than that enjoyed by the priests of any other
religious community.

In 1852 I visited their sacred temples. In one of them
is Booddha reposing, carved out of the solid rock, and ten
yards long, the temple being built over the god, while on
the exposed part of the rock outside is the grant, engraved
in Cingalese, by which the kings of Kandy conferred its
rights upon the temple. The government agent, with two
native authorities, each having a key, has custody of the
precious relic, the tooth of Booddha, the possession of which is
supposed to confer the rights of sovereignty over the island
of Ceylon. Unfortunately, one of the authorities was absent,
so I could only see the outside of the chest which contains
the relic. I should have been allowed to see it, the rarest
of favours, had it not been for the absence of this functionary.
There are six chests or coffins of pure gold, one within
another, the outer, or seventh, being of silver gilt, with a
great number of precious stones, its form being somewhat

conical, and its height about three feet. It is enclosed
within iron bars, with the three locks I have mentioned.
The tooth was taken by the Cingalese in the rebellion, but
was recaptured. The King of Siam offered, it is said,
£70,000 to £80,000 for the tooth, so great is its prestige.
There are a good many priests in the temple, but the tooth
is not left in their care, and there is always a guard of
British soldiers in the neighbourhood.

The tropical trees and shrubs in Ceylon, the magnificent
fruits and flowers, remind you of a nursery hot-house on the
largest scale, but a hot-house has no gorgeous butterflies
floating about, no songs of birds, no lizards glancing along
in the sunbeams, no little black children, with their flashing
eyes, ivory teeth, and long pendant hair, in absolute and
utter nakedness ; no men looking just like women, for they
all wear tortoise-shell combs, some of them very large and
tall, as I remember the fashion when I was young. Then
the women, with a single piece of muslin, or sometimes a
short jacket and loose under garment, pass along with their
little ones clinging to their hips, for they seem never to
carry an infant in their arms, as in Europe, or on their
backs, as in China.

The temperature was delightful (in January) and the
scenery enchanting, especially where streams make their
way down from the distant hills, whose very brows are
crowned with gorgeous vegetation.

JAVA.

No greater political blunder was ever committed by
British negotiators than the cession to the Dutch of the
fertile regions of Netherlands India, while we retained a
portion of their West Indian colonies of incomparably less
value. The teeming population, the prolific soil, the excellent roads, and the fine harbours of Java give it advan-

tages rarely enjoyed by any colonial possessions. The resources of Borneo, one of the largest islands in the world,
are for the most part undeveloped, Sumatra being in the
same condition, while in neither have the aboriginal tribes
submitted to the Dutch, who only hold a few spots where
the civil is supported by the military rule. Banca, small
as it is, gives a large revenue to the mother country, being
one of the few places producing that important metal which
brought the ancient Phœnicians to the Cornish Stannaries.
The population of the Dutch archipelago is said to be
nearly thirty millions of souls, and if the choice were offered
to me of being viceroy of these dominions or King of Holland, I should not hesitate to prefer the former dignity. So
rapid is the communication from the excellence of the postal
service, that in 1853 I was conveyed in a carriage from
Batavia to Buitenzorg, a distance of forty miles, in less than
four hours, almost all the way being an ascent. Many
extraordinary public works were accomplished by General
Daendels, who was the Governor-General under Napoleon, and
had much of his character. On one occasion, finding that
the road to Bandong went round the foot of a mountain for
a considerable distance, he collected the native chiefs, and
told them he must have a direct passage made, over which
a carriage could travel. They answered that this was impossible, and that there would be a great sacrifice of human
life, on which he observed that roads put an end to intestine
wars, and that it was better that lives should be sacrificed
on useful works than in useless feuds, while as regards the
impossibility of the work, he should order a gallows to be
erected, and would hang every chieftain in the country if
the road was not ready in six months, when he meant to
travel over it. The menace did not fail of its purpose, for
the road *was* made, and he *did* travel over it. He issued
an arbitrary decree that, whenever he passed, all travellers

should alight under pain of undergoing a public flogging, but a member of his government, who conceived that his high position freed him from the obligation, having omitted to do so, Daendels ordered him to be seized, and the ignominious penalty was inflicted upon him. The official felt the insult so deeply, that at a party which he gave soon afterwards, he proposed as a toast " death to General Daendels." This having been reported to the Governor-General, he invited the offender to meet a large party at the palace, and such invitations having the character of commands, the outraged functionary took his seat at the table. The Governor-General then himself proposed a toast, "to the death of General Daendels," on which the official, without any hesitation, said, "I drink your toast." The General, hearing this, offered him his hand, told him to uncover a dish on the table in which were two loaded pistols, and observed, " You say to my face what you have said behind my back, I honour your honest courage, and claim your friendship. You and I should otherwise have met, and one life would certainly have been sacrificed had you shown any poltroonery." Though probably in these days acts so tyrannical could not be practised towards any European, yet the natives and the Chinese have often to complain of the irresponsible despotism exercised by the Dutch functionaries.

The number of settlers from the Flowery Land is nearly a hundred and fifty thousand, and when I was in Java, I learned that there was only one China woman among them. I knew a wealthy Chinese merchant at Samarang who exercised authority over ten thousand men of his nation. He received me with some ostentation, met me with a considerable escort some miles from his abode, and conveyed me in a state-carriage, which had belonged to one of the viceroys, to the place of my destination. He gave me a grand entertainment, to which all the principal officials and leading inhabitants were invited. I had known him in China, and had been able to afford him some protection from the exactions of the Mandarins. One of the objects of his visit was to obtain the consent of his wife to accompany him back to Java, but such is the stigma attached to the abandonment of her country by any female, and such the surveillance exercised by the clan to which she belongs, that no exertions and no money sacrifices enabled him to effect his purpose. This is not the only case which occurred during my residence in China of the failure of such attempts. I was requested by a Chinese, who had made a large fortune in the Straits Settlements, to endeavour to accomplish the removal of some female members of his family, he being willing to pay a large sum for the purpose, but, although it is supposed that there is no high Chinese official who cannot be tempted by a large bribe, in this instance also, there was nothing but failure, for the mandarins dared not encounter the obloquy which the removal of a female would have certainly created. Yet the emigration of Chinamen to various parts of the east must amount to many millions. In the city of Bangkok alone there are reported to be more than a hundred thousand, while the whole number settled in the Siamese dominions is believed to exceed considerably a million, a similar state of things existing in the islands of the Indian archipelago, where the great success which attends persevering exertion, accompanied by temperance and economy, makes the Chinese the subject of distrust and dislike to the aborigines, who have few of the qualities which lead to the accumulation of wealth, and who labour as little as they can, and then generally only for the supply of their daily wants.

At Bandong I took up my abode with the Toemenggong or Regent, who wore rich diamonds, and a golden dress

sparkling with precious stones. Everybody, including all
the servants, crouched to the ground whenever he appeared. His government (always subject to the Dutch,
however), was over one of the richest and most picturesque
regions I have ever seen, and the people seemed extremely
happy. He invited me to be present at the marriage of his
wife's brother. We were introduced with music and artillery into a large hall, in which were Moosulman priests all
on their knees, while in the centre sat a youth with a golden
helmet, his breast bare, but the rest of his body oppressed
by the burden of gold ornaments, splendid robes, and a
quantity of diamonds and other jewels. The principal
priest came and knelt before him, two others kneeling behind on small carpets. Attendants came in, and covered
the young man with a white sheet to remind him of the
vanity of worldly pomp, while the high priest read, or sang,
from the Koran all the verses which speak of marital
duties. He alone was allowed to touch or to come near
the bridegroom, on account of his exalted rank, while the
others bowed their heads to the ground from some distance.
Then the attendants brought in the bride, a rather pretty
and modest looking girl, whom they unveiled, and she too
was encumbered by jewels and splendid garments. She sat
on a chair on the right side of her husband, now and then
glancing timidly round, while offerings were presented, and
betel-nut distributed to the attendant priests. The bridegroom came to receive his father's blessing, and that of the
other gentlemen of the family, the Regent among them. I
gave him a hearty shake of the hand, and we were
then escorted from the bridal chamber with torches and
music.

I visited the volcano of Tang-koeban-praoe, and was
accompanied by a troop of mounted men in the liveries of
the Regent, and by a great number of petty chiefs, who,

with their followers, turned out to escort us. Music was prepared in the villages, and, on reaching the foot of the mountain, I should think a hundred attendants went with us through the vast woods which we had to penetrate. The forests were gloriously beautiful with trees covered with flowers, ferns twenty or thirty feet high, orchids hanging down from the branches, and singing birds around, but when we reached the upper regions, all was desolation, the trees being scathed and stripped by the eruptions of the volcano, whose sulphureous outpourings filled the atmosphere. We went to the top, and looked into the crater, where the hot waters were boiling and bubbling from the depths below. The wildness of the place is as wonderful as the Eden-like look of the forests beneath, and there is a vast expanse of scenery visible in the distance.

At Cheribon I went to see the tombs of the Sultans, which are a strange mixture of the old and the modern, the beautiful and the grotesque. They are reached through a plain with splendid trees, and are surrounded by tessellated walls, on which Chinese porcelain-plates of all sizes, and Dutch tiles with Scriptural pictures, exactly such as amused my childhood, are among the ornaments, with all sorts of vases and jars, the government allowing three thousand rupees yearly to keep the tombs in repair. The innermost is deemed holy, being that of the founder of the dynasty, and is locked, no Christian being permitted to enter. At one place where we halted, about eight miles from Koeningan, the musicians and people were congregated under an immense and much-venerated tree, on measuring which, at three or four feet from the ground, we found its girth to be sixty-three feet. The gardens and grottos of the former native rulers at Cheribon were laid out by a Chinese architect, whom the Sultan murdered in order that he might make nothing so beautiful for any one else. They are all

in ruins, having been shaken by an earthquake, but resembled exactly what I had seen in China, and what one
observes in Chinese pictures and porcelain.

The people all looked meek and docile, robberies being
very rare, and though they sometimes run what is called
" a-muck," killing and wounding every one they meet, I
was told this only happened when they were under the influence of opium, and that the outbreak was generally
caused by some motive of jealousy. Throughout the Tegal
district I saw at every station a curious fork for catching
such unruly people, the sharp spiked points fixed along
each branch of the fork being the prickles of a certain
species of bamboo.

After visiting the famous temple of Boro-Buddor, I went
to see the Merapi, or eternal fires, places where flames are
constantly bursting forth from the earth's surface, sometimes through waterponds, and at others merely through the
soil, the hydrogen igniting when it comes in contact with
the atmosphere. Then, accompanied by a great number of
native chieftains, we went to the Moddenvell, a vast pond
of liquid mud, which the action of the internal fire tosses
up in violent heavings, like a huge caldron. Its appearance
for a moment is smooth and quiet, and then with loud
noises the liquid mud is hurled into the air, agitating from
one side to the other the pond's vast extent. Some of the
ponds are in the centre of hillocks, which have been raised
by the falling mud when hardened by the action of
the sun.

At Toeban I inspected a tree eighty-six feet in circumference, a single trunk nearly two hundred feet high, called
in Malay the Randor Alas—the wild-cotton tree, I believe.
I visited the tombs of the ancient sovereigns, and a beautiful bath overshadowed by tall banyan trees, and descended
into a grotto of almost boundless extent, whose alleys and

arches represent an infinite variety of forms, and as we were accompanied by many men bearing large lighted torches, the effect was sublime.

While I was at Pasoeroean, the Resident, a warm-hearted Dutchman of the old school, invited me to accompany him to the Bromo volcano situated in the wild and wondrous scenery of the Tengger Hills. We started before daybreak, and saw the volcano blazing in the dark distance, lightnings and thunder bursting from the neighbouring mountain. Preceded by horsemen bearing torches, and lighted by those of the peasantry as we went along, our carriage took us to the foot of the Bromo, where we found chairs, with roofs and supported by bamboos, and with no less than sixteen bearers to each, which conveyed us over roads, and through ravines and woodland-passes which often looked perilous. How the bearers made their way with their bare feet over sharp rocks and stony places, through deep mud, masses of lava, the roots of forest trees, and numerous other impediments, I know not, but they are patterns of docility and good humour. We breakfasted at Torarie, 5,373 feet high, and then proceeded to the volcano through the grandest forest scenery, looking up to heights and down into depths covered with all the magnificent vegetation of the tropics. The people brought wild raspberries from the woods, and I saw many a white rose in the banks and braes. At last, from the top of a high headland, we looked down upon what is called the lake of sand, it being the crater of an extinct volcano, and after descending about half a mile on foot along a most precipitous and crooked path, I leaning on the arm of one of the native chiefs, who took as much care of me as if I had been his father, we reached the sandy sea, and traversed it for three miles to the bottom of the Bromo volcano. Supported by my friendly Javanese, I mounted two hundred and forty steps to reach the top of the crater, and looked down upon the smoke issuing from several parts of the vast basin.

I visited the island of Banca, which, for its extent, is one of the most populous and productive of the Dutch settlements, the tin found in it being of excellent quality and in great abundance. The only workers in the mines are Chinamen, of whom there were about five thousand employed, their general term of engagement being five years, while their industry enables them to save sufficient to purchase a small farm in their native land, to which they are so passionately attached that their corpses are taken back to be interred in the places occupied by their departed forefathers. The Government informed me that the supply of emigrants was always equal to the demand, and that it was considered a privilege in China to emigrate to Banca.

My visit in Java was to the Governor-General Deymaar van Twist, from whom I received every courtesy, and was accompanied by one of his aides-de-camp in my explorations. Our hosts were generally the native chiefs, among whom we had an opportunity of witnessing the mode of living which, as to their meals, seemed characterized by the use of an enormous quantity and a great variety of heating condiments. I saw as many as twenty sorts upon a waiter, and undoubtedly something is required to give piquancy to the rice, which is the foundation of all their culinary preparations. The Dutch functionaries live in their own homely style, varied in some cases by *recherché* French cookery, but generally the simplicity of ancient manners is maintained.

At Buitenzorg I was invited to an exhibition of biology. After failing with five persons, three soldiers, whom the biologist saw for the first time, and who were sent for by the commander of the regiment, were, after certain passes and processes, placed so completely under the control of the biologist that they lost absolutely all liberty of action. At his command they slept and woke, visited Holland, described the places they saw, and drank of whatever beverage he ordered them to partake, cold water being turned into hot punch, madeira, port wine, and sundry other drinks. He set them down to dinner before an empty table, pieces of wood being turned into knives and forks. They cut up their meat and potatoes, appeared to eat the dessert (out of empty plates), picked up cherry after cherry, throwing the stones away, and giving, as they thought, fruit to those who were near. They were ordered to skate, and seemed to put on their skates, complaining that the ice (the floor) was so difficult to skate upon. They were taken to a menagerie, when one suddenly exclaimed that the door of the tiger's den was open, and he ran away in an awful fright, saying that the beast was following him. Another was made to fancy that he was drowning at sea, exhibited all the marks of fear, and took to swimming for his life. They were made dumb several times, and no menace, even of their commanding officer, whom they recognized, could extort a word. Things changed their colour at the command of the biologist, and a large sum of money was offered if they would strike him, which they made many an effort to do, but the hand was always arrested before it reached him. They were, as it were, fastened to the ground limb by limb, and even one finger after another, and were released in the same way, after incredible but vain efforts to relieve themselves. They could not break a rush, or even a straw, upon their knees with all their force, till allowed to do so. One was made to believe that he was playing on a drum, another on a hand-organ, and when the latter was requested to sing, though he protested he could not, such was the power of the biologist that he compelled him to do so, the singing being most grotesque. One was made a corporal, and began to command the others, showing his

Q

chevrons with great delight, but was disappointed on awaking to find that he was only a private. Another was made to see the girl whom he was courting, and who was in Holland. Again, another was told that the biologist would heat a florin which he placed in his hand, and declared that it grew hotter and hotter, till at last he flung it down, being unable to hold it any longer. Being ordered to let drop a handkerchief which they held, it was impossible for them to do so, and when allowed to let it fall, they could not pick it up again. They were ordered to tie it in a knot, and made many efforts to do so, but in vain. The three were employed some time in endeavouring to blow out a candle, which was close to their mouths, but, in spite of all their attempts, their breath always passed on one side or the other. They all made several trials at putting a small stick into an empty bottle, but could not find the way to its open mouth. These are only some of the strange things exhibited, the performance lasting some hours. They could not in the slightest degree account for the power exercised over them, but said it was absolutely irresistible. The biologist was a marine officer—modest and intelligent.

SIAM.

One of the most interesting parts of my public life was my visit to Siam in 1855, of which I published an account in two volumes, called " Siam and the Siamese." There had been many attempts on the part of the United States of America, of the Governor General of British India, and of the English government, to establish diplomatic and commercial relations, but they had utterly failed. Sir James Brooke, the Rajah of Saráwak, had visited the Meinam, and endeavoured to open a correspondence with the Siamese authorities, but his reception was so unfriendly that he was compelled to break off all negotiations.

The country was crushed by monopolies, almost every article
of produce was made an exclusive property, and there were
only two vessels engaged in the foreign trade. An obstinate
and ignorant illegitimate son had succeeded to the throne ;
but on his death the nobility clamoured for the recognition of
the legitimate descendant, a remarkable man, who had
retired from public life, and made his person sacred by
becoming a Booddhist priest, and withdrawing to a convent,
where for eleven years he devoted himself to the study of
Sanskrit, Pali, and other Oriental tongues. He learned
Latin from the French Catholic Missionaries, at whose
head was Bishop Pallegoix, the author of the Thai dictionary
and grammar, and of one of the best accounts of Siam ; and
English from the American Missionaries, who for many
years had a Protestant Propaganda in Siam, where, if truth
be told, they laboured with little success.

The new King, who was a most enlightened, sagacious,
and enquiring man, had been a correspondent of mine, and
received in an amiable spirit the overtures I made him. I
informed him—which indeed he knew well, for he had a
pretty accurate knowledge of Oriental and European politics—that I had a large fleet at my disposal, but that I
would rather visit him as a friend than as the bearer of a
menacing message. He wrote to me to request that, in order
not to alarm his subjects, I would come with a small naval
escort, so I steamed to the Meinam, with two vessels of
war, one of which, the " Rattler," conveyed me and my
suite to Siam.

We were advised by the American Missionaries that I
must expect to fail as other envoys had failed, that the Siamese were preparing barricades on the river, and giving
other evidence of an unfriendly spirit, that the Court was
hostile to strangers, and that our conquests in India had
awakened and seemed to justify their apprehensions.

Arrived at the mouth of the river, I sent my secretaries to the capital, where they had little reason to be pleased with their reception, as they were kept in a sort of imprisonment, and not allowed communications beyond their abode. The King, however, determined to send down one of his steamers to Paknam, to ask more specifically the purposes of my mission, and to beg that they might be put in writing for his information. A similar request had been made to Sir James Brooke, who had complied with it, and was soon involved in an irregular and entangled controversy. My answer was a refusal to enter upon such correspondence, as it might involve me in making demands which it might be inexpedient or impossible for them to grant, and exclude topics which it might be important for both parties to introduce. I said I should prefer some preliminary conversation, in which they could explain to me their position and objects, and hear from me what I thought we might reasonably expect from them.

The negotiations were thus opened, but many difficulties arose which had to be vanquished. They wished the ships of war to remain at the mouth of the river, to which I could not consent, as, independently of their being necessary to my comfort, they and their officers were requisite appendages to my mission. Then the Siamese requested that the guns might be left in their keeping, while the ships ascended the river, a condition equally inadmissible. Next the King sent down a number of royal barges, magnificently adorned, in the shape of dragons and peacocks, with gold and crimson silk drapery, to escort me to the city in all dignity, as if we were Siamese of the highest rank. I accepted the proffered courtesy, but requested that the "Rattler" should follow in our wake. After a day's delay, this point was conceded, but they wished to impose another condition, namely, that no salutes should be fired, as this might frighten the people. I urged, however, that it was out of the question for us to see the flag of the White Elephant (the Siamese ensign) flying on the palace without saluting it, and that I expected a return salute of seventeen guns, but I suggested that the King should announce by proclamation our intended arrival as friends, and that the salutation of his flag was a respect paid to him by the Queen of England. I added that it would be wise to send some of his State Officers on board the " Rattler," to witness the ceremonies, and then matters were comfortably and peacefully arranged.

On arriving at the court, however, a new perplexity awaited us, as no man was allowed to approach the king's person with any weapon, but I informed them that we always wore swords when received by our sovereign, and I was able to show that M. Chaumont, who had been the ambassador of Louis XIV., had worn his sword in the presence of the then king, and that I was the representative of a monarch certainly as great as the sovereign of France. The king sent for me at night, and conducted me secretly to the audience-hall, where I settled with him all the terms of precedence, respecting which he was glad to be instructed, as he would know how to arrange matters for other ambassadors who might follow me. I said that I could not ask the officers of Her Majesty's naval service to divest themselves of an ornament which was a part of their official costume, in which they were bound to show their respect for a foreign power.

The King's throne was an elevated recess, regally adorned. He wore a high, splendid crown, with many precious stones, and held his sceptre in his hand, while near him were the members of the royal family, which comprised then forty or fifty sons. We passed to the centre of the hall, all the nobles being on their faces in the presence of their monarch.

A cushion had been provided for me to sit on, while my suite stood around me. I made my address to the King, but though His Majesty understood English, it was translated into Siamese for the benefit of the audience, while the king's answer was translated from Siamese into English, that all the replies might be intelligible to our party. The following day similar ceremonies were performed in the presence of the second King. There was an interchange of presents, and I was sorry to see that the telescope which was among the gifts sent by the Queen, was far inferior to those which the King had, already in his observatory. Among other presents which His Majesty handed to me was one which he said was of greater value than all the rest. It was a golden box, locked with a golden key, in which were some hairs of the tail of the sacred white elephant tied with floss silk. The possession of a white elephant is considered a high privilege, it being believed to be one of those incarnations in which Booddha loves to dwell, an emblem of purity, though the skin is not white but of a coffee colour. The elephant is kept in a beautifully ornamented stable, is fed upon sugar-cane, is waited on by Siamese dignitaries, and, whenever it goes forth to bathe, is covered with splendid drapery, preceded by music, and accompanied by reverential crowds.

After the reception, the King sent for me to visit him privately in his apartments, and said he had understood perfectly every word in my address except one, of which he desired an explanation. He had no garment on but his shirt, and held a child on his knee, utterly naked, but wearing a wreath of fragrant white flowers. He was fond of his children, and wrote me a letter five months after my visit, which began, " Plenty of Royalty! five children have been born to me since you left."

The Siamese laws about etiquette are so rigid that no

man is allowed to cross a bridge if a noble be passing on the
water below, and if an individual of inferior rank is found
in an upper apartment when visited by a superior, he must
either descend, or the superior, instead of ascending the
staircase, makes his entrance through the window, in order
to maintain a more elevated position. A curious exhibition
of this feeling occurred on board the " Rattler," when a
member of the royal family visited her. He saw in the
cabin several images of Booddha, over which the sailors were
accustomed to walk upon deck. He showed great distress
at what he deemed a profanation, and offered a large sum
of money for the idols, as it would have been a merit
recognised in a future state of existence to have released the
emanation from the godhead from a state of ignominy. I
was not able to comply with his request, and informed him
that, with the feelings of Christian people, it was quite
impossible to give any security that the images of Booddha
would not frequently be placed in a similar position. It is
remarkable, however, that the King repudiated all the
teachings of the Bonzes, which are inconsistent with the
discovered truths of natural philosophy, particularly those
of a geographical and astronomical character, to the study
of which he had specially devoted himself. He had a large
collection of telescopes, quadrants, and other instruments,
was able to calculate an eclipse, and had himself published
an almanack for the use of his people. He insisted that the
vulgar errors which are prevalent in Siam now, as they were
formerly in Europe, are not warranted by the earlier revelations of Gautama, who lived about the time of Confucius
and Herodotus, and is deemed the last incarnation of
Booddha manifested to the world. It is remarkable that a
similar philosophical spirit distinguishes the reformed
Brahmins of India, who repudiate the corruptions found in
the Shâstras, and aver that there is no authority for such

adulterations in the more ancient and far more sacred books, the Vedas. Among the Reformed Hebrews, there is a similar determination to reject the teachings of the Talmud, as having no divine authority, while even in the Christian Church, many are bringing into the field of discussion opinions which, a few centuries ago, would undoubtedly have been deemed heterodox and heretical. In China, the learned Confucians treat with utter contempt the hundreds of volumes of legendary rubbish which have been introduced by the Booddhist and Taouist priests. In fact, a new spirit of religious investigation pervades the whole eastern and western world, and, in the course of a few centuries, will no doubt modify opinions now deeply rooted and widely spread.

The king of Siam used to express an opinion that what he called *the Superior Intelligence* had given different religions, each specially adapted to the locality and people to whom his will had been conveyed. He put no impediment in the way of the teachings of either Catholic or Protestant missionaries, saying, what was most true, that they had made few, if any, converts among his people. There are at Bangkok a considerable number of professing Catholic Christians, but they mostly belong to the mixed races, the descendants of the Portuguese, while the few converts whom the Protestant missionaries claim are to be found principally among the Chinese settlers. There is probably no nation, with the exception of the Cingalese, so attached to Booddhist rites and doctrines as are the inhabitants of Siam. Every Siamese passes three months of his life in a convent, where the priests instruct him in the creed of Booddha, and it must be acknowledged that as a race, the Siamese Bonzes are incomparably more intelligent than those found in China, or any of the remoter regions of Eastern Asia. Time has produced great changes in the action of different sects, for, though Christians only are now to be found sending forth teachers to carry on the work of conversion, there was a period when the missionaries of Booddhism covered the face of China, made their way to the court, and persuaded millions of men to embrace their faith. Though the Mahommedans, after the death of the prophet, despatched their priests to the Flowery Land, they were less successful than the advocates of Booddhism and Brahminism, who came from India.

The Mormons have exhibited much zeal in the propagation of their extraordinary revelation, and boast of having made from sixty to seventy thousand converts in England and Wales alone—a greater number probably than the Protestant missionaries could claim in all the regions of the East. While I was Governor of Hong Kong, an American, who looked and spoke as if he came from the back-woods of the United States, visited me, charged, as he said, with a special mission to China, and, producing his credentials, said that if I would listen to him, I might effect a wonderful religious revolution. " Signs, and wonders, and miracles," he added, " have accompanied our progress, and evidence of divine approval is seen in the immense multitudes that have joined our standard." I replied, "Though I am much occupied with public business, work now a miracle in my presence. Turn this pewter inkstand into stone, walk on the ceiling with your head downwards, or do anything supernatural, and I will acknowledge at once the authority which you represent." " Ah!" said he, "you are but one of a faithless and unbelieving generation," and he left my presence. I heard afterwards that he went to the parade-ground, haranguing an auditory, of whom scarcely any understood a word that he said, and inveighing bitterly against the incredulity and deafness of the place. He ended by speaking of his poverty, and a British sailor, touched by commiseration, flung some money towards him

as a charitable contribution. Of the future fate of this
adventurer I never heard.

On one occasion the King of Siam delivered over a great
number of Anamite prisoners to Pallegoix, the Catholic
Bishop, telling him that he might convert them to Christianity if he could.

I may add in conclusion that the Anglo-Siamese Treaty
has brought most beneficial fruits. The number of vessels
engaged in foreign trade has been centupled, the sides of
the Meinam are crowded with docks, the productive
powers of the land have increased, and with them the
natural [augmentation of property, and the rise of wages.
The number of Chinese who are settled in Siam have greatly
aided the natural developement, and intercourse with
Europeans has not introduced, as in many parts of the
world, the deteriorating effects of intemperance. Siam is a
country of progress, and is sending forth her youth to be
educated in the best schools and colleges of Europe. The
Siamese, like the Japanese, are more aware of the advantages of Christian civilization than are the proud Chinese,
but even upon China that civilization is not without its
beneficent influence.

THE PHILIPPINES.

A serious attack of the intermittent fever, which is the
chronic malady of many parts of the east, compelled me in
1858 to seek the remedy of a sea voyage, and I determined
to visit the Philippine Islands, into which a more liberal
policy had lately been introduced.

In these islands Spain possesses a great treasure, and at
some future time they will become one of the greatest em-
poriums of commerce, and one of the widest fields for the
production of tropical articles. The number of islands is
very large, and in fact not fully ascertained, as only a few

of them have been wholly subjected to Spanish dominion, while, even in these, authority is maintained by the occasional presence of military force. Even the friars, with all their missionary zeal, have not penetrated into the interior of any of the larger islands. In Mindanao the Spaniards only possess some territory on the coast, while the native chieftains, Mahommedans, and idolators retain almost all the inner regions. Manila, and a few other commercial ports, particularly those of Iloilo in the island of Panay, and Sual and Lingayen in the northern part of Luzon, two places which (with Zounboanga) have been lately opened to foreign trade, are giving evidence that these fertile regions are making their way out of obscurity, and that they will ere long prosper in the sunshine of a brighter day.

Their ancient condition was indeed a miserable vassalage. They wore the heavy chains imposed by an unenlightened monopoly, and were placed under the sway, and exposed to the oppressive legislation, of new Spain, which laid upon the Philippines a yoke more intolerable even than that imposed upon herself by the tyranny of the mother country.

In those times the islands were not self-supporting, but drew for large deficits upon the resources of Spanish America, their trade was confined to the narrowest limits, and that trade, though so small, was restricted to a privileged few. But the improved spirit of the age, and the progress of free-trade principles have led, though slowly, to a considerable relaxation of the ancient monopolies. Many European and American merchants are now settled, especially in Manila, and have brought with them capital and experience, giving a great impulse to the general prosperity. These improvements are small indeed compared with the capabilities of the soil. Any quantity of land can be obtained without the payment of rent, and though the character of the natives is generally careless and indolent,

some of them have been giving a better example to their
fellows, and have begun to learn that industry is the parent
of wealth, and that wealth brings with it many blessings
and enjoyments. Many examples fell under my notice,
and I found Indians, moved by the love of gain, who were
increasing their plantations year by year, there being a
ready sale for the fruits of the soil. The Philippines are
no longer a burden to Spain, but in fact contribute a large
amount of revenue annually to the home treasury. In
truth, while the finances of the Spanish peninsula have
been in a most disorderly state, the Philippines have revelled
in a considerable excess of income; every functionary has
been regularly paid, and every engagement righteously ful-
filled, and yet, compared with the productions of Cuba, the
value of the exports from these islands is small and unsatisfactory. The meddlings of the Madrid Cabinet, the constant changes of Governors-General, which have been the
result of the quarrels of faction at home, the inattention
and delay which these valuable colonies have met with at
the hands of the sovereign authorities, and the restraints
put upon the action of those whose local experience entitled
them to attention, are among the causes which have prevented the greater developement of the latent resources of
the Philippines.

The friars possess much influence over the people, and
might, if they pleased, give a great impulse to industry,
but they seem rather concerned in maintaining their ecclesiastical authority, and there is no part of the world in which
there appears such a prostration of the understanding and
the will to priestly domination. The most opulent of the
regular orders of clergy are the Augustines, who possess
large tracts of land in the islands, and are said to be liberal
landlords. Next, the Dominicans, then the Franciscans, and
last of all the Recoletos or barefooted monks, who, though

smaller in numbers, are not wanting in authority, the archbishop, when I visited the Philippines, being one of their
order. Out of Manila there are no hotels, and it is to the
friars principally that the traveller must look for the exercise of hospitality. I found that hospitality boundless, the
spacious convents and the gardens attached to them providing for something more than the ordinary wants of life.
In many localities the padres possess the best horses and
handsomest carriages that are to be found, and enjoy revenues far larger than they are able to expend. A friar,
who was exceedingly popular in the locality where he lived,
once invited me to a dinner at which he said he would
show what he was able to effect in the way of a festive
entertainment. No doubt he drew largely on the liberality
of his neighbours, but he placed upon the table a dinner
which might have satisfied a Parisian gourmand, at which
a great number of his friends were assembled, and they
carried on their revelries for several hours after I quitted
the house.

Two characteristics have especially excited the attention
of all travellers in the Philippines—the ostentatious display
of the religious processions, and the universal passion for
cock-fighting which everywhere prevails among the native
inhabitants. The church ceremonies are most costly. I
witnessed a procession in honour of the Immaculate Conception which, I was informed, was nearly a mile long, the
whole line being crowded by votaries, each bearing a lighted
wax-candle. There was a long succession of Madonnas,
glittering with ornaments, and adorned with jewels to the
value of many thousand dollars, borne upon the shoulders
of devotees. Crowds of the secular and regular clergy,
with many members of the different sisterhoods, accompany
these exhibitions, multitudes of children, dressed in white
garments, and often representing the angelic hosts, being

among the attendants, while the great civil and military authorities are also not wanting. There are large escorts, too, of cavalry and infantry, and the programme of the arrangements in the official gazette sometimes occupies whole pages. I have heard the ecclesiastics boast that in no part of Christendom can be seen such a display of devotion, and that the reverence for the Virgin is greater in these islands than in any other part of the world, yet among the natives there is much hidden dislike, and many of the vestiges of ancient idolatry are to be found in the phraseology which they employ. I have heard it said that the most binding oaths are those made in the names of the heathen gods whom they formerly worshipped, and many superstitious practices have traditionally come down from their ancestors, having had an origin long anterior to the Spanish invasion. In the writings and in the conversations of the Papal priesthood complaints are often made of the hypocrisy and mendacity of the aborigines, and many curious examples are given of their untrustworthiness and insincerity. At the same time they have their apologists and advocates, and very different judgments have been formed, even by those who have had the same opportunities of observation.

Cock-fighting is the general amusement of the natives, and long before the break of day the game-cock's clarion is heard reverberating from every side, its noisy crowing continuing till the setting of the sun. There is no town or considerable village in which there is not a *galleria* or cock-pit, invariably crowded with spectators to witness the bloody fights between these bipeds, which are armed with steel spurs, so sharp that their encounters are frequently fatal. I have seen the Indians bearing home a triumphant chanticleer, to whose wounds they pay more attention than they would to the indisposition of any member of their family. If an Indian's hut take fire, he will neglect his wife and children in order to preserve his favourite bird, to which he is as much attached as the Arab to his high-blooded horse. The government derives a considerable revenue from the cockpits, which are the scenes of much gambling and of frequent quarrels. Every characteristic of the game cock is, with the Indian, a subject of study, the colour and disposition of the feathers, and even the scales on the legs and the shape of the claws being favourite topics, while money will not purchase from his owner a cock who has been a successful warrior.

I ought to mention among the notabilia of these islands the enormous production of ducks by artificial heat. The eggs are placed in sawdust, which is kept constantly warm, and at the same temperature. Every day multitudes of ducklings come forth, and are sent to the ponds belonging to the proprietor, where they are fed on mollusca, which are found in large quantities in the water. Strange stories have been circulated by some credulous travellers, who have asserted that the eggs are incubated by the natural heat of the bodies of Indians employed to sit upon them, a story having about the same authority as the fable that there are birds in the Philippine islands which make their nests in horses' tails, where their offspring are naturally and regularly hatched.

One of the great charms of the Philippines is the forest scenery. Magnificent trees are covered with beautiful, and often fragrant flowers, while many varieties of orchids hang their insect-resembling blossoms in festoons from branch to branch, and from tree to tree. Then the multitudes of many-coloured butterflies, beetles, and other insects give vitality to the scene, and the waterfalls which dash down from the mountain tops bring music to the ear. The equinoctial rains and perpetual sunshine give an enormous impulse to vegetable life, and I have heard that bamboos half-a-foot in diameter grow to twelve inches in twenty-four hours ; while the production of fungi is still more rapid. Of course no inhabitants are found in the depths of the mountain solitudes, of which so many utterly escape the penetrating eye of man. One cannot but be amused by the grotesque and picturesque shapes of the trees, which seem to divert themselves by putting forth every fantastic form. There is sometimes great difficulty in making one's way through the wild scenery, but the Indians carry with them large knives, which they use for many purposes, and rapidly remove the branches, even in the thickest parts of the woods. Sometimes the mud is so deep that it is diffi-cult to make one's way through it, and I have had thirty or forty attendants, embedded up to their thighs in mire, en-gaged in extricating my palankeen from so disagreeable a plight.

The inhabitants of the several islands are very different in character. The languages spoken in Luzon are Tagala and Bisayan, but in the ruder and less accessible parts the idioms are very various, and consist of a small number of words and very few letters. Like the rude islanders of the Pacific, they have only five consonants and three vowels, and these are not very distinctly pronounced. The Negritos, or little black men, found in the interior of the Island of Mindanao, are among the very rudest of the human race. They build no houses, and dress no food, but live in trees, and eat reptiles and fruit. Immense numbers of Chinamen, but without Chinawomen, have settled in almost every part of the Philippines, penetrating into parts which the Spaniards have not conquered, nor even dared to invade. They have intermarried with the natives, and their presence may be traced in the greater industry exhibited in the families where they have been domiciled. Among the aborigines, I do not remember seeing any evidence of manufacturing industry, but looms are generally found in the cottages of the Chinese.

There is not much difference at Manila between the temperature of the summer and the winter months. They divide the year into the hot and the rainy season, and there is a refrain which says that the Manila year is made up of " Seis meses de polvo, seis meses de lodo, y seis meses de todo "— "Six months of dust, six months of mud, and six months of everything."

SKETCHES OF VARIOUS CELEBRITIES.*

LOUIS PHILIPPE.

My acquaintance with Louis Philippe dates from more than half a century ago. I had been an intimate friend of General Dumouriez, who was closely connected with Broval, the Private Secretary of the Duke of Orleans, and in the year 1822 I was introduced to the Duke through Broval, and was frequently received by His Serene Highness, both at the Palais Royal in Paris, and at his country seat at Neuilly.

I have never seen a happier family than was that at Neuilly. Though, naturally enough, the Duke thought much and talked much of the prominent public events of the time, he was mainly.occupied with his domestic affairs and the management of his large property. The whole scene was that of a prosperous country gentleman—an affectionate happy husband, the father of a numerous and promising progeny. I was the first foreigner who saw the King after he had been acknowledged by the British government. A singular accident occurred, which was mentioned at the time in some of the newspapers, and was deemed by some ominous of Louis Philippe's fate. When we entered by that room in which there was a picture representing Louis Philippe when engaged as a teacher of mathematics in a Swiss family—I believe David was the painter—the King met us in a most excited state of delight at the announcement which had just been made to him by the British envoy. There were several ancient ornamented

* A few of these sketches have, I believe, previously appeared in print.

armchairs there, and with his own hand the King drew three of them to the centre of the room, and saying to us, " asseyez vous—asseyez vous," he sat down so violently in the middle chair that it broke down, the King falling on his back. He was raised up by the Prefect and myself, and Odilon Barrot said, " voyez ! vous êtes entouré d'amis," but the incident was not a very pleasurable one to the incipient monarch. He was only disturbed for a moment, and talked, as he was accustomed to do, most glibly.

The faults of Louis Philippe were as prominent and as unmistakeable as his virtues, but his faults damaged his public reputation, and led to his overthrow, while his virtues were only felt in his immediate social circle. If his failings leant to virtue's side, it may be argued, they did no mischief to others, while they were meant to benefit his race. This is not so. His passion for money was such a weakness as to lead him into errors of whose consequences he never made a calculation, and from which he could never recover. He was constantly dreaming about augmenting the wealth of his family, and was always hunting for bargains in the investment of his property. He had reports made to him of "lots" which were to be purchased cheaply, and bought many " lits de mer," in order that he might recover lands from the encroachment of the waters. He was perpetually talking of the insufficiency of the grants for the Civil List, and was not pleased when I told him that the Chambers had dealt more liberally with him than our Parliament had dealt with the British Monarchs.

I had represented to the King, who was not a Free Trader, and to the Baron Louis, the Minister of Finance, who was a most earnest and conscientious supporter of commercial freedom, the desireableness of strengthening the *entente cordiale*, to use the phrase of M. Guizot, who, by the way, uttered the flattering words, but by his acts showed how little he was disposed to give effect to them. I had shown how much the political unity would be promoted if the commercial intercourse between the two countries could be based on a liberal treaty of commerce. Lord Clarendon (then Mr George Villiers) and I were named the British Commissioners to meet Baron Fréville and M. Tanneguy Duchatel, afterwards Minister of the Interior. Notwithstanding repeated assurances of the King's desire to aid us, we had abundant evidence of his duplicity. He was alarmed lest the introduction of British iron should depress the value of his forest property, as the French smelting furnaces of that time employed only wood. He employed Oudard, his Private Secretary, to report on the extent of sacrifice he might have to make, and finding it considerable, the British Commissioners had little hope of success. The government had proposed as the French Commissioner, David, the head of the Custom-House, and the most determined enemy of free-trade, with whom we refused to act. We remained for some months at Paris, constantly thwarted by M. Thiers, and by the intrigues and sinister interests of Ministers, Peers, and Deputies who were manufacturers of iron, and who exercised great influence in the Chambers. The sister of the King, Madame Adelaide, was a partner with Marshal Soult, the Duke of Dalmatia, in iron-works, and they furnished supplies for the State. It remained for Mr Cobden to accomplish the work in which we had so signally failed, and in which he would have failed too, but for the courageous and omnipotent support which he received from Napoleon III. Had Louis Philippe shown more honesty and more sagacity, his dynasty might at this moment be occupying the throne of France. His short-sighted and selfish policy met with an appropriate recompense.

No man ever exhibited more markedly than Louis Philippe the deteriorating effect of power. The man who can enforce his opinions, and put down controversy and contradiction by his position, he whose will can influence the will of other men, without the necessity of bringing his understanding to convince the understandings of those he seeks to influence, will, as the shorter way of settling any question, feel it sufficient to say "sic volco—sic jubeo." And the infirmity of loquacity grew upon him. On one occasion he sent for me to discuss some matter of interest at the Tuileries. I went. He talked, and talked, but never approached the subject on which he wished to consult me. He was accustomed to interlard his conversation with bits of foreign languages, several of which he spoke well. I think he called the Duke of Wellington "comme vous autres Anglais disent a Puss in Boots," and when speaking of his own possession of the crown, he added " Possession, vous savez, is nine points of the law." In reference to some question of war, he said he should not be betrayed like the Spaniards by a cry of "a la guerra ! a la guerra! Españoles!" He complained bitterly of the Duke of Wellington's refusing to give him a command in the army during the Peninsular War. He had a high notion of his own military abilities, and there was no subject on which he was more eloquent than the battles of Valmy and Jemappes, where he had fought under Dumouriez. Though Dumouriez served under the Republic, he was never a Republican. The convention, no doubt, mistrusted him, and when the commissioners summoned him to Paris to answer for his monarchical weaknesses, he arrested them, well knowing that if he obeyed their mandate, the guillotine would have been his doom. The allies were as unwilling to co-operate with him for the establishment of a constitutional monarchy, as he was to carry out their despotic views. The " Mémoires " written

by himself may be accepted as a fair picture of his opinions
and an honest report of his doings.

I witnessed strange sights immediately following " les
glorieuses journées de Juillet 1830." Then it was that
Louis Philippe, with his umbrella in hand, walked about
the streets of Paris, unaccompanied by any servant—the
citizen more than the king, the king absorbed in the citizen.
Then it was that I saw the whole of the Lafayette family at
court, the King stifling them with kisses, beginning with
the old General, and going through the line of his descendants. Then was the time of the " monarchie entourée
d'institutions républicaines." Then were the cries mingled
—from one side, " Louis Philippe parceque Bourbon," and
from the other, " Louis Philippe quoique Bourbon." Then
was it loudly proclaimed that he was the son of his father,
L'Égalité, who had so boldly placed the big tri-colour cockade
in his hat, and whose taint of blood and life of folly had
been more than expiated by his death. Lafayette, less
distinguished by strength of mind and sagacity than by
his amiable temper and courteous manners— in fact he was
a *preux chevalier*, who would have been distinguished in
the chivalric ages—was only taught by sad experience the
duplicity of the King. When Lafayette's influential position
as Commander-in-chief of the National Guard gave the King
some disquiet, lest his authority should be used to strengthen
the republican against the monarchical principle—the King
managed to persuade the General to resign his high post, on
the ground that his *moral* was greater than his *military*
influence. I ventured, when Lafayette reported to me
what had been done, to say, "and so the King persuaded
you that a man *without* a sword is stronger than a man
with a sword ?" On his death-bed, Lafayette confessed to
me that he had been deceived, that I had appreciated Louis

Philippe's character better than he, and that he had trusted him when he deserved no confidence.

It was clear to me that Louis Philippe altogether mistook his position, and fancied his dynasty was firmly established in the mind and the purposes of the people. He listened unwillingly to any representations as to the errors of his policy, received and welcomed the pleasing pictures of his popularity which his courtiers painted, and was utterly blind to the indications which, previously to his downfall, were perceptible on every side to everybody. On one occasion, when I reminded him that monarchs were often misled by the flatterers who surrounded them, he retorted that the mob had its flatterers too—a truth, no doubt, but the flatterers of the mob are less mischievous than the flatterers of the monarch, and their influence is counteracted and controlled by other popular influences favourable to good government, and even to monarchy itself. I remember once, when at the Tuileries, he pointed to the troops on the Place du Carousel, and spoke of them as the supporters of his throne. How little did he recognize the fact that the army of France has never hesitated to abandon the Republic, the Empire, or the Monarchy, when public opinion has declared itself unfriendly to either. The French army is not the army of a monarch or a ministry, or of any particular form of government. It is thoroughly imbued with the national feeling, and in moments of popular enthusiasm shares that enthusiasm and becomes its instrument.

The King so little understood the position of a Constitutional Monarch that he often boasted of carrying matters against the opinion of the Ministers by his personal will. He said to me, " am I to sit in Council, and be a nullity like the Queen of England?" to which my reply was "Sire ! vous faites des questions ministérielles des questions monarchiques. You involve yourself in responsibilities which had

better be avoided." And yet he had a great idea that he
was a master of the art of kingcraft, and that he could
carry out his personal policy by a machinery of his own.
He never concealed his opinion that he was the only person
who could pilot the State vessel through all the revolutionary storms. In one of his outpourings he said, " Il n'y a
que moi qui puisse mener cette voiture là "—meaning the
State carriage—and when I answered, " Mais, sire! si vous
la versez ?", he was much displeased, and retorted to Casimir
Perrier, from whom I heard it, " Bowring m'a dit des choses
vertes." Up to a certain time, he received me most con-
fidentially. I have been summoned to his boudoir when
he was shaving himself, for I believe he did not employ a
barber ; but in a later part of his reign his courtesies were
wholly discontinued, and I never intruded on him during
his exile.

At the Revolution of 1848, a list was found headed,
" Hommes à moi," and it is well known that he had corrupted the Chamber of Deputies by honours and emolu-
ments, a very great number of them having obtained places
and decorations for themselves and their dependents. Electors and elected were equally bribed. At the time of the
negotiation of the unhappy Spanish marriages, he carried
on a private correspondence with his minister at Madrid,
Bresson, who afterwards committed suicide ; and in a conversation I had with him at the Tuileries, he pulled out
from his side-pockets a quantity of papers, and said, " Croyez
vous que mes ministres aient vu cela ?" He certainly had
not the *ars celare artem*. As far as my experience went,
his sister Adelaide was the only person who had any real
influence with him. His talkativeness and obstinacy increased with his age. As a country squire, he would have
held an honoured position ; as a monarch, he was beneath
mediocrity. He would have quarrelled with England, and,

under Thiers' impetuosity, would have willingly gone to war, but he *dared* not. I doubt if he trusted anybody, though he believed he could control everybody.

There is little merit in delineating his character, and it may be prognosticated that posterity will be pretty well agreed as to his demerits and his deservings. 1871.

LEOPOLD I., KING OF THE BELGIANS.

Whatever may be the future fate of the Duchy of Saxe-Coburg as an independent State, the blood of the princely family which there rules is now intermingled with that of almost all the imperial and royal races of the civilized world. The population of Coburg, united with that of Gotha (added to it in 1825, and nearly double in amount), does not exceed 150,000, or less than that of a second-rate European city; while the House of Gotha can claim a ducal ancestry scarcely extending back beyond the period of two centuries. Now, when the position of the Coburgs in the political field is contrasted with that of the Bourbons of France and Italy, that of the Vasa in Sweden, of the Stuarts in England, and other wrecks of ancient royalty, the chances and changes of time become indeed matters of great marvel as regards the past, and of perplexing speculation in reference to the future.

Time was when the rise and fall of dynasties depended wholly on the results of the battlefield. The conquered being crushed, the conqueror seized the contested crown, and seated himself on the vacated throne. But other influences than the sword have decided, and are more and more likely to decide the fate of sovereigns. Beyond a certain amount of misrule, public patience will not tolerate the grave faults of those in authority. The beheadings of some kings, and the deposition and expatriation of others, have shown how little sacredness attaches to the person of a sovereign, even if they have not destroyed all reverence for rights divine. New views of the relations between governors and the governed have brought the mightiest as well as the meanest before the inexorable tribunal of public opinion.

Leopold was the first of a royal dynasty, and has fixed it on a foundation more likely to be durable than the assumption of ruling " by the grace of God," or by the titles conferred by the Pope of Rome. Royalty is subject to the same conditions of chance and change which surround all human institutions, and if, in ordinary circumstances, monarchs are treated, as they have a fair title to be treated, with more indulgence than their dependents, it has been sometimes found that they become the objects of bitterer hatred and severer condemnation than those less fawned upon and less flattered than themselves.

I enjoyed more or less of intercourse with King Leopold during the fifty years of his public life, and, not long before his death, had a most interesting conversation with him on his personal history during that half century, in whose remarkable events he had taken so active and so useful a part. I had an occasion then particularly, as I had often had an opportunity before, of studying the grounds of that quiet and benign influence which he had so habitually exercised in the interests of peace, and in the service of his race, and which, though the marks of pain and exhaustion were still visible, enabled him to look back, not only with serenity but with self-gratulation on his own marvellous history, on the elevation of his family, and generally on the position and prospects of European affairs. His nature— not, however, so unimpassioned as it has sometimes been deemed—had been subdued by age, toil, and suffering, to a singular complacency, and enabled him, like one harboured in a port of safety, to recall to his grateful memory the storms in which many had been wrecked, but through which he had passed, not with safety and dignity alone, but in triumph.

I may briefly revert to the question which was the immediate occasion of my last visit to Laeken, as it had been referred specially by the ministers to himself, and its solution was characteristic of his peace-seeking and peace-loving nature. It had reference to an article in a treaty of amity and commerce, by which it was provided that, if there were any difference of opinion between the contracting governments which could not be satisfactorily solved by diplomatic correspondence, there should be no appeal to arms—*ultima ratio legum*—but that such differences should be referred to the friendly arbitration and decision of some neutral power. It was the first European Treaty into which such a condition had been introduced, and there were many objections, principally on account of its novelty. It is a general but somewhat hasty assumption, both of monarchies and republics, that they are sufficient for the maintenance of their own authority and dignity, that they ought to reserve to themselves the power of insisting on the reparation of supposed wrongs and the recognition of invaded rights, and that it does not become the pride and self-sufficiency of a nation to surrender to others the solution of controversies which it can settle by its own unaided strength. Such an opinion Lord Palmerston had invariably interposed, when on more than one occasion it had been suggested that it would be a noble example to be given to the world if a country so powerful as Great Britain would take the initiative of declaring her willingness to submit to arbitration the *vexatæ questiones* which have so often led to fierce contests, associated with all the uncertainties of war, but with the certainty at least that the evil passions of envy, hate, and jealousy, will be fanned and fostered, the peaceful rela-

tions of commerce interrupted, the taxes fearfully augmented
—for great nations, as the Duke of Wellington declared,
cannot engage in petty strifes—and, as a result far more
sad, that the loss of money, the sufferings of individuals,
families, and peoples, might all be provided against, and
prevented, would governments allow, in cases of controversy, an appeal to some equitable and disinterested authority. " C'est une question *humanitaire*—ainsi soit il," was
the king's decision, when his ministers asked for his award.
Well do I remember the phrase, and though I believe the
word is not to be found in the dictionary, where it well
deserves to be, the arbitration clause was introduced into
the Belgo-Hawaiian Treaty of friendship and commerce,
and has since been adopted in the treaties with several
European nations. Its adoption is at all events one step
towards the establishment of an International Tribunal—
that great desideratum—which will, in process of time,
propound and administer a code of international law ; for,
whatever may be the power of a *lex non scripta*, authori-
tative international law there is none.

Among the foolish schemes of a very foolish sovereign
was that of disposing of the hand of his daughter—of the
heiress to the British Crown, without that daughter's consent. Now, if there ever were a woman with a will of her
own, and whom it would have been impossible to bend to
a despotism which disregarded her feelings and affections
in the most susceptible part of her nature, that woman was
the Princess Charlotte ; and even had no more attractive
lover than the Prince of Orange been presented for her
acceptance, the Prince of Orange most assuredly would
never have obtained her hand, and still less have won her
heart. Neither in person—for that was mean and un-
attractive—nor in any moral or intellectual superiority, did
the young Dutch prince recommend himself. He had every

possible advantage, the warm patronage of the lady's father, and of the ministers of the Crown, and what was perhaps of more importance to him, the personal knowledge and approval of the Duke of Wellington, whose aide-de-camp he had been, and with whom he had creditably served. He had, too, the recommendation of belonging to a family with which the Protestant sympathies of England had been long associated, and was the future representative of that " Oranje boven," the utterance of which had not been without its importance in overthrowing the Napoleon dynasty. His rival was a youth of a comparatively obscure race, a younger son of one of those petty States which represent the discordant elements of Germany, and which are in process of inevitable absorption by that tendency to union and unity which makes similar elements gravitate to and finally mingle with one another. Great nations are formed, and constantly grow greater by drawing towards them the inferiorities that surround them, whether inferior in physical strength or intellectual power. This irresistible " tide of tendency " has lately been strikingly exhibited in the creation of the Prussian kingdom, while, on the other hand, the failure of the attempt to dissever a smaller portion of a great empire from the larger may be studied in the events of the federal war in the United States.

The mind of Leopold, modified as it was by English and French associations, the result of the study of books and intercourse with men, was markedly of the German type, and though he spoke fluently, but somewhat slowly, the languages of what have been called the two great rival nations, and was well instructed in the history of both, there was a paramount Teutonic influence traceable in his phraseology, which showed that he thought in German, · even while his utterances were in the idioms of France or England. Even at his table, German was the accepted and

preferred tongue, unless when courtesy to guests, or diplomatic usages, made the employment of French or English
more becoming. The affinity between High and Low
Dutch, or in other words, between the Saxon and the
Flemish, both derived from Gothic roots, is so great that
the knowledge of one would render easy the acquisition of
the other. Of the three languages spoken in Belgium—
French, Flemish, and Walloon—the Flemish is the most
extensively used among the people. I am not aware that
Leopold ever ventured to employ the popular idiom in any
public discourse, or in any communication with the Flemings.
The presence and government of the Hollanders had given
to the dialect of Flanders no small encouragement from its
very close resemblance to the Dutch. Indeed, while Belgium
was linked to Holland, and they formed together the
Netherlandic Kingdom, the Flemish was quite as much the
official language as was the French, and many of the deputies of Flanders used the vulgar tongue in their parliamentary
debates ; but, as the French represents a higher civilization,
occupies a far more extensive field, and is recommended by
a more rich and varied literature, there can be no doubt that
the French will gradually supersede the Flemish, not only
from its greater value as a language, but because it is the
organ employed by the State, and represents the riches and
the rank of the capital, for, except in the lower districts of
Brussels, to speak Flemish would be deemed something
worse than unfashionable. French has become the organ
of the government, and all the influential newspapers, almost
all the remarkable publications, the more eloquent preach-
ings from the pulpit, the dramatic exhibitions, and the
national songs, bear testimony to the intrusion of the French
language upon Flemish ground. Parliamentary oratory is
almost exclusively French—indeed there is scarcely a statesman of mark who has employed any other tongue for the

display of his political power. The nationality of the Belgian, his alienation from the Dutch alliance, is more marked by his repudiation of their tongue. Holland, in which the home-feeling is intense and immoveable, will long retain *de Hollandsche Taal;* but that portion of the Netherlands which was wrested from her by the revolution of 1831, will in a few generations adopt the language of Paris, to which all others will be subjected, or in which they will be absorbed. Already the Brabanters pride themselves, in that the French of *la bonne Société Bruxelloise* is as pure as that which, according to Chaucer, in the schools of one metropolis was *not* spoken—at all events not in " Stratford le Bowe,"

" Where French of Paris was to them unknowe,"

and certainly the Belgian French is more classical than that of many departments of France, where the *patois* tone and type influence the pronunciation of the national tongue.

Nothing could be more fortunate to Leopold than to have resisted the temptations which the crown of Greece offered to his ambition, an offer singularly attractive at a time when the uprising of Hellas from her long apathy had awakened the impassioned sympathy of the world. Canning had, in his youthful enthusiasm, hailed the hope of her resurrection, and Byron had flung his heart, and soul, and voice, and fortune into the movement, by which she seemed to prove that something better than a " blush " was to be found for Greeks, and for Greece something brighter than a " tear." But Leopold had penetration enough to see that the anarchical elements which stood in the way of the reconstruction of the Hellenic Kingdom might be too strong to be subjugated by his energies, and perhaps had even the foresight to anticipate that he might be called to a higher mission. Be that as it may, it was fortunate for Belgium,

for Europe, and for the world, that Athens was not chosen
for the display of his talents for government, and that
Brussels *was* so chosen.   Leopold was chosen too when
many rivalries were in the field, when it was notorious that
Louis Philippe had an absolute passion for seating his
children on adjacent thrones.   Fond as he was of intrigue,
and never losing sight of family interests, his views upon
Belgium would have been willingly accepted and endorsed
by the French people, had not a very steady purpose of
independence become the popular Belgian policy—a policy
looked upon with something more than complacency by the
European Powers.   Moreover, Louis Philippe was wholly
wanting in moral courage and confidence, and always
shrank from the dangers which might have followed any
adventurous daring.   He was indeed well satisfied with an
arrangement by which, soon after the nomination of Leopold
to the kingly power, the eldest daughter of the Orleans
royal race was selected for the Belgian queen.

The position in which Leopold was placed was one
which demanded two special, and not always concurring
qualities—calmness and energy—calmness to form a clear
and distinct estimate of what was needful to be done, and
energy to subdue the difficulties that opposed themselves
to the accomplishment of a steadily defined purpose, and to
give to that purpose substantial effect.   The national feeling
insisted on terminating the connection between Holland
and Belgium, a connection in whose enforced infliction not
the slightest regard had been paid by the Congress of
Vienna to the wishes and opinions, or to the prejudices of
the Belgians, a people more numerous, though perhaps less
national, than the Dutch.   It is true that the prevailing
feeling was not wholly divested of the sympathies which
grew out of a common language, and a common literature,
for the Flemings have always considered the Netherland

authors as belonging to, and reflecting glory upon, themselves. Still, the influence of French writers over Brabant and the provinces in which French was spoken, was stronger than that of Dutch literature over the Flemish provinces. The Catholic religious element, while it presented a serious barrier to any strong sympathy between the two nations, was not the less a subject to be dealt with by a Protestant prince whose Protestantism would naturally be supposed to give influence to the party with which he had been connected from his birth upwards, and his attachment to which could only have been strengthened by his alliance with that English princess who would undoubtedly have a right to be deemed, should she ascend the throne of England, as the very head of the Protestant religion in Europe, and indeed of the whole world. It is only in weighing the heterogeneous and opposed elements with which Leopold had to deal, that the sagacity of his mind can be properly appreciated in so disposing of them that they were combined in a regard for his person, and a disposition to support his government. Not to offend the priestly party, while strengthening the growth, and helping the extension of a general educational system, and at the same time not to alienate or offend those who looked upon priestly interference as mischievous and intolerable, was indeed no easy task. It is true that, from time to time, each party took umbrage at the too much or too little that was done, but neither party had ever any ground for complaining that the kingly authority was exercised in an unbecoming or unconstitutional manner.

Leopold was singularly fortunate in the choice of his agents and representatives, of which a remarkable evidence was seen in the person of Sylvain Van de Weyer, so long his minister plenipotentiary at the Court of St James. Van de Weyer was the son of an obscure Juge de Paix, and his mother kept a *librairie* at Louvain. He obtained some

s

eminence as an *avocat*, and by his writings and speeches made himself obnoxious to the Dutch, and was marked out for political persecution, which obtained for him notoriety and fame. In 1830 he became a member of the Provisional Government in Brussels, of which De Potter was the President, and, though speaking English marvellously well for one who had never put his foot in England until he came hither, sent by the Republican party, he soon, by his firmness and sagacity, won his way to the good opinion of our leading politicians, and especially of the ambassador of Louis Philippe, Talleyrand, who constantly spoke of the young diplomate in terms of high laudation. The Duke of Wellington was struck by the *undiplomatic* frankness and ability with which the youthful envoy treated the great interests confided to his advocacy. Van de Weyer formed a very correct estimate of the tendencies of public opinion at home and abroad, soon detached himself from the Republican party, and attached himself to the cause of monarchy as represented by Leopold, to whose service he devoted himself with unswerving faithfulness. His marriage with the daughter of Mr Bates, the opulent managing partner in the house of Baring Brothers, brought to him all the consideration that wealth could give, while his love of books and literary studies secured for him a very honourable position in the world of letters. It was happy for him that Great Britain was the field in which his talents found their exercise, for in Belgium the *morgue aristocratique* would have rebelled against his elevation, as it did when for a short season he was invested with ministerial authority at home.

There is no country in Europe where opinion has been so thoroughly revolutionized on the subject of Free Trade as Belgium. The woollen and cotton manufacturers of the Flemish provinces were among the most ardent advocates

of the protective system, while the greater and more growing mining and agricultural interests advocated the removal of restrictions. Moreover, the interest which, after
all, ought to be preponderating and paramount—namely,
the interest of the consumer, distinctly perceived that the
national well-being would be best promoted by low tariffs,
and extended foreign commerce. Towards this object, and
the promotion of the sound principles of political economy,
the views of Leopold were constantly turned. He spoke
with much delight of the conversion of the Belgian people
to wholesome and profitable notions on the subject of trading intercourse. In fact, if the revenue could be spared, or
other means of taxation be provided, there is a disposition
among the Belgians to abolish custom-houses altogether,
and to allow the exit and entrance of all merchandize without any fiscal interruption, whether to levy an impost or to
impose a condition. Happy will be the nation which shall
first give the noble example, and splendid its reward will
be, of allowing to the whole world the privilege of unre-
stricted communication, and which shall have the courage
to say—"Bring to us your superfluities; we shall impose
no tax upon their import—take in exchange what we have
in excess, no duty shall be levied on its export; our markets shall be to you and to everybody what your home-
markets are to one another; as far as we are concerned, we
will make international what has hitherto been only
national, and as far as commerce is concerned, extend to
all people the privileges of a common fraternity," Such a
solution of fiscal and financial controversies would indeed
be the introduction of a happy millennium, whose advent
will perhaps be hailed by a not distant generation.

As the vital forces of nature overpower all resistance, as
the rays of light proceed in straight lines, notwithstanding
temporary interruptions or refractions, as the electric fluid

runs through the wire-conductors as far as they reach, so we may anticipate a day, however remote, when all human energies, brought into the arena of industrial and beneficent action, will display themselves in full and unmolested power, and the laws of a sound political economy will be recognised as the most solid basement for the prosperity of nations.

The two opposing elements—subjection to ecclesiastical authority, and free thought with its various tendencies— are pretty evenly balanced, and come into immediate contact with one another in Belgium. There can be no doubt as to the tendencies of public opinion. The hold of the clergy upon the peasantry is very strong, and made much stronger by the attachment of many of the old families to the Church of Rome, while the priesthood puts forward its claim to be the director and controller of the national education. Its power is at the same time greatly augmented by its association with the religious rites of baptism, marriage, and burials, though it is the civil registration that constitutes the legal validity of the ceremony. Added to these, the monopoly of the pulpit, and the omnipresence of the confessional, give the ecclesiastics instruments of action and influence which are denied to the laity. Wise and popular political insti-tutions, a free press, cheap and accessible means of locomo-tion, a low rate of postage, and a teeming and industrious population are all co-operative to diffusion of knowledge and of civilization, while it is certain that Catholicism must either move with the onward march of mind, and reconcile itself to new phases of religious thought,—in other words, must be combined with the colour of the times,—or it will be supplanted by other systems more in harmony with that social futurity to which everything is tending, whatever may be the temporary obstructions and delays.

The best of Belgian society is not easily accessible to

strangers, nor, when they are admitted within the social circle, are the predominant influences very distinctly traceable in their many ramifications. The Parisian habits of *grands diners*, *soirées*, and *réceptions diplomatiques* have made their way to the capital of Belgium only on a small scale. There are few brilliant conversationists, indeed, *l'art de causer* is little studied. The Belgians are not wanting in a costly hospitality, though it is for the most part of an exclusive character. There has been none of the levelling, none of the equalizing, such as the French Revolution introduced even into the *salons* of Paris, where, though the old family *morgue* has maintained itself in certain inaccessible circles, known as those of the Quartier St Germain, the very best intellectual society is often honoured by the presence of distinguished men emanating from and belonging to the unopulent and even the prolétaire ranks. The courtesies of intercourse, the polite phraseology addressed from one grade of society to another, and by people of the same grade among themselves, evidence how widely the true spirit of *égalité* has interblended itself with the forms and usages of daily life—even more so than among nations whose institutions are avowedly democratic and republican. Belgium is not emancipated from caste prejudices, but to have mastered them, modified them, and, still more, to have made them subservient to the peace, prosperity, and progress of the Belgian people, was perhaps the most memorable recompense of the wise rule and administration of Leopold the First.

There was always in the mind of King Leopold a longing, a feeling (for which the Germans have in *sehnsucht*,[*]

---

[*] The Portuguese have a word, *sandades*, which has no synonym in any other language. The French translate it by " regret de l'absence "—" doux souvenir "—" juste mémoire," as they render *sehnsucht* by " désir constant," and " souhait animé," but the very variety of these interpretations shows how little they represent the real meaning of the words.

literally sigh-malady, a more emphatic word than we possess) — there was a longing which led his thoughts towards Claremont. The gardens and conservatories there were called upon to furnish fruits and flowers for his table, and I have had not unfrequently a dinner-invitation from the Court, with the appendix " *le panier de Claremont est arrivé.*" It will be remembered with what a high-minded sense of propriety the king returned to the British exchequer all that was voted him as a yearly revenue by Parliament, except that portion which was necessary to keep in proper condition the grounds and gardens of that spot whose memory was so dear to him. Few places will teach more emphatic lessons than that charming chateau. It was the witness of Leopold's elevation to a height of singular felicity and influence, and contrasted sadly with the melancholy reflections that the fallen Orleans family must have often uttered, and more frequently felt, as they wandered through its walks. Leopold never sank downwards in the whole of his career. From the moment in which the Princess Charlotte stretched to him her welcoming hand, and accepted him as the chosen one of her affections, his good fortune never deserted him, but led him step by step till he culminated in kingly power, and founded a dynasty likely to last longer than that of the Bourbons, with all their historic prestige.

There was one topic on which the king was always pleased to dwell—the means of increasing the salubrity and beauty of the capital. The improvements which he introduced during his reign, without such enormous pecuniary outlays as have been required from the Parisians, and as have entailed upon coming generations such heavy responsibilities, will make that reign distinguished in future times. For, though opulent, Brussels has not the con-centrated wealth of the French metropolis, nor does the

Belgian government possess the centralized despotic power which would enable it to carry out even beneficial changes without the concurrence and support of public opinion, and of the representative orders who have to be consulted. Whole districts have, however, been covered with commodious residences, beautiful hotels, and public edifices, the population has gone on increasing, the facilities of communication have been greatly extended, railways, cheap postage, and electric telegraphs have added to the national wealth and to the general well-being, and it may be confidently asserted that there is no part of Europe with fewer subjects of complaint, or with greater cause for self-gratulation as to its present and its future than the Belgic kingdom. And when this tranquil and happy state of things is contrasted with the internal troubles and tumults which have so frequently disturbed the public peace, with the miseries of personal and local feuds, with the plagues of foreign invasion, and, from its geographical position, with its having so often been the battlefield of wrangling Europe, the present tranquillity of Belgium is all the more remarkable— the best evidence that the well-being of the people has been provided for, not only by the satisfactory action of the legislative and administrative bodies, but by the wisdom of the supreme power.

A striking evidence of the genuine simplicity of Leopold's nature was seen in his attachment to his country abode at Laeken, which he much preferred to the palatial residence in the capital. In the grounds and gardens, and in the less adorned but very comfortable apartments of his country home, he found much more that was domestic and social than was compatible with the greater glare and splendour of the metropolitan city. Though he visited it for state receptions, for diplomatic intercourse, and for those public displays which are associated with the functions of monarchy, he always returned with renewed enjoyment to the comparative retreat and seclusion of his beloved rural domicile. Not that he was in any way reserved or inaccessible—quite the contrary—for not only did he willingly and cordially receive all those with whom he had to do in private or public life, but there was a courtesy and kindness in his habitual bearing which were singularly winning, and which in his presence left everybody at his ease. He spoke, as has been noticed, gravely and deliberately, but with a very pleasing emphasis. Both his French and English had a very slight touch of Germanism, alike in accent and forms of expression—not that anything inaccurate or ungrammatical could ever be detected, but that his thoughts seemed moulded in a Teutonic type, and preserved in their expression somewhat of their normal character when translated into any other tongue. It is impossible to graft upon the stock of early education any offshoots which shall not have something in them of the original stamp. Thoughts, like streams, flow in their wonted channels, and even should they be diverted from that course, they will bear with them the character with which they were impregnated at the fountain-head. The style which is said not only to represent, but to *be* the man, will reflect early associations as assuredly as the bending of the twig will decide the form of the branch.

Among the less important characteristics of King Leopold was this. He seemed to have an affection for old garments, not from any niggardliness—of which I never heard him accused—but from the mere force of habit, which becomes, as it were, a portion of every day's continuity. Many men confess to a certain weakness in favour of old shoes and old hats, and it is a subject of reasonable complaint that when they become most comfortable, when every toe has found its own particular niche, or when the hat has become plastic enough to accommodate itself to every undulation of the brow, the faithful servant is dismissed on account of some hostile criticism, and a new hat is introduced which pinches the forehead, or a new pair of shoes which inflict agony upon the feet. Now, up to the time in which absolute raggedness demands the expulsion of a favourite bit of ancient costume, one may be allowed to hesitate about its rejection—and certainly the gold lace upon King Leopold's *froc* had lost· its lustre long before it was dismissed—1868.

GEORGE CANNING.

Minutes of a conversation with Mr Canning, 16th January 1824.

On my entering, Mr Canning rose and shook me by the hand, apologising for not moving. " I have a good deal of gout yet, though I'm better. Take a seat." I said that I had written to him when he was in the country, asking for an interview on the subject of the Malta loan ; but that I had also wished to communicate to him *vivâ voce* some information I had received indirectly from the Duke of Orleans, of language used by Chateaubriand with respect to him (Mr Canning) personally, and which it might at that time have been important for him to be acquainted with, as it was of a most unfriendly character, and at a time when there were external marks of good opinion between the parties. Mr Canning was very much excited by this, and, lifting himself up, asked when such language was used. I said, " it was some weeks ago," on which he nodded his head significantly. (Chateaubriand's words were, " I prophesy that Mr Canning will not much longer direct the Cabinet of St James.")

I then said that when I before solicited the honour of an interview, I wished to make him master of many extraordi-

nary facts which the agitation of the loan for the Knights
of St John had brought to my knowledge, as I wished to
show him how Russia had been using this military Order
for carrying into effect her projects of aggrandisement in
Greece and Turkey.   I had seen the correspondence between the agents of the Order who were sent to Verona and
Prince Metternich, showing that the sovereigns looked with
much complacency on the re-establishment of the Order.
I mentioned that the Order had been for years a mere instrument in the hands of Russia.   Paul was the last Grand
Master, the insignia and archives of the Order were deposited at Moscow, almost all the late admissions of knights
had been from among the Russian nobles, and the scheme
of Russia was no doubt to arm herself with the Order for
carrying into effect her plans upon Greece.   Mr Canning
asked what had prevented the completion of the contract for
the loan ?   I told him that the first cause was the misunderstanding between the contractors of the agent for the Order
—the second was probably the interference of the Greek
Committee, who, finding the loan was assuming the name
of a " Greek loan," and being well assured that the Greek
government was no party to it, published an advertisement
declaratory of this fact.   Mr Canning asked what security
they offered ?   I said, " The estates of the Order."   " Was
this," said Mr Canning, " a security ? "   I replied that it
was deemed so by the contractors, for I heard from their
own lips that their lists were completed, and the whole sum
subscribed.   I added that it was certain that the French
government regarded the loan with complacency, for it
was within my knowledge that the Duchess of Angoulême
had made several applications for the admission of knights,
and that the last Chapter had been held at Paris.   " Was
there some stipulation for the cession of some islands to the
Order ? " inquired Mr Canning.   " Yes ; Cyprus and Rhodes

were mentioned. They formerly claimed the Negropont and the bailiwick of the Morea, and I imagine it was believed the British government would consent to their establishment, on their quietly giving up all claim to Malta, which we hold with a flaw in the title, they, its former possessors and heirs, never having consented to its cession." Mr Canning looked exceedingly surprised, and obviously checked some rising feeling.

Mr Canning said, " I should tell you that the informa tion you formerly gave me (respecting the intrigues of Russia in the West Indies) has turned out to be correct, and we have found that the individuals whose names you gave me were really engaged, but we could not ascertain that there was a treaty for the cession of an island." I said I believed the principal agent (Colombel) was now dead, but that another individual had been since sent by Russia to treat with Boyer.

I then said, "The immediate object, sir, of my wishing to see you was to represent to you the state of Greece, and to communicate a number of facts which might perhaps be important in assisting a prompt decision on the part of the British government. We have news down to the 7th December, by which it appears that new triumphs on the part of the Greeks have closed the present campaign, and have decided finally the independence of Greece." " I believe," said Mr Canning, " that they are now convinced at Constantinople that the struggle is a hopeless one for them." I said, " Sir, it is not Turkey, but Russia that the friends of Greece have cause to fear. The Greek insurrec-tion was originally planned at St Petersburg, where Ipsi-lanti, Hepites, and others received their instructions. The Russians have sent several agents to the Morea, they have been in constant intercourse with the *Kapitanoi*, they have kept the Metropolitan of Greece (Ignatius) long in their

pay, and through the Hetairist Society at Warsaw they have
long sent supplies into Greece. Now, the Greeks can have
no chance of independence against Russia, except in alliance
with England, and to England they are stretching out their
arms, and would make any sacrifice to obtain its amity, for
they feel that the interest of England and the independence
of Greece are closely allied." "The situation of Turkey,"
said Mr Canning, " is one that is sufficiently perplexing to
us. The peace of Europe hangs on a thread, and we know
that, with the monstrous power of Russia, Turkey would be
overwhelmed, and Greece too, whenever Russia chooses to
put her armies in motion. A war with Turkey would be
popular in Russia—popular with the army, popular with
the people, if popular opinion can be said to exist in a
country so governed, but we have the Emperor's pacific
assurances constantly repeated." " Then, sir, if the power
of Russia is to be feared, why allow Turkey to exhaust herself in a fruitless struggle ? and would it not be a sound
policy to create in Greece a strong and popular government
which might be an effectual barrier against Russia ?"
" Yes," said Mr C., " that would be a proper argument for
English policy, but what language could we hold to Russia
to obtain her consent, knowing as we do that she can con-
quer Turkey and Greece when she pleases ? " " Russia has
fomented every insurrection in Greece, she has made the
treatment of the Greeks the prominent ground of complaint
in all her discussions with the Porte, and has always professed to be the advocate of Grecian independence. She
would hardly put in a direct claim to the sovereignty of
Greece, but, if the worst came to the worst, France would
be disposed to oppose her. The French government has
sent two agents to Greece lately to ascertain the state of
affairs, and has always in its official journal (*Journal des
Débats*) advocated the Greek cause. The possession of

Greece by Russia would give her at once that without which she is not to be feared as a naval power—namely, ports open all the year round. The Russians would be disposed to introduce a monarch into Greece (and they have already mentioned the son of Gustavus Adolphus). Such a monarch —a stranger, for no one could be found with any pretensions among the Greeks themselves—must be the blind instrument of the Holy Alliance, of which he would of course be a member." "Will you," said Mr Canning, "give me substantive evidence of the facts you have mentioned with respect to the proceedings of Russia which I may lay before others?" "Yes; I will also, if you please, communicate in confidence the substance of conversations between Pozzo di Borgo and Colonel Stanhope, the former of whom is on his way to Italy." "No! I do not wish to have anything from that Mr Stanhope. I believe Pozzo di Borgo is not gone to Italy, though he has large estates there. Does any government exist in Greece which is generally obeyed? We understand that in the Islands they refuse to obey the executive body." "The fact is, sir, that there is great insubordination among the *Kapitanoi*. They possess wealth, they have all that has been plundered from the Turks, and they overawe the senate of the executive. This evil will be removed when a loan shall be put in the hands of the really virtuous party." "I suppose a loan can now be easily effected?" "Yes; many subscribers have already come forward." I then referred to the expected arrival of the Deputies, and mentioned that Orlando had been President of the Senate, and was an Islander (Hydriote), and Luriottis, a Peloponnesian, and said I hoped he would honour them with an audience. He hesitated, but at last said, "No; I think not. Everybody knows what passes here. I suppose the object of their coming—the principal object—is to raise a loan, which they probably *will* raise."

"That is their principal object certainly, but they will also
be most desirous of ascertaining on what terms they can
obtain the friendship and alliance of this country. Would
it, sir, be too much to hope for your interference to stop the
effusion of blood, to prevent the continuance of a struggle
which will exhaust both ? If you will suggest anything to
the Greeks, I will answer that it shall receive their most
solemn attention, and, if it be consistent with their honour
and their interest, that it shall be carried into effect." He
answered, " A mediation of this sort, if rejected, would probably involve the interfering mediator in a war. What are
the views of the Greeks with respect to their independence ?" I said, " I imagine their independence must be
recognized in an unqualified form, but it is not impossible
that they might consent to make some pecuniary remune-
ration to the Porte for that unqualified recognition." Mr
Canning, " There seem two ways in which the matter might
be considered. First, could not the Greeks be in a situation of qualified dependence, as in Wallachia and Moldavia ?
or would they be disposed to pay a tribute for the unqualified recognition of their independence ?" I said, " I imagine
they would not be satisfied with the former, for there could
be no security with such a government as that of the Porte,
unless such a power as England was the guarantee—that a
yearly tribute would be intolerable, but that a loan might
be raised in this country for the final redemption of their
country from the Turkish yoke ; but meanwhile, the Porte
was losing time, and that the boundaries to which the
Greeks would now consent would be advanced much further
north if the struggle continued, and that Macedonia itself
would be probably freed." Mr Canning said, " Would they
make the Isthmus of Corinth the boundary line ?" " Certainly not—much more is freed. A line must be drawn
across somewhere to the south of Macedonia."

1 then spoke of the conduct of the British consuls in the East, and said that I hoped the changes in Greece would put the consulates into the hands of the government instead of a monopolizing Turkey company. "It is only about fifteen years," said Mr Canning, "since we sent even an ambassador." I mentioned that Green of Patras had supplied the Turks with stores, that £20,000 of his bills had just come back protested from Constantinople for supplies for the service of the Turks, and I expressed great indignation at such conduct. "He is not directly under our control," said Mr Canning, "but we did give one of them, and I think it was Green, a very hard rap. I am glad of the fact you mention, because we can quote it at Constantinople, where they speak of the interference of Englishmen on behalf of the Greeks. You will then give me some evidence of the facts of Russian interference without betraying your authority." "Yes, sir; and allow me to say in reference to Greece, that your situation is one enviable beyond the conception of envy. It is a subject which every mind like yours must enter on with something like enthusiasm. The enthusiasm that exists you contributed to create, and what you dreamt of as a boy, you may *do* as the minister of England." He bowed his head very graciously. "I see," he said, "D. Lyall has published his work on Russia." "Yes; and it contains many curious facts, though written in a bad style. His comparing the political state of Russia to a decayed wheel, where, the spokes being equally rotten, no one gives way, is very good."

I gave Mr Canning some information with respect to Mavrocordato's character and the affection of the people for him, of the constitution of the Senate and their proceedings, of the progress of the campaign, &c. He thanked me, and my interview, which lasted more than an hour, was ended by his saying, "I shall be very glad to see you again." We shook hands, and I left him.

LORD PALMERSTON.

Memorandum of a Conversation with Lord Palmerston on 18th *Dec.* 1848.

I stated to him that it would be of great importance that I should be able to say to the Chinese Authorities that I had seen the Queen before my departure. He answered that there was a general rule, through which he could not break, that no persons under the rank of Ministers Pleni-potentiary should have special audiences, that the Queen was unwilling to have her privacy disturbed at Osborne House, and that he had been obliged to negative several requests similar to mine. He thought my having been so long in Parliament, and so much in the public eye, with my literary reputation, would give me all the consideration necessary in the eyes of the Chinese Authorities.

I asked him whether he would consent to give me the title of President, so as to place me in a situation equal to that of the American representative. He said that might be a matter for future consideration, but that at present the existing arrangements could not be disturbed.

I enquired whether, in case of obtaining access to the in-terior of the town, which might necessitate some ostentatious array, he would be disposed to make an allowance for extra expense so incurred. He said that he should favourably consider such an application, admitting it to be reasonable, and saying that similar allowances were made at Constanti-nople and elsewhere. He said that, if convenient, he should be glad if I could be ready to depart by the January steamer, in order to be present when, according to the terms of the treaty, the town of Canton was to be opened to the British ; that there would be great resistance to their being admitted ; that he did not think their admission should be peremptorily insisted on, if it were likely to lead to a rupture, or a war, as the object would not be worth the sacrifice; but that he thought, as regarded the Consul, the right *should* be insisted upon, which might lead in due time to the admission of British subjects in general. He desired me to state my views specifically in this matter.

I told him, generally, that while we ought to be very cautious in making a demand upon the Chinese, that demand, once made, should not be retracted—that, as the greater portion of the opulent Chinese merchants lived without the walls of the city, admission within the walls did not appear to me a matter of sufficient importance to be insisted upon, if pertinaciously resisted by the Chinese; but that access to the government authorities by the Consul was absolutely necessary for the comfortable despatch of business, and for those verbal explanations which tended so much to facilitate a friendly understanding. He agreed in this, and said it would be right to insist on access to the authorities, and to persevere until that point was carried, even though menaces and the presence of an armed force were necessary.

I enquired whether, if there should be invincible repugnance to the admission of British subjects at Canton, he would be willing to waive the right, if other concessions were made by the Chinese, such as the surrender of Chusan. He said there were various opinions as to the value of Chusan, and objections from the difficulty of defending it; but he still felt that Hong Kong was too near Canton, and would be willing to entertain favourably any suggestions I might be able to convey. He wished me to write to him privately on these or any other matters of interest.

He told me that two important mistakes had been made by Sir Henry Pottinger. First, in not insisting that if there were any misunderstanding as to the treaty, the English, and not the Chinese text should be taken as the authority;

T

and secondly, that he had not required that Chinese ships from *all* the ports, and not the five only, should be permitted to trade with Hong Kong.

We discussed, at much length, the subject of the internal duties, by the imposition of which the Treaty of Nanking was practically violated, and he said it must be one of my principal objects to get them removed, to the state at least in which they were before that Treaty. He said also that a practical monopoly had grown up, in violation of the Treaty, by which another *Hong* had been established, granting to fifty or sixty merchants the sole privilege of introducing certain articles, on the plea that this was necessary for the security of the Chinese revenue. To the removal of these and similar impediments to a free interchange, my attention was specially called.

I suggested to Lord Palmerston that, as there were very different usages in the five ports of China, it would be desirable that I should visit the various ports, with a view to the adoption of the best system, and assimilating the whole to that system. Lord Palmerston said that he should not object to this, provided it were done in concurrence with Mr Bonham, the Superintendent of Trade, with whom he wished me to confer on the subject.

The two points which were particularly pressed on my attention by Lord Palmerston were the removal of internal impediments to commercial transactions, and the placing the consular relations with the authorities of Canton on a proper footing.

DUKE OF WELLINGTON.

I have mentioned that I had in my boyhood a peep at Nelson in a shop at Exeter. Of the military hero, with whom we have been accustomed to pair the naval victor, I had some experience and knowledge, and have more than once somewhat disagreeably crossed his path. In 1828 I was recommended by the Financial Committee of the House of Commons (Alexander Baring, afterwards Lord Ashburton, being the Chairman), to be appointed a Commissioner to enquire into the state of the public accountancy with a view to its reform. It was proposed that Messrs Brooksbank and Beltz of the Treasury (we should have been three *Bees*) should be nominated by the Government, and that I should come in without prejudice in favour of routine, and bring into the field that practical knowledge which I possessed. The Duke of Wellington struck my name out of the Commission, saying he would never consent to the appointment of such a d——d radical. The then Chancellor of the Exchequer did his best to support me, but the Iron Duke was inexorable, and Mr Peter Abbott was selected to fill my place. The whole affair was an abortion, the Commissioners quarrelled, the officials prevailed for a time, and the public accounts were rescued from any substantial reform ; but, thanks to the perseverance of Sir Henry Parnell, a commission, consisting of himself, Lord John Russell, Sir James Graham, Sir James Kemp, Mr Edward Ellice, &c., was appointed on a change of ministry, and I was made the Secretary of the Commission. It produced the report on the Exchequer which was laid before Parliament in 1832, and which became the foundation of all the improvements which have been introduced into our financial records—whose last triumph has been in the act which requires the payment of the *gross revenues* of the State— the revenues without any deduction—into the Exchequer, thus giving Parliament an absolute control over the whole national expenditure.

I have been told that I afterwards gave offence to the Duke of Wellington by the efforts I made in Parliament to abolish corporal punishment in the army. The Duke did not willingly surrender an opinion, or part with a prejudice, yet, though for some time he stoutly held by the necessity for flogging for the preservation of discipline, on the ground mainly that the soldier was made of bad moral materials, I had the pleasure of hearing from his own lips an avowal (made in the House of Lords), that he did hope that corporal punishments might be wholly superseded in the British army. They have been nearly superseded without any injury to its efficiency, and much of pain, disgrace, and suffering have been spared. The officers connected with the ancient system of severity, who do not willingly surrender any portion of their corrective coercion and power of punishment, will continue to prognosticate all sorts of mischief to the military and marine services if men pretend to be wiser than their forefathers. It is the stale, the ever repeated fallacy which stands in the way of all improvement, but the sophism dies away as the sceptical pass from the stage, and so the great tide of reform rolls forward—the mighty tide of tendency.

Though party bitterness never forgave Sir Robert Peel the changes in his opinions and policy, those of the Duke of Wellington, though equally marked and prominent, seem not to have been recorded or remembered, or were lost sight of in the blaze of his military services. For, as regards the Test and Corporation Acts, the emancipation of the Catholics, the repeal of the Corn Laws, the question of Free Trade, and other matters, his desertion of the Tory or Conservative banners was quite as marked and quite as decided as that of the right honourable Baronet, and, considering the unbending nature of the Duke, those desertions were even more remarkable. The fact is he understood very little, if anything, of the questions of State policy, beyond the immediate field of his own personal responsibilities and duties. Of political economy he was supremely ignorant, yet his strong common sense enabled him at last to recognise some of its fundamental truths. His speeches on economical subjects teem with puerilities and absurdities, without ingenuity in conception or in expression. Of the ends and objects of government he had formed no philosophical estimate, nor dreamed that authority had any other duty or function than to cause itself to be respected and obeyed. The people were altogether a cypher in his eyes, except as grouped round the sovereignty. All his sympathies were with rulers, whatever was the character of their rule, and he cared nothing for subjects, whatever might be the nature of their subjection. But when dangers menaced the " ruling few " from the action of the " serving many," he had the sagacity to discover that those dangers justified and demanded concessions. His patrician spirit could discover that it was not safe to detach the commanders from the plebeians of the rank and file, without whom staffs and commissioned officers would cut a poor figure in the field, and so, far from being an impediment, he became a valuable instrument in forwarding a legislation disagreeable and hateful to his nature, but submitted to under the responsibilities of a high influential position.

LORD MELBOURNE.

On my return from Germany, where I represented Great Britain at the meeting of the Zoll Verein in Berlin in 1839, I accompanied a deputation to Lord Melbourne to represent that while the Corn Laws existed, there was no chance of obtaining any commercial concessions from the German States until those laws were abolished ; upon which Lord Melbourne said to the deputation that " I was mad, and fit for Bedlam " to propose anything so utterly unreasonable. Events have told a different tale.

On another occasion, when my name was introduced,

Lord Melbourne exclaimed, " Dr Bowring! d——n him,
why, he collared a prime minister!" which was the ex-
aggeration of a true story. When, with Lord Clarendon
(Mr George Villiers), I was sent to negotiate a commercial
treaty with France, M. Thiers had consented to an arrangement for the removal of the prohibition on the importation
of the finest qualities of cotton twist, and had promised
us that the ordinance announcing the removal of this prohibition should appear in the *Moniteur* of the following day.
It did not appear, upon which I made my way to M. Thiers,
and, taking his coat quietly and laughingly, I told him that
we had been seriously compromised, having announced his
formal engagement to our government, and I said, " Mon
ami, il faut que l'ordonnance paraisse sans rétard." He
made some lame excuse about " difficulties " (which no
doubt had emanated from the King, who professed free-
trade principles, but hated them at heart, and had himself
a pecuniary interest in many monopolies), but ended by
saying, " bien! ça se fera," and the ordinance appeared the
next day, so the collaring at all events was to some purpose.—1853.

LORD BROUGHAM.

Jeremy Bentham once said to Lord Brougham—

"O Henry! what a mystery you are !
Nil fuit unquam tibi tam impar!"

And, on another occasion, " Harry! when you want to
study insincerity, stand opposite a looking glass." I found
in Bentham's handwriting these words—

"Frailty! thy name is woman,
Insincerity! thy name is Brougham."

And yet Bentham had a great affection and a great admiration for Brougham, and very frequently invited him to his

table, to which also Brougham sometimes invited himself, especially when he was about to make a speech on law reform. I find one of his applications in the following shape—" Grandpapa, I want some pap ; I will come for it at your dinner hour." Bentham often expressed to me his surprise that Brougham seldom or never referred to the sources of his inspiration by mentioning his name, or lauding his writings, but, after Bentham's death, I happened to be in the library of the House of Lords, when Brougham had in his hand a large roll of paper, which I believe was a Codification Bill. He gave me laughingly a rap upon the ribs, exclaiming, " Here he is, here is our old friend Jeremy."

There was something very charming in Lord Brougham's conversation. It was playful, varied, wise, witty, full of anecdote and novelty, and overflowing with vanity. His forgetfulness was extreme. He once asked me to breakfast. I went, but he had gone out long before the breakfast hour, and told the servants they were not to expect him till dinner, and he afterwards, when I reminded him of his invitation, and of my disappointment, said with great simplicity that he had forgotten it wholly.

I think I may, at all events, say that my political career had been tolerably consistent, yet I found among Bentham's papers, which, as his executor, fell into my hands, a letter addressed to him by Brougham telling him to beware of me, as I was no better than a tool of the Tories, and by no means to be trusted, and this was written at a time when Brougham assured me he was exerting himself on my behalf, in order to secure my nomination to a professorship in the London University. It was an era in my life in which the pressure of adversity was hard upon me, and when Bentham's kindness was a plank of salvation to me. I believe the emotions excited in my mind were afterwards

made intelligible to Brougham himself when, as Lord Melbourne's executor, he turned over the correspondence of
some of his bosom friends, in which he found expressions
not very flattering to his self-love.—1853.

LORD HARDINGE.

When the inquiry into the conduct of General Darling
as Governor of Australia was before a Select Committee of
the House of Commons, Sir Henry Hardinge was the M.P.
who was the recognised advocate and friend of the accused.
It is always understood that an accused man shall have
some such defender.   On one occasion Sir Henry used his
privilege of having the room cleared, and, as it appeared
to me, pressed with cruel severity on one of the witnesses.
I said that I did not think he would have carried on the
examination as he did had the eye of the press and the
public been upon him.   He thought the remark was
damaging to his honour, and sent the Judge Advocate
(Nicol) to me the next day, asking explanation and satisfaction.   I replied that I meant no reflection upon him
which would not apply to any man, for I thought the presence of auditors and spectators a necessary protection to
the administration of justice.   He was satisfied, but I had,
I believe, no intercourse whatever with him till years after,
when, being Governor-General of India, he wrote me to
say that as he was intending to patronize the most distinguished youths among the civilians, he had fixed on a son
of mine as the first object of his attentions, and had invited him to Barrackpore.   Now this was a delightful
exhibition of a noble spirit.—1853.

DANIEL O'CONNELL.

Daniel O'Connell, during the early part of my connection
with public affairs, was a prominent actor in the political

scene. His rude, robust, impassioned eloquence produced a greater impression upon assembled multitudes than that of any other man of whom I have had any knowledge. I was with him on the Calton Hill at Edinburgh, when he harangued an incredible gathering of the people, who seemed to roll to and fro, like waves in a storm, under the magic influence of his oratorical powers. It was a sudden outbreak, descriptive of the magnificent scenery of that remarkable locality ; the hills, the sea, the ancient and the modern city, upon which the sun was brightly shining, were the themes of his outpourings, and they lost nothing of their effect from the strongly Hibernian pronunciation which distinguished them. When he came into Parliament, it was said that the Irish demagogue would lose all influence there, but his ready and original wit, and his vituperations—often coarse and personal—obtained for him a ready attention on the part of the honourable House. He was sometimes singularly felicitous in his illustrations, two of which I have mentioned under the head of " Parliamentary Recollections."

It was O'Connell who gave a national character to the discontents of his country. He worried the English government by the menace of dissolving the Union, and found this to be a chord which met with strong sympathy among the Hibernians—the talisman by which all their grievances would be redressed. There were many who believed that, if he could have effected the repeal, he would have shrunk from the responsibility ; but, vile as were the means by which that union was brought about, and disgraceful as was the conduct of many who were prominent parties to it, there are few, I suppose, who would not now acknowledge that the connection of Ireland with Great Britain has been a blessing to both countries. As a law-reformer, O'Connell rendered great assistance to the cause of progress.

I have in my possession some of his letters, of great length,
addressed to Jeremy Bentham, whom he held in the highest
esteem, full of admirable matter connected with this
important topic. The injudicious conduct of the government in their persecutions, and the abuse in many of the
English papers of the " big beggar man," naturally enough
exasperated a proud and sensitive mind.

He was a charming companion. Educated at Douai, he
was an almost fanatical Catholic, wore a scapular upon his
bosom, and showed immense reverence for the Papacy and
the priesthood. His nature was so impulsive that, though
he must have regarded the character, both public and
private, of the Prince Regent with dislike and distrust, he
rushed into the water to welcome him when honouring
Ireland with his visit. His parliamentary influence was at
one time incredibly great. He brought several of his sons,
a son-in-law, and his nephew into the House of Commons,
and these formed but a small part of the persons who owed
their seats to his intervention. When Joseph Hume very
prudently refused to incur the expenses of a contested
election for Middlesex, O'Connell found a seat for him in
an Irish borough. The charge against him of avaricious
selfishness in receiving the contributions of the people as a
recompense for his many professional sacrifices was unreasonable, inasmuch as he lost much more than he gained
under the new arrangement, but with his death his influence
passed away, and his name and fame have been strangely
forgotten.

He left his body to his country, but directed his heart to
be sent to Rome as evidence of the strength of his attachment to the Catholic faith. He had a great zest for the
enjoyment of the beauties of nature, especially in their
wilder character, and I have heard him describe with poetic
enthusiasm the delight with which he saw and heard the

waves dashing upon the coast of Kerry, and led his beagles to the chase in the neighbourhood of Derrynane Abbey. His character was an incarnation of his country, and it seemed as if all the faults and virtues, the foibles and eccentricities of the Emerald Isle had been mingled and moulded into his individual self. He was greater than Demosthenes in Athens, Cicero in Rome, or Mirabeau in France. In his domestic relations he was honoured and beloved. He was of gigantic size, which was the more remarkable when compared with the small stature of Richard Lalor Sheil, who stood next to him in the estimation of his countrymen, and whose shrill and feminine voice formed a singular contrast to the deep and sonorous tones of the more formidable agitator.

O'Connell had an intense dislike to Disraeli. He was one of six members of Parliament who, on the right honourable's first appearance in the field of public life, commended him to a radical constituency on the ground of his attachment to liberal principles. He afterwards called him "a recreant deserter," and hurled at him the scathing denunciation of being "the direct descendant of the impenitent thief." Yet evidence may be seen in Disraeli's political career that there is an under-current in his mind of democratic opinion, of which his speeches in favour of reform, avowing that he would go further than the liberal party, his coquetting with the Manchester school, when by their aid he hoped to continue to hold the reins of Government, and the distrust with which he is spoken of by the representatives of the old Tory régime, afford abundant evidence. That, if an opportunity occurred, he would imitate the conduct of Sir Robert Peel, and incur the opprobrium of having deserted his party, I cannot doubt ; but there is not in him that stability and honesty which distinguished the man who had the courage and the truthfulness to avow that he had been converted to the principles of free trade by the irresistible arguments of a political opponent, Richard Cobden, and this avowal was the more remarkable, as on a former occasion Sir Robert had even accused Cobden of something like an encouragement to assassinate him by holding him up to popular reprobation as an enemy of the people. I remember few things with greater complacency in my House of Commons' experience than that speech in which he said that his cup of life would be sweetened by the thought that he had cheapened the poor man's daily bread. Had his life been spared, I have no doubt he would have originated many other important reforms. Long before he announced his purpose, the workings of his mind were manifest in his conversations with others, in which he sought to elicit information on subjects to which his thoughts were directed. I have seen him perambulating the Queen's Square Place garden with the venerable sage (Bentham), discussing matters of law-reform, and I have reason to think great changes were contemplated by him in the ecclesiastical field which, in due time, would have developed themselves, had it been the will of Providence to maintain him in his high position.

RICHARD COBDEN.

Cobden's name has obtained far too much celebrity, and his history is too well-known to sanction any observations of mine upon either. I deem him one of the most privileged, as he deserves to be one of the most honoured of his race. No man has ever been called in to exercise more important functions, and no man's exertions have been more successful in their issue, or more unpretending in their display. No doubt he has been rewarded by proofs of the most general sympathy. Those were indeed for him proud moments when *The Times* announced the existence of the Anti-Corn-Law League as a great fact, and when Peel avowed that Cobden was the apostle who had converted him from the errors of his ways in the field of political economy. Cobden has been tried by heavy domestic sorrows in the loss of his only son—an affliction far more hard to endure than the endless vituperations of which he has been the object. His strength has always been found in his advocacy of sound principles to be carried out in their full extension. No surrender of a truth—no compromise with an error. Yet he has always been willing to take reasonable instalments towards the payment of a just debt, he has never sacrificed an obtainable good in the pursuit of an unapproachable better, but has felt that every step forward is progress, leaving less to be done than if that step had not been taken. This is practical philosophy and sound wisdom—it is a disarming of the enemy to employ against him the weapons he has surrendered. Then again, there has been on Cobden's part no jealousy or distrust of fellow-labourers—on the contrary, they have been most cordially welcomed to co-operate.—1861.

C. P. THOMSON (LORD SYDENHAM).

Among the public men whom I have been instrumental in bringing into the field of politics was Charles Poulett Thomson, afterwards Lord Sydenham. He was a young Russia merchant of considerable sharpness and sagacity, and had made himself acquainted with the principles of political economy. He had an ambition for public life. I introduced him to Joseph Hume, and through him he was introduced to the electors of Dover, and returned by them to Parliament. He became useful to Lord Althorp, brought much commercial knowledge and aptitude for business into the field, made his way to the Vice-Presidency, and afterwards to the Presidency of the Board of Trade, and became

Governor-General of Canada. But he was by no means a man of high capacity, or of remarkable stedfastness and soundness of opinion. Happily the tide of his interests rolled in the current of his knowledge. He abandoned Dover to represent Manchester, and his connection with that free-trade citadel, in which popular opinion was becoming more and more patent, and more and more enlightened, gave Thomson an influential status in the government, in parliament, and in the country. Yet he was not the man to conceive, and still less to undertake, anything essentially grand. His free-trade schemes were puny, hesitating, and imperfect. He ought to have anticipated Peel in his nobler and wider conceptions, but that was beyond his grasp. He was ever querulous, impatient, and unteachable when anything was suggested of a more comprehensive and embracing character than a policy founded on an instinct of self-preservation appeared to warrant. This is the curse of party factions. They look mainly to their own safety, and will only cede so much to public opinion as will enable them to hold exclusively the reins of power. If public opinion demand anything which imperils a party object, they will despise and oppose that opinion. Thus it is that concessions which might be gracefully and becomingly made, are extorted by an irresistible pressure, and parties lose the reputation they might acquire by what may seem a self-sacrificing course of action. But party-selfishness had generally destroyed public confidence, which looks with almost equal indifference on both sides of the House, and no wonder.

Thomson obtained a peerage, which died with him. He suffered much from gout, and died at an age which might have opened to him very bright prospects, but perhaps he was not winged with strength for a higher flight than that to which he reached—1853.

TALLEYRAND.

From Talleyrand I received once a very gracious compliment. He said I was the only man who ever made an
intellectual treaty. During my residence in Paris in 1830,
a proposal was approved of, both by the French and English
governments, that there should be a yearly gratuitous interchange of the literature of both countries, and that such
interchange should not be interrupted by war, but that the
vessels bearing the books should pass unmolested. The
British minister endeavoured to purchase from one of the
Scotch universities a right then enjoyed to a copy of every
book published, but the negotiation failed, and the object
was not accomplished. An arrangement was, however,
made between the Chamber of Peers and the House of
Lords for the mutual communication of all parliamentary
documents. I was the victim on this occasion of a shabby
act of *petitesse* from M. Guizot, then Minister of Public
Instruction in France. M. Semonville, the Grand Réferen-
daire of the French Chamber, proposed to him that, as a
testimony of the value set upon my services, the grand
edition of Denon's 'Egypt,' published at the government
cost, should be given to me, but M. Guizot said he thought
it was too liberal an acknowledgment. M. Semonville then
suggested that the volumes of the " Antiquities of Greece,"
a work of less value, might be presented, but excuses were
made, and I did not receive it. I heard of the steps taken
from M. Semonville himself, and have reason to believe
that M. Guizot was influenced by a dislike towards me
resulting from some strong expressions I had used, and
which had been repeated to him, condemnatory of certain
acts of his administration. Guizot is by nature a stern,
narrow-minded, pedagogical man. With all his asceticism,
he had the strongest thirst for power, and with all his pro-

fessions of liberalism, he was a decided despot. He was furious in his moderation. He laid down his principles of government, which he called free and constitutional, but he exacted for them the most slavish deference.

When Talleyrand was ambassador from Louis Philippe to the British Court, he occupied the house in Hanover Square in which Lord Grey had lived, and in which he fancied he saw that human head which entered the room, looked at his lordship, and then took its departure. Talleyrand said he had never been honoured by the presence of the mysterious visitant, and that he liked a haunted house just as well as any other; and I remember saying to him, " The spirits are afraid to encounter you." Talleyrand's conversation was terse and sententious. His readiness was wonderful, but the few words he uttered showed often re- markable sagacity. What could be more biting than his answer to the minister who said to him in his diplomatic perplexity, " Je sens tous les tourments de l'enfer "—" Eh comment ! déja ? " What more embarrassingly flattering than the reply to Madame de Stael, who, in responding to some perhaps overstrained compliments to her intellect, said, " But, Prince, if Madame Récamier and I were both to fall into the water at the same time, which would you save ? "—" Madame ! vous sauriez nager." His chin and mouth were usually buried in the folds of a large white cravat, and the effect was odd when he raised his head to utter some sharp witticism. I was once dining with him— the Duke of Kent was one of the guests—the cuisine was exquisite, and the wines particularly of the very finest quality. The Duke, lauding one of the specimens, asked the Prince its age, and he answered, " Il est aussi vieux que moi," and it appeared that it was the produce of a vintage gathered in the very year of his birth. Before Thiers had attained his celebrity, he mentioned him to me as a young politician who had a "grand avenir" before him, and he spoke admiringly of the talents of Van de Weyer, who was then entering upon the cares of public life. Jeremy Bentham was once the subject of conversation, and he said he had known many able men, but, as a *man of genius*, Bentham overtopped them all. Bentham and he had been acquaintances in the earlier period of the French Revolution. It was at the time of Mirabeau's great oratorical successes, for many of whose most splendid speeches, Dumont of Geneva, Bentham's French interpreter, furnished the materials. I had occasion to bring the statesman and the philosopher together after a separation of forty years. I mentioned to Bentham the language in which Talleyrand spoke of him, and he asked whether he would accept a dinner-invitation to the hermitage. Talleyrand said he would give up any and every engagement for the pleasure of meeting his ancient acquaintance. They met, and an amusing and instructive colloquy took place between one of the busiest actors in the great scenes of the world, and the almost inaccessible recluse whose life was given up to meditation and study. 1861.

LA FAYETTE.

La Fayette was called by the Royalists during the early part of the French Revolution the "Grandison Robespierre," than which no designation was ever less deserved; for, though sometimes weak of purpose, and seduced by the flattery of the Court on the one hand, and the desire to win popular applause on the other, a more sincere and incorruptible man never appeared on the stage of public events. The republican tendencies of the young enthusiast were displayed in his visit to America where, going to assist the so-called rebels in their resistance to monarchical despotism, he was received as if he had been an angelic visitant.

U

The head of one of the first families in France, he flung aside his title of Marquis, detached the aristocratic *De* from his name, and adopted all the forms of commonwealth simplicity. Loaded with evidences of American gratitude, he returned to France, and could scarcely fail to be selected as a leader in the great liberal movement. His counsels, had they been listened to, might have saved the King from destruction, but, as in the case of the Stuart Charles, the Bourbon Louis disgusted his best friends by his faithlessness and treachery, and became another example of the truth of the ancient maxim, " The gods infatuate those they mean to overthrow." That he should have escaped amidst all the dangers that menaced him, obnoxious as he became to the Court, and distrusted by the mob, is not among the least remarkable of the events of that wonderful chapter in history. He bore serenely the rigours of his imprisonment at Olmütz, and became again all-influential when the three glorious days of July called him prominently forward.

In his family relations, he was one of the happiest of men, and it was a delightful privilege to be his guest at his country seat at La Grange, where, surrounded by a numerous family, he was the object of universal affection and reverence. No doubt he was sadly disappointed by the course of action pursued by Louis Philippe, who, to him, more than to any man, owed his regal position. His disappointment was shared by Lafitte, Du Pont de l'Eure, and the other great men, who created an influence which soon became too strong for their control, but the field is too wide to be here explored.—1861.

BARRY O'MEARA

said—" I saw the Duke of Sussex yesterday. He told me I had killed Lord Castlereagh. That will console me for the rest of my life."

DUMOURIEZ.

General Dumouriez, in whose eyes yet sparkled that extraordinary vivacity which led Charles IV. of Spain to say—"aquel Francesito tiene los ojos endiablados," was talking to me over old times, and throwing the spirit of his genius over all his narratives. He said—"When I was first introduced to Paul at Petersburg, I found him, with Alexander acting the part of a page, and the courtiers before him, arranged in straight and formal lines according to their rank. He said to me, 'How comes it that you—vous autres Français—do such fine and glorious things, and gain such splendid victories? What can I do with a sty of pigs like these?—un tas de cochons comme voila?' pointing to his court. I answered, "C'est par l'impulsion de la gloire, l'appliquant à recompenser la bravoure et à punir la lacheté.' 'Bah,' replied Paul, 'de la gloire ! ! ! Parlez de la gloire à ces cochons là,' and swept away abruptly as usual." The next time he went to court, Dumouriez was nearly hidden behind a column, when Paul entered, with the Empress hanging on his arm. He was dressed in his usual uniform, with white silk stockings and white kid gloves. He marched on, and, perceiving Dumouriez, smiled, and when he came opposite to him, turned off at right angles, dragging his wife, and shouting, "Général! je vous présente ma femme," which being said, he turned off abruptly, and hastened forwards. Paul's vehemence of character is well known, and when irritated, he seemed to have all the ferocity of a demon. A young lady of whom the Emperor was enamoured—Nellidoo was her name—was once present during one of Paul's paroxysms (she was, Dumouriez said, small and short, and ugly as himself, but with l'esprit d'un diable). She seized him violently with both hands by the collar, and dragged him

to a mirror, to which she pointed, exclaiming, " See what
a horrible countenance you have." Paul sprang upon the
glass, and broke it into a thousand pieces with his feet.
" Now Sire !" said she, " you have only multiplied your
hideous figure !" She was banished, and her recall could
not be obtained. " Paul," said Dumouriez, " gave me his
picture, which I gave to the Prince Regent (George IV.)
I visited Gustavus Adolphus in his closet. He had the
smallest room and the biggest sword I ever saw, so that he
was constantly tumbling over it, or obliged to hug it in his
arms in order to move about. He consulted me about his
campaigns, and took out of his pocket a vile little map of
post-roads, by which he began to explain his military plans,
but it was so small, that Pomerania, to which all his projects were directed, was not there. However, he talked on.
He had a plan for making Stralsund an impregnable fortress,
and meant to build bastions, &c., of the bricks of the merchants' houses, which he said he would destroy. Il n'avait
pas le sens commun.

" Meyer was not satisfied with my translation of his
little book on France. Klopstock said to me, however,
" Meyer aime trop à farder. Il veut trop peindre en beau.
Vous l'avez fait parler un langage plus raisonnable."

" My grandfather had thirty-two children, every one of
whom reached the age of twenty-two, and often twenty-
five or twenty-six grown-up children sat at his table.

" I was omnipotent when I had little claim to the good
opinion of my country. I won the battle of Jemappes.
They disorganised my army, took all power out of my
hands, and sacrificed me."—1822.

Dumouriez died on 2d March 1823 at Turvile Park, aged
eighty-four, his last days having been made comfortable by
a liberal allowance from the then Duke of Orleans, which
enabled him to keep a carriage. The General had, I believe,

a pension of £1000 a year from the British Government, with whom he was in intimate communication, and for whom he drew up a plan of defence against the menaced French invasion. At his death, his papers were purchased by the Government from his executors. The accusation that he had sold himself to the enemy was certainly groundless, for he was almost penniless when he quitted the army, and subsisted for some time in Germany by the use of his pen before he emigrated to England. I left London in the vain hope of finding him alive, but found him a corpse. He had enjoyed life to the very last, and a few hours before his death, had walked to the window, and looked over the green common with complacent and delighted satisfaction. I had hoped for one glance from those bright eyes, but they were closed, and for ever. He was dead, stiff, calm, and silent. He who shook empires, frozen as a wintry clod. The spirit of Jemappes stilled and voiceless. A short time before his death his hands were often observed to be closed. "Que faites vous, mon Général ?"—"Je me recueille," I am harvesting myself. What a harvest! The Catholic priest behaved manfully. Le Dieu said, " the General believed in God, and in a future state. He did harm to none, but good wherever he could. We will not have his last moments tormented with cruel questionings." The priest crossed his eyelids with the holy oil (extreme unction), in silence,—and the General died.

He had seen much of kings, and estimated them at their value. Take an anecdote of his of the present Emperor of Austria (1823). When the news of the taking of Mantua was brought to him, he opened the letter, and seemed to read it attentively. He snatched at the sheet suddenly, exclaiming, " I have caught him." A fly had just pitched upon the sheet, which the wary monarch had entrapped. He threw down the sheet unfinished. Who shall say, " Aquila non captat muscas" ?—1823.

LÉON FAUCHER.

France, more perhaps than any country in Europe with
the exception of Turkey, presents examples of the most remarkable changes associated with the history of her public
men. In the fall of the aristocracy, as in the rise of men
of the people, many lessons are to be found of the strange
chances which mortal flesh is heir to. Léon Faucher's history is a very singular one. His character was marked by
great buoyancy of mind, integrity of conduct, perseverance
in the objects of his ambition, and a courage not to be re-
pressed by any misadventure. He was born in obscurity,
and the pangs of poverty were augmented by family dissensions, which led to the separation of his father and mother;
but even in his earlier studies, he gave evidence of intellectual superiority, and carried off many of the prizes
that were accessible to competition. But the small town
of Limoges offered too narrow a field for his genius, and
having great facility in composition, he made his way to
Paris, where a ready writer seldom fails to find employment
for his pen. He determined to establish a newspaper, but
had certainly not estimated the difficulties attending such
an enterprise in a capital where the public press is in the
hands of influential and opulent men, and where most of
the principal journals represent the opinions of large political sections of the community. He failed, and his failure
involved him in debt, led to his imprisonment, and reduced
him to such straits that he was often obliged to ask for a
meal from the bounty of his friends. He had scarcely where-
with to shelter himself from the inclemency of the weather,
and was obliged to.pledge his little possessions in order to
keep body and soul together. But his indomitable perseverance never abandoned him, and his literary reputation
grew by the production of a number of papers in the

periodicals, in which he treated subjects of finance, political economy, and other matters which occupied the French mind, and in which he exhibited great sagacity and varied information. The breaking down of the barriers between the different States of Germany in the great federation called the Zoll Verein led him to conceive of a similar custom-house union between France, Belgium, Spain, and Switzerland. It was a natural proposal to come from one who had been an early apostle of free-trade, and who saw more facilities in binding the smaller nations to France, than in emancipating France and England from the heavy fetters which obstructions and monopolies had placed upon both. His great desire, however, was to get into the Chamber of Deputies, which he naturally thought would afford him the widest sphere of useful action. He made four or five unsuccessful efforts, being generally defeated by some representative either of the agricultural or manufacturing interests of France, but he ultimately effected his purpose, and became one of the most useful of deputies, for, though he could scarcely be called an eloquent man, his sound arguments and valuable statistics gave weight to his opinions, and, in committees especially, his services were most invaluable. He had travelled in England during the time of the great anti-corn-law agitation, had made the acquaintance of many of our most eminent free-traders, returned to France more firm than ever in the sound principles of political economy, and gave his opinion to the world in several papers of great excellence.

He married Miss Wolowska, a sister of the lecturer on political economy, well known in the world of literature and public affairs. In 1848-49, Faucher became one of the French Cabinet, and was also made a member of the Institute. His political opinions, though republican, were not extreme, and he was unfriendly to the action of universal suffrage. He showed some restlessness and impatience under the sway of Louis Napoleon, then President of the Republic, and of course was not long allowed to occupy his official position. He died of pleurisy in 1854. His "poor tenement of clay was o'er informed," and he bore about him evident marks of exhaustion and weariness. The pecuniary difficulties which had overshadowed his earlier life had been removed, and though his style of living was always simple, his home afforded him all the felicity which a happy union could bring. Madame Faucher's patriotism and love of her country were such as may be said to characterize almost all Polish women, and while her husband's memory will long be honoured for his personal virtues, he will be deemed one of those who gave no small impulse to the progress of reform at home, and the brotherhood of nations abroad—1861.

ARLÈS DUFOUR.

Amiable alike in all the relations of private life, and respected in his public career, Arlès Dufour of Lyons has ever been most loved and honoured by those to whom he has been best known. It is impossible to estimate the amount of good done by a man of intelligence, activity, and strong convictions, in a sphere where his intellectual superiority gives him pre-eminence. Arlès was not only an earnest promoter of every philanthropic project in Lyons, but one of the most efficient advocates of the great principles of Free Trade in the Chamber of Commerce, and through the public press. It is to the honour of Manchester, and the cotton-interest, as to that of Lyons, as representing the silk-trade—these being the most interesting and the most advanced of the manufactures of the two countries—that they have struggled for emancipation, and have been the faithful exponents of the soundest political economy. They have not only furnished irresistible arguments, but the statistics of important and conclusive facts, and in their prosperity and self-sustained strength have given admirable lessons to the world. Some of the most instructive documents which have been published emanated from Arlès' pen, and if men like Chevalier Frederick Bastian, and some others, have been better known, it must be attributed to the circumstance that they have been, not anonymous writers, but open and avowed partisans of opinions which have of late years been spreading through society like a new revelation of truth and soberness.

Arlès owed much to the influence of the St Simonians, among whom the Père Enfantin was the object of his special reverence. Whatever tares and weeds may be found in the harvesting of this strange community, there was in all their teachings abundance of the good and prolific seed of a genuine and generous philanthropy, which has produced excellent fruits in many of the leading minds of France. International hatreds have disappeared wherever the St Simonian creed has prevailed, and with it the conviction has spread that love, not hatred, peace, not war, unchecked commercial intercourse, not repulsion, are the motives by which nations should be influenced, and the objects for which they should strive—that if God, in His all-wise providence, has given to each people its advantages of climate, soil, and production, it was not for selfish but for cosmopolitan ends—it was that the superfluities of each may be interchanged with those of all others—it was in a word, that benefits and blessings might be maximized over the widest space, and for the whole human family. Men like Arlès become the apostles of this genuine Christianity, and if the little candle throws its beams afar, the light that is set on high cannot be hid, and, fed by heaven's flame, will burn and brighten for ever and ever.

It would be an interesting task to discover and disclose the gems of truth and words of wisdom which exist in the teachings of *all* the founders of new religions. Even among the Mormons there is something to be learnt. For example, "To say 'I cannot,' is to condemn yourself to helplessness—to say 'I will try,' is the way to accomplish wonders—but to proclaim 'I am determined to succeed,' will work even miracles." * So in the St Simonian creed, how much of practical good sense is there in the command-ment, "To each the labour according to his talents, to all the recompense according to their deserts." These, like Bacon's great aphorism, "Look to the end †—let experi-ence be fruitful, authority barren"—or Bentham's " maxi-mize aptitude, minimize expense"—"seek the greatest good of the greatest number"—these, and other such are as pole-stars to guide our way. They constitute a higher code of instruction than is to be found in contradictory proverbs, and represent the concentrated deductions of a sound and stable philosophy.—1861.

D'ARGENSON (VOYER)

Said, " It is necessary that an influence be given to the wealth gained by industry equal to its importance in society, and that hereditary wealth possessed by indolence and laziness be reduced in its influence to the point of its comparative worthlessness.

---

* By the last returns given by M. Rémy in his *Voyage au pays des Mormons* (Paris, 1860), the number of Latter Day Saints is estimated at 186,600—of whom 33,000 are in the British Islands, 80,000 in Utah, 40,000 in the United States, and the rest scattered over the world. In France, only 500 are re-ported to exist.

† I do not know that Jouffray's maxim " The best criterion of morality is the course which best secures the universal end "—or the aphorism proposed by some French writers, " Duty is that which looks to the universal end with a view to the general good"—practically differs from Bentham's theory, though the phraseology is more diffuse.

" Buonaparte was not eloquent. He had a wonderful effusion of words, and was remarkably verbose. He talked, and talked, and talked, and it was only now and then that he talked with talent. In such a mass of talking, of course there fell something from him worth recording, and it was always recorded. But on great occasions, when eloquence might have materially served him, he was generally obscure and wordy. He erred in the gross—he erred in the details of his conduct. He hated liberty, and spurned the principles on which his greatness was built. He wanted to blend extremes—old civilization with liberal institutions. He re-created nobility, he re-introduced expensive farces and delusive follies, and would unite them with the stern simplicity of republicanism. He would be crowned by the Pope, and he would have had the *ampoule* of the Holy Spirit if he could have managed the trick. He married an Emperor's daughter, to show that he made common cause with monarchs. All this was blindness. He ruined his country and ruined himself.

" He had, after all, no great discrimination. Gourgaud told me that when his escape from St Helena was plotted, he refused to seek an asylum in the United States. He exclaimed, ' Je n'aime pas les Américains. Ils me vendraient.' "—1822.

FOURNIER PESCAY

Said, " I lived three years with Ferdinand, and his brother and uncle at Valengay. Carlos was a poor superstitious wretch—Antonio half an ass and half a pig, ignorant and brutish. Ferdinand was the vilest, and coldest, and most abject piece of servility I ever met with. He rose at 7—when ready, his valets were called to assist him at his wardrobe, and I was introduced. He never varied his form of salutation, ' Bon jour, comment te portes tu ? '

After his chocolate, the correspondence and newspapers were brought, the former having always been examined before. The first things that arrested his attention were the enigmas and charades, and he cried out 'Devine ça.' When found out, he never would believe that the guess was right, but said 'We shall see to-morrow,' and that was always part of the morrow's business. He generally read the prayers himself, and when pleased with anybody, would say, 'Tu iras avec moi à la messe.' (In Spain, the King always uses the second person singular). He dined with his brothers at 12 o'clock, and afterwards slept (the siesta) till 4, when he played at cards, but would never learn any game but 'la mouche,' the game of the most common and vulgar classes. He used to translate the journals for his uncle, who understood no French. It was I who wrote the famous letter in which he entreated Napoleon to call him *his son*, and to give him his sister in marriage. I entreated him on my knees not to do so foolish a thing, but he insisted on it, though he afterwards declared that the letter was sent to him ready-written by Buonaparte. When the Emperor received it, he burst out laughing, and said, ' Combien ils sont vils ces Bourbons ! ' Napoleon sent the letter to the *Moniteur*, but never deigned to answer it.

"His mistresses were the washerwomen and servant girls who visited his apartments. At dinner he delighted himself with reading the inscriptions on the bon-bons, and making others read them. C'était un véritable enfantillage. He went out every day, except when it rained in torrents, and his invitation was invariably ' Voulons nous aller nous promener.' "—1822.

COUNT PORRO

Said, " I had once a singular conversation with the Pope, who said to me, ' Murat is a very good fellow, but

I'll tell you what passed on one occasion between him and
me.' He said, ' Holy Father! I have a favour to ask '—
' Well, what is it ? ' ' I hope, Holy Father, you are disposed
to grant it.' ' Yes, if it is reasonable.' ' I want you, Holy
Father, to excommunicate the Carbonari.' ' No ; that I
cannot do.' ' Holy Father, you wish well to me, and this
would be serving me.' ' Well! I will do it, on one condition.' ' What is that, Holy Father ? ' ' I will excommunicate the Freemasons at the same time.' ' No! no! Holy
Father.' The truth is Murat was a Freemason."—1822.

N. PICCOLO.

Piccolo was a Greek who honoured his country, and, overflowing with fine and generous emotions, devoted thought
and action wholly to the liberation of Greece. He wrote
that fine appeal to the English, which was published in
1821 in the *Examiner* and other papers. It was an unsuccessful appeal. He observed—and it was observed with
truth—that the love of liberty is much less extensively
circulated in England than in France. It is less understood
here. Our people, deceived by vague declamations about
" our glorious constitution "—" wisdom of ancestors "—and
other delusions, rivetted in their minds from childhood upwards, have really a very imperfect notion of good government. They are badly off, and wish for change, but they
do not see how all-important it is that the change should
be erected on a popular and extensive principle.

I enjoy those orientalisms and ancient usages which are
still preserved among the Greeks. When I was travelling
with a Sciote in the South of France, our affections had
blended, and we were about to separate with mutual regret.
He proposed that we should go into the woods to seek some
rivulet, and wash each other's feet, as Jesus did, as a token
of love. I am not one who can resist such appeals to the
heart.—1822.

FOSSOMBRONI.

Fossombroni was prime minister when I was in Tuscany.
He was a very clever man, but of course lost in the narrow
sphere to which his abilities were confined. Buonaparte
said of him, " C'est un géant dans un entresol." He often
was very happy in his talk, and had much influence with
the Grand Duke Leopold, whose unbending gravity was not
always pleasing to the more lively and imaginative minister.
On one occasion when Leopold was encouraging Fossombroni
to point out any of his political mistakes, the minister said,
" V. A. ha un difetto." " Cosa è ? cosa è ? " enquired the
Prince, " V. A. non sa ridere"—your Highness cannot
laugh. The services Fossombroni rendered to his country
by draining and filling up the Maremma are beyond all
praise. Under his auspices, health supplanted disease, and
fertility superseded barrenness, the fetid marsh became a
fruitful plain, and vast tracks where disease and death
reigned were made habitable and salubrious.

SONNET TO COUNT FOSSOMBRONI.

" If sovereigns throw a glorious light on story,
    When peace and peaceful triumphs mark their reign,
They too shall reap their portion of the glory
    Who led them on—nor led them on in vain.
Blest he whom years have crowned with honours hoary,
    Whose memory, tracking life's long path again,
Sees—not war's footsteps barbarous and gory,
    But flowers and fruits and harvests in the plain,
Which he hath planted ! Statesman ! thou shalt cull,
    In Chian's vale and the Maremmas wide,
Laurels of brighter green, and nobler pride,
    More lasting, more divine, more beautiful,
Than those men wreathe around the warrior's brow,
    Thine the true conquests—the true conqueror thou."

                                        Florence, 30th Dec. 1836

MINA*

Said, "During the war of independence, I kept up a correspondence with Carlota (the Queen of Portugal, and sister of Ferdinand), who wanted above all things to become Regent in Spain, and then Queen, to accomplish which she would have sacrificed brothers and sisters, husband and children. Her daughter, the wife of Don Carlos, is her image, just as bad, and has a hundred *queridos*. When I went to call on Don Carlos at the palace, he called her 'Maria Francesca!' She came in—a dirty sloven, her hair tangled, a common cotton gown on, and said to me abruptly, 'Ah! Mina! mama te quiere mucho-mucho. Has tenido una larga correspondencia con ella?' 'Si Señora.' 'Si, mucho te quiere, mucho. Ha roto algunas cartas tuyas, pero muchas guarde, muchas.' 'Pues, yo, Señora, todas las guardo.'"† A friend of Mina had great influence over her, for she had committed herself by her letters to him. He told me that she had several times hinted that to reign was worth shedding some blood for. She did not care for a few heads rolling, be they whose they might.

"How did you manage your correspondence with the Queen of Portugal," I asked Mina. "By special couriers. She said the Empeanado and I were the only men in Spain who could do the thing, and she wrote me thirty-six or thirty-four letters. In one, she offered me anything I could ask. I sent copies of all her letters and of all my answers to the Regency, and she found it out at last. If she caught me, she would flay me." "Tell me what passed in your interviews with Ferdinand?" "I saw him first in 1814,

---

* The well-known Spanish Guerilla partisan.

† 'Ah! Mina! mamma loves thee much. Hast thou had an extensive correspondence with her?' 'Yes, Señora.' 'Yes, she loves thee much. She has destroyed some of thy letters, but keeps many, very many.' 'And I, Señora, keep them all.'

after the war of independence. He sent for me, and said, ' Mina ! mucho deseaba verte '—I wished much to see thee. I said, ' Your Majesty has only to command my presence.' ' I am very glad to see thee. How do things go on ? ' ' Your Majesty is surrounded by knaves and flatterers, bringing on the perdition of Spain.' ' Yes ! I have many flatterers, what shall I do ? ' ' Dismiss them all, and seek trustworthy and honest men.' ' I'll do it instantly.' He then began to vituperate Eguia, and the other ministers, and said he would form a new list.

" Castaño came to me very much perplexed. He had an affection for me, and I for him. He said, ' Son of mine, son of mine, you must not talk thus at Court. You don't know how to behave yourself. You should not sow dissensions and enmities thus.' ' I suppose *you* do not talk in this style, but I cannot talk in any other. A king has no more in him to me than any other man.' I was only a few days in Madrid. I was wretched there. I would rather live in the free air, or the mountains, or anywhere. ' *Did* he change his ministers ? ' said I. ' No.' ' What do you think of Ferdinand ? ' ' A timid, trembling knave.' When I spoke to him, the perspiration ran over his brow. He would have done anything—anything. He sent for me in 1822. I arrived post, and before I visited my lodgings, covered with dust as I was, I went to the palace, and asked to see the king. He was with one of his mistresses, and appointed me to come in the morning. When I was introduced to him, we talked of the insurrection in Catalonia, and I said I would soon put *that* down, but that his Majesty ought to know that the heads of the faction were not in Catalonia, but in Madrid. Everybody felt it was necessary that the ministry should be changed, and different members were to be proposed, but there were some names which were so hateful to the king, yet so necessary for the people, that no one would venture to propose them. Abisbal was wanted as Inspector-General of the army. The king hates him cordially, yet he is the only man in Spain fit for that office. No one would propose him. Nerva Pambley said he could not—dared not. I said, 'What! you won't propose, from men's fear, that which is so necessary for the country?' 'El Rey me echarà un ajo.' 'Well, throw another at him, or come down to the Cortes, and say the king has insulted you while you were discharging your duty, but speak firmly. Does he sweat when you speak to him? (He hace S. M. sudar?)' I went to the king, told him that Abisbal must be appointed, and brought back the order, written in pencil by Fernando himself.

"When I was at Madrid, charged with the affairs of the *Tribunal volante*, which had been established during the war of independence, but whose decrees the tribunal had refused to sanction, in consequence of which many thousand families were in a state of great distress, I went to the Minister of Grace and Justice, and urged his expediting the matter. He hesitated, asked for time, and would not be hurried. I went to the king, and said, 'This decision, your Majesty, can and must delay no longer.' 'Let us talk with the Minister of Grace and Justice.' 'I cannot answer for your Majesty's safety if it is not despatched.' 'But,' said the king, 'must I approve of all they have done? How do I know what iniquities I may sanction?' 'The thing, please your Majesty, has been for a long time before the Minister of Grace and Justice. Every cause was decided by judges, and I have approved them. Six thousand families of Navarre and Aragon are clamorous. There can be no longer delay.' The king took a pencil and ordered the minister to despatch the matter. 'Will your Majesty authorize me to say that it must be despatched immediately?' 'Yes!' It was eleven o'clock at night. I went

x

instantly to the minister's house, who said it was impossible then, that his secretaries had left the office, that the time was unreasonable, that he must examine the affair, &c. I said, ' Sir, will you or will you not obey the king's orders instantly ? ' I will not be put off (for I knew that, if he saw the king, the order would be changed). He said the decree was by far too comprehensive. I replied that I would not leave the place until he expedited the order. He sent for his secretary, and ordered him to prepare the despatch, with which I went at six in the morning to the king, who signed it. I called on the Infante, Don Carlos, who said to me, ' Mina, vas a Cataluña contre los facciosos ? '—' Si Señor '—' Jode los, jode los.'

" ' Do you know the Infante Don Francisco ? ' ' Yes, I lived with him for a long time.' He once said to me, ' My brother (the king) is not a constitutional—I am. Do the people like me ? Have I any party ? ' (for, though a miserable fellow, he has much ambition). I said, ' You have, sir, the party of the Spanish nation.' He was prodigiously delighted, and wanted to give me two fine horses from his stables, which I refused. I would not have it said that I received favours from the princes."—1825.

ECHEVERRIA, J. T.

Echeverria came to Europe with Revenga to induce the Spanish government to recognize the independence of Columbia. His health had been shattered by his sufferings in the patriotic cause, he having been shut up for many months in a mountainous and desert spot with nothing but roots and wild fruits to exist on. Bentham endeavoured to persuade him to use his influence with the Columbian government in favour of the cession of a part of the Isthmus of Darien to a company, to be called Junctiana, who should undertake to make a water communication between the

Atlantic and the Pacific, and to allow equal privileges of transit to all nations, but Echeverria would not hear of the alienation of a foot of land belonging to the Republic. —1822.

CORAY.

τῷ γέροντι κόραη, as he called himself. I saw him in August 1821. The sons of Greece were gathered round him, and he was listening to the different tales they brought of the progress of the struggle with the Turks. " I foresaw all this, but I believed it would take place when my pilgrimage was over. I foresaw it ; " and tears flowed fast from " the old man's " cheeks. " No, no," said the young men who were about him ; " you shall return to Greece, and we will build you a monument." A smile of grateful joy played upon the old man's countenance, and every tongue had some accent of kindness and of congratulation.—1822.

HASUN EL D'GHIES.

Hasún el D'Ghies was a liberal, fine-hearted Moosul-man, learned, and impatient to do good to his country (Tripoli). He complained of the great injustice done to it by the publication of the Tully correspondence. He appealed to his own dress, that he had always worn, as a proof of the carelessness of the details. He had been reading Vattel and Bentham (in his translator's " Traité de Législation "), and I found the pages covered with Arabic notes.

" To what extent might reform be introduced in Tripoli," he asked, " without giving umbrage to the Holy Alliance ? I want to introduce a more liberal system. It must be represented to the monarch as a guarantee for his personal safety—to the people it would recommend itself. Adopted in Tripoli, it would spread to Tunis, and so fly along the coast. I have prepared the following Arabic decree to prepare men's minds for it.

"People! beloved people! whom God hath committed to my care! Hearken now to my voice! It shall be a sound of sweetness to your ears. Opening on a former day the Book of Life, for so did God ordain, I read in it this sentence—' Ruler! act not purely of thy own will. That which is of moment do it not but with wise and honest counsellors.' No sooner had I read these words, than it seemed to me as if a film had fallen from my eyes. I looked up, and lo! all the errors of my past life stood as it were arrayed before me. I trembled, and should have sunk down at the sight, had not the same divine words which thus brought to my eyes the evil, brought with them the remedy. On a sudden, it seemed to me as if the prophet were looking down upon me, and that not with hand, as when he delivered to our forefathers the book of truth,— not with hand, but with tongue and lips, he spake to me these words—' My son, adore God, and listen to the prophet. Thou hast erred, I will set thee right. Thou hast been severe, I will make thee gracious. Thou hast been selfish, I will make thee generous. Thou hast been weak in mind, I will make thee wise. Thou hast been in peril, I will make thee safe. Thou hast been weak in power, I will make thee strong. Thy power would end with thy life, but I will continue it even to the end of time. The power of those that come after thee shall thus be bounded, but thine own power shall receive increase. Yea! it shall receive increase, for that obedience which those who went before thee were wont to receive from fear, *that*, and more also, shalt thou receive from admiration, love, and gratitude. Do that which I command thee, and the whole multitude of the faithful throughout the earth shall look up to thee, they shall envy thee until they imitate thee, and all generations to come shall bless thee even as a second prophet from whose word they will have received a being compared to which the state of all who went before thee was a state of affliction, fear, and darkness. Ruler! thou takest upon thee to provide for the wants of thy people, and thou knowest not what they are. Thou callest upon them to obey thy will, and they know not what it is. My son! Thou shalt call the people around thee, and thus shalt thou know their wants. Thou shalt call around thee men chosen by the people, and, when thou hast heard their counsel, thou shalt profit by it. Thou shalt cause thy will to be written in a book, and wheresoever the book of my laws shall be kept, the book of thy law shall be heard. Thou shalt divide thy kingdom into districts, and from each district thou shalt call unto thee a wise man, the man whom thy people shall have chosen. In each district thou shalt place a judge. At his right hand shall lie the book of my word, and the words of those concerning whom it is written in the Table of Brass that in all ages they shall come after thee. The seat of the judges shall be on high, and shall be in the presence of the people. Under them shall sit at all times two men, or three men, as the case shall require, also taken by lot among the fathers or sons of families. Without these men he shall do nothing. On each occasion he shall pass such decision as, in his own judgment, shall be according to the law, and according to the facts that have come before him, but whatever these men shall see good to say, shall in the first place have been heard. Thus doing, thou shalt be loved as sovereign never was loved before thee, for never before did people receive from a sovereign such gifts as thy people shall thus have received from thee. Thus doing, thou shalt be safe against adversaries from within, even as no sovereign before thee was ever safe, for that safety which other sovereigns have

sought in fear, thou wilt have received from love.   Thus
doing, thou wilt be safe against adversaries from without,
even as before thee no sovereign ever was safe, for, seeing
thy people clinging to thee, while their subjects flee from
them, they will see that, instead of assailing thee, those
whom they would lead or send against thee would cast
themselves at thy feet, and beg to be received into the
number of thy subjects.   The yearly growing wealth which
God has given to thee as sovereign, thou shalt divide into
two parts.   One thou shalt continue to receive for the sub-
sistence of thyself and thy family.   This thou shalt not
thyself increase.   The other shall be diminished or increased
as necessity calls, and the receipt, as well as disposal thereof,
shall be according to that which thou, after hearing the wise
men from the people, shall have ordained.'

"People ! I know not as yet whether what it seemed to
me that I then saw and heard was the truth, or whether it
was but an illusion and a dream.   When the men of your
choice shall stand before me, we will pray with one voice
to the Almighty, and His will shall put aside all clouds,
and make the truth more manifest to our hearts.

"Thereupon, if at all, comes the charter containing the
Declaration of Rights which it confers or acknowledges."—
1822.

DEÀK FERENCZ.

To unite discordant parties in a common action—to har-
monize hostile passions into a sympathizing enthusiasm, is
a privilege and a power granted but to few, and their successful exercise may be accepted as evidence of high capacities, both intellectual and moral.   Among the men who,
out of elements apparently irreconcileable, have produced a
fusion of thought and feeling, co-operative in the great work
of national regeneration, the name of Francis Deàk stands

prominent, the leader in and the peace-giver to the Magyar land. It is not surprising that in Hungary there should be some men of merit and of mark, who stand aloof at the extreme points of legitimacy and of liberalism ; men who, on the one hand, have maintained the divine and inalienable rights of monarchs, and, on the other, those who look upon the claims of legitimacy as utterly irreconcileable with the freedom and well-being of nations ; but that any influence should have been able, in the troubled political arena of Hungary to have done what Deàk did for the conciliation of all except the most determined royalists and the most inflexible republicans, is a fact which is well worthy of thoughtful attention.

So little was the origin and early history of Deàk known out of Hungary, that his very name was ordinarily mispronounced, and he was denominated *Dik* or *Dak*, whereas the veritable representative letters to convey the proper sound in English would be *Deeauk.* At court, when first introduced to His Majesty, the Emperor made a preliminary inquiry, " 's ist wohl noch ein sehr junger mann ? " The simplicity of the imperial questioner became a standing joke in evidence of the extraordinary ignorance which prevailed in Vienna as to the existing state of public feeling, and the individuals who represented it most prominently in Hungary. It is more to the influence of this supposed " very young man," who had really reached the meridian of life, and whose name was in every Magyar mouth, than to any other circumstance, that the preservation of the Hapsburg dynasty is to be attributed. But it had been the policy of Austria to extinguish the Magyar name, and of her representatives of the Metternich order, to absorb in the Vienna circles, or to annihilate altogether, everything anti-Teutonic. If, in the struggle with Prussia, Austria had obtained the victory, imperial Germany might have subjugated, or, in the progress of centuries, have established a permanent ascendancy over the Magyars, Lombards and Czechs. Happily for the peace of mankind, and the progress of civilization, the higher Prussian intellects carried off the prize of sovereignty among the German races, and Austria has been compelled to remove her authority eastward, and may probably discover in Pesth a more powerful centre of concentrated action than in the now somewhat humiliated Vienna.

For more than three centuries, the policy—one might safely say the passion of Austria—was directed in Hungary to one simple object, namely, the extirpation of the Magyar nationality, and, whether by cajoling and coercion, by bribes of place, power, and title on the one side, or by the most cruel oppressions and unrelenting punishments on the other, to invite or to compel submission to the imperial decrees. Shortsighted as the policy may be which insists on absolute prostration, and brings a pitiless vengeance on all the disobedient, its machinery is very simple, easily understood, and as easily directed by its administrators. Its requirements are, "bend or be broken."

Descended from an ancient Catholic race, noble, though not of the higher ranks of nobility, Francis von Deák was born on the 13th October 1803 in Kahida, in the county of Zala, on the hereditary estate of his family. Three personages have been most conspicuous in the struggles which have agitated Hungary for the last forty years, and which have culminated in the establishment of popular representative institutions, or, as the Hungarians are more wont to boast, in the restitution of ancient rights and liberties. These three were Count Stephen Szécsenyi, "our great Count"; Deák, "our great Deputy," as the Magyars call them; and Kossuth, of European fame. Szécsenyi, by an act of suicide, passed from the stage; Kossuth condemned himself to exile, and to an obscurity strangely contrasted with the idolatry of which he was the object, when a people, maddened to despair, saw no hope but in the violence of revolutionary explosions ; while Deák, by the exercise of more genial and conciliatory attributes, though without any abandonment of purpose or sacrifice of principle, has brought the great national work to a successful issue.

The sagacity of Deák consisted mainly in this, that he had equally the discretion to be silent, and the courage to speak, when the popular interests were best served by either. Those who wisely wait are more valuable auxiliaries than those who rashly act, and to wait patiently sometimes demands a courage more heroic and a self-mastery more perfect than do the most desperate acts of valour.

In 1825, Anthony, Deák's elder brother, nominated as a deputy to the Diet, and summoned away by a death-sickness, said, in taking leave of his colleagues, " Be comforted, I am not he that should come. A younger brother will follow me, who in his little finger has more power and patriotism than I possess in my whole frame." Francis Deák was at that time only twenty-two years old, and was nominated to succeed his brother as the deputy for Zala in the Diet of 1825. It was in that Diet that Count Szécsenyi roused the dormant nation from its long slumbers, and uttered words in the hall of the magnates which found a loud echo in every part of Magyar land, " Hungary is not, but Hungary shall be." His were not words alone, but he declared that he would devote the whole of his revenues, amounting to sixty thousand guilders, to the advancement of the popular cause. His example was contagious. Two statesmen of influence soon associated themselves with the generous movement. Baron Wesselóny (who had been denounced at Vienna as the deceiver and betrayer of the people), and the orator Paul Nagy, came prominently forward to lend to the movement all the weight of their authority.

The radical reforms which these patriotic leaders proposed were staggering to the privileged orders to which they belonged. They demanded the absolute abrogation of the exclusive privileges of the nobility, equality before the law, and no exemptions from the discharge of common obligations, whether fiscal, social, or political. The suggestions were denounced as madness—the suggestors were deemed madmen. To call upon the untaxed nobility to sacrifice one-tenth of their incomes, to require that twenty thousand families of the hereditary aristocracy, of which six-sevenths were of Magyar race, should mingle in common citizenship with the fifteen millions of the people and the peasantry, seemed a most preposterous demand. But eloquence, self-sacrifice, and popular enthusiasm, accomplished the great work. It was not, however, without fierce strifes and bitter sufferings on the part of the advocates of the national emancipation, that, after a struggle of twenty-three years, a majority of the Diet proclaimed the abolition of exclusive privileges, and equality of all Hungarians in the presence of the law.

In 1825, the overthrow of the monopolies of the nobles was prophesied by an ancient senator to be "the suicide of the Hungarian people." Deàk then declared with great emphasis that for his part he would only be satisfied with the most radical reforms carried out to their remotest consequences. Every eye was turned towards the youth whose strong words were uttered with such remarkable calmness. Those strong words have been made the test of many a political project, and their utterer has become the most efficient and the most trusted leader of the party of progress.

In the years 1832 to 1836, the Diet was principally occupied in denouncing the infractions of the laws, and the

violations of the constitution. Representations and remon-
strances were in vain addressed to the supreme authorities,
and the parliamentary discussions became impassioned. In
this session, the tranquil, thoughtful, and impressive eloquence of Deàk obtained for him the never-claimed but
generally acknowledged leadership of the reform party.
The elevation of the peasantry and the equalization of taxation were his principal topics. The government became
wroth with the exhibition of the national feeling, and began
its despotic work. The Diet was dissolved. In 1837,
Lovassy and Kossuth were arrested. Lovassy died in prison.
Kossuth was detained for three years, their crime being the
publication of the debates of the Diet. A fit representative
of Austrian despotism, Pulsky, was nominated to the High
Chancellorship of Hungary.

The Diet met again in 1839. The reaction against the
despotism of the government had become stronger and
better organized, and Deàk was the recognized centre of
the movement, which rolled with him, and revolved around
him. It seemed then as if the many turbulent and noisy
streamlets were all flowing into one majestic river, whose
irresistible course was onwards towards the great ocean of
freedom, and the year 1840 appeared to bring with it peace
and conciliation.

A considerable effort was made at this period, under the
influences of Szécsenyi, to give an impulse to the material
prosperity of the nation. " Let us become rich, and we
will make ourselves free," was the device of the hour. It
operated to some extent as a diversion from political action,
and was dexterously turned to account by the Vienna party,
who, if they could have absorbed a prosperous and opulent
Hungary into an Austrian centralization, would have done
much to extinguish that Magyar nationality which had
always been an object of distrust, if not of abhorrence.

Kossuth's journal, the *Pesti Hirlap*, helped wonderfully to arouse the popular mind. The elections of 1843 were conducted with extreme violence, and led to the spilling of blood, and to the rejection of Deàk in his native *Comität*, and he retreated for a time from the tumultuous arena. He was then denounced as cowardly, though sagacious, " Böles de nem bátor," but there is sometimes more bravery in abstention than in action, and the service of waiting may be more efficient than that of taking a precipitate part.

The retirement of Deàk from the field of political action, and his silence—when speaking would neither have served his country nor his country's cause—his resolve to wait for better times and fitter occasions, was the dictate alike of the experience of the past, and a correct foresight of the future. His absence, indeed, was a more emphatic protest against existing abuses than his presence would have been. Even one of his most earnest opponents (Zséndenyi) gave utterance to the words, " The purest character of the nation is wanting to the Diet." If, as has been said, the ear of Heaven is most open when *Pii orant tacite*, a nation may be believed to be listening to a patriot whose dumbness was more eloquent than his words. So strong was the feeling towards him that, when in 1847 he was *not* nominated to the Diet, his wonted place was left unoccupied—a voiceless protest against what was thought to be a national injustice. His health, however, unfitted him for any laborious exertion, so he quitted Hungary for a time, and travelled through most of the countries of Central Europe. Kossuth became the leader of the advanced section of the Liberals. More eloquent than Deàk, he had less aptitude for the direction of public affairs. In 1848, Deàk returned, under Batthyany's ministry, to take the post of Minister of Grace and Justice, and never were the two attributes more satisfactorily displayed than when personified in Deàk. He did more than any man to conciliate the non-Magyar portion of the Hungarian population. To the Magyars he said, "He who will free himself must be just to others." To the Slavonians, "Labour with us that we may labour for you." His functions were exercised a little more than six months. Austrian reaction had embittered the Magyar mind. Deàk was one of the deputation who visited Vienna to represent the grievances of the Hungarians. It is known how scornfully they were repelled. The Magyar capital was invaded by hostile Austrian armies, and the national ministry was scattered. Some of the most distinguished of the Hungarian nobles sought an interview with Prince Windischgrätz in his camp, but he refused to see them, and sent back the insulting answer, "I hold no intercourse with rebels."

It were sad to follow the fortunes to prison and to the scaffold of the then courageous chiefs of the popular cause. Only a few days ago, the official journals of Pesth announced that four of the leading men of Hungary, whose death-warrants Francis Joseph, the Emperor of Austria, had signed, and who escaped the hands of the executioner by flight, were welcomed with smiles and gratulations by the same Francis Joseph, the King of Hungary. In January 1849, Deàk withdrew himself from public notice, to serve while waiting in his rural seclusion, and for twelve years appeared to be almost forgotten. In those twelve years 2127 persons were sentenced to death, nearly ten times that number were thrown into prison, and 4652, among whom were many of the wisest, the noblest, and the best of the Hungarian race, were condemned to wander in foreign lands. Did Deàk's inaction give some hope that he might be won over to forward Austrian policy? He was invited to Vienna. His answer was a memorable one to the minister (Bach), who received him with words of courtesy, spoke at

length of his purposes, and desired to engage the co-operation of Deák, who listened without the intrusion of a single
word ; and when the discourse was ended, calmly replied,
" Your Excellency must forgive me, I know nothing but
the Hungarian constitution. Provisionally, at least, that
constitution has no existence, and I have none."

And he returned to his rural abode, now and then visiting
Pesth, and occupying two obscure chambers. His conversation was very reserved, though his person was accessible.
His moderate income of about £500 was not only sufficient
for all his individual wants, but enabled him to lend assistance, not only to friends less fortunate than himself, but to
those of whose misfortunes he only accidentally heard.
Surrounded by those whose more impassioned natures often
led to the bitterest outpourings of hate and indignation, he
preserved his calmness, but did not lose his influence.
Szemere said of him, " He lies as if smitten in an accursed
land, a silent oracle, to which none can appeal, and which
seems wholly disregarded." But the silence befitted the
time. Meanwhile, misrule reigned uncontrolled, but not
without the complications of debts and difficulties—debts
that could not be paid, and difficulties that could not be
subdued. The Italian war sadly shook the rotten edifice,
and from the southern side of the Alps a light burst forth
upon Hungary. Pressed on both sides—by the conservatives, who would fain have saved the Empire from
humiliation—and by the radicals, who saw in that humiliation their own best hopes of redemption, Deák resisted the
demands of both ; but the extreme urgency of the crisis
brought him to Vienna, where, in December 1860, he and
Eötvös had a private audience with the Emperor-King.

The path of efficient usefulness seemed now opening
before him, and the ground cleared around him. The
counsels he then gave led to the Royal Rescript of 16th

January 1861 addressed to the Diet, to which he prepared the elaborate and emphatic answer. The reformation of the Civil and Criminal Codes was cordially discussed, and the influence of Deàk, now the representative of the Magyar capital, was widened and strengthened to all the Hungarian frontiers, and far beyond them, through the Austrian dominions, and, it may be asserted, very far beyond the extremest limits of the Fatherland.

The radical party, unwilling to make concessions, and dissatisfied with the tone of the Royal Speech, would fain have avoided any response beyond the acknowledgment of its utterance. Deàk acted as moderator between the servility of one extreme and the scornful bearing of the other, and prepared an elaborate reply which, while preserving all the forms of respect and courtesy, abandoned none of the great principles or positions which are the basis of liberty. There are few examples in the political history of nations in which the thoughtful judgment and personal influence of a single man have served to draw all political passions into the calm receptacle of one single pure and honest mind, and to mould those passions into a common action. Deàk had, however, one great element to deal with—the universal feeling of nationality which pervades the Magyar race. Every effort to absorb that nationality in Austrian Imperialism had resulted in failure, and still less chance had the attempts to annihilate it. The Pragmatic Sanction of 1729 had irrevocably associated the sovereignty of the Hapsburg family with the fullest recognition of Hungarian rights and Hungarian laws, and indeed the conditions were but a renewed guarantee for the maintenance of the ancient constitutional privileges which had been reasserted two centuries before. But the unity of Magyar feeling was no recommendation to the Viennese. Other considerations, the results of many humiliations, and the dread of still greater

humiliations, compelled the inexorable to yield, and the
" never surrender " of the obstinate was made dumb in the
presence of that necessity, which has for its authority no
law, and needs no argument for its support.

This stern necessity, which again called together the so-
often humiliated Diet, made it so irresistibly triumphant in
1865, that the absolute independence of the Magyar Orzag
was proclaimed by the Austrian Emperor, and the fundamental conditions recognized that Hungarian Representatives
should alone be allowed to tax *the Hungarian people, and
that the military forces of Hungary could only be disposed
of by the national will.

It was indeed a marvellous result that, immediately after
the battle of Königsgrätz, the Austrian Autocrat felt himself
compelled to summon together no less than nineteen representative assemblies—seventeen on this, and two on the
other side of the Leitha, appealing to every fragment of the
Empire that was left unconquered, to help the Fatherland
in her sorrow, shame, and repentance.

A national ministry, amnesties for the exiled and condemned, forgiveness of past injuries on the one side, promises
and oaths on the other, and a general jubilee have inaugu-
rated a better and brighter futurity. Transylvania is united
with Hungary by a natural fusion of laws and languages.
Croatia resumes her ancient fraternal relations. As the connection of Austria with the German element is more and
more enfeebled—as it must inevitably be by that longing
for German unity which has found its intellectual, moral,
and military centre in Berlin—the force of events will drive
Austria from her occidental weakness to her oriental
strength.

Deàk has had his reward, far richer and more honouring
than the patronage and perquisites of office. A torch-light
ovation of the most distinguished of the Hungarian youth

was the becoming acknowledgment of his multitudinous services, his thorough disinterestedness, and popular virtues. The fate of Hungary is in the hands of the Hungarians. May we not hope that their wisdom will consolidate what their patience and their patriotism have achieved.—1868.

JEREMY BENTHAM.

Not to speak of all that I owed to excellent parents, two men have exercised more than any others an influence on the formation of my character. Dr Lant Carpenter was the guide and instructor of my early youth, as Bentham was the admiration of my riper years. The teachings of Bentham were naturally of a more philosophical character, more original and striking. Many of his axioms could not fail to make a deep and permanent impression. The phrase which he acknowledged to have borrowed from Dr Priestley's writings, "the object of governments should be the greatest happiness of the greatest number," has been adopted as the device of a large political party. He always spoke with great admiration of Lord Bacon, whom he considered to be the first philosopher who had laid down the principle that all theories should be subjected to and tested by the crucible of experiment. "Let experience be fertile and custom be barren" was one of his favourite phrases. "*Respice finem*" was another, which he found in Bacon's works, where a famous aphorism constantly attributed to the great Chancellor, "Knowledge is power" is not to be discovered, and I am afraid that the experience of man, especially in the times antecedent to Bacon, would but too frequently show that knowledge was but weakness, and that the power of superstition and ignorance was the stronger of the two.

The life of Bentham was one of singular happiness. He had never a moment unoccupied, and was constantly engaged either in writing, or in having the most interesting

Y

publications, and particularly voyages and travels, read to him by one of his two amanuenses, always directing marginal notes to be made of the most striking and instructive passages. When called to the bar, where he was a bencher of Lincoln's Inn, his susceptibilities were tried by being called upon to defend cases which he thought indefensible, and not being satisfied with being required (using his own words) to prove that black was white, or that white was black, according to the usages of professional men, he found it desirable to abandon his profession, and on his father's death he took up his abode at the paternal domicile in Westminster. He spent a few years at the beautiful retreat of Ford Abbey in the west of England, having James Mill and his family for inmates. Bentham seldom left his home. His exercise, in which he was always accompanied by the guest who dined with him (for he said that more than one distracted conversation) was round his garden, and he called this recreation his anteprandial circumgyration. Overlooking the walk, and belonging to Bentham, was the house in which Milton lived while Secretary to Oliver Cromwell.

A few years before his death, Bentham visited Paris, where his name was universally known to the learned through Dumont's translations of his writings, translations which, though exceedingly popular in their style, do not always accurately represent the original thoughts of the author. He received in Paris the most flattering welcome. His bust was taken by David of Angers, who made the statue of Washington, in the capital of the United States, the façade of the Madeleine, and other renowned sculptures, and General Foy, on being introduced to him, said, " Vos mœurs et vos écrits sont peints sur votre visage." His countenance so greatly resembled that of Benjamin Franklin that David Ricardo purchased a bust of the American, supposing it was intended for the English philosopher. So much was Bentham in advance of his age, that Sir Samuel Romilly recommended him not to publish several of his works, as he felt assured that printing them would lead to prosecution and ˌimprisonment. Many of his writings I have not deemed it safe to give to the world, even after his death, so bold and adventurous were some of his speculations, but they remain in the archives of the British Museum, and at some future time may be dragged into the light of day.

The services of Bentham as a law-reformer are now no longer disputed. I have found the groundwork of some of the most important improvements in our judicial legislation in his writings. His masterly views on the laws of evidence, many of his suggestions on prison discipline, on the poor-laws (such a field of abuse in his days, and so much ameliorated now), may, with many others, be mentioned in connection with this topic. Codification, or the bringing the vast and confused mass of written and unwritten law into order and harmony, was one of the great objects he had at heart, and he said that no glory that Napoleon had ever acquired would equal that of his going down to posterity with his five codes in hand. Bentham's "Defence of Usury" was written while on a visit to White Russia to his brother Sir Samuel, then a General in the Russian service, to whom the merit is due of introducing the celebrated machinery for making blocks at Portsmouth.—1861.

NOTES OF CONVERSATIONS WITH BENTHAM.—1822-24.

I found Bentham with his fine locks—straight but silvery—which used to hang over his shoulders, as if they had been chopped with a hatchet,—but that tall and magnificently-formed forehead, that serene and playful expression

of countenance, that earnest interest in everything which
bears a relation to human happiness, unchanged.

We talked of the Conciliatory Courts of Denmark.
Bentham had lent his history of them (a French edition)
to Horner, who promised to write an article for the *Edinburgh Review*, but Horner died, and the book was lost.
In 1795 it was decreed in Denmark that no lawsuit should
be brought into the courts of justice, except after an
attempt at conciliation. Conciliatory committees were in
consequence established, and in 1797 they were introduced
into Norway. In 1798 they were formed in the colonies,
though, in fact, a similar plan had existed ever since 1755.
In the capital, the committee is formed of one of the judges
of the chief tribunal, one municipal magistrate, and one
popular representative. In other towns, and in the colonies,
it is composed of two individuals chosen by universal
suffrage out of six who are proposed as candidates by the
authorities. In the country, the bailiff (prefect) is compelled to act the part of mediator, and to name two citizens
where he personally cannot interfere. In Norway, one of
the two must be chosen among the respectable peasantry.
In 1820 a statement was published, by which it appears
that of 39,777 lawsuits, 36,872 were settled by the Conciliatory Committee, and only 2905 had been referred to
the tribunals. Scarcely any one example of abuse or injustice has occurred. I mentioned that when a similar
scheme was proposed in England, it failed merely on account
of its popularity. I believe it was at Newcastle. The
decisions had given so much reputation to the conciliators,
that the office became one of aristocratic ambition, and men
were introduced, not because they had aptitude to decide,
but interest to be selected. "A proof," said Bentham,
"that pecuniary recompense is not necessary to obtain
public services."

Bentham's conversation is often desultory, but he throws into every remark such originality and power that his observations might serve as texts which require volumes for their development. I will give a few examples.

"Good government only requires 'aptitude maximised, and expense minimised.' When I first began to think, I was perplexed and confounded by what seemed to be a barrier to all improvement—influence. It exists universally, and could not be got rid of. I was relieved when I discovered that influence is no evil—no necessary evil. The influence of one man's understanding upon another man's understanding is good. It is only the influence of *will* upon *will* that is baneful.

"Lord Holland told me that the cabinet was divided into three degrees or classes of confidence. The first, called the cabinet, consisting of all the members; the second, the correspondence of five or six individuals, among whom the despatches of the ambassadors, &c., circulate; and the last the 'post-office,' consisting of only two or three members, who had the privilege of stopping all letters in the post-office.

"Utility did not communicate an idea on which all men were agreed. It does not seem to have an immediate connection with enjoyment. 'The greatest happiness of the greatest number' has superseded it in my mind. That is intelligible to everybody. Rey of Grenoble said, 'the definition is not perfect. It should be the greatest and *most permanent*, for a whole people may be influenced by a temporary delirium of joy, and yet that joy be founded on circumstances leading to misery.' 'Well, then,' I replied, 'that happiness is not the greatest happiness which wants a permanent character.'

"George III. hated me cordially. With Pitt I was on terms, but the malevolence of the former frustrated the

intentions of the latter towards me, and prevented the fulfilment even of the most solemn contracts. The origin of
the King's hatred was this :—*He* had written in the Leyden
Courant (the then European journal), a dull and prosing,
but most mischievous letter to induce the King of Denmark
to make war upon Russia, without any motion whatever.
The only ground—the fallacy—was the repetition of the
idea 'check—check—check.' I answered the letter in the
indignant strain which Junius had made so popular. I
poured upon it a storm of contempt. I signed 'Anti-
Machiavel.' The King discovered that I was the writer, and
ever after put his veto upon everything I proposed, so that,
in spite of acts of parliament, in spite of the protection and
the warm encouragement of several ministers, I was always
sacrificed.

" It would be a good service to publish an edition of the
speeches delivered in Parliament, with a statement at the
foot of each of the particular fallacy employed for the purposes of deception. People would soon learn to apply this
mode of judgment.

" Bingham is heartily tired of the law and of its cheatery.
More credit is obtained for defending a bad cause than a
good one. Rhetoric and delusion are the only currency.

" The great value of our English law-records consists in
their proposing almost every possible case which can be
the object of legal decision. The cases have wonderful
variety. The decisions are often unjust, absurd and decep-
tive."—July 1822.

Bentham pays no visits, yet when I told him that Sir
Robert Wilson had an interest in the Columbian loan,
he hurried off to his house, having had information that
the loan would probably not be recognised. He pursued
him from house to house, left a note saying that somebody

should sit up for him all the night through, and showed an anxiety as restless as honourable.—1823.

Bentham said—"Botany is greatly superior to mineralogy. One may distribute what one discovers and do good. Seeds may be sent over the world, but stones won't grow."

Though Bentham always speaks slightingly, and even insultingly of poetry, he has made verses. I once told him I would prove to him that there was poetry in his character, and talked of the enthusiasm and delight he felt in anticipating the progress of the "greatest felicity principle." I endeavoured to prove that much of this was imaginative. He lifted up his stick, and laid it gently on my shoulders. These lines are Bentham's, and were written in 1780.

Memoriter Verses expressive of the Elements or Dimensions of Value in Pleasures and Pains.

> "Intense, long, certain, speedy, fruitful, pure,
> Such points in pleasures and in pains endure.
> Such pleasure seek, if private be thy end.
> If it be public, wide let them extend.
> Such pains avoid, whichever be thy view,
> If pains must come, let them extend to few."

" Intellectual aptitude without moral aptitude is a nuisance."

" What are you doing now ? " said I. " I am dragging nobility through the dirt."—1822.

He was full of the notion of having his head preserved in the style of the New Zealanders, and had sent to Dr Armstrong to consult him about it. Experiments are to be made, and Armstrong is to get a human head from Grainger, the anatomist, which is to be slowly dried in a stove in Bentham's house.

Bentham was very angry with the judges, their opposition to *publicity* having wrought his mind to indignation. He said, " The worst of pickpockets is better than the least bad of the judges. They never open their mouths but to lie, to tell money-getting lies." He laughed again at my poetry, at all poetry, at all poets. Some man had sent him a volume. He said to me, "Now steal it, and publish it as your own."

He looked over his memorandum-book, which he calls his *Facienda* and *Dicenda*, "Let me see if there are any *dicenda* which are not *dicta*."—1824.

LORD BYRON.

I never had the advantage, during his lifetime, of a personal acquaintance with Lord Byron. After his death, his body was consigned to me in a puncheon of rum, which came from Missalonghi, whence it was transferred to a leaden coffin, which lay exposed to the inspection of the privileged for some days in Great George Street, Westminster. He was buried at Hucknall Torkak, near Newstead Abbey, his ancestral seat, and a curious controversy afterwards arose as to the proprietorship of an album which I gave to accompany his corpse. It became valuable in consequence of the many distinguished persons who visited his sepulchre. The heirs of the sexton claimed it, because he had obtained the signatures ; the clergyman said it belonged to him in virtue of his office, that being the position of all property brought within the walls of the church ; while the wardens claimed it, as trustees, under their parochial authority. The matter was referred to me, but, as I had not anticipated that the book would have a pecuniary value, I had nothing to say under the unexpected circumstances that had arisen. It was really a curious topic for the wrangling of lawyers. I believe it was ultimately decided that the property was parochial, but vested in the Rector as the temporary custos.

It was after some correspondence with me that Lord Byron determined to proceed to Greece, and to give his services, both personal and pecuniary, to a cause which was at that time arousing a general European enthusiasm, and which his previous visits to that country had disposed him to sympathize with in all the passionate earnestness of his character. He was indeed "sated at home—of wife and children tired," as he himself expressed it, "sated abroad, all seen, but not admired," when the Greek Revolution replaced his morbid feelings by a new and unexpected excitement. He met with many vexations and disappointments, being often deceived by the cupidity and mendacity of intriguing Greeks, but he found some of the Klephthoi faithful—the ragged ones, as he denominated them—and found no reason to distrust Prince Mavrocordato and a very few of the leading men. The history and the results of the campaign are too well known to require any reference from me, but few auxiliaries gave a greater impulse to the patriotic movement than a Romaic translation of that emphatic and touching song found in "Don Juan." "The isles, the isles of Greece, where burning Sappho loved and sung," the last, and one of the most touching of Byron's compositions, was written on his thirty-fourth birthday, a short time before his death, and was sent by me to the *Morning Chronicle* for publication. "'Tis true this heart should be unmoved, since others it has ceased to move."

I doubt if there was ever a character made up of more contradictory qualities than that of Byron. He was sometimes generous to excess, and at others inconceivably mean. He would in the course of the same day spend thousands of pounds on any object that interested him, and gather together and place in a cupboard the remainder of the logs which had not been used. He seemed to live in a perpetual vibration between what is divine and demoniacal. Had his autobiography been published (and he thought he had taken every security for its publication after his death), it would have thrown much light upon the aberrations of a genius which seemed always in a state of transition from darkness to light, and from light to darkness.

His poetry will live as long as our language endures— the records of a mind agitated by the fiercest commotions, and finding for them the most eloquent expressions. Though bursting into violent declamations against tyranny, he was essentially an aristocrat, and proud of tracing his "life-blood to the parent lake." His intrinsic dislike to the Tories, who were in the ascendant in his time, is everywhere to be seen. Nothing more scathing was ever written than his "Vision of Judgment"—his picture of the reign of George III., who "ever warred with freedom and the free," and his most vehement onslaught on the Poet Laureate, a portion of which Mr Murray felt himself bound in prudence to suppress. The expunged passages in "Don Juan" contained ridicule on Romilly's death.

Byron, wherever he went, left strong impressions behind him, carrying with him his eccentricities, prejudices, and passions. A friend of mine at Leghorn possesses the table upon which he wrote, sloped like a desk, and the bed on which he slept, and where I, too, haunted by the recollections of this strange genius, have often sought and found repose. The bed is of somewhat fanciful form, carved and gilded, while in the footboard is the family escutcheon, with the motto "Crede Byron." The bed is surmounted by a dome, à la Turque, from which the mosquito-curtains fall, and the corners are decorated with pendant plumes. Compared with beds usually found in Italy, it is of large dimensions.

The Countess of Guiccioli, with whom Byron lived in Italy, did not appear to me remarkable either for her genius or her beauty, and had often to complain of the outbreaks of his violent temper. I have heard that a young woman at Venice, whose fierce black eyes he has been known to describe, held him in bondage by the impetuosity of her nature.

His life was sacrificed to the ignorance of the medical men who attended him in Greece, and who, in the Sangrado style, bled him copiously when he was in a very exhausted state. He would seem almost to have foreseen the result of this mis-usage, for he exclaimed on one occasion, "I fear the lancet much more than the lance."—1861.

SIR WALTER SCOTT.

I paid a charming visit to Sir Walter Scott at Abbotsford. It was at the time when he was struggling with his pecuniary difficulties, and he often spoke of the annoyance caused him by his "domned debts." But the desire to free himself from his embarrassments led to immense exertions on his part, and probably to the overstraining of his intellectual powers. The profits he made at this time by his writings—it was in the hey-day of his Waverley glories—were such as have rarely been realised by any other man. He received in one year between £30,000 and £40,000, and I recollect hearing from his publisher in Edinburgh that he had paid him nearly £120,000 in all. It would be a curious inquiry to ascertain what has been the greatest amount of pecuniary benefit realised by popular works in English. Mr Cadell once mentioned to me that the works of three authors (each of whose names began with the letter B) had been far more productive than any others, and these were Burns' "Justice," Blair's "Sermons," and Buchan's "Domestic Medicine," which left a profit of £100,000. No doubt there was in Scott's case the heart-sorrow of regret that he had not satisfied himself with the enormous advantages his works produced, but that, to add

to his income, he should have engaged in trading opera-
tions, such as paper-making, leading to bill-accepting and
all sorts of anxieties ; but none of these cares affected his
outward cheerfulness, and his reception of his friends was
in the highest degree hospitable and generous. His style
of living was even luxurious, his table was covered with
every delicacy, and in the little usages were many characteristics of Scotch nationality. Unadulterated whiskey of
the finest quality was dealt out to the guests in miniature
tubs called quarths, and he supplied his visitors with cigars
and tobacco of the rarest kinds. He had a good deal of the
pride of family, and was fond of saying that he stood next
in rank to his chief, the Duke of Buccleuch. He would
point out the picture of an ancestor, who was such a partisan of the Stuarts, that he vowed he would never allow his
beard to be cut until that family was restored to the throne,
so of course he went down to his tomb unshaven. When
Scott was dining with King George IV., whom he welcomed to Scotland in a poem which obtained a short-lived
celebrity, beginning, " Carle, now the king's come !", he
was somewhat embarrassed by an inquiry as to what would
become of his allegiance if the Stuarts were still in existence. He answered, that " he rejoiced that he had now to
decide on no such a question." It is known that the king,
when Prince Regent, ventured to ask Sir Walter if he were
the author of the Waverley Novels—a very unbecoming
question assuredly, but it was evaded by something like a
denial.

Scott's habits were most regular. He rose early, and
gave several hours to literary labour before breakfast, which,
I think, was at ten o'clock. He would then take a ride with
his guests, followed by his favourite dogs, and wielding a
whip which he cracked with all the light-heartedness of
youth. His conversation on these occasions was most fasci-

nating, and full of wit and originality. He had tales to tell of every mountain, valley, plain, and stream. He accompanied me to Melrose Abbey, and on my referring to his beautiful description of its appearance by moonlight, he said, " Let me tell you, I never saw the Abbey after set of sun." He gravely asserted that the ghost of Byron had appeared in his library, and pointed out the curtain from behind whose folds Childe Harold had introduced himself. In that library was a silver urn containing ashes which Byron had sent him from Thermopylæ, and in it were originally some autograph verses which some scoundrel stole from their place of deposit—an act of inconceivable turpitude, inasmuch as their exhibition must have covered the thief with infamy. Scott was exceedingly proud of the graceful foot of his younger daughter, and in more than one of his novels has spoken of a fine foot as a most attractive appendage to female beauty.

In Sir Walter Scott's time political hostilities were particularly rife, and the most violent personal vituperation was the order of the day. *Blackwood's Magazine* was the local organ of the party who have since taken the name of Conservatives, though a periodical called *The Beacon*, to whose establishment Sir Walter was a party, was the channel through which individual resentments found even stronger expression ; but so powerful were Caledonian hospitality and kindness, that strangers found no difficulty in making the acquaintance of men of all shades of party and politics, and in my own case, whether among the high-flown faction which rejoiced in the designation of Tory, of whom Scott and Professor Wilson were the two most distinguished chiefs, or among the Whigs grouped round Jeffrey, who spoke by the mouth of the far-famed *Edinburgh Review*, I found a sympathy and a kindness quite as great as any I received from the philosophical Radicals, with whom I most especially sympathized, and whose opinions found expression in *Tait's Magazine*, and several newspapers which had a large circulation among the working-classes. I was not unfrequently invited to the singular revels well known by the name of the *Noctes Ambrosianæ*, the descriptions of which are among the happiest and most characteristic records emanating from John Wilson, and in which I have several times found myself mentioned with great kindness. Strange scenes indeed they were, in which the quantity of tumblers of whiskey-toddy consumed could not easily be calculated.. It used to be reported that the Professor's indulgence in this favourite tipple sometimes kept him to the house for several days, unshaven and unshorn, after the "jollifications;" but Wilson was a most interesting and intellectual man, and most popular among the students of the University, all of whom did homage to his genius. He was accustomed to escape from the free life of the city to the mountains and the lakes, where hunting and fishing, and especially the latter, braced and invigorated him.

THOMAS MOORE.

Tom Moore, the playful and light-hearted, was among my acquaintances. It is superfluous to say how agreeable such an acquaintance was. I scarcely know whether he obtained most applause from those finished productions, known by the name of "Irish Melodies," in which he brought new words to adorn the popular music of his country, or from those fugitive pieces which had reference to the party politics of the day, and in which a playful wit was as sparkling as in the cotemporaneous outpourings of Byron, in whose writings were manifested his more intense feelings of hatred to the ruling influences of the times. On one occasion I experienced great generosity from the "Bard of Erin." He published in the *Times* a bitter attack upon me, entitled "The Ghost of Miltiades," but when a common friend assured him that he had done me great injustice, he immediately consented to suppress the publication of the poem. He accused me, however, while I was the editor of the *Westminster Review*, of having inserted a censorious article upon his "Life of Lord Byron." That article was, however, written by a gentleman equally acquainted with the noble bard and his biographer, and I considered it a part of my duty not to refrain from publishing any honest opinions on the writings of either foes or friends. Moore said I invited him to my house at the very time when I carried in my pocket a loaded pistol, which was to be fired at him—no doubt an ingenious way of attaching blame, but it is a sufficient answer to say that, if I allowed him to be attacked where I deemed him worthy of animadversion, there were many other occasions on which I was his defender and advocate.—1861.

MRS OPIE

Said, "Richard Lovell Edgeworth was very desirous that I should introduce him to Mrs Siddons. I did so, and I shall never forget the magnificent stride with which he walked up to her, 'Madam, I shall never forget the impression you made upon me—'twas forty years ago—when I saw you act the part of Lady Townley.' The lady drew herself back, violently agitated, shook her fan with the greatest rapidity, and said hastily, 'Never acted the part in my life, Sir! never acted the part in my life,' and turned away with a terrible frown. Edgeworth shrugged up his shoulders, and walked slowly away repeating, 'J'ai manqué—j'ai manqué !' 'Twas a delicious scene."

Mrs Opie's habits are very singular. At Norwich she lives in seclusion, attends at the Quaker meeting-house, and visits nobody. When she comes to town, her house is

the scene of an eternal levée, and who is so busily gay as
Mrs Opie?—1822.

MRS BARBAULD.

There was in my earlier days a very interesting group of
people dwelling at Newington, not far from the mansion
which was Dr Isaac Watts' domicile when living under the
protection of Sir Thomas Abney, to whom he addressed the
exciting lines,

> "Live, my dear Abney, live to-day,
> Nor let the sun look down and say
> 'Inglorious here he lies.'
> Stretch out thy wings, and give thy name
> To immortality and fame,
> With every hour that flies."

I believe, however, that Sir Thomas' title to immortality
mostly hangs upon his connection with the bard of the
sanctuary, and with that cemetery which bears the appellation of Abney. William French, the actuary, and author
of the astronomical "Evening Amusements," who had been
expelled from Cambridge for his heterodox opinions, was a
leading personage in the attractive circle, to which belonged
Dr Aikin and his sons, of whom Arthur obtained some
celebrity in the world of science.   Charles is known to
many juvenile readers as he for whom Mrs Barbauld, the
most distinguished of the family, composed a book for
children, beginning "Come hither, Charles, come to mamma."
The mother was a daughter of Gilbert Wakefield, the
classic, who was punished by an imprisonment of two years
in Dorchester Jail for a libel in saying that "a right
reverend prelate felt as embarrassed as a donkey whose
attention was distracted between two competing bundles of
hay."

Mrs Barbauld's prose hymns, which I heard from the

lips of my parents, appeared to my childish imagination the perfection of pathos and poetry, and I deemed it a great privilege afterwards to be in close intimacy with her, while I was much flattered by some complimentary verses which she addressed to me, and which will be found among her published compositions.

Mrs Barbauld's hymns and devotional pieces are among the most beautiful religious compositions in our language, and many of the former have obtained a permanent place in the collections that have been made both for public and private worship.

Dr Aikin's "Evenings at Home" had much celebrity in their day. Their value of course has been much diminished by new scientific discoveries, yet they rendered good service in popularising such topics, and suiting them to the capabilities of youthful minds.

ELIZABETH BENGER.

Among the literary celebrities of the last generation was Elizabeth Benger, who wrote memoirs of Royal Personages, some novels, and other works, which obtained a fair share of attention in their day.

She was a believer in a metempsychosis, and often claimed me as an acquaintance in an earlier stage of existence—a pleasant speculation at least, and I never repudiated the fancy. I was young, and on most topics we very cordially sympathised. She was an enthusiast for truth, progress, and liberty, and her conversaziones were attended by many of the London literary stars.

HELEN MARIA WILLIAMS.

Among the literary celebrities of the French Revolution was Helen Maria Williams, at whose house were wont to assemble the most distinguished of the liberal writers of

z

France, her own reputation giving considerable éclat to these meetings. She wrote some of the most beautiful hymns in our language, was a prisoner under the *reign of terror*, and published a work on the French Revolution, which is full of the most touching incidents, and adorned with specimens of the ardent and pathetic poetry, the product of French genius under the excitement of those most mysterious days. A. Humboldt was much attached to her, and committed to her care the publication of some of his most elaborate works.

She had two nephews, Athanase and Charles Coquerel, whom she educated, and who both attained considerable fame, one in the theological, and the other in the political field. Athanase was for some time the preacher in the Protestant Church at Amsterdam, and married the daughter of a Swiss gentleman, the only person I have ever known on the continent to adopt the dress and profess the opinions of the English Quaker. Miss Williams maintained intimate relations with her English friends, was familiar with the great lights of the Revolution, and her conversation was most instructive, entertaining, and varied. All her sympathies were on the side of freedom, and though she was not so prominent as to be persecuted by the Emperor, like Madame de Stael, she was the object of a good deal of suspicion, and narrowly watched by the police, who are at all times, unhappily, an instrument in the hands of despotic, and sometimes even of representative governments. In fact, they form such a part of the machinery of administration on the continent that the Emperor Alexander, at an audience which he granted to the head of the London police, expressed his astonishment, and almost his incredulity, when he was informed that the police of Great Britain did no political work for the State, but were solely employed in the protection of individual persons and property from outrage. —1861.

THOMAS NOON TALFOURD.

Judge Talfourd, the author of "Ion," was in his youth a zealous Unitarian. He married the daughter of John Towell Pratt, who edited the large edition of the works of Dr Priestley. Talfourd used in his early days to take a very active part in evening discussions held by the young men belonging to the Gravel-Pit Congregation at Hackney. It will be remembered that he received his death-stroke on the bench when he was delivering judgment. He was a great admirer of the poets of the Lake School, especially of William Wordsworth, and wrote several of the reviews which helped to establish Wordsworth's reputation, which Byron so bitterly attacked, saying of his most elaborate work that it was—

> "A drowsy, frousy poem called the Excursion,
> Writ in a manner that is my aversion."

It is not the less true that Byron drew largely upon Wordsworth's resources, of which abundant evidence will be found in the 3d and 4th cantos of " Childe Harold." The passionate verdicts given, both *pro* and *con*, in reference to Wordsworth, Coleridge, and Southey, may now be looked back upon with some wonder, but all three had made themselves obnoxious to the charge of renegadism. Wordsworth had accepted the office of stamp-distributor from Lord Lonsdale ; Southey, after attempting to suppress his demagogical drama of " Wat Tyler," became a violent Tory, bringing a hot partizanship into the ranks to which he fled, and Coleridge, a Tom-Paineite in politics, and a preaching Unitarian, ended by adopting all the doctrines of orthodoxy. Talfourd's intercourse with his " Lake " friends was however never interrupted, nor was his personal attachment at all cooled by the changes in their views.

COLERIDGE, SOUTHEY, AND WORDSWORTH.

Our judgments of those who differ from us are often more uncharitable and severe than just and discriminating. Coleridge always seemed to live in the dreamy regions of cloudland, and it was difficult to follow him through the mazes of his misty eloquence. At table, his harmonious periods fell from his lips like water from a fountain. Every now and then he was observed to put his finger and thumb into his waistcoat-pocket, from which he took an opium pill, which he clandestinely conveyed to his mouth, and so he seemed to feed his gentle, and often most touching oratory. But Southey was above all men the man who made literature his business. He toiled without intermission from day to day. History, biography, reviewing, prose and poetry, were receiving daily contributions from his indefatigable pen. The last time I visited the Lakes, Wordsworth dissuaded me from paying a visit to the shattered and broken man. " If he remember you," said he, " it will be with thoughts of pain, in reference to the breaking up of his mind. If he do not, the interview will be yet less desirable." Wordsworth had formed a very exalted opinion of his own poetical merits, and when the " Ettrick Shepherd " visited him, and began a sentence with the words, " We poets," Wordsworth interrupted him, and exclaimed, " Poets! " laying a strong emphasis upon the terminating letter, as if it were a profanation for any other man in his presence to share his bardic glories. He was fond of having his poetry quoted, received even extravagant laudation as a fit tribute to his genius, loved his sister the more dearly because she often recited his verses, and himself not unfrequently pointed out the beauties of his own versification to his listening guests.—1861.

N. T. CARRINGTON.

My recollections of Carrington are of a modest, melancholy man, who sought rather encouragement to converse than to manifest any disposition to be heard. He did not give me the impression of his being happy, nor indeed was he, for he said he sought the relief of poetry from the monotony of a schoolmaster's life. His verses, though flowing and correct, are somewhat monotonous, and in many of them he borrows the thoughts, and employs the identical words of the leading poets of the day. What follows is a favourable specimen.

> " I love the summer calm, I love
> Smooth seas below, blue skies above,
> The placid lake, the unruffled stream,
> The woods that rest beneath the beam.
> I love the deep, deep pause that reigns
> At highest noon o'er hills and plains,
> And own that summer's gentle rule
> Is soothing, soft, and beautiful.

> " But winter, in its angriest form
> Has charms,—there's grandeur in the storm,
> When the winds battle with the floods,
> And bow the mightiest of the woods.
> When the loud thunder, crash on crash,
> Follows the lightning's herald flash,
> And rocks, and spires, and towers are rent—
> 'Tis startling, but magnificent.

And yet it may be remarked that thunder and lightning are not characteristic of the winter season. These verses are formed on the model of Thomson's " Seasons."

One of the most characteristic of Carrington's poems, called " Holiday," is given in the notes to his " Dartmoor." It is really pathetic, such as only a poet and a schoolmaster could have written. There is a pretty local description of the port of Plymouth, of a June morning, of the wanderer who, without anxiety, enjoys the beauties of nature, and the contrasted personal application closes in these flowing strains:—

"What are his joys to mine? The groves are green,
And fair the flowers, and there are ever seen
By him the mountain's breast, the hills, the woods,
Grass-waving fields, and bright and wandering floods.
The lays of birds are ever in his ear,
Music and sylvan beauty crown his year.
But if to him the rural reign have power
To fill with joy the swift-revolving hour,
What rapture must be mine, so seldom given
To feel the beam, and drink the gale of heaven!
For, O! I love this nature, and my eye
Has felt the witchery of the soft blue sky.
Bear witness, glowing summer! how I love
Thy green world here, thy azure arch above.
But seldom comes the hour that snaps the chain,
To me thou art all beautiful in vain.
Bird, bee, and butterfly are on the wing,
Songs shake the woods, and streams are murmuring.
But, far from them, the world's unwilling slave,
My aching brow no genial breezes lave;
Few are the gladsome hours that come to cheer
With flowers and songs my dull unvarying year.
Yet when they come, as now, from loathèd night
The bird upsprings to hail the welcome light
With soul less buoyant than I turn to thee,
Prized for thy absence, sylvan liberty!—June 1825.

1861.

DR WOLCOT.

If not to be reckoned among the purest, Dr Wolcot was in his day one of the most popular of verse makers, and some of his *hits* upon George III. were of the hardest the " good old king " ever received. He was born at Dodbrook in 1738—indeed he has told the world this in the inscription for his tomb, when he announced that—

> "On this shall future generations stare,
> Who come to Dodbrook, and to Kingsbridge fair."

Dodbrook is a sort of appendage to Kingsbridge, in which latter place he received his early education in the Free School founded by Crispin, the prosperous Exeter merchant. He went afterwards to a grammar-school at Bodmin, in Cornwall, but nothing interesting or important marked his early life. He was apprenticed to a medical uncle, who sent him to Normandy, that he might acquire the French language. He visited a London hospital as a becoming close to his professional studies, but seems to have had more passion for poetry than for physic, a passion not favoured by his uncle and aunts, his father having died when his son was eleven years old.

When, in 1767, Sir William Trelawney was made Governor of Jamaica, he patronized Wolcot, who accompanied him to the island, having obtained the degree of M.D. from the University of Aberdeen. But the whites were too few and too poor to give him much encouragement, and the Governor suggested that he might be appointed to a lucrative living, if the incumbent, then seriously ill, should leave a vacancy. So the doctor came to England, and was ordained by the Bishop of London, but, on coming back to Jamaica, found that he had waited in vain for the shoes of the dead man, who had recovered from his illness and resumed his duties. Dr Wolcot obtained the small curacy of Vere, but his principal employment—no doubt the more attractive— was to act as master of the ceremonies to Sir William. A man less fitted for a religious teacher could scarcely have been stumbled on. His clerical duties were wholly neglected, and he returned to England in 1768, accompanying the widowed Lady Trelawney.

He was as little fitted for a doctor of medicine as for a
doctor of divinity. He could better epigrammatize than
prescribe, preferred ridiculing to healing, and had a keener
eye for mental or personal obliquities than for corporal
infirmities. He located himself in sundry places in Cornwall as a practitioner, but was a practitioner without practice. One good service he did while living at Truro. He
found out Opie the painter, whose chalk figures on a barn-
door arrested the attention of the observant critic. He
sent some of his songs to William Jackson, the eminent
organist of Exeter, whose

> "Time has not thinned my flowing hair,
> Nor bent me with his iron hand,"

and some other glees, will not be permitted to die. In
1778 he published his "Epistle to the Reviewers."

The doctor was a very discontented man, and gave expression to his dissatisfaction in many ways, especially in
his "Tristia, or the Sorrows of Peter," where he pours out
his grievances on the attention of the King, his Ministers,
the Bishop of London, and sundry political celebrities,—
heading it with Horace's complaint,

> "Ploravere suis non non respondere favorem
> Speratum meritis,"

he (Peter) being the *genius* and the *virtue* rewarded by
cold neglect. His complaints are amusing enough, but
somewhat exaggerated, the theme being that, generally,
poets get less of solid pudding than of empty praise.
George III. is, as might be expected, the principal target
against which his arrows are directed. He professed to
have no very soaring ambition—

> "Dread sir ! your bard's ambition soars not high,
> To take Pitt's place, or join the Privy Council,
> But yet a warbling goldfinch, such as I,
> Might pick some hemp-seed, taste a little groundsel."

He petitions most imploringly for a pension, which indeed he obtained and lost. His silence could be purchased, but not his song. He pleads his poverty, dilates on his merits, shows that he had served his country, and his country's statesmen, consoles himself that Erskine has been made Lord Chancellor, but that all sorts of unworthy men have been advanced to high honours. He, the poet, passed over, while catgut-scrapers, and canvas-daubers are elevated to dignities. Then he abuses the reviewers who had abused him, the paltry paragraph-spinners whose want of discernment had depreciated Pindar. He forgives Charles Fox, because he is William Pitt's opponent, but reminds him that while he had the distribution of the loaves and fishes, nothing whatever had been flung into the poet's plate. Pitt had threatened to hang him, but he scorned the *Willi*ppics of the Premier. He has a friendly word for Sheridan—belabours "Cobbler Gifford," and such "cobbling" fellows—calls Eldon "Old Puzzle," "who cannot distinguish a fly's foot from a tiger's paw,"—"full of wig-wisdom and deep doubts,"—laments that in hunting *Dame* Fortune, he had been taken in by *Miss* Fortune—asks the sympathy of Porteous, the Bishop of London, as a brother poet, and tells him to order the parsons who are lodged in the British Museum, to abandon the lousy birds and quadrupeds, and the musty manuscripts, and to attend instead to the souls of their parishioners, offering himself as a practical curator. He consults the goddess, who tells him that he is entitled to a high seat on Parnassus, for with golden lines he instructs, illumines, and adorns her pages, but recommends him to get a seat in a Cornish rotten borough if he wants advancement—tells his Cynthia that he is merciful, uses his toe and not scorpion-whips—tells the Bee that their fates are similar, one to be smoked, and the other starved to death. He pursues the

same career for more than one hundred pages of self-lauda-
tion and abuse of other people. He is worse treated than
the organ-grinder, or other street exhibitor, and says the
discoveries of gold have not relieved his poverty, and
opines they will prove a curse to the nation.

Then he laments his celibacy. He could afford to keep
a wife, but had poetized and pleaded with many fair ones
in vain. They were venal, and he had discovered that
they were vain· and valueless. He was a virtuous man,
and why should he seek alliance with the vices of woman-
hood? He has discovered that critics are bats, but of an
inferior race, as they live upon damnation. The world is
going to the dogs, and all that is good—his poetry especially—is condemned. Eloquence is aped. Statuary is
stoned to death. What's the use of his speaking? The
Court is his foe. Why did he mock the Sovereign? He has
suffered, but he must eat and drink. Why don't they take
pity? He has praises and sighs to sell. In his " Tristia "
the following verse is good. It is to Lord Nelson with
his Lordship's night-cap, that caught fire on the poet's
head at a candle as he was reading in bed at Merton :—

> " Take your night-cap again, my good lord, I desire,
>   For I wish not to keep it a minute.
>   What belongs to a Nelson, where'er there's a fire
>   Is sure to be instantly in it."

Lord Nelson was one of his heroes, but his eulogium on
Shakspeare is one of the finest ever written :—

> " Here while I wondering turn o'er Shakspeare's page,
>   I read, midst visions of delight, the sage
>   High o'er the wreck of worlds who stands sublime.
>   A column in the melancholy waste,
>   Its cities ruined, and its glories past,
>   Majestic in the solitude of time."

His vanity breaks out in multitudinous forms. He will

have it that Cornwall and Devon will claim the honour of being his birthplace, as the cities of Greece fought for that of having cradled Homer, and cries out—

> " Ye men of metre,
> Hide your diminished heads at Peter."

His " Odes to Academics " show generally a very sound appreciation of the merits and demerits of the painters of his day.   He recommends West not to attempt things beyond his reach—laughs at Fuseli for attempting to rival Sir Joshua, and for dreaming that he has caught a shred from the mantle of Michael Angelo—chastises Loutherbourg for his *volcanic* eruptions — hails young M'Lean as an artist of promise—expresses high admiration for Wilkie, who will imitate Hogarth in wit and humour—Turner, he says, will leave his rivals far behind—lauds Bacon, the sculptor—rejoices that Garrard can and ought to despise Academic honours—sees the muse of Sculpture awakened in Nollekens, and laughs at " The Heads " who seek distinction by exhibition on the R.A. walls.

He pours out his diatribes on the once renowned Mrs Clarke, the heroine of ducal story.   He celebrates the Carlton House fête, to which he was not invited, and thinks that, as Sheridan is taken in favour, Peter should not be neglected.

Wolcot's vanity is irrepressible.   Peter is always the prominent picture.   He writes to everybody about himself, and he is the central orb round which kings and subjects, and indeed the whole creation, move.   His pension, his prophecy, his paintings, his praise, his censure, and his criticisms are to annihilate all other topics.   The desire to silence such a critic was quite natural.   Nobody likes to be laughed at, and it is not all laughter, for he sometimes uses a whip of scorpions, and lashes sore places with the delight of a Mephistophiles. That in those libel-hunting days he should have escaped unscathed can only be attributed to the fear of giving wider circulation to his incisive jokes, many of which remain indelibly associated with the blunderings and stutterings of the " Good King George." In our days much of the licentious boldness which characterises his verse would not be tolerated. Moore laid it on with a lighter and more graceful hand, but opinion compelled the " Little Tom " to suppress much that he had written, and in his later days he became more refined and decorous. It is amusing now to read the adulation — " fulsome " used to be the word — with which Peter belauded the Prince of Wales, merely to spite his royal father and mother. All the tittle-tattle of the Court, every bit of scandal he delights in, expatiates on, and versifies. Except that he was a favourite at Court, one can hardly explain his vituperation of Sir Joseph Banks, whose chace after a butterfly called the Emperor of Morocco is humorously told. William Pitt is delivered to damnation in the epistle to a falling minister, and to him is devoted a clever imitation of Horace's Ode XII. (Book I.). The " heaven-born " could hardly complain of having applied to him—

> " Quid prius dicam solitis parentis
> Laudibus ; qui res hominum ac deorum
> Qui mare et terras, variis que mundum
> Temperat horis ? "

His " Subjects for painters " has Fontenelle's motto—

> " Qui veut peindre pour l'immortalité
> Doit peindre des sots."

The " Ode to the Devil," complimenting his Satanic majesty on his successes, is full of variety and fun.

Mrs Levi demanding from the theatre-manager the shilling back because her son had fallen into the pit, and had "not seen the show," is very good. His expostulatory "Odes to the Peers," though overlaboured, has many pungent stanzas. Poor Sylvanus Urban is very shabbily treated, but this is a natural return for the criticisms of the *Gentleman's Magazine.* In his "advice to a future laureate," he suggests, with what propriety, the honour might be conferred on him. The complimentary epistle to James Bruce, Esq., the Abyssinian traveller, has some interest now when Abyssinia, the sources of the Nile, and Dr Livingstone occupy so much of public attention. The "Rights of Kings, or loyal odes to disloyal academicians," is in the usual stream of obloquy. There are eighteen such odes, followed by one to Thomas Paine, and another to "My Ass," honoured with his own name Peter. He laughs at Dr Parr, whose vanity was flattered when he praised himself. Of the king's ignorance and precipitancy he gives an instance, which if "non vero è ben trovato"—

> "Who's this ? who's this ? who's this fine fellow here ? "
> ",Sesostris," bowing low, replies the Peer.
> " Sir Sostris ? Hey ! Sir Sostris ! 'pon my word,
>   Is he a Knight or Baronet, my Lord ? "
> " One of *my making ?* what ? my Lord ! *my making ?*
>   This, with a vengeance, was mistaking."

"More money" is a remonstrance with Mr Pitt for new demands for the king. There is an amusing dialogue between George III. and the Head Master of Eton, to whom his Majesty addresses all sorts of ridiculous questions as to the domestic habits of Cæsar. It is called "The Progress of Knowledge." The Eton boys turn the king into ridicule, so that the monarch "bade to schools a long adieu."*

Dr Wolcot could say bitter things. He liked to be

---

* " Bade to schools a long adieu !
    Of Eton journeys gave the idea o'er,
    And, angry, never mentioned Cæsar more."

thought a sarcastic wit. A friend of mine who was introduced to him, was not of the most perfect shape, and on
receiving him he said to the introducer, "You have
brought me a greyhound in a dropsy." He was willing
only to wound, but was not afraid to strike, and he was
careless of the wound inflicted if he could obtain the credit
of being able to shoot a poisoned arrow.

Many characteristic anecdotes are told of Peter. On one
occasion, there was a large party gathered together for a
picnic, to which he was not invited. As he deemed himself the most important person in the locality, he was very
angry, and determined to find some way of exhibiting his
displeasure by annoying the guests. He learned where
the basket was that held the provisions for the festivity,
the most prominent object being a large apple-pie. He
took off the crust, devoured the apples, and replaced
them by stones, placing upon them an abusive piece of
poetry, a mode of revenge in which he was accustomed to
indulge.

On another occasion, when he had returned from Portugal, he told two venerable aunts that, being desirous of
giving them something better than an ordinary present, he
had managed to obtain two angel Seraphim and Cherubim,
and had carefully preserved them for the service of his
highly respected relatives. They expressed great delight
at the novelty and value of the gift; "but, alas!" he said,
"a melancholy accident has happened. We had a terrible
storm at sea. There was a great uproar among the crew
and the passengers. The angels quarrelled, took to fight-
ing, and pulled out one another's eyes. I could not offer
you the dilapidated relics." My informant said that the
ancient ladies believed every word of their nephew's communication.—1872.*

* This article on Dr Wolcot was written in October 1872, and appears to
have been Sir J. Bowring's last composition.

ALEXANDER HUMBOLDT.

Alexander Humboldt's name will hold an exalted place among the celebrities of the first half of the nineteenth century. My personal acquaintance with him began at the dinner-table of Cuvier in the Jardin des Plantes in Paris, and I may mention by the way, with reference to the great French naturalist, that his brain, when weighed after death, was reported to be the largest upon record. I sat next to Humboldt, and was struck by the excursive character of his conversation. I was not aware of the name of my neighbour, but having asked Cuvier for an introduction to him, he revealed the fact that it was with Humboldt that I had been engaged in a colloquy which interested me much. Not to speak of his travels with Bonpland, his " Cosmos " is one of the most comprehensive and suggestive of contributions to literature and science, not only bringing a vast amount of knowledge from regions he had himself visited, but drawing from the researches and experience of others deductions the most valuable. Yet it was somewhat strange to me to find how much the habits and duties of a courtier were mingled with the condition and abstract studies of the sage. Singular was the contrast between Humboldt in his own residence, surrounded by philosophical instruments, pursuing the most profound investigations, and the same Humboldt transferred to the presence of kings and queens, and learned in the strict and rigid ceremonials of a German Court. I have been more than once extricated from embarrassment as to my own conduct by the kind and judicious advice which I received from him. Independently of his thorough mastery of the discoveries of science, he was fond of the *belles lettres*, of works of art, and not unfrequently referred to the great geniuses of the Italian schools. Dante was one of his favourite authors. His correspond-

ence with learned men was most extensive, and it has been
seen by the publication of some of his writings that he could
now and then indulge in a strain of sarcastic bitterness.
He certainly, had his opinions prevailed with the late King
of Prussia, would have given to the politics of that government a liberal tendency.   Such may be the future career of
the Prussian monarchy, and it would undoubtedly be acceptable to the higher intellects of the nation.   It seems scarcely
natural that Austria should take the lead in popular reforms, and thus occupy a position higher than that aspired
to by the more cultivated spirits of northern and eastern
Germany.   There were certain ideas in the mind of the
late King of Prussia, which showed a disposition to assimilate the constitution of his monarchy to that of Great
Britain.   He once discussed with me the desirability of
creating an hereditary peerage resembling our own, the
elements of which would, however, certainly not be found
in the Prussian dominions.   Probably the more intimate
union with the English Court, and intercourse with British
subjects, may lead to beneficial changes.   At all events, the
flow of opinion is in that direction, and to it we may confidently look for the solution of many a political problem.
—1861.

NIEBUHR AND SCHLEGEL.

Niebuhr was one of the most interesting men with whom
it has been my lot to hold intercourse.   Those who are
acquainted with his history of Rome need no evidence of
his industry and erudition, but what struck me most was
the extraordinary sagacity with which he spoke of Irish
affairs, at that time so complicated and embarrassing.   The
son of a distinguished father, he inherited all his activity
and more than his knowledge, turning to excellent account
advantages given him by a long residence in Rome as

Pru sian Minister, so that he had occasion by his own observation to form an excellent estimate of the value of tradition, and to compare the existing monuments with the tales of the remotest times. There was sometimes a good deal of asperity in his criticisms, and in one of his controversies with A. W. Schlegel he used the phrase, " May he eat the bread of bitterness." His home was one of the greatest simplicity, the supply of furniture small, and altogether of an uncostly style, in which there was a great contrast to his adversary Schlegel, who was quite a man of the world, and lived somewhat ostentatiously. I remember a suite of servants, all clad in light-blue liveries with silver facings, and have seen their master at many of the Courts of Europe representing all the fashion of the passing hour. German literature owes much to Schlegel for his translations of the dramas of Shakspeare, which gave the latter's name a wonderful popularity in Germany, a country where it is at least as highly appreciated as at home, and the reaction has extended far and wide, for no man now in France or Italy would venture to represent the bard of Avon as merely an inspired barbarian, a title with which he was frequently honoured down to the beginning of the present century. Since the time of Homer, no man has ever held the mind in such enchantment as " our great heir of fame," and it is no profanation to say that neither the Iliad nor Odyssey, nor the Eneid of Virgil, are likely to leave impressions so lasting on future generations as the works of our own Shakspeare.—1861.

BUNSEN.

Bunsen was not only a most learned, but a most religious man, devout sympathies being a part of his very nature. In his domestic relations no man was ever more loved. My acquaintance with him began more than a quarter of a

century ago when he was Prussian minister at Rome, where
he succeeded Niebuhr. The legation was then on the top
of the Tarpeian rock, where Protestant service was regularly held. Bunsen's speculations have been deemed bold
and sceptical, but they are such as must approve themselves to all attentive students of ancient history. As no
men of intellectual cultivation would in these days accept
the Mosaic account of the creation in its literal sense, so it
is impossible to deny that Bunsen has demonstrated from
the Egyptian annals that four thousand years at least must
be added to the period given in the Old Testament as the
epoch between the time of Noah and the Pharaonic dynasties. The date of the erection of the pyramids can be
pretty accurately ascertained, and it took place within a few
generations of the deluge. Now, it is quite impossible that
such an innumerable quantity of workmen (Herodotus represents them to have been seven or eight hundred thousand)
should have been collected among the descendants of a
single family. There are many theories by which the facts
may be accounted for. The flood was perhaps partial, for
there is no reference to it in the most undoubtedly ancient
histories, those of China.

Bunsen has furnished many materials for serious thought
in the field of historical inquiry, and has helped to rescue
Protestantism from the charge of being as intolerant in its
claims to infallibility as the Church of Rome itself. He is
but one of many interpreters, and the example of men like
him whose attachments to the teachings of the Gospel, and
whose reverence for the character of the Saviour cannot be
for a moment doubted, must exercise a permanent influence.
Bunsen had much at heart a federal union between the
German and Anglican Churches, but the elements are far
too heterogeneous. They have small sympathy for each
other, and little that is common in their constitution. It is

not likely that the Germans would ever recognize the high-flown pretensions of the English Episcopacy, or reconcile themselves to the incredible distinctions between the salaries of the bishops and those of the subordinate clergy. Nor does the union of Church and State find much approval on the Continent, where in most Protestant, and even in some Catholic countries, the clergy of all denominations are looked upon with an equal eye.—1861.

LAMARTINE.

In the year 1831 I was engaged with Lord Clarendon (then Mr George Villiers) as Commissioner for the negotiation of a Commercial Treaty with France. At that time Louis Philippe professed an earnest desire to increase intercourse, and to extend trading relations with England. A grand opportunity was lost at the Congress of Vienna when, if our statesmen had had the slightest idea of the best means of securing the peace, and advancing the prosperity of nations, they would have removed the barriers which Custom-house legislation placed in the way of the friendly exchange of those articles for the production of which different localities have their various aptitudes. But the statesmen of the day were occupied in far less popular negotiations. They were settling dynasties, they were parcelling out nations, and were dealing with millions of men to whom they promised freedom as if they were serfs or slaves. But the progress of time has undermined, and the tempests of agitation have blown down the ill-conceived and hastily-constructed edifice. The French Bourbons, whom it was the main object to establish upon the French throne, have been driven out, and the Buonapartes, whose exclusion from that throne was the primary object of the then victorious sovereigns, are now reinstalled by an irrepressible determination of the popular will. Belgium has

been wrested from Holland, Italy from Austria, and the
records of those arrangements which seemed so triumphant
have, in the course of less than half a century, been torn
into pieces and scattered to the winds. The voices which
cried out to the enthralled universe, "This is to be your
future condition!" the decrees which proclaimed to the
advancing tide of civilization and progress, "Thus far shalt
thou proceed, and no further," have been issued in vain.
The world moves on in its grand cycle of advancement, and
the triumph of Free Trade must be deemed one of the
noblest evidences of that advancement.

But already, in France, sinister interests had created, and
public legislation patronised and protected many a pernicious monopoly, and our mission met with small success.
The French Commissioners were not ill-affected. One, the
Baron Fréville, was a man of little strength of character,—
the other, Duchatel (afterwards a Cabinet Minister), an
intimate friend of Guizot, was a doctrinaire, more desirous
of making himself agreeable to the king, than of promoting any great national object. The king himself was a
deceiver throughout. He was a large forest proprietor,
and could not reconcile himself to the losses he anticipated,
should the importation of English iron lessen the value
of the timber employed in the manufactures of the French.
Then, in the House of Peers and the Chamber of Deputies,
were the most potent possessors of those privileges which
excluded foreign articles from fair competition with the
national productions. They maintained that the markets
of France belonged by rights to Frenchmen, and that
foreigners were but intruders there. Independently of the
resistance we met with in the highest quarters, almost all
the subordinate functionaries were bitter enemies of commercial liberty, and the remembrance of the old quarrels
with Great Britain made the introduction of our goods

particularly obnoxious to French policy. It was in northern France, however, that this hostility was principally displayed. The Lyons Chamber of Commerce, much influenced by that enlightened man Arlès Dufour, the representative of the silk manufacture, an industry the least protected and the most prosperous in France, never failed to proclaim the sound doctrines of political economy. In Bordeaux also spoke out most eloquently the vineyard proprietors, having as their organ Henri Fonfrède, whose father perished on the scaffold with his friend and leader Brissot. One of the most important and valuable of the agricultural interests of central and southern France had been long sacrificed to the manufacturing interest of the north, but the hope that the English market might be made accessible to them gave a great impulse to their efforts, and there was a moment in which many of the Gascons openly avowed a desire for fiscal separation, and that they should be subjected to tariffs less inimical to their well-being.

About this time I visited most of the wine-districts of France, and will mention a few facts as amusing as instructive. The average production of the four clarets of the first quality does not exceed about 400 tons per annum. These are called *premiers crus*, and are represented by the Médoc vineyards of Lafitte, Latour, Chateau Margaux, and Chateau Haut Brion. It is a curious fact that, while the English were possessors of Gascony, the wines now universally recognised as of the best order were so inferior that it was made a condition, in order to dispose of them, that a certain quantity should be taken by those who desired to purchase the then superior wines of Blaye. It is believed that more than 30,000 tons are sold in the different markets of the world under the favoured names. In Champagne, the two most distinguished vineyards—that of Aï

for the sparkling, and that of Sillery for the still champagne—produce very small quantities, though there is no
wine-merchant who will not agree to provide a supply to
any extent. I was informed that there are five countries,
England, Russia, France, Turkey, and the United States of
America, any one of which consumes more than the whole
of the genuine produce of Champagne, so that at least
four-fifths of the wine drunk under that name is either
made in other districts, or artificially manufactured.
While on a visit to M. Ouvrard, the proprietor of the most
celebrated of the Burgundy vineyards, that of Romanée
Conti, he informed me that, though the wine was nominally
sold at every restaurant in Paris, and is to be found in the
lists of all the principal dealers in wine, he never sold a
bottle, the vineyard producing only a few tons which he
kept for his own private use, and for presents to a small
number of privileged personages.

At this period I made the acquaintance of Lamartine,
and visited him at St Pol, a beautiful estate he possessed
in the neighbourhood of Macon. His father was originally
in the service of the Court, and Lamartine received a
thoroughly monarchical education. It is not for me here
to follow the stages of thought which ended in his becoming
the most distinguished of French Republican advocates.
Study and travel developed and adorned the rich resources
of his mind, and I believe his integrity to have been as
incorruptible as his intellect was bright and glowing.
Nothing in political history is grander than his display of
courageous eloquence at the Hôtel de Ville, when a furious
mob flouted the red flag in his face, and he bared his breast
to the menaced attack on his life. Sufficient justice has not
been done to this most remarkable man, but his name will
stand out hereafter among the most prominent bas-reliefs
of heroic story. I can never forget, when I was the object

of an intemperate attack from M. Joubert in the Chamber
of Deputies for having acted as an incendiary on my visit
to the wine-departments, with what an earnest enthusiasm
I was defended by my illustrious friend. Like Scott, he
had been visited by great reverses, and, like Scott too, had
been moved by those reverses to incredible mental labours.
He has had some family sorrows. He married an English
lady, and they lost their only child while travelling in the
Holy Land. Of his adventures there, the account of his
visit to that strange personage, Lady Hester Stanhope, is
singularly amusing. Nothing flattered her vanity more
than to be the object of attention from a great celebrity.
It would be too long and laborious a task to criticize, or
(more becomingly) to eulogize the multitudinous contributions to literature which have emanated from Lamartine's
pen. Examples are not rare in France where men of letters
are leading actors in the field of political strife. Among
the most illustrious will Lamartine be ranked.—1861.

MADAME DE STAEL.

Madame de Stael was a perfect aristocrat, and her sympathies were wholly with the great and prosperous. She saw
nothing in England but the luxury, stupidity, and pride of
the Tory aristocracy, and the intelligence and magnificence
of the Whig aristocracy. These latter talked about truth, and
liberty, and herself, and she supposed it was all as it should
be. As to the millions, the people, she never inquired into
their situation. She had a horror of the canaille, but anything of *sangre azul* had a charm for her. When she was
dying she said, " Let me die in peace ; let my last moments
be undisturbed ; " yet she ordered the cards of every visitor
to be brought to her. Among them was one from the Duke
de Richelieu. "What !" exclaimed she indignantly, " What !
have you sent away the *Duke?* Hurry. Fly after him.

Bring him back. Tell him that, though I die for all the world, I live for *him*."—1822.

JULLIEN, M. A.

No man's mind was ever so completely occupied with one idea as Jullien's with the *Revue Encyclopédique*. He runs over the chimes ten times a day, and scarcely relieves the dullness with any note of variety. The *Revue* is to him the very centre round which all civilization turns. He knows everybody, and presses everybody into the service of his book. "You can do this and that," as if all men's hands and all men's talents waited his bidding. Jullien said, "When Mercier wrote his vehement and eloquent book against lotteries, Bonaparte said to the Minister of the Interior, 'Give Mercier a good place in the lottery-department.'—'Quoi! Votre Majesté ne sait elle pas qu'il a écrit contre la loterie?'—'Oui. Il dit qu'elle n'est bonne à rien. Prouvez lui qu'elle est bonne à quelque chose.'"—1822.

FRANZEN, F. M.

In a little secluded village of Sweden (Kumla, near Örebro) I found this sweet poet and most amiable man. He was surrounded by the children of the peasantry, to whom he communicated daily instruction. His large and interesting family delighted me. The eldest daughter, who had never seen an Englishman before, spoke our language with singular purity. We read Shakspeare together, and she seemed to feel every sentiment, whether touching or sublime, of our master of the stage. I have seldom passed a happier day, for it was passed in witnessing happiness and in communicating it.

KARAMZIN, H. M.

I expected to see an affected and self-complacent man.

In his early writings there is such an overstrained and exaggerated sympathy, such a parade of sentimentality and exquisiteness, that I had no idea such a mind would become robust and energetic. He talked of his travels with animation and eloquence. He introduced his children, to each of whom he had given the name of a nation. There was a little round-faced Tatar-like child whom he called "The Chinese." Another, with a curly flaxen head, and cheerful rosy cheeks, was "My English Boy." Karamzin's wife pleased me by the readiness of her wit, and the variety of her conversation. Of Alexander, Karamzin spoke in terms of unqualified eulogy, and said he had sent for him, before his "History of Russia" was written, to command that no respect for his imperial person should on any occasion warp his views, or induce him to deface the fair and honest representations of truth.—1822.

ADELUNG.

At Adelung's table, at St Petersburg, there were often most interesting individuals. I there first met Hepites, the Greek Physician, who so often risked his life in seeking remedies for the plague. Our intercourse, though irregular and broken, still continues, and I have had many occasions to admire the ardent zeal and patriotism which he has been for years directing to the enfranchisement of his country. His friendly feelings towards me were thus expressed :—

> " Σε ιδα εις τας οχθας της Νεβας,
> Σε ξαναιδα εις τας οχθας της Σενας,
> Εγω εις του Ταμητος τας οχθας σεζητουσα,
> Καλω ανταμωσιν εις τας οχθας του Ευρωτα."

> " I saw you (first) on the banks of the Neva,
> I recognised you on the banks of the Seine,
> I sought you on the banks of the Thames,
> I invite you to meet me on the banks of the Eurotas."

The particular attention which has been paid in Russia
to the history of languages is well known. There is a
curious book by Adelung on the subject. The laborious
undertaking of Pallas originated with Catherine, and Adelung showed me the first conception of the work in the
handwriting of that most extraordinary woman. It is a
list of words, nearly similar to that adopted by Pallas, which
was sent wherever Russia possessed a channel of communication. After ·Pallas came the elder Adelung, whose
"Mithridates" has become a standard book on language.
F. Adelung's catalogue is far more extensive, and is no
doubt the most perfect list that has hitherto been formed.
It is rather a strange fact that nations seem to attend to
this subject in the very infancy of their literature. Next to
those of Russia, the writers of the United States (Du Ponceau,
for instance) have done most to advance the inquiry.

When Voltaire had published his history of Peter the
Great, there were such innumerable errors in the orthography of the proper names, that Catherine directed her
secretary to write to the witty Frenchman. His reply was
laconic enough : "Je lui désire moins de bêtises, et à sa
langue moins de consonnes."—1822.

CRAS, H. C., AND MEYER.

Among the many interesting men whom I met with in
Holland, Cras was one of the most interesting. He must,
I think, have been more than an octogenarian, but there
was a power and a cordiality about him which delighted
me not a little, and I regretted that I could not accept the
offer, which he had come in person to make, of sharing an
English 'bif stck' at his table. But I did sit at his table
when he was surrounded by the most learned men of his
country, and I shall not forget the enthusiasm with which
an ancient cup passed round on which was a Latin inscrip-

tion, repeated by all the guests, consecrating the principles of, and renewing the pledges to truth and liberty. Cras' Latinity was remarkably pure. He died soon after I quitted Holland in 1819.

The introductions I took from my old and venerable friend Bishop Gregoire led me very much among the Jews of Holland. I found them strikingly intelligent, their minds richly stored with languages and literature, but almost universally sceptical. The families of Peninsular descent were well acquainted with the fine language of their ancestors, and they talked with singular enthusiasm of the renowned romantic land, the love of which has always been one of my passions. Meyer, whose history of jurisprudence has become a standard book, was Secretary of State to Louis Buonaparte. His person, if my recollection deceive me not, was very fine, and his power over language remarkable, as were his shrewdness and pointed conversation. He talked with raptures of the French language as being of all others the best adapted for legislation, the most refined, and the most pliable. My opinion is quite the reverse. I regard the Gallic branch as the meanest and the poorest derived from the Roman root. It borrowed little from Franks and Normans, it has enriched itself from no local or provincial sources, and a bar has been erected against all improvement by the stupid decree that no word shall be considered legitimate which did not exist in the time of Louis XIV. To our language hundreds and thousands of words have been added since then, and it marches onward with the march of knowledge. Let any one take the compounds of our nervous and flexible idiom, and endeavour to transfer them into a French form, and he will find it impossible ; *e.g.*, belief—unbelief—misbelief—disbelief. The shades of distinction cannot be conveyed to a Frenchman in his own tongue. The tenses of French verbs are feeble and inexpressive, they confound necessity with free-will, and are metaphysical monsters. To have made the French language universal, as Buonaparte projected, would have been as baneful to the interests of science and wisdom as universal empire would have been to public security and happiness.—1819.

CONDE, JOSE ANTONIO.

I never saw a man so modest and retiring as Conde. How should I? There was scarcely ever perhaps an instance of such trembling diffidence as his mind exhibited. He was frank and communicative, and though his communications were of a singularly original character—for the Arabic literature of Spain, to which he was devoted, has found no modern writer to rival him—they were always made with striking simplicity. He wanted only poetical feeling to be the *non plus ultra* of European Arabic scholars. The MSS. of the Spanish Moors are full of verses, and the soul of poetry is diffused over the whole of these most interesting records. Conde felt their strength, and could convey it to others, but he had no sense of harmony beyond the mere vibration of the rhymes. His friend Moratin's elegy on his death is one of the sweetest lyrical produt ions of modern times.

1.

"Te vas, mi dulce amigo,
La luz huyendo del dia ;
Te vas, y no conmigo,
Y de la tumba pia,
En el estrecho limite,
Mudo tu cuerpo está !
Y á mi que debil siento
El peso de los años,
Y al cielo me lamento
Di ingratitud y engaños
Para llorar te ; misero !
Largo vivir me da.

"My friend, and dost thou leave me
In darkness and despair ?
And am I left to grieve me
While thou art mouldering there
In mute and sad forgetfulness
Within thy narrow bed ?
I, 'neath the burden bending
Of long and sorrowing years,
My plaints to heaven ascending
Of toils, deceits, and fears,
And mourning thee, life's pilgrimage
Is dark, long, full of dread.

2.

" O fuéramos unidos
Al seno deleitoso
Que en sus bosques floridos
Guarda eterno reposo.
À aquellas almas ínclitas,
Del mundo admiracion ;
O solo à mi llevára
La muerte presurosa,
Y tu virtud gozára
Modesta, ruborosa,
Y tan ilustres méritos
Ufana la nacion.

" O would we were united
In those celestial bowers,
Where we might rest delighted
Midst ever fragrant flowers,
Among those spirits glorified,
Whose memories here remain.
Or had I gone before thee,
To see the hand of fame
Shed all its laurels o'er thee,
And thy retiring name
Blushing beneath the gratitude
Of our maternal Spain.

3.

" Al estudio ofreciste
Los años fugitivos,
Y joven conociste
Cuanto le son nocivos
Al generoso espiritu
El ocio y el placer.
Veloz en tu carrera,
Al templo te adelantas,
Donde moral severa
Dicta sus leyes santas,
Y en ellos, digno interprete,
Llegas à florecer.

" Thy early spring-tide given
To study and to thought,
Pleasure and luxury driven,
As things which profit nought.
Thou didst withstand their blandishments
In steady dignity,
That fane of glory seeking
Where sternest virtue lives,
And there, sublimely speaking,
The law of wisdom gives ;
And thou wert her interpreter,
And she was proud of thee.

4.

" Ciñieronle corona
De lauros immortales
Las nueve de Helicona—
Sus diafanos cristales
Te dieron, y benevolas,
Su lira de marfil,
Con ella renovando
La voz de Anacreonte,
Eco amoroso y blando,
Sonó de Pindo el monte
Y te cedió Teocrito
La caña pastoriL

" The smiling muses wrought thee
A fadeless laurel crown ;
Their sweetest songs they brought thee,
And made those songs thy own.
And in thy hand, obsequiously,
They placed their ivory lyre.
Thy touch anew created
Anacreon's joyous strain,
And Pindus' Mount repeated
Its former notes again.
And then we saw Theocritus
Salute thee and retire.

5.

" Febo te dió la ciencia
  De idiomas diferentes,
  Y el resono y afluencia
  Que usaron elocuentes
  Arabia, Roma, y Atica
  Supiste declarar.
  Y el cantico festivo
  Que en belica Armorica
  El pueblo fugitivo
  Al numen dirigia,
  Cuando al feroz ejercito
  Hundió en su centro el mar.

" Thine were the countless treasures
  Of many a varying tongue,
  And music's sacred measures
  And eloquence of song ;
  Arabia, Rome, and Attica
  Brought all their gifts to thee.
  Thou heard'st the anthem glorious
  From Egypt's shore resound,
  While onward passed victorious
  That wondrous sea which drowned
  The chariot and the charioteer,
  'Twas Israel's victory.

6.

" La historia, alzando el velo
  Que lo pasado oculta,
  Entrega à tu desvelo
  Bronces que el arte abulta
  Y codices y marmoles
  Amigo, te explicó.
  Y de alli de las que han sido
  Cuidades poderosas
  Se cuantas dió al olvido
  Acciones generosas,
  La edad, que vuela rapida,
  Memorias te dictó.

" Where proud inquiry falters,
  Securely thou didst lead,
  Midst pyramids and altars,
  And memories of the dead.
  It was the pride of history
  To lift her voice for thee.
  She told of many a ruin,
  The strange vicissitude,
  She saw thine eye pursuing
  The generous and the good,
  And bade her favourite rescue them
  From dark obscurity.

7.

" Desde que el cielo airado
  Mostró en Xerez su saña
  Y al suelo derribado
  Cayó el poder de España
  Subiendo al trono Gotico
  La prole de Ismael ;
  Hasta que rotas fueron
  Las ultimas cadenas,
  Y tremoladas viéron
  De Alhambra en las almenas
  Los ya vencidos Arabes
  Las cruces de Isabel.

" She took thee to the ages,
  When victory led the Moor,
  And read those chequered pages
  Of joy and sorrow o'er,
  When the dark sons of Ismael
  Sat on the Gothic throne,
  Until the chains of slavery
  Were broken by the enslaved,
  And the red flag of bravery
  Above the Alhambra waved,
  And our triumphant Isabel
  Called rescued Spain her own.

8.

" A ti fué concedido
Eternizar la gloria
De los que han distinguído
La paz o la vitoria
En dilatadas epocas
Que el mundo véo pasar.
Y a ti de dos naciones
Ilustres enemigos
Referir los blazones,
Hazañas, y fatigas,
Y de candor historica
Dignos ejemplos dar.

" And thou hast given to story
Eternal being now,
And stamped of shame or glory
The signs upon her brow.
O'er the vast desert wandering
Of long departed days,
Alike the friend and foeman,
Thy honest judgment share.
And Moor, and Goth, and Roman,
Thy stern reproof must bear.
And honour, valour, chivalry,
Obtain thy glowing praise.

9.

" Europa que anhelaba
De tu saber el fruto,
Y ofrecerle esperaba
En aplausos tributo
La nueva de tu perdida
Debe primero oir.
La parca inexorable
Te arribató á la tumba
En eco lamentable
La boveda retumba,
Y alla en tu centro lobrego
Sonó ronco gemir.

" The world, of thee unworthy,
Stood gazing on thy pen,
And wreathed a garland for thee
In smiling pride—and then
Was told thou had'st abandoned her,
And that thou wast no more.
Alas ! for death hath swept thee
Into its depth of gloom.
We saw the eyes that wept thee,
We heard thy echoing tomb,
And O ! they now close o'er thee
The heavy grating-door.

10.

" Ay ! perdona ofendido
Espiritu, perdona !
Si en la region de olvido
Ciñes aurea corona,
Y sus virtudes solidas
Tienen ya galardon.
No de una madre ingrata
El duro ceño acuerdes
Que nunca se dilata
La existencia que pierdes
Sin que la turben perfidias,
Envidia, y ambicion."

" Forgive, offended spirit !
Forgive—for, where thou art,
The golden crown of merit
Is thine—thy gentle heart
Shall soon forget thy destiny,
While here a wanderer.
Of thy ungrateful mother
Forgive the frowns austere,
And wounds of friend and brother,
While thou wert lingering here.
But envy, hate, or perfidy
Can never enter there."—1822.

ST. SIMONIANS.

When I was in Paris after the Revolution of 1830, I made the acquaintance of a remarkable group of men, the St. Simonians, who were then exciting much public attention, and exercised no small influence over the press. The formula round which they were gathered was to this effect, "To each his work, and to each according to his work." Sceptics they all were, but though they held the writings of their founder in great reverence, they never pretended that they represented a supernatural revelation. They were a set of socialists, bound together by the strong bonds of brotherhood, and recognising as their head Père Enfantin, their father and high-priest, who was encircled by a kind of priestly hierarchy. They had their church and a regular service in the Rue Taitbout, but their doctrines were deemed so subversive, that they were suppressed by the intervention of state authority. Among their leaders, were many men who afterwards reached high distinction in the state, and occupied important social positions. Michel Chevalier, who is well known as the enlightened and generous judge of British institutions, and the honest interpreter of British interests and British policy, to whom the initiative of the movement which resulted in Cobden's famous treaty of commerce is mainly due, and who had been rewarded by the Emperor in being called to the Senate — and Emile Perrain, the head of one of the great commercial associations of France, who has amassed a colossal fortune, were among the eminent names. Various public functionaries, directors of departments, and some of the principal managers of railway companies, and other industrial undertakings, owed their first reputation to their connection with the St. Simonian movement.

In the pursuit of a chimera, which they called woman,

great numbers of the St Simonians migrated to the Levant, especially to Egypt, where they obtained employment under Mehemet Ali Pasha. Some professed Mahommed-ism, submitted themselves to Moosulman rites, and took up their abode in the Turkish quarters of Cairo, while some even accompanied the caravans in the pilgrimages to the holy cities, and one of them, whom I knew, was denounced as an untrustworthy convert, and was cruelly ill-treated on on his way to Medina. The profession of Islamism no doubt furthered ambitious views, and the general commander-in-chief of the Syrian armies, well known as Sooleiman Pasha, was a Colonel Sève, formerly an officer in Napoleon's legions. Whether the fascinations of the harem, or curio-sity respecting Mahommedan inner life, or other motive was the cause, it is an undoubted fact that several Englishmen have become renegades to their Christian faith. One man I knew at Constantinople, the son of a respectable London merchant. At Aleppo the head of the dancing dervishes was a Scotchman, and in Alexandria the dragoman of the British Consul-General openly professed Mahommedanism, married women of that creed, and directed that his children should be educated in the faith of the prophet. At Cairo our Consul-General ascertained that great preparations were being made for the reception of an Englishman, but he managed to get him arrested for debt and sent away from the Egyptian capital, in order to avoid scandal, especially as the conversion of an Englishman was deemed a most memorable triumph. Among the Maltese, great numbers have been found ready enough to abandon their Christian calling, and it is most strange, yet not less true, that scarcely an instance can be found of the conversion of a Moosulman to any of the forms of orthodox Christianity.

The appearance and disappearance of St Simonianism among the cultivated minds of the French is a phenomenon

2 B

worthy of remark. Unlike Mormonism, and the impostures
of Brothers and Joanna Southcote, which made their way
wholly among the most ignorant and credulous of professing Christians, St Simonianism may be said to have num-
bered high intellects. This can only be attributed to the
fact that, amidst much dross, there were grains of pure
metal, and that their field of teaching was not wholly
covered with tares. It were well indeed if Christians would
recollect that there never was a religion exercising any influence among thoughtful and philosophical men which had not
in it some element of truth, and, consequently, of stability.
—1861.

REV. ROBERT ASPLAND.

Mr Aspland was the Unitarian minister at the Gravel-pit
Chapel at Hackney.   He was, I believe, the son of a Cam-
bridgeshire farmer, was educated in orthodox opinions,
which he abandoned, and became one of the most distinguished preachers, and a recognised authority among the
religious body with which he was connected.   He was the
Secretary to the British and Foreign Unitarian Association,
and the editor of the "Monthly Repository," which was
for many years the principal literary organ of the Unitarians.   In all movements for the extension of religious
liberty, such as the repeal of the Corporation and Test
Acts, he took a most energetic part.   He was the founder
of the Nonconformist Club, a body of Unitarians, mostly
men of letters, who met monthly to discuss the religious
phases of the times, one of them usually being charged with
the preparation of a paper on some historical or polemical
topic.   Many of these papers were published in the
" Monthly Repository."   There were in the Club some
remarkable men, namely, Edgar Taylor, who translated the
" German Popular Tales," and published an admirable ver-

sion of the New Testament, founded principally upon Griesbach's text,—his cousin Richard, known by the name of the *Classical Printer;* Samuel Parkes, author of the "Chemical Catechism," a popular work in its day, which gave the writer for many years an income of £500 ; William Johnson Fox, whose talents were afterwards transferred from the pulpit to the senate ; Dr Southwood Smith, then best known by his "Essay on the Divine Government," and afterwards by his public services at the Board of Health ; Christopher Richmond, a barrister, and an able and interesting man, and some others unknown to fame beyond the circle of their religious community. There was a strong bond of union between those who professed an unpopular and heterodox faith, and who were the objects of no small amount of opprobrium from their orthodox brethren. But time has somewhat modified the harshness of condemnatory judgment. When I was in the House of Commons, of fourteen Dissenters, I think thirteen belonged to the Unitarian community.—1861.

REV. THOMAS BELSHAM.

The chapel in Essex Street, London, was originally built for the use of Theophilus Lindsay, one of those excellent men to whom their conscience is a law, and who resigned the vicarage of Catterick, in Yorkshire when his convictions could no longer reconcile themselves to the ritual and the doctrines of the Anglican Church. He was succeeded by the Rev. Thomas Belsham, and the congregation became one of considerable influence, numbering some members of the Peerage, among whom was the Duke of Grafton, and others of the aristocracy. It is notorious that there is in the bosom of the Church itself a great amount of heterodoxy, and no one can have been admitted to intimate and confidential intercourse with the higher intellects of the age without failing to discover that there is much heretical pravity among them. An indifference to religious questions in general, a yielding to the tide of tendency, and a wish to maintain a social status in a country where a certain amount of opprobrium and degradation has been generally associated with dissent, are among the causes and the apologies for much real dishonesty. Mrs Barbauld used to say that in opulent families the carriages of the third generation always carried their possessors away to the national Church. The disabilities and persecutions however, to which Nonconformists were subjected had some advantages, for, in consequence of their exclusion from official positions in the State, those who were not members of the Establishment usually devoted themselves to commercial pursuits, in which they were mainly successful. The Jews became traffickers in money, while the Huguenots, persecuted in France, brought with them in their flight to England the silk manufactures of France, and in Spitalfields, Norwich, Coventry, and other places introduced new industries. In the great manufacturing towns dissenting families were at the head of many of those vast establishments which have given to our fabrics their world-wide reputation, and which are the great aliment of commerce abroad, the means of employment to busy millions at home, the source of enormous wealth, and the impellers of a growing civilization. In Manchester the Heywoods, connected with the cotton ; in Leeds, the Marshalls representing the flax ; in Derby the Strutts at the head of the local fabrics, were only the principal Presbyterian or Unitarian families of those places. I recollect when I was very young, that, in the chapel where my ancestors were wont to worship, the principal merchants and manufacturers of the staple woollen trade at Exeter were members of the congregation, but at the moment when I write, not one of their descendants, myself excepted, occupies a place in that once distinguished seat and school of heterodox Christianity. My own family professed, and were persecuted for their Puritanism. When the intolerance of the times prohibited their assembling for religious worship either in public edifices or private dwellings, they held their gatherings in remote and secret places. I have found a representation from the Bishop of Exeter to the Archbishop of Canterbury, in the time of James I., denouncing a turbulent and unmanageable nonconformist, one John Bowring, from whom I am directly descended. I possess a licence granted to a John Bowring, in the time of William and Mary, authorising him to use his house at Chulmleigh for the purpose of religious worship. He was in the woollen trade, and issued a token, bearing the date of 1670, and an inscription, " John Bowring, Chulmleigh, his halfpenny," which is ornamented with the device of a wool-comb, to designate his business, which was that of my progenitors down to my father's days. No less than three Directors of the Bank of England, leading partners in great London houses—the Barings, the Gibbs, and the Heaths—are descendants of men formerly engaged in the Exeter woollen trade. In my earlier days, I found the name of Exeter (Exon was its usual designation) familiar as a household word among foreign traders. In China, the long ells, a species of coarse serge, still manufactured by the hand-loom in Devonshire, are greatly preferred to the power-loom productions of Yorkshire. They are used, not only for winter clothing, but for the lining of carriages, for flags and ornaments, and for many domestic purposes. Such was the reputation of the East India Company that bales of long ells, bearing the marks of that great association, were received in every part of China unopened, and passed as currently as coin at an understood value.

In the United States of America, where no privileges or

disabilities of any sort attach to the profession of any special religious views, the open avowal of Unitarian opinions is far more generally diffused than in Great Britain. The most distinguished university, that of Harward in New England, may be deemed the principal school for the teaching of Unitarian doctrines, but, though Boston is the locality in which the most eminent of their preachers and professors have had their residence, there are a considerable number of Unitarian churches in other great cities of the Union. The chaplains to Congress have not unfrequently been ministers attached to that creed, and the most eminent of all American authors, Dr William Ellery Channing, has been most probably the man of all others instrumental in giving to the faith he professed a reputation through the literary world. His writings have been translated into several languages, and long before his remarkable sermons attracted such general admiration, his essays on Napoleon and Milton, which, if I mistake not, were published in the *North American Review*, had given him extensive fame. George Canning pronounced upon Channing's works a high and emphatic eulogium, and Rémusat has borne similar testimony in his preface to his life written in French, and published in Paris, by an English lady. I saw much of him on his visit to England. He had been staying with Southey at the Lakes, who had influenced him most unfavourably and unfairly against the whole body of English Unitarians, whom he was taught to consider as wearing a cloak of Christian profession for the concealment of a latent scepticism and infidelity. He then, as always, held negro slavery in utter abomination as the stain and stigma of his native land, but he excused himself from giving vent to his opinions, on the plea that such avowal would destroy the influence which he exercised over his fellow-citizens. Afterwards, however, he came to the nobler and bolder decision that it was his bounden duty not to conceal his views, and he gave to them a full and fervid expression, and assuredly the events that have occurred in the American common-wealth have demonstrated how important it is that the convictions of the wise and the good on a subject so full of sin and shame should not be suppressed.

The favourite theme of Mr Belsham was that Unitarianism, while it repudiated the doctrines which have been the subject of controversy in the Christian Church, recognized all the great outlines on which all Christians are agreed. Many have denied the Trinity, but all admit the unity of the Godhead; many repudiate the divinity, but all recognize the humanity of Jesus Christ; some deny the orthodox interpretation of the miraculous conception, but all admit that he was the son of his mother Mary. The doctrines of original sin and the terms of salvation have been the subject of much controversy, but no Christian denies the frailty of man, the resurrection of Christ, and the benefits which his mission has conferred upon the world.

Mr Belsham was a most agreeable, social companion, and was an object of great personal esteem among a large circle of friends. His sister married the Rev. T. Kenrick of Exeter, a distinguished preacher belonging to the school of Dr Priestley, and the father of one of the most eminent scholars of our day, the Rev. John Kenrick of York.—1861.

ABBE GREGOIRE.

The Abbé Gregoire, Bishop of Blois, well known by the title of "L'ami des noirs," was one of those great moral powers which repose, as it were, in the silence of seeming inaction till the day of change. He was feared, and dreaded, and harassed more than others, because his influence was not of a tangible character. Pure and unpolluted amidst all changes, he was a stern, unswerving, yet gentle and exemplary Republican. No man was more vehemently abused than he during the period when the restored Bourbons occupied the throne of France. He was denounced by the Royalists as the regicide—the episcopal regicide—but I believe he neither voted for the death of Louis XVI., nor for any other penal sentence of death, for he was in favour of the abolition of all capital punishments ; and I have heard him again and again aver that he wished the king to be the first example of the abrogation of the right of society to dispose of human life. He was a firm advocate of the liberties of the Gallican Church, called a Jansenist, but associated with a large body of clergy who, though avowing themselves Catholics, were and are desirous of circumscribing and limiting the Papal power. Gregoire was a most eloquent man, and was mainly occupied with the question of negro emancipation, his enthusiasm on behalf of the blacks being exhibited in impassioned and emphatic expressions. His sympathy for them was intense, and he was one of the most courageous and active coadjutors of Clarkson, Wilberforce, Allen, and the other abolitionists. He had gathered together a large library of works written by people of colour, and a very curious collection it was, consisting, if I recollect aright, of two or three hundred volumes, among which were books of which female negroes were the authors. Hayti furnished large contributions, and the newspapers of that island were certainly conducted with no small ability. In Gregoire's house the most interesting people of colour were habitually congregated. I remember many who had a considerable reputation in France and Europe. Pescay, the physician under whose care and keeping Napoleon placed Ferdinand VII. of Spain while a prisoner in France, was a black man, and as there is no doubt that he was expected to play the part of reporter and spy, his appointment may be

deemed good evidence of the value attached to his capacity
by the sagacious French ruler. General Roche was a half
caste, but I have heard his military talents extolled. To
say nothing of Dumas, there has been one instance at least
of a man of colour having carried off a prize at the French
Institute, but my experience would not enable me to endorse the opinion of the good Bishop that the intellectual
aptitudes of the blacks are equal to those of the whites. I
believe, however, that in some regions they are superior to
those of the long-haired inhabitants. When I was in Egypt,
a Nubian had to undergo the operation of losing his leg.
He showed extraordinary courage while in the hands of the
surgeon, and, on being complimented on his self-possession,
exclaimed, "Did you suppose me to be no better than a
fellah (native Egyptian)?" In the boats on the Nile, black
men are often in command, and exercise a somewhat despotic authority over the indigenous crews. Having had a
good deal to do with black youths under the process of
education, I conclude that, though up to a certain point,
they are even more teachable and ready than Europeans of
the same age, it is very difficult, if not impossible, to raise
them above that point, so as, for example, to bring them to
understand complicated mathematical problems, and to
pursue high studies in astronomy, or any of the abstract
sciences requiring long and profound attention. I remember that when the King of Hayti was compelled to abdi-
cate, and his queen with his daughters fled to Europe for
safety, Gregoire set his heart upon bringing about a marriage
between one of the ebony beauties and a young and favourite
literateur, Benjamin Laroche, who was compelled to seek an
asylum in England when the Bourbon police was pursuing
him. He was well known in the literary world by his
translations of Shakspeare into French. He did not fall
into Gregoire's views, and, to say the truth, the young lady

was of a somewhat passionate temperament, and would have led her husband an uneasy life.

Gregoire was an object of great dislike and suspicion, and, unless my recollection fails me, was expelled from the Chamber of Deputies after the Bourbon restoration, but he went on in his forward path undaunted and unmoved, his mind always occupied by some plan and purpose of benevolence, every species of human sympathy and virtuous exertion being in turn the object of his thoughts and cares. The slave trade, prisons, schools, hospitals—everything, in short, which excited his beneficent solicitude—the independence of his church, the enfranchisement of Jews, and the abolition of persecution, all were subjects for his religious exertions—his mind, as well as his pen, being extraordinarily active.—1861.

RÁM MOHUN ROY.

Strange changes have been going on in most religious communities, and the spirit of reformation seems to be making its way alike in the Oriental and the Western world. There is a general conviction that, whether due to the craft of kings or of priests, the teachings of the great instructors have been distorted and corrupted, and that the nearer we approach them and their times, the more purity will be found in their doctrines, and a closer adhesion to the principles of truth and morality. Among the Booddhists, tens of thousands of volumes exist, the depositaries of unauthorized traditions and incredible theories; the reformed Jews are repudiating the writings of many Hebrew commentators; and Christian churches are refusing to admit the testimony of the " Lives of the Saints " and the untrustworthy records of miracles, the belief in which may have well suited an ignorant age, but which will not bear the test of critical examination. The reformed Brahmins

contend, and with much reason, that the Vedas contain
nothing derogatory to the Divine character, and give no
sanction to the idolatrous rites now practised in the Indian
temples. When I attended the worship of the Vedántas
in Calcutta, I saw nothing and heard nothing to which a
believer in the unity of God could object. There are, I
believe, at this moment from three to four hundred temples
in which reformed Brahminism is professed.

Rám Mohun Roy was perhaps the most illustrious, and
certainly the best known of these Brahminical reformers.
I do not believe that he was a Christian, or that he
really admitted the evidence of the miracles, and especially
of the resurrection of our Saviour; but his "Precepts of
Jesus" is a beautiful testimony to his admiration of the
character of the Messiah, of whom he always spoke with
reverence, as one of the greatest instructors of our race.
When he determined to visit Europe, he did not dissolve
the link which bound him to Brahminism, or repudiate any
observance necessary to the maintenance of his position.
His family violently opposed his leaving Calcutta, his wife
especially, and his son, Rám Prasád Roy, was compelled by
the strong influences exercised to remain in Bengal, where,
by the way, he is an eloquent pleader in the Supreme
Court, and a Vakeel of the Government in British India.
He speaks English, as did indeed his father, with admirable
purity.

Rám Mohun Roy naturally found his sympathies drawing
him more closely to the Unitarian than to any other religious
body. He did not avoid controversy, but, in order not to
give offence, he perhaps sometimes allowed it to be supposed
that he was making concessions which were far indeed from
the convictions of his own mind. In fact, I have heard
him called orthodox by those who knew little or nothing of
his genuine opinions. No one could be more desirous than

he to strengthen the bonds which unite India to Great
Britain, and he would have been glad to have been the
herald of a succession of Brahminical visitors. Another
followed him, Dwárkánáth Tágore, whose presence made
some sensation in England. He was a merchant, but as
his commercial adventures were not fortunate, he naturally
enough lost much of his influence. At this moment I
believe the best known of the Bengal Vedántas is the Raja
of Burdwán, but all Rám Mohun Roy's schemes were
thwarted by his death, which took place at Stapleton
Grove, near Bristol, while on a visit to Miss Castle, in
whose grounds he was buried, but when the property
passed out of the hands of the family, the corpse was
removed to the cemetery at Arno's Vale, where he rests in
peace.—1861.

MEZZOFANTI.

Knowledge of languages is a very vague expression,
meaning everything between what is little—more—much—
and up to such perfect knowledge as is possessed by a
cultivated native. The list presented to the Philological
Society at their meeting of the 2d inst. (Jan. 1863) by Mr
Watts is an ill-digested assemblage, sometimes of the same
languages under different names, but, altogether, exhibiting
the utmost confusion, both as to the character and the
classification of different tongues.

Mezzofanti had studied with greater or less attention
most of the idioms taught by the Propaganda, and those
idioms are far more numerous than those cited in the
Athenæum. What struck me in my intercourse with the
Cardinal was the accuracy of his ear, and the correctness of
his pronunciation, together with his acquaintance with
many obscure dialects confined to small localities. Of those
of Spain, for example, only two are mentioned, viz., Spanish,

i.e., Castilian, and Catalan, whereas he certainly had knowledge of thrice that number of dialects spoken in the Iberian peninsula. Of Italian, three are reported—Italian, *i.e.*, Tuscan, Sicilian, and Venetian—a small proportion only of those with which he was familiar. So, again, he had attended to several of the Philippine dialects, only one of which, namely Tagal, is spoken of. Mezzofanti, I am sure, never pretended to *know* the various dialects of the Chinese, of which the names are (very confusedly) given. He *knew* the Mandarin, *i.e.*, the court or literary language, well, but I remember when a friend of mine, who had been conversing with him in that language, broke off into Cantonese (one in the list), Mezzofanti said, "That is not the Hwan-hwa" (the literary tongue), but he could not carry on the conversation in the Canton dialect. The most profound philologist whom I have known was Rask of Copenhagen. The philologist who made himself acquainted with the greatest number of dialects was the elder Adelung.—1863.

LANGLES.

France is the country of false and undeserved reputations. Literary and conversational piracy is universal. Every man appropriates to himself whatever he can lay hold of, and everything is exhibited on the surface. They all wear the clothes of their intellectual wardrobe on their backs, and carry about in ready money all their knowledge of books or things.

Langles lived and died with a prodigious reputation for erudition, yet he was an ignorant quack, who supported himself by what he stole from others; but, in transferring it to himself, he had the cunning either to alter its character, or now and then to conciliate its owner by a puff. The secret of his reputation was to talk with every man on the subject of which that man was particularly ignorant. He would talk to a Persian of English books, and drive an Englishman per force to Ispahan.

Raynouard is another man whose fame is out of all squares with his deserts. He has published five volumes on the Troubadour poetry, yet he knows little about it—of the best of the Troubadours, those of Spain, he knows nothing, nor of the Minnesingers of Germany.

There are men in France, however, whose talents are infinitely *above* their reputation. Fauriel is one of these. He was for years the *cher ami* of Madame Condorcet. He overflows with gentleness, kindness, and wisdom. A new race of men has grown out of the French Revolution. Sedateness and quiet thought have planted themselves deeply, and are spreading widely. The tumultuous ones are the old and the young, but the generation now in its ripe manhood is admirable.—1824.

J. MILFORD.

John Milford was the descendant of a family which migrated to Exeter from Thorverton, where they possessed an estate called Dunsallis. They had been connected with the staple manufactures of the county. The first of whom records now remain was Richard, who was born in 1704. Among his sons was Samuel, who was the father of Samuel Frederick, born in 1759, and John, born in 1761. The latter had eight children, the eldest of whom was John, the present possessor of Coaver. It was John Milford who, in 1812, sent me to Spain as his representative. He was a man of singular expression of countenance, with large bushy powdered chevelure. He had a habit of putting up his spectacles on his forehead when about to say something severe—a power not wanting to him—and his energy found now and then expression in terms somewhat intemperate. He had certain canons which he laid down for his

commercial code. Among them were, "Obey orders"—
"There is no resisting force major." He rather prided
himself on the incisive character of his correspondence.
There was in those days a sort of rivalry between men of
business as to who could write the best style of letter.
An Exeter merchant, John Cole, had a great reputation on
this score, and boasted that he put the eloquence of Junius,
of whose compositions he was a diligent and devoted
student, into his epistolary mercantile intercourse. It was
a grand thing to get hold of a few antitheses, and to bring
a little political sagacity into the regions of profit and loss.

Few men more enjoyed the pleasures of the table than
John Milford. He drank his port-wine out of an enormous
glass, and was fond of introducing double-quart bottles,
called magnums, which were appropriated to wines of the
highest reputation—the bees-wing representing age (often
a great delusion and a fraud), and *body*, meaning strength,
the produce of alcohol, a characteristic which has little to
do with real vinous excellence, and is, indeed, incompatible
with it.

LORD ERSKINE.

In the latter part of his life, Lord Erskine was accustomed
frequently to come to my counting-house, and to sit there
for a long time discoursing on his "travel's history," but
there was little left of that fine and fiery eloquence which
characterized his youth. Only once do I remember anything particularly striking in his conversation. We were
driving to my house in a hackney-coach, and he began to
talk of the evidences of Christianity. He became greatly
excited, his mind expanded more and more, and at last he
burst into such a strain of oratory as I never heard. His
eye flashed with light, and he spoke as if inspired, the tones
of his voice too being singularly beautiful.

He was a most zealous and efficient labourer in the cause
of the Greeks, not that he had much knowledge or judgment—for what he wrote on the subject was vague and
declamatory—but there was a charm about his name which
was transferred to the cause, and the master-string of his
mind, vanity, had been touched, its vibrations trembling to
the very end of his existence. I believe one of his latest,
perhaps his last letter, was addressed to me from Scotland
on the Greek insurrection.

· Lord Erskine said, "When the Emperor Alexander
came to England, Lord Granville told me that the
Emperor wished to see me. I went. He received me
with particular attention, and said he was very anxious to
make my acquaintance. He spoke English as well as you
do. 'You are a friend and correspondent,' he said, ' of my
most valued friend La Harpe.' ' Yes, sire.' ' Is he a regular correspondent?' 'Yes, a very kind one.' 'Has he
been so of late?' ' Well, if your Majesty will cross-examine
me, I must own that he owes me a letter.' He put his
hand into his pocket, and drew forth a letter addressed to
me. ' Yes, there is his answer. I intercepted it that I might
have the pleasure of making it the means of knowing Lord
Erskine.' I gave Alexander all my writings and speeches,
which he received with many expressions of satisfaction.

"Once when I was with La Harpe at the Emperor's
Court, it was an hour before dinner time. La Harpe said,
' You cannot dress here. Go into that alcove, and you will
find some papers to amuse you.' There was a box of letters
from Alexander, one of them written immediately after his
accession to the throne. It said, ' I tremble when I think
of the responsibility which weighs upon me—that the
happiness of so many millions depends upon my conduct.
I should be wretched if I did not hope that the instructions which you (to whom I owe more than to any other

living being)—the instructions you have given me, would influence my conduct.

"At the time when I assisted Lady Huntingdon to resist the interference of the church-bigot who put her into the Ecclesiastical Court for opening her place of worship in Clerkenwell, the present king used often to abuse me for encouraging sectarians, saying, 'God d——n it, Tom! you are the wickedest fellow in existence. I wonder God Almighty suffers you to live.' And now the King is a Methodist himself. My sister, Lady Anne Erskine, sent for me in 1778 to defend Lady Huntingdon, who imagined that, as a peeress of the realm, she had a right to be protected in her worship, but I told her that the Toleration Act gave her no protection. 'What shall I do?' said she, looking at her shabby dress, 'I who have spent all for the promotion of the Gospel? What shall I do? I who have reduced myself to this?' I told her she must shelter herself under the Conventicle Act, which she did, and sent me an inkstand of pure gold as a mark of her gratitude.

"The king was accustomed to pour out such vollies of abuse on Lord Eldon, that I once took the liberty of saying, 'Forgive me, Sir, but you should not use language so violent of a gentleman in such a situation.'

"When Ashhurst was said to 'throw light upon the laws' by his decisions, I replied,

> "'Ashhurst throw light upon the laws!
> Yes! 'tis through his lautern-jaws.'"

1823.

2 c

APPENDIX.

LIST OF THE PRINCIPAL WRITINGS OF SIR JOHN BOWRING.

1. Contestacion à las Observaciones de Don Juan B. Ogavan sobre la esclavitud de los Negros—1821.
2. Observations on the Restrictive and Prohibitory Commercial System from MSS. of Jeremy Bentham—1821.
3. Details of the Arrest, Imprisonment, and Liberation of an Englishman—1823.
4. Russian Anthology—1820-23, 2 Vols.
5. Matins and Vespers—1823.
6. Batavian Anthology—1824.
7. Ancient Poetry and Romances of Spain—1824.
8. Peter Schlemihl (translation from Chamisso)—1824.
9. Hymns—1825.
10. Servian Popular Poetry—1827.
11. Specimens of the Polish Poets—1827.
12. Poetry of the Magyars—1830.
13. Cheskian Anthology—1832.
14. Deontology—1834.
15. Minor Morals—1834, 35, 39—3 Vols.
16. Observations on Oriental Plague and Quarantines—1838.
17. Jeremy Bentham's Life and Works—1843, 11 Vols.
18. The Decimal System in Numbers, Coins, and Accounts—1854.
19. The Kingdom and People of Siam—1857, 2 Vols.
20. A Visit to the Philippine Isles—1859.
21. Translation from Petöfi—1866.

To the above may be added a great number of Articles in *The Westminster Review, The Foreign Quarterly, The Cornhill Magazine, Once a Week, The Monthly Repository, All the Year Round, The Fortnightly Review, The Theological Review,* and other periodicals. He also contributed several articles to the Transactions of the Devonshire Association, of which he was the first President.

LIST OF DIPLOMAS AND CERTIFICATES

GRANTED BY VARIOUS SOCIETIES TO SIR JOHN BOWRING.

1. Accademia Costante d' Italia, ... 1821
2. Turin Unanimium Societas, ... „
3. Philanthropic Society of Greece, ... 1824
4. Lecuwarden Constanter Genootschap, . . . 1828
5. Groningen Academy, ... 1829
6. Islenzka Bokmenta Felag, ... „
7. Åbo University, ... 1830
8. Eclectic Society, ... „
9. Société Française de Statistique Universelle, . . „
10. Sociedad Economica de Guatemala, . . . 1831
11. Académie de l' Industrie, ... 1832
12. Hungarian Academy of Sciences, ... „
13. Hull Literary Association of the Friends of Poland, . „
14. Société Montyon et Franklin, ... 1833
15. Schleswig-Holstein Lauenburgische Gesellschaft, . . „
16. American Antiquarian Society, ... 1834
17. Institut Historique, ... „
18. Bayerische Akademie der Wissenschaften, . . 1836
19. Schweizerische gemeinnützige Gesellschaft, . . „
20. Bataviaasch Genootschap van Wetenschappen, . . 1853
21. Nordiska Oldskrift Selskab, ... 1854
22. Royal Geographical Society, ... „
23. Institut d' Afrique, ... 1857
24. Société Impériale d' Horticulture, . . . „
25. New York Historical Society, ... 1858
26. Real Sociedad Economica de Filipina, . . . 1859
27. K. Königliche Geologische Reichsanstalt, . . . „
28. Anthropological Society of London, . . . 1863
29. Zoological Society of London, ... 1867
30. Ancient Order of Foresters, ... „

RECENT BIOGRAPHIES.

CHARLES KINGSLEY,

HIS LETTERS AND MEMORIES OF HIS LIFE.

EDITED BY HIS WIFE.

With a Steel Engraved Portrait, Illustrations on Wood, and a Fac-simile of his Handwriting.   Sixth Edition.   In Two Vols., Demy 8vo, cloth, price 36s.

JOURNALS OF COMMODORE GOODENOUGH,

DURING HIS LAST COMMAND AS SENIOR OFFICER ON THE AUSTRALIAN STATION, 1873-75.

EDITED WITH A MEMOIR BY HIS WIDOW.

Second Edition.   One Vol. square Post 8vo, cloth, price 14s.

MEMOIRS AND LETTERS OF SARA COLERIDGE.

EDITED BY HER DAUGHTER.

With Index and Portrait, Revised and Corrected.   Third Edition.   Two Vols., Crown 8vo, cloth, price 24s.   Cheap Edition, with Portrait, cloth, price 7s. 6d.

LIFE AND LETTERS OF ROWLAND WILLIAMS, D.D.,

WITH EXTRACTS FROM HIS NOTE BOOKS.

EDITED BY HIS WIFE.

With a Photographic Portrait.   In Two Vols.   Large Post 8vo, cloth, price 24s.

HENRY S. KING & CO., LONDON.

RUSSIA AND TURKEY.

MAJOR RUSSELL'S NEW BOOK.

RUSSIAN WARS WITH TURKEY.

Second Edition, Crown 8vo, with 2 Maps, 6s.

" Major Russell's narrative is exceedingly good, and he possesses the far from common gift of placing military events before us in clear relief and harmonious order."—*Times.*
" Major Russell is well known as an accomplished student of the art of war; he displays, in addition, the impartiality, breadth of view, and power of logical induction which are the characteristics of a statesman. Both soldiers and statesmen will do well to follow Major Russell through the history of former wars between Russia and Turkey. Some interesting speculations on the probable strategy of the contending parties are also given."—*Athenæum.*

With Map, Large Post 8vo, 12s.

THE RUSSIANS IN CENTRAL ASIA.

BY BARON F. VON HELLWALD.

TRANSLATED BY LIEUT.-COL. THEODORE WIRGMAN, LL.B.

"The conclusions drawn from the facts we have analysed above are not so very extravagant or unfair ; he considers that Russia never loses sight of two main objects, the establishment of a vast commercial monopoly in Asia, and the solution of the Turkish question. To affect unconcern or indifference in the teeth of the evidence arrayed by the author would be a mistake even more lamentable than the remedy of impotent bluster or unreasonable counter claims."—*Saturday Review.*
" We have reason to thank Her von Hellwald for his highly interesting and in the main right-minded work, which is by far the best on this subject which has been produced in England."—*Pall Mall Gazette.*

Crown 8vo, with Map, 6s.

RUSSIA'S ADVANCE EASTWARD.

Based on the Official Reports of Lieut. Hugo Stumm, German Military Attaché to the Khivan Expedition.

BY CAPTAIN C. E. H. VINCENT.

To which is appended other information on the subject, and a minute Account of the Russian Army.

Lieut. STUMM was the only recognized foreign participator in Russia's advance eastward, which caused such alarm in England. The book is an expressly authorized translation of his Reports to the German Government.

" Captain Vincent's account of the improvements which have taken place lately in all branches of the service is accurate and clear, and is full of useful material for the consideration of those who believe that Russia is still where she was left by the Crimean War."—*Athenæum.*

Two Vols., Medium 8vo, 36s.

THE CRIMEA AND TRANSCAUCASIA.

BY CAPTAIN J. BUCHAN TELFER, R.N.

With Numerous Illustrations and Maps.

" The beauty of the type, the gloss of the paper, the number and almost photographic appearance of the illustrations, seem to stamp it as belonging to the . . . hierarchy of books *de luxe.*"—*Spectator.*
" The whole of it is very instructive reading. Although both the tours which he describes were carried out in the course of very rapid travel, yet he is not one of those sensational writers who make a story of their hasty observations and superficial impressions. Captain Telfer is at home in Russian society. He has carefully studied most branches of the literature of the countries he visited, and has made himself thoroughly master of their history. Both volumes are so replete with valuable matter in great variety that we cannot profess to do more than indicate the nature of their contents." *Saturday Review.*
" He is a most conscientious guide and shrewd observer, and introductions to Russian officials of high position gave him access to sources of information which remain sealed to ordinary travellers. The author has succeeded in producing a readable and at the same time a most instructive book. Every page shows the experienced traveller, the man of broad views and of culture. The illustrations are all that could be desired."—*Athenæum.*

HENRY S. KING & CO., LONDON.

BOOKS FOR THE LIBRARY.

PRINCIPLES OF MENTAL PHYSIOLOGY.
By W. B. CARPENTER, M.D., F.R.S.

Fourth Edition, illustrated, 8vo, 12s.

THE PHYSICS AND PHILOSOPHY OF THE SENSES.
By R. S. WYLD, F.R.S.E.

Illustrated, Demy 8vo, 16s.

PHYSIOLOGICAL AESTHETICS.
By GRANT ALLEN, B.A.

Large Post 8vo, 9s.

ETHICAL STUDIES.
By F. H. BRADLEY.

Large Post 8vo, 9s.

A DISCOURSE ON TRUTH.
By RICHARD SHUTE, M.A.

Large Post 8vo, 9s.

REASON AND REVELATION.
By WILLIAM HORNE, M.A.

Demy 8vo, 12s.

RECONCILIATION OF RELIGION AND SCIENCE.
By T. W. FOWLE, M.A.

Demy 8vo, 10s. 6d.

THE CHILDHOOD OF RELIGIONS.
By EDWARD CLODD, F.R.A.S.

Crown 8vo, 5s.

THE OTHER WORLD.
By THE REV. F. G. LEE, D.C.L.

New Edition, 2 vols., crown 8vo, 15s.

ESSAYS ON THE ENDOWMENT OF RESEARCH.
By VARIOUS WRITERS.

Square crown 8vo, 10s. 6d.

CONTEMPORARY EVOLUTION.
By St GEORGE MIVART, F.R.S.

Post 8vo, 7s. 6d.

PESSIMISM: A HISTORY AND A CRITICISM.
By JAMES SULLY.

HISTORY OF THE EVOLUTION OF MAN.
By PROFESSOR E. HAECKEL.

HENRY S. KING & CO., LONDON.

THEOLOGY.

F. W. ROBERTSON, M.A. (of Brighton). *New and Cheaper Editions.* SERMONS, 4 Vols., 3s. 6d. each; LECTURES ON EPISTLES TO THE CORINTHIANS, 5s.; NOTES ON GENESIS, 5s.; LECTURES AND ADDRESSES, 5s.

STOPFORD BROOKE, M.A. SERMONS, 1st Series, 9th Edition, 6s.; 2nd Series, Third Edition, 7s.; 3rd Series, *Shortly.* CHRIST IN MODERN LIFE, 9th Edition, 7s. 6d.; THEOLOGY IN THE ENGLISH POETS, Third Edition, 9s.

H. R. HAWEIS, M.A. CURRENT COIN, 6s.; SPEECH IN SEASON, 3rd Edition, 9s.; THOUGHTS FOR THE TIMES, 9th Edition, 7s. 6d.; UNSECTARIAN PRAYERS, 2nd Edition, 3s. 6d.

J. BALDWIN BROWN, M.A. THE HIGHER LIFE, 4th Edition, 7s. 6d.; ANNIHILATION IN THE LIGHT OF LOVE, 2nd Edition, 2s. 6d.

SAMUEL DAVIDSON, D.D. THE CANON OF THE BIBLE, 5s.; THE NEW TESTAMENT, translated from the latest Greek Text of Tischendorf. New and Revised Edition, 10s. 6d.

J. LLEWELLYN DAVIES, M.A. THEOLOGY AND MORALITY, 7s. 6d.

LORD STRATFORD DE REDCLIFFE. WHY AM I A CHRISTIAN? Fifth Edition. 5s.

H. HAYMAN, D.D. RUGBY SCHOOL SERMONS, 7s. 6d.

PERE LACORDAIRE. LIFE. New Edition, 3s. 6d.

PREBENDARY LEATHES. HULSEAN LECTURES FOR 1873; THE GOSPEL ITS OWN WITNESS. 5s.

P. LORIMER, D.D. JOHN KNOX AND THE CHURCH OF ENGLAND, 12s.

CARDINAL MANNING. ESSAYS ON RELIGION, &c., 3rd Series, 10s. 6d.

DANIEL MOORE, M.A. CHRIST AND HIS CHURCH, 3s. 6d.

DAVID WRIGHT, M.A. (of Clifton). WAITING FOR LIGHT, 6s.

HENRY S. KING & CO., LONDON.

www.ingramcontent.com/pod-product-compliance
Lightning Source LLC
Chambersburg PA
CBHW030816110726
47900CB00006B/1637